Clara's Three Lives

Alex Amit

To Y., who walks by my side

Contents

The First Life

In 1923, hyperinflation developed in Germany due to the difficulty in meeting World War I reparations established in the Treaty of Versailles, as well as uncontrolled money printing. A loaf of bread that cost 250 marks in January reached a price of 200 billion marks by November 1923. The streets were filled with strikes and demonstrations.

Chapter One

Berlin 1923, When Money Had No Value

Five years after the end of the Great War, which would later be called World War I

"Frau Hoffmann, you have exactly half an hour to pack your belongings and leave the apartment before I call the police," Herr Schulz angrily says as he stands before my mother in our apartment hallway, his hands clutching the bundle of banknotes she had given him moments ago.

"Herr Schulz, I beg you, you know I'm not the type of woman who asks for mercy. I'm only asking for a few more days—we will get the money." Mother stands before him, straight-backed in her simple blue dress. I can see her lips trembling un the weak light of the yellow hallway lamp.

"You're already two weeks late on the rent, Frau Hoffmann, and this money isn't enough. I don't intend to wait any longer." Herr Schulz waves the notes he's holding. He's wearing a light button-up shirt and tie. Despite the early summer evening, I can see sweat stains spreading under his arms. He smells of cheap cigarettes.

"Please, give me two more weeks to settle the debt. You know all prices have risen and nobody has enough money," Mother continues trying to convince him, maintaining her upright posture. Her gray hair is carefully combed back and held with pins. It had been brown before the Great War. Her eyes have grown dimmer too.

"Frau Hoffmann, I warned you months ago and notified you a week ago that the rent would increase. You've had plenty of time to arrange for more money," he tells her, stepping back toward the open apartment door behind him.

I glance past him at the hallway wall, painted in a flaking grayish-white. Are the neighbors hearing this argument?

"And if you can't make the payment, then I'll find someone who can," he continues addressing her. "Do you think I can afford to pity you? I need to look after myself." He shifts his gaze to me. "What about her? Doesn't she work? How old are you anyway?" he asks me while his eyes examine my neck and chest, covered by a simple gray summer dress.

"Fräulein Clara, sir. I'm twenty-six and I have a good job," I answer, trying to stand as straight as Mother despite his scrutinizing gaze making me uncomfortable. "I work in a shoe workshop near Hackescher Bahnhof. I have steady employment. We both work," I add. We need this apartment, despite its small size and the permanent smell of mold.

"Fräulein, women your age should be married by now," he says, lowering his gaze to survey my entire body as if there's something defective about me. I feel myself shrinking, fighting the urge to step back. I've hated the word 'Fräulein' for years now.

"Herr Schulz, my daughter will marry only when she finds the right man, not a minute before," Mother responds aggressively, positioning herself in front of me, shielding me from his small, examining eyes.

"I'm a landlord, Frau Hoffmann, not a matchmaker, and I don't care who your daughter marries or when. You have half an hour to leave the apartment, and this money is mine," he angrily answers, stuffing the banknotes into the pocket of his brown trousers. "Take all your things and disappear. I'll come back to make sure you're not here—you and your daughter—and if you still are, I'll call the police," he adds in a quiet voice like a snake's whisper, and exits through the open door.

We both stand in silence as the sound of his footsteps echoes on the wooden stairs as he descends. Mother just gave him our entire weekly wages, and still we're left without a home.

The moment Herr Schulz's footsteps vanish down the stairs, Mother approaches the open wooden door of our apartment and closes it, making sure to lock the bolt. Then she passes by me and goes to the only bedroom in the apartment. After a moment, she returns with the round silver alarm clock that usually sits on the nightstand beside our bed, and places it on the wooden table in the dining corner. This isn't the first time we've had to leave a rented apartment because we don't have enough money; I'm used to it by now.

"I'll start in the kitchen," I tell her as I approach the wooden drawer in the kitchen and open it. I take out the knives and forks, placing them in a metal pot that belongs to us. Then I remove the cardboard box from the cabinet, containing the precious silver cutlery Mother had inherited. She meticulously polishes them every few months with rough cloth dipped in wood ash, even though we never use them. I take these and the rest of the kitchen utensils to the bedroom. There I place them in the center of the bed that Mother and I share, and bundle them in a towel so they won't scatter.

"No one speaks to my daughter like that," she mutters to herself as she forcefully opens the heavy wooden dresser drawers and dumps their contents onto the bed.

"Everyone talks like that, more or less. They don't mean it," I answer while removing our few clothes from the wooden wardrobe in the corner of the room: two wool coats, several dresses, and a few camisoles, brassieres, and bloomers. We don't need much time to vacate an apartment.

"They never mean it," she grumbles. "They just look with their eyes and stretch out their hands to receive money, or some other compensation," she continues to speak quietly while bundling all our clothes inside an old sheet and placing it on the bed.

"Is there anything else?" I ask, looking around. The clock that sits on the kitchen table shows we have nine minutes left.

"Did you pack everything from the kitchen? You didn't forget the silver cutlery?" She examines the small bedroom covered in peeling wallpaper, light green with gray stripes.

"Yes," I answer, also taking the silver clock from the kitchen table. We have seven minutes left.

"Let's go. I don't want to see him again," she says, standing on one side of the bed while I stand on the other. The bed belongs to us; all the other furniture belongs to the landlord.

Together we lift the heavy bed, and slowly walk down the hallway to the entrance door. We lived in this house for nine months.

The difficult part is getting through the front door, and although the bed isn't wide, we have to tilt it slightly to cross the threshold and exit into the corridor. Thankfully it's still early, and some of the neighbors haven't yet returned from work.

We're both panting as we carry the bed down the stairs. Only one of the neighbors opens her apartment door and watches us curiously. I lower my eyes and concentrate on my fingers gripping the iron bars of the bed. They're white from the effort. I just want the neighbor to not say anything, to not ask why we're being evicted, to not pity us. I just want us to not make much noise as we slowly descend the wooden stairs and leave this building. The main thing is that we leave and disappear from here, that the neighbors forget about us. "Just one more floor," I tell Mother. She's breathing harder than I am. She's not young anymore; she's already forty-eight. If we had a little money, I would suggest we find a man to pay to help us carry the bed and our belongings instead of her.

The first time we left an apartment, when I was still a little girl, I remember a big man with black hair who helped Mother carry the bed out of the apartment. I remember Mother wore a light blue dress with small flowers, and she told me to sit on the bed while they held it in their large hands. I'd held the metal bars tightly, careful not to fall, and imagined it was a boat sailing in the blue sea, rocking between the waves like the picture in the only book of poems I had, from which Mother would read to me before turning off the light.

Just a few more steps down the stairs and we'll reach the street, and I'll be able to put down this heavy bed. My hands are aching.

Outside the building, we both walk down the street and place our heavy bed, loaded with our belongings, on the sidewalk against the wall of one of the houses. "There, he won't get our money anymore. Clara, do you have any money left?" she asks while her hand momentarily rubs her back. My back hurts too. I should have tried to find a young man to help us for free, although Mother wouldn't have agreed to that.

"I have a little bit left. This is it." I take several banknotes from my dress pocket and give them to her. "We paid the rest to Herr Schulz."

I watch as she slowly counts the bills. Her rough fingers, covered with small cracks from years of doing laundry in wealthy homes, pass one bill after another in her wrinkled palm, while her lips mumble and calculate the amount. I wish so much that we had more, but we both know it's not enough. We didn't have enough to pay Herr Schulz, and we don't have enough to pay someone else.

When she finishes, she raises her head and examines the street around us, then looks back at me with a sad expression. Her brown eyes are framed by wrinkles that appeared in recent years. "Did you remember to take the silver cutlery?" she finally asks, her lips trembling slightly again.

"Yes," I tell her, and place my hand on the towel covering the small cardboard box on the bed.

"Give them to me." She extends her hand toward me, and I silently open the towel and hand them to her. The silver utensils make a delicate tinkling sound inside the box as she holds it with both hands.

"Stay here and watch our things. I'll find us a new apartment. I'll also find better work, and I'll get them back," she quietly says, more to herself than to me, and walks away down the street. I follow her with my gaze until she disappears among the people, and for the first time since being evicted from the apartment, I look around.

The late afternoon sunlight breaks through the clouds, illuminating the upper parts of the gray buildings on one side of the street. Even the peeling plaster is momentarily painted in shades of yellow. The laundry hanging outside windows on lines adds patches of brown, blue and green above the street that's still wet from the earlier rainfall. A tram moves slowly on its metal tracks down the middle of the street, and a black car with gleaming silver headlights quickly passes, overtaking it. A horse harnessed to a wooden cart pulls it at a slow walk, its hooves making a gentle noise on the cobblestones. A man in a suit riding a bicycle rings his hand bell as he passes the cart. I watch him, but then he returns my gaze and I become embarrassed, lowering my eyes. What must he think of me, seeing me sitting like this on a bed in the middle of the street?

Another tram crosses the avenue at a slow pace. I hear it moving over the tracks with a metallic screech, but I don't dare raise my eyes. Are all those respectable men in suits sitting comfortably in the tram now looking at me? Are they lifting their gaze from their evening newspapers and examining me? I keep my eyes lowered and study the gray pavement stones on the sidewalk. I feel so conspicuous, like the caged pink flamingo at the Berlin Zoo before the war, when I was a child. It had stood in the center of the cage, and all the people had stood there pointing at it and laughing. Some children had even thrown small pieces of bread at it. Father had told me then that it was nice for it to stand alone in the middle of the cage, and that we couldn't release it to fly back to Africa. Eventually we left its cage, and eventually my father left us too.

I mustn't think about the people on the street passing by and looking at me. Mother will soon return and tell me that she has found us a new apartment, like last time. We're already used to it.

"Fräulein, how much are you selling the bed and what's on it for?" I hear a voice and raise my eyes. An elderly man with uncombed white hair, wearing a dirty black cloth coat and a flat cap, stands there looking at me. He holds the halter of a thin brown pack horse tied to a wooden cart, on which boxes and several chairs have been placed.

"The bed and the things on it are not for sale," I firmly say to him, straightening up as much as I can. My eyes suspiciously examine his dirty hands. I need to be careful, lest he try to snatch something from me.

"I'll pass by here tomorrow too, Fräulein, and then I'll offer you less," he says to me, laughing wickedly as he starts to walk, pulling the horse behind him. I don't want anyone to call me Fräulein.

I follow him with my gaze until he becomes a gray spot among the cars, cyclists and cargo wagons, as well as the tram approaching from the direction of the city center. I need to be more careful and watch over our things so no one tries to take them. I sit in the middle of the bed and place my hands on our few possessions. They're safer this way. This is how I imagined myself sailing on a boat across the stormy ocean when I was a child.

A wail causes me to look down at a dirty stray cat cautiously approaching me, stopping at a safe distance.

"I don't have any food to give you," I tell it, but then I notice two policemen approaching me from down the street, and I feel my entire body tense. Did Herr Schulz call the police to deal with us?

They walk toward me, wearing thick dark blue coats adorned with gleaming gold buttons and round helmets with the police emblem on their heads. Their black boots strike the pavement stones, and the batons stuck in the leather belts at their waists move slightly with each step, as if waiting to be grabbed and raised high. I hurry to get off the bed and stand as straight as I can. What will I tell them when they take me with them? Why hasn't Mother returned yet?

As they approach, the taller of the two officers fixes his gaze on me and offers a small smile. He has a magnificent black mustache, and says something to the second officer who is shorter than him. As he speaks, he raises his hand slightly in my direction, but I can't hear what he's saying. I take a deep breath. I will convince them that we're not guilty and that we paid Herr Schulz everything we had.

A green truck passes on the street and honks, but I don't focus on it; I watch the policemen approaching me, and lower my gaze to the shiny black leather of their boots. They'll reach me in a moment.

To my surprise, they say nothing when they draw near. They merely survey me with their eyes and continue walking, passing me by and moving into the black entrance to the building, disappearing into the darkness a moment later. I breathe slowly and go back to watching the people passing through the street. They don't seem so frightening to me anymore, and I allow myself to look at them too. The sun has already set.

A muffled scream comes from the dark entrance to the building, like that of a wounded animal. I turn my gaze toward the sound, and after a moment I see the two policemen who passed me earlier emerging from the building entrance. They are firmly holding a young woman in a simple brown dress similar to mine, and they drag her into the street. Her light hair is disheveled, and blood flows from her nose, staining her lips with cherry-colored lipstick.

"It's about time, you immoral woman, we don't need women like you here," an elderly woman follows behind her and shouts, raising her hand threateningly. I flinch backward slightly, even though she's not threatening me.

I look at the immoral woman, and our gazes meet for a split second before the policemen holding her arm pull her further down the street. Two buttons on the back of her dress are torn, revealing her pale skin. Her loose, light brown hair sways from side to side as she tries to match her steps to those of the policemen forcefully holding her. I can't stop watching her.

Three children, about six or seven years old, come out of the building and run behind the policemen and the woman. They follow them with laughing calls, careful to keep a safe distance from the policemen but trying to get close to the woman and hit her. One of them holds a wooden stick in his hand, which he waves above his head. What did she do? That thing that men always want? I feel the cool wind suddenly striking me and I hug myself tightly, rubbing my hands together to warm up. When will Mother return?

The sky turns dark, and the street lamps light up, painting the buildings with weak patches of yellow. The horses carrying cargo wagons disappear, along with the black cars and the men riding bicycles. Only a red tram continues to occasionally pass down the tracks in the middle of the street, its lights shining in yellow dots like a pair of eyes. I'm cold. I look around and stand up, moving from side to side to warm myself.

Finally I see Mother approaching me. "Let's go," she says, smiling at me tiredly. "I found us a new apartment for the coming days, it's not far." And we again begin to carry the bed through the street. At least we'll have somewhere to sleep tonight.

"The apartment is here, on the third floor," Mother tells me after some time, and we turn toward the entrance of a building similar to the one we left.

In the courtyard near the entrance is a muddy puddle, remnants of firewood left over from winter, and laundry hanging above our heads. Here too, the plaster peels in the stairwell just like in the previous building. The air carries the scent of cabbage soup.

We slowly climb up the wooden stairs; my hands ache and I'm exhausted. Thankfully it's already late, and there are no neighbors standing in their doorways eyeing us, examining us with their gazes. On the second floor, a woman stands in the corridor, her hands gripping the railing. She's a small, thin woman with carelessly-gathered gray hair. Her chin and nose are sharp like a bird's, and she scrutinizes us curiously as we climb, breathing heavily on the stairs.

"Good evening, are you the new tenants?" she asks inquisitively.

"Good evening," Mother answers her, "I am Mrs. Hoffman, and this is my daughter Clara," she indicates me with a nod.

"I'm Mrs. Vogel. All the neighbors here are long-term residents. We insist that tenants don't change every couple of months. There are buildings that look like train stations, but not here," she tells us without extending her hand in greeting. Her eyes examine the belongings piled on the bed with interest. She doesn't offer to help us either.

"Nice to meet you. Have a pleasant evening," Mother responds, and turns her gaze to me. "Come, Clara, just one more floor."

"Have a good evening, Mrs. Vogel," I politely answer with a smile. The sound of classical music seeps through the closed wooden door of one of the apartments. Just one more floor and we'll reach the apartment where we'll spend the night. I'm tired. "One... two... three..." I\m counting the wooden steps we have left to carry the heavy bed when footsteps and a boy's voice sound behind me.

"Good evening, can I help you?"

I turn around. He's a young boy, about sixteen or seventeen, and he bounds up the stairs below me with large steps until he stands close to me. He's slightly taller than I am, his blond hair somewhat disheveled, and his body is thin like all those boys who haven't yet completed their growth.

"Yes, please, thank you," Mother wearily smiles at him.

"I'm Bruno," he smiles back at her as he passes by me and takes her place, gripping the heavy bed where she had been holding it.

"Let's go," I say to him, and he and I continue climbing the stairs.

"We live beneath you, across from Mrs. Vogel's apartment," he says without gasping for breath. "We're the Koch family. The apartment with the music—my father loves loudly listening to music," he adds with something like an apology. A few more stairs and we'll reach our floor.

"I'm Clara, and this is my mother Mrs. Hoffman," I answer while catching my breath and pushing the bed up the last stairs. At last, we reach our floor.

"Thank you very much, young man. You were raised well," Mother thanks him as he stands and places the bed at the entrance to the apartment.

"You're welcome. Happy to help," he bids us farewell. "And don't mind Mrs. Vogel. She's always gossiping and full of complaints. Good night," he adds with a smile and descends the stairs.

"We'll remember that. Good night," I smile at him and watch his back as he goes down the stairs. Mother is still breathing heavily. We both are. Mother is too old to move apartments like this.

I stand there, looking at the wooden door of our new apartment. The wood has peeled in several places, and on the wall next to the door is a name someone has erased. I can't identify what was written. It doesn't matter; we probably won't be here for more than a few months anyway.

"Are we waiting for the landlord?" I ask Mother.

"No," she pulls a key from her dress pocket, "he already took what he was owed when he showed me the apartment. Besides, he won't fix anything that's broken. He was very clear about that," she says as she opens the door and we enter.

It takes Mother a moment to find the light switch. Only her footsteps are heard in the darkness, until a weak yellow lamp suddenly lights up in the corridor, and I enter the apartment and look around.

It's similar to the previous apartment, just smaller and older. The short corridor at the entrance leads to a living room, with a bedroom to its right and a small kitchenette to its left. The bedroom is covered with peeling beige floral wallpaper with mold stains near the floor, a dark brown wooden wardrobe, and a scratched mahogany dresser. The living room is slightly larger than the bedroom, with two wooden chairs and a low table in the center. The kitchenette contains a cabinet, a dirty work surface, a sink and a small iron stove. I smile wearily. We don't need a bigger place, this is enough for us.

We place the bed in the bedroom and silently begin to arrange our belongings. The most important thing is to organize everything, to transform the empty rooms into a place in which we live. To know that this is our place, that we can forget the previous home we were in just as I've already forgotten all the homes before it.

After the kitchen and bedroom are organized, Mother sits in the kitchen and takes out a pencil and the brown notebook where she keeps the household accounts. I sit beside her and watch as she opens a new page in the notebook, draws a line, and writes 'New Apartment' above it. Her cracked fingers tightly grip the pencil.

"We'll manage to get by," I tell her as I rise to fill the kettle with water to make us some tea.

"I know," she answers while continuing to stare at the blank page. "We have no other choice."

Afterward we wash our faces, undress and lie down together in the narrow bed, pressed close to each other. We've been used to sleeping like this for years now.

Before turning off the light, I place the silver alarm clock on the nightstand. Tomorrow morning the hammer will forcefully strike the bells, and I'll get up for work just like every day. We'll manage to get by. We have no other choice.

Chapter Two

The Shoe Workshop

The next morning, I briskly walk down the awakening street. Mother has already left for the house where she works as a laundress. My fingers tightly grip my wool coat to protect against the cool wind. Across the street, a bakery worker unloads sacks of flour from a wooden cart hitched to a patient, waiting draft horse. A lone truck with a gray tarpaulin cover passes by with a noisy rumble, leaving behind the smell of burnt gasoline.

Before reaching the Hackescher Bahnhof train station, I turn onto one of the smaller streets. I enter through the metal door of the shoe workshop, one entrance past the blacksmith shop, in the three-story red brick building.

"Good morning," I greet the other girls, hanging my coat at the entrance and sitting at my station in front of the industrial sewing machine. All the girls quietly speak to one another in the cold hall. I look at the clock hanging above the workshop manager's office. I have one more minute.

"What happened to you, that you arrived so late?" one of the girls turns to me and whispers. "We thought something had happened to you."

"I was delayed this morning," I whisper back. I don't want to tell her about yesterday.

Precisely a minute later, the work supervisor Mr. Konrad comes out of the workshop manager's office, looks at his wristwatch, and announces: "Good morning, girls, start working." And we all fall silent.

The small hall fills with the rattling of sewing machines and the whistling sound of the gluing machine. Three lamps hanging from the ceiling illuminate the workshop space with a weak yellow light. Even the tall, dust-covered windows allow only a little gray daylight to penetrate inside.

I lean forward, holding the piece of leather under my fingers and pushing it toward the needle as it rapidly moves up and down. The most important thing is to work precisely and keep the stitching straight. I mustn't think about the broken window in our new bedroom, through which the wind had blown all night. I'll receive my next paycheck in the coming days, and I'll look for a glazier to replace the window. For tonight, I'll put a piece of cloth up to stop the wind. I'll buy us food with the money I receive today. Yesterday we barely ate.

"You need to work more precisely, Clara. This stitch is crooked. I don't have extra leather to waste on poor work," Mr. Konrad surprises me as he extends his fat fingers toward the men's work boot I'm currently sewing. He looms over me, and I feel my body freeze. He reeks of cigarettes, shoe glue and sweat.

"I'll try harder, Mr. Konrad," I answer, shifting slightly in my chair; I don't want him to touch me.

"Don't give me reasons to dock your wages," he says, and places his hand on my shoulder for a moment before moving on to check the next worker.

"Yes, Mr. Konrad," I answer, trying to ignore the sensation his hand left on my shoulder. I need to concentrate on my work; I need this job. We all need this job.

I lower my gaze again and focus on my fingers, which hold two pieces of tough leather and guide them to the sewing machine's needle as it continuously moves in rapid motions. The main thing is to avoid getting distracted and making mistakes. I can't afford to have Mr. Konrad angry with me. The most important thing is to get through the workday and receive my wages at the end of it.

"Break," Mr. Konrad announces at exactly twelve o'clock, and the sewing machines fall silent. We all rise from our chairs and go out to the workshop courtyard to warm ourselves in the pleasant sun.

"What happened, Clara? You were almost late today," another worker asks me as she bites into her sandwich. The other women also take out fruit or small pastries, and bite into them.

"Yes, the alarm clock didn't ring. Luckily I woke up in time," I answer. I'll eat later, at the end of the workday, after I get my wages.

"I thought you went out with someone, and that was why you didn't show up," someone else joins the conversation and laughs.

"Who? Clara? Clara doesn't go out with men," another answers, and I smile awkwardly. I don't like them talking about me.

"Come with us to the club, Clara. There are nice men there, they buy us drinks and dance with us. I'm sure you'll find someone who'll like you," one of the girls says as she turns to me. I don't think she means it.

"Those men at the clubs only want one thing," one of the girls answers her with a smile.

"I'm willing to give it to them for a ring," the first responds and laughs. I lower my eyes and smile embarrassedly. I wish I were less shy, like them. I wish Mother had a man living with her and not just me.

"Clara won't come with you, she's looking for a gentleman who doesn't exist in reality," another joins the conversation.

"She's right, there are no gentlemen left. The war took them all," someone replies, and we all fall silent.

A gust of cool wind passes through the small courtyard and makes me shiver. I remember the women in black dresses who used to stand by the walls of the Defense Ministry downtown, reading the notices posted there, searching through the lists of names. I was a young girl then, and looked at them with apprehension, afraid to one day be like them.

"At least the war is over," someone says, breaking the silence.

"Yes, at least the war is over," I agree.

"Clara, promise me you'll think about coming with us to the club," one of them turns to me. She has light hair, pulled back, and freckles on her cheeks. "It's not good to be without a man."

"What's there to think about?" Hildegard joins the conversation, bowing her head for a moment as she lights a cigarette for herself. She's about my age, and her brown hair is gathered in a blue-gray scarf. We started working at the workshop around the same time.

"This doesn't concern you. We were talking about clubs. You don't like going to clubs," one answers her.

"You don't need to go to clubs, you need to come with me to protests," Hildegard says, exhaling the foul cigarette smoke toward us. "We all work here at the workshop like mice under Mr. Konrad's flute, while he steals part of our wages and trades the shoes on the black market. The government wastes all our money and prices rise, and no one has money to buy anything."

"You don't know that he's stealing from us," one of the workers replies in a whisper.

"Believe me, I know enough," she angrily answers. "And believe me, I also don't have enough money for food, like you, and believe me, men will continue to control us until we make a revolution."

"We need to get back. We have one minute left," someone quietly says, and we all hurry back into the work hall. Even Hildegard tosses the cigarette she's smoking to the floor, crushes it with her shoe, and enters with us. Sometimes I wish I had the courage to speak like her.

"Work begins," Mr. Konrad announces as he stands beneath the large clock. Once again my fingers grip the tough pieces of leather and push them into the track of the sewing machine.

"End of day," Mr. Konrad announces later, and we all stop working. Silence falls over the workshop, interrupted only by the sounds of chairs as we all rise from our sewing stations. A gray afternoon light filters through the dirty windows in the upper part of the workshop walls.

We all stand in line in front of Mr. Konrad, and wait to receive our wages. Soon I'll be able to buy food for Mother and myself. I smile. Today I'll buy us something tasty.

One by one, Mr. Konrad passes between us, a cigarette stuck in his mouth, handing out our banknotes.

"You were late. I'm docking you two hours today," he says to one of the workers standing in line, and takes several bills from the stack, stuffing them into the pocket of his blue overalls.

"I have a sick child. I was waiting at the doctor's," she says to him in a weak voice, her hand still outstretched to receive the money owed to her.

"Then let the doctor pay you for those two hours," he cruelly answers, the brown cigarette trembling between his lips.

"He's a corrupt man," Hildegard, who is standing in front of me in line, whispers to me with a voice full of hatred. "He's stealing her money, he's taking it for himself. You should listen to me. We need to shut the workshop down and go out to protest," she adds.

"Did you say something?" Mr. Konrad asks her, looking at her with the cigarette stuck in his mouth and his hand holding the stack of bills.

"We are a republic. The war is over, and the empire is over. We're allowed to say what we want. And women have the right to vote," she turns and answers him, raising her chin as she does so.

"Yes, that's the reason the streets are full of women looking for work, because women forgot that everyone needs to fulfill their role, and women still don't manage work," he answers. "Women started talking too much," he mutters, and places the banknotes in the outstretched hand of the worker waiting for them. "Don't be late tomorrow," he tells her. "I can always find a new worker to replace you."

"Yes, sir. Thank you, sir," she says to him as she leaves the workshop. Mr. Konrad advances and stands in front of Hildegard.

"Here you go." He forcefully places the money in her outstretched hand. Ash from the cigarette in his mouth falls onto the sleeve of the light blue work dress she wears.

Hildegard's hand grips the bills, and she takes them and turns her back to him, walking toward the metal door of the workshop.

"No thank you?" he calls after her.

"We women have equal rights. We're done being polite," she answers him without turning around and exits the workshop, her brown hair escaping from beneath the scarf on her head. I wish I were as brave as her.

"What about you, Clara?" He places the banknotes in my outstretched palm, his fingers brushing mine for a moment.

"Thank you, sir. See you tomorrow," I say to him, snatching the bills and turning to leave. Past the metal door of the workshop, I rub my fingers hard against the rough fabric of my simple dress, trying to cleanse the feeling of his greasy touch. But I mustn't think about that. Soon I'll buy myself food, that's all I'm thinking about now.

I enter the bakery and close the glass door behind me. The door bell rings with a gentle chime, and the shopkeeper raises his tired gaze from behind the display case.

He's older than me, about fifty, and his light bald spot gleams in the light of the lamp hanging above the small, dim bakery. His brown shirt contrasts with the white apron he wears.

I look at the nearly-empty display case. The few loaves of bread are arranged in two straight rows, but those sweet pastries that had been there since the war ended disappeared after prices began to rise. We're not the only ones who can't afford to buy them.

The price tags display numbers full of zeros for a loaf of bread. The price hasn't stopped rising in the last two months.

"Can you sell me bread for the old price?" I look at him while tightly gripping the bundle of bills between my fingers.

"I'm sorry," he answers, placing his large palms on the counter. "You know how it is, the price of flour rises every day too. I can't sell at the old price to anyone."

I go back to looking at the row of white wheat bread loaves displayed in the front of the case. It's been so long since I've chosen them. They're too expensive.

The door bell rings again as the bakery door opens, and a woman about my age dressed in a simple brown wool coat enters, followed by two workers in blue overalls. The two men say something to each other, talking about demonstrations or a strike. The woman and the workers stand behind me and patiently wait. I need to decide. The money won't be enough for all the food I wanted to buy today.

"Please give me half a loaf of rye bread," I point to the simple bread. Half a loaf will be enough for today, for Mother and myself, and there will also be enough money left to buy potatoes and maybe some sausage.

"Just half a loaf?" he asks me, making sure he heard correctly.

"Yes, please," I answer, and place the money on the counter.

The baker takes the paper bills and counts them quickly. Then he bends down and takes a loaf of rye bread out of the display case. With a sharp motion, he cuts it in half using a knife, returns half to the display case, and wraps the other half in brown paper. The two workers continue to talk quietly among themselves. Are they looking at me as I wait? Do they and the woman in the brown wool coat have enough money to buy a whole loaf, or even white bread?

"Have a nice day," the baker says to me, and hands me the half-loaf of bread. I take it, pass by the woman and the workers, open the bakery door, and exit onto the street. Maybe the sausage seller will agree to sell to me at yesterday's price, I'll argue with him more.

Later, on the way home after buying sausage, cabbage and potatoes, I stop in front of the gleaming glass window of the only confectionery on the boulevard. I've remembered it since I was a child.

On the other side of the glass, sweet pastries are arranged in straight rows. From a distance I hear the shout of a newspaper boy announcing that a wave of strikes and demonstrations will begin because of rising prices, but I ignore him. I focus only on the apple strudel and cinnamon rolls in the display window.

I slowly approach the window, almost touching it, and stop. I close my eyes and imagine the sweet pastries in my mouth, just like I imagined when I was a child.

Mother never bought me apple strudel from the confectionery; she never had enough money, but I didn't mind. Every time I walked home from school, my fingers aching from Mrs. Schattner's ruler that she would mercilessly strike me with, I would stop by the confectionery's display window, close my eyes and imagine that I was a respectable lady in a sky-blue corseted taffeta dress, eating apple strudel.

Like a castle in fairy tales, everything happening around it in the streets seems not to affect the sweet smell of cooked apples and cinnamon coming from behind the closed confectionery door. I remain standing with my eyes closed, allowing myself to imagine the flavors. From a distance I hear the shouts of the newspaper boy who continues to tell of the strikes, the clicking of horse hooves on cobblestones, the rumble of black cars, and the muffled roar of a tram passing on the track, slightly shaking the street.

"Excuse me, madam," I hear a male voice and quickly open my eyes. A man slightly older than me, dressed in a blue suit and wearing a fedora, stands before me while holding the hand of a young lady about my age wearing a fashionable green dress.

A shiny black car with a convertible roof is parked on the street a few steps behind them on the road.

"I'm sorry," I say to them and move backward. The man politely smiles at me while his companion surveys me indifferently as he opens the confectionery door for her, and they enter. The scent of cinnamon hits my face for just a moment before the door closes, and I breathe it in, turn around, and continue on my way home. I have a bag full of food that I bought; even the sausage seller gave me a small discount. That's what matters.

While walking, I get confused for a moment and start walking toward the old house, but then I remember and turn onto the new street, enter the correct front door, and climb the wooden stairs.

"Mother?" I ask as I enter the apartment and close the door behind me.

"Yes, I'm here," she tells me as she comes out of the bedroom, holding a gray rag in her hand.

"There's food and some money left," I tell her, and put the cardboard bags of food and the banknotes on the kitchen table.

Mother takes the brown notebook down from the kitchen shelf and, with neat handwriting, writes the amount in pencil. Then she takes the banknotes, rolls them up and puts them in a tin box on the shelf. I'll bring more money tomorrow.

Later, we both sit playing cards after dinner. The lamp in the corner of the living room casts a crooked shadow on the floral wall, but the house is much more organized and clean.

"The Koch boy, Bruno, was right about what he told us yesterday," Mother says, and places a card on the table. "Mrs. Vogel from downstairs likes to talk."

"What did she tell you?" I ask as I place a counter card.

"About all the neighbors," Mother answers, and places another card. "And she also asked questions. She likes to stand in the stairwell and ask questions. To know what's happening."

"Did she ask about us?" I ask, and take a card from the deck.

"We raise questions," she answers, and also takes a card.

Three gentle knocks on the door cause me to raise my gaze from the cards and look toward the hallway. Who could it be? Mother and I look at each other, and I put the cards down and get up to open the door.

Before me stands a tall, thin woman about Mother's age, around fifty. In the dim light of the stairwell's yellow lamp, I can make out the small creases at the sides of her eyes. She wears a simple black dress that contrasts with her fair face. Her nose is small, and her eyes are brown. Her dark hair, streaked with white strands of gray, is neatly gathered.

"Good evening," she says to me in a quiet voice as I hold the door almost shut.

"Good evening," I answer, examining her suspiciously. She holds a glass jar in her hands, which are wrapped in leather gloves.

"I live down the hall, across from you. I just wanted... to welcome you."

I look at her, surprised, and open the door a bit more. We've never been welcomed when moving into an apartment. People would always look at us suspiciously and wonder how much money we had.

"Thank you," I awkwardly say to her after a moment.

"This is for you." She extends the small glass jar in her hands to me. "Some cookies I made," she adds, and smiles at me.

"Thank you very much," I say to her again. "That's... very kind of you."

"You're welcome," she nods. "My name is Hanna Schneider."

"My name is Fräulein Clara, Clara Hoffman," I answer, and hold the jar of cookies in my hand. They emit a scent of cinnamon, like the smell from the magical confectionery on the boulevard.

"When I was young and came to Berlin, the neighbor gave me a box of cookies, and I wanted to preserve the tradition. Have a good evening, Fräulein Clara." She smiles at me again, and it seems to me she's as embarrassed as I am.

"Good evening, Mrs. Schneider. Thank you very much." I bid her farewell with a smile.

After I close the door, I return to the kitchen table and place the cookie jar on it.

"Who was that?" Mother asks me while looking at the jar on the table among the cards.

"Mrs. Schneider, the neighbor at the end of the hall," I say, and take two cookies out of the jar, giving one to Mother and putting one in my mouth. The sweet taste of the cookie makes me smile and close my eyes in pleasure. It crumbles in my mouth, and I slowly bite into it.

"She's a widow," Mother sighs. "Mrs. Vogel talked about her. Her husband died from Spanish flu after the war. Mrs. Vogel said his heart couldn't withstand the grief." She slowly eats the cookie in her hand.

"What grief?" I ask. I was also very sick then. It was the winter after the war. People had shut themselves in their homes, and the streets had been filled with black carriages with wooden coffins. There'd been a smell all around that I couldn't explain; I think it was the smell of fear.

"Their son," Mother sighs again. "He was killed in the war in 1916, at the Battle of the Verdun. Mrs. Vogel talked about her a lot."

"What else did she say about her?"

"That she has a glove and hat shop in the city center, but Mrs. Vogel doesn't buy from her."

"Why?" I look at the cookie jar and struggle with the urge to take another. I'll take another one tomorrow.

"Because Mrs. Vogel doesn't purchase from Jewish shops," Mother says, and takes the cards she'd placed earlier off the table. "Shall we continue playing?"

Later, as we lie in bed, I think about the taste of Mrs. Schneider's delicious cookie. We hadn't had Jewish neighbors in the previous house, nor the one before it. We'd never received gifts from neighbors at our previous homes either. Mother has long since fallen asleep and is breathing peacefully, but I can't fall asleep. What will Mrs. Vogel tell the rest of the neighbors about us?

The following evening, there is a stronger knock at the door.

"Clara, open the door," Mother tells me as she tidies the bedroom.

I remove my apron, my fingers still damp from the water in the sink. I straighten my dress and approach the door, carefully opening it.

Before me stand two men – one older, about Mother's age, broad-shouldered, his dark coat meticulously ironed. He wears a white shirt and tie, and a hat on his head positioned at exactly the right angle. Behind him stands a young man about my age with short wheat-colored hair. He is also wearing a white shirt and brown tie. His gray eyes observe me with a cold gaze. Neither of them is smiling.

"Fräulein," the older one says in a low voice, "Gustav Koch, City Housing Department. I am responsible for this building – maintenance, order, proper behavior and reports. You could say I'm a representative of the municipality. We live on the floor below you." He stands there examining me, surveying my simple dress as if I'm up for inspection. "This is my son Walther. He accompanies me," he says without further explanation.

I mumble hello awkwardly.

"May we come in?" he asks, in a tone that suggests only one answer to this question is possible.

"Please," I say, and move aside to let them pass. Why have they come?

They both pass by me through the narrow corridor and enter the living room, looking around. I feel embarrassed about the sparse furniture and the peeling wallpaper. They don't speak to each other, just observe as if mentally recording what they're seeing, so they can fill out a written report after they leave.

"I heard you move in two days ago, you and your mother," he says, glancing for a moment toward the kitchen. "We like to know who lives here. There is order in this building, and that's not to be taken for granted in times like these." He is speaking to me but continues to look around, as if recording the details of the meager furnishings in his head.

"We haven't had time to organize the apartment yet," I answer awkwardly. Did Mrs. Vogel tell him about us?

Mother comes out of the bedroom and stands before him. For a moment she lowers her gaze, but then straightens up, looks into his eyes, and greets him politely.

"Hello, Mrs..." Mr. Koch introduces himself slowly, but after a moment he turns back to look at me, then at his son, as if contemplating what he'll say next. "You understand," he continues as he slowly walks toward the small window facing the street, "in times like these, someone needs to maintain order." He moves the curtain and peeks outside. "Berlin has been changing since the war. Too quickly. People are demonstrating, there are riots..." he continues to speak quietly as he looks out the window. "There are those who support the Communists. They roam the streets with red flags and want a revolution."

His son Walther doesn't say a word, just stands in the room straight as a post, his hands behind his back.

"We're not Communists," Mother answers as she stands upright. "I was born here in Berlin, not in Moscow."

"You know," Mr. Koch moves away from the window and looks at his son, "it used to be clear who the landlord was, who the tenant was. What was allowed, and what was forbidden. Today everything is blurred, everyone thinks they can do as they please. The government allows things to happen. It shouldn't be this way."

My fingers grip the hem of my dress as I look at Mother. She stands before him and examines him in silence.

"For example, at the end of the hall on this floor," he continues to speak in a low tone, as if casually reporting, "lives Mrs. Schneider, a Jewess. A very sweet woman, of course. She has a shop selling hats and gloves near Hackescher Market. Someone once allowed her and her husband to open a shop. But not everything that's approved is proper, one needs to supervise and check." He surveys me, and I feel the tension in my body under his gray eyes. "I don't hate anyone," he continues, "but when you're responsible for a building, you learn to look beneath the surface, to arrange things. To identify who is loyal to the Aryan race, and who might want to stab the nation in the back. To identify problems before they grow." He turns away from us again and looks out the window. "Fortunately, I check on things, to make sure she knows her place," he speaks, seemingly to himself, as he looks out to the street. His son Walther stands erect the whole time, examining our facial expressions as if trying to study us.

"I'm sure she's a loyal German," Mother answers, and Mr. Koch turns from the window as if surprised by her response.

"Have you already met her? Mrs..."

"Mrs. Hoffman," Mother replies.

"Mrs. Hoffman..." he gives her a small smile. "You should know it's my job to meet, to identify, to get to know others, to decide who's loyal and who isn't. What's your name, Fräulein?" he turns to me.

"Clara," I answer, almost in a whisper.

"Clara, a beautiful name." He nods as if making a note in the invisible notebook he surely keeps in the inner pocket of the dark coat he wears. "Mrs. Hoffman, Clara..." He nods at us as if to indicate that his visit has ended. "I hope you'll be quiet, orderly tenants, and if there's a problem, you're welcome to contact me. We're like one big family here. Order is important to me," he says, and turns to leave, his son behind him.

They approach the door and open it without waiting for me to do it for them, or for us to bid them goodbye. But as he stands in the open doorway, Mr. Koch suddenly stops and turns around, as if remembering something. "Ah, of course, I forgot to introduce him properly," he says, placing his heavy hand on his son's shoulder. "My son Walther," he proudly says. "He served in the army in the Great War, not at the front – he was stationed here, in Berlin. At Headquarters. Important, precise, responsible work. Not everyone was capable of doing it."

His son's face remains inscrutable as he stands proudly, and his eyes survey me. His cold gaze creates a feeling of discomfort in me, as if he were a wolf examining whether it's worthwhile to waste his time hunting me.

"He's a good boy," Mr. Koch adds, his hand still resting on his son's shoulder. "Not like those who complain all day about failure in the war – we don't cry, we continue and will change the situation. We will restore Germany's strength, we will make it great again." He continues to speak as his eyes move from me to Mother, who stands beside me. "The problem is with those who want to take us over, with their money and their red flags, but we will fix and change that. Berlin needs people who work, not parasites who live at the expense of the German people." He finishes speaking and removes his hat, adjusts it under his arm, and then nods briefly. "Have a pleasant evening, Mrs. Hoffman, Fräulein Clara. I'm sure you'll fit in nicely here."

With confident strides they turn and walk away, their steps heavy as they descend the stairs.

I stay there with the door half-open until I hear their apartment door close one floor below us. There's a cool evening breeze in the hall that gives me goosebumps.

When I finally shut the apartment door and re-enter the house, Mother says to me: "Clara, I think you should return the glass jar to Mrs. Schneider and thank her."

I stand in front of Mrs. Schneider's door and knock gently. What will I do if she wants to invite me in? Perhaps we should keep our distance from her? I think about Mr. Koch's words.

I hear footsteps from inside the apartment, and after a moment Mrs. Schneider opens the door just a crack, peeking through it. When she realizes it's me, she opens the door wide. She's wearing a simple, dark blue housedress, and her hair is neatly gathered. Suddenly she seems smaller and more vulnerable than yesterday, when she stood at our doorway and brought us the cookies.

"Good evening," I say to her, and hand her back the small glass jar. "Thank you for the cookies, they were very delicious."

"You're welcome," she says, taking the jar. Her small fingers hold and gently stroke the little container. I have a feeling she wants to say something more to me, perhaps to invite me in or continue talking with me. But she says nothing, and I remain silent too. After a moment, I thank her again and bid her goodbye.

Only a few steps separate her apartment door from ours. For a moment I think I can still hear the footsteps of Mr. Koch and his son descending the stairs, and although I know I'm imagining it, I feel a sense of relief when I open the door to our apartment and go inside, locking the bolt behind me.

"Mother," I ask her later when we're playing cards at the kitchen table, "what do you think of Mr. Koch's son?"

"I think he'll be exactly like his father in a few years," she answers, examining the cards she's holding.

"And what do you think about his father? About Mr. Koch?"

"Mr. Koch is looking for prey," she tells me after a moment. "We won't be it," she adds, and briefly raises the cards she's holding as she looks at me.

"So why didn't you answer him when he was in our apartment?" I ask.

"Because there are people who terribly love to be in charge of words in the air; such people only love their own words," she answers, and takes a card from the deck on the table.

"There's something frightening in his talk about wanting change," I tell her as I take a card.

"He doesn't want change," she answers. "He wants to force other people to change."

"He loves the order of Kaiser Wilhelm II, maybe he wants to restore the empire."

"I have a feeling he wants to crown a new emperor." She puts down a series of kings on the table. "But it doesn't matter anymore to all the young men who already died in the war. They died for the previous Kaiser," she says as she throws down a card.

"I think Mrs. Schneider is afraid of Mr. Koch," I tell her, though I have no reason to say this. After all, Mrs. Schneider and I didn't talk at all.

"She's Jewish. No matter how much she tries to be loyal, there will always be those who see her as a foreigner."

"We're strangers in this building too, it's not for nothing that Mr. Koch paid us a visit."

"The problem with people like Mr. Koch," Mother says as she places all her cards on the table, "is that they think life is only black and white. They're sure they're on the side of white, but in the end they bring only blackness with them."

A few days later, I'm at the workshop, sitting at my sewing table and stitching men's work boots. Only the noise of the sewing machines can be heard in the hall. Out of the corner of my eye I occasionally see Mr. Konrad walking between the tables and the hunched girls, but because of the noise I can't hear his footsteps. Each time I don't notice him, I feel my body tense. I mustn't think about it, I must think about the black leather I'm holding. I can't give him an excuse to scold me again or lean over me. My eyes focus on my fingers gripping the needle as it rapidly rises and falls. I don't raise my gaze; I smell the stench of the cigarette he's smoking. He must be standing close to me now. I breathe slowly and continue to sew. After a while he moves on. I see his shoes as he continues walking across the concrete floor stained with oil and glue residue. I lower my gaze again and concentrate on my fingers, firmly gripping the tough leather and pushing it toward the needle.

A few more minutes pass, with only the noise of the sewing machines and the hissing of the gluing machine heard in the hall. Then loud talking suddenly begins. I raise my eyes and see Hildegard rising from her workstation and standing in front of Mr. Konrad, saying something to him that I can't understand.

"Sit in your spot, you're a worker like everyone else, and you'll do what I tell you," he angrily says to her. The other girls also stop sewing and watch them.

"Don't touch me, you belong to the generation of corrupt masters, those who take money that belongs to the people and put it in their pockets, those who exploit the workers, those who trade on the black market," she shouts at him, her hands raised in anger toward him.

"Take your seat and get back to work, this is your last warning," Mr. Konrad shouts as he throws the cigarette stuck in his mouth onto the concrete floor.

"We are the people, we'll deal with capitalist pigs like you when we bring down this corrupt government," she shouts back at him. Then she goes to the entrance of the workshop, takes a large piece of paper out of her coat pocket, and unfolds it into a paper poster. **Enough of hunger – rise to revolution!** is written in large red printed letters on the paper she waves in her hands. The symbol of the hammer and sickle has been drawn above them. "Come on, girls, it's time, strike now," she walks among us and roars while holding the poster above her head. Her hair is a bit disheveled, and her eyes gleam with anger.

"You're fired now," Mr. Konrad shouts as he advances toward her and raises his hands to grab the poster she's holding above her head.

"Don't touch me," she shouts back and moves backward. "Come on, Clara," she calls to me. "Come on, Gerda," she calls to another worker. "Come on, girls, it's our time for revolution."

I remain standing in my place and look at her with apprehension. I know she's right. I know Mr. Konrad is a terrible person, but what about my job? I can't risk my job. I need the money, otherwise we'll have nothing to eat.

The other girls also remain standing in place. We all look at her and at each other, searching for a hint of how to act. But no one steps forward to stand with Hildegard. Only the sound of her breathing and footsteps can be heard in the quiet hall as she slowly walks backward and away from Mr. Konrad, her hands raised above her head.

"Come on, girls," she shouts more weakly. "Come on, Clara, you need to be with me," she shouts and looks at me.

"Come on, to the manager's office, your show is over," Mr. Konrad manages to catch her near the workshop's brick wall. His large body almost covers her. He forcefully grabs her arm and drags her after him to the manager's office in the corner of the workshop. They both enter the small room, and he closes the door behind him. We all remain standing, watching them through the glass windows of the small room. No one sits down and returns to work. I feel as if my legs are welded to the floor, unable to take even one step. Through the transparent windows we can see Mr. Konrad waving his hands in front of Hildegard while the manager watches them from behind his desk. They look to me like actors in a silent film where you can only guess what's happening inside by the movements of their hands. Finally, the manager's office door opens again and Hildegard comes out, with Mr. Konrad behind her. He extends his hand, pushing her forward toward the exit.

"Don't touch me," she turns and shouts at him as she walks ahead of him. But it's no longer a shout of pride, rather more like the whimper of a wounded animal.

She slowly passes between us while Mr. Konrad walks upright behind her. When she passes me, she tries to look into my eyes, but I lower my gaze to the stained concrete floor. I can see her simple brown shoes, and his large black ones as he follows her. I should join her, but I feel my legs can't move.

By the door, she stops and turns around, shouting at us: "Why aren't you joining me? What do you think, that they'll keep you here for much longer? You're women, you're cheap labor, it's convenient for them to employ you now, but when the situation gets a bit harder they'll fire you. They don't care about you. Don't touch me," she says to Mr. Konrad. "I'm leaving on my own."

I watch her take her coat, her eyes surveying us one last time. I could still join her and call for equality, but I know I don't have the courage. My fingers fidget with the rough fabric of my dress. I can't join her. I must stay and work.

Hildegard goes outside, and Mr. Konrad slams the workshop's metal door shut behind her before turning to us. "Back to work," he shouts at us. "Unless someone else wants to join her? There are plenty of women outside who want to take your place."

One of the women sits at her workstation and starts her sewing machine, and another after her, and another. I sit back in the chair too, lowering my eyes to the sewing machine, gripping the tough leather fabric and continuing to sew. I did the right thing by not joining her. I need this job.

Only the noise of the sewing machines and the whisper of the glue machine pistons can be heard in the workshop hall. I can smell his cigarette again as he stands behind me, close to my station, and watches me. I can feel him.

"Clara," he says to me after a while as he leans toward me, his mouth stinking of cigarettes, "I want you to stay and organize the storeroom at the end of the workday."

All the women take their wages at the end of the day. Only I remain sitting at my quiet sewing station, watching them leave single file through the workshop's heavy metal door. Why did he choose me to organize the storeroom? Does he want to find a reason to fire me too, because Hildegard called out my name? Does he want to make sure I won't complain like she did? He knows I'm docile and I always do what he wants.

The last woman in line receives her wages and leaves the hall. Even the manager turns off the lights in his glass office that looks like a cage, and only Mr. Konrad and I remain in the quiet workshop hall.

Mr. Konrad walks around the workshop, turning off the lights. I can hear the quiet sound of his shoes.

"Come," he says to me when he finishes checking the empty workshop, and I begin to follow him.

Only one lamp remains lit in the hall. In the dimness, the metal machines for cutting and gluing shoes look to me like forest monsters watching me from the darkness, examining me as I walk toward the storeroom at the back of the hall. I could have refused, but I need the job and the money. I have no other choice. I walk slowly. It seems to me the quiet metal machines are watching over me, making sure I don't turn around and run away. Only the sounds of our shoes are heard on the concrete floor as Mr. Konrad places his hand on the storeroom door at the back of the production hall, opening it and turning on the light.

"Put these shoes there, in the corner," he instructs me while remaining standing at the entrance to the storeroom.

I do as he says, working as fast as possible. I just want to finish and leave this place. Mother is probably waiting for me at home.

Even though he doesn't try to come closer, I feel my whole body tense at his presence.

He lights a cigarette for himself and throws the burnt match on the floor. "I hope you weren't thinking of joining Hildegard," he says to me as he exhales cigarette smoke.

"No, sir," I answer, bending down and taking a few more shoe boxes. Why is he talking to me? Is he setting a trap for me?

"Women shouldn't engage in politics," I hear him say behind me. "These shoes, put them by the door in a pile, they're for tonight's shipment."

"Yes, sir," I answer, and continue to arrange the shoeboxes as he asked.

"I don't need subversive Communists in my workshop."

"No, sir," I agree as I organize the last shoeboxes and stand up, rubbing my hands together. "Is there anything else you need?" I ask, trying to stand upright before him like Mother would.

He looks at me and smiles slightly. Then he puts his hand into the pocket of his blue work pants.

"These are your wages." He places a bundle of bills in my palm.

"Thank you, sir," I say as I take the bills, turning toward the exit.

"Wait," he calls after me.

"Yes, sir?" I stop and turn around, feeling another wave of tension.

"This is for you too." He approaches me, again putting his hand into his pants pocket and taking out a few more banknotes. Then he takes my hand and places the additional banknotes in it. "Don't think I don't pay for what I get; maybe you'll want to come organize the storeroom again in the future," he says to me as he releases my fingers.

"Thank you very much, sir," I say. I lower my eyes, hurrying to walk out of the workshop. Despite the money I've received, and despite not having done anything wrong, I feel dirty. I hope he'll call someone else next time. I have a bad feeling about this money.

I hurry to walk down the street, but as I approach the main boulevard, I hear shouts and sounds of a demonstration. The newspaper boy has been shouting in the street in recent days that there were going to be demonstrations.

Chapter Three

Carousel

The main boulevard is blocked with protesters. They have their backs to me, marching away from the city center toward the neighborhood, and I have no choice but to push my way through them.

They fill the street—hundreds, perhaps thousands—I can't count them all. I slip between them, trying to make my way to the open street while pressing myself against the building wall. Their shouts surround me, and for a moment it seems I'm being swept away in the current, drowning among them. Everyone around me looks identical, wearing the same work clothes as mine in shades of gray and brown. Most of the men are wearing berets, others have their wheat-colored hair flying wildly from side to side in the cool breeze as they vigorously move their heads. The women wear gray dresses and thin wool coats, most with scarves on their heads, faces bare of makeup. For a moment I spot someone in the distance who looks like Hildegard, and I begin forcing my way toward her. If only I could speak with her, I could apologize for not joining her. I'd explain that I support what she did, but I had no choice—I need this job.

I push through people, trying to move forward, but they shove me as they advance. "Hildegard," I shout with all my might toward the woman with the blue-gray scarf, but she doesn't turn around. "Hildegard," I call out again.

"Bread for workers! Down with capitalism!" the people around me roar repeatedly, their lips moving in the uniform rhythm of thundering drums as they raise their fists to the gray skies.

"Hildegard," I shout, pushing through them, trying to advance as much as I can. The smells of sour sweat, rotting market vegetables, grease and fuel hang around me. The crowd closing in on me makes me anxious. For a moment it seems someone is trying to snatch my side bag with my daily wages, and I bend down, clutching it tightly.

"We will not pay the Republic's debts to the capitalists of Versailles," a dark-haired woman shouts as she stands beside me. I lift my gaze from my bag and search for Hildegard, but she's vanished, and despite looking in all directions I can no longer spot her. Above my head, red banners wave with anti-government slogan, along with red flags topped with hammers and sickles.

"Police ahead!" someone shouts, and people stop walking, though they continue yelling and raising their fists upward. I manage to push forward between them, further and further. I must move ahead and get out of here. I feel the people around me will drown me at any moment.

Step by step I advance, pushing or being pushed—I'm no longer sure which. One of my hands grips my bag tightly while the other tries to clear a path, until I reach the front line of the demonstration and look ahead. Before me stands a row of police officers in blue uniforms and helmets. They hold batons and block the way to the rest of the boulevard, but behind them the street is quiet and calm. The protesters behind and beside me shout at them, but fear moving forward. I need to get past the police, I need to get home.

With slow steps I emerge from the rows of protesters and walk to the side, trying to reach the edge of the street and pressing myself against the gray apartment building wall. I don't belong with the protesters, I'm not one of them.

My eyes focus on the policemen's hands, covered in black leather gloves as they grip their batons. Some nervously swing them from side to side.

"Where are you going?" a large policeman with a magnificent black mustache adorning his face angrily asks me as I approach them. His eyes examine me suspiciously.

"I just want to cross to the boulevard, I'm not protesting, I'm returning from work," I answer, showing him my bag.

He looks at me for another moment, examining me with his brown eyes. "Go ahead, get out of here. We'll deal with these anarchists soon," he finally says. He moves slightly, allowing me to pass through the line of police blocking the boulevard.

I hurry away from the demonstration toward home, trying to leave the noise behind. Everything seems crazy and illogical lately, everything trembles. Like when I was a little girl and Father took me on a rowboat in the Tiergarten and rocked the boat hard, and I felt nauseous and vomited.

Rain begins to fall, and I breathe deeply and hurry down the side street toward our apartment. I just want this day to end and to reach home.

As I enter the building and begin climbing the stairs, Mrs. Vogel stands there on the second floor, watching me. I must greet her politely.

"Good afternoon, Clara," she returns my greeting. "How's the new apartment?"

"It's comfortable," I answer courteously.

"I noticed you barely brought anything with you from your previous home," she quietly says, stepping a little closer to me as if expecting me to confide in her about where we came from and what possessions we own.

"We don't need much, we make do with little," I reply. Was she the one who'd reported our arrival to Mr. Koch? How much can we trust her?

"People these days don't know how to be content with little," she tells me softly, "that's the reason for all the commotion in the streets. And what about Mr. Hoffman? Is he away on business and will be joining you later?" she asks, in that quiet voice of hers that sounds like an owl's whisper.

"It's just my mother and I living in the apartment," I answer. It's none of her business that Father left us years ago.

"I see..." she whispers, and waits for me to tell her more, but I remain silent. "A good husband can always help support the family. Especially in difficult times," she finally says.

"Have a pleasant evening, Mrs. Vogel," I say, and turn toward the stairs.

"Clara, have you met the other residents in the building yet?" she asks, and I stop again and turn to face her.

"I believe so, Mrs. Vogel," I smile politely.

"They're all nice people, I'm sure you've already noticed that," she continues.

"Yes, Mrs. Vogel, they're nice people."

"I understand Mr. Koch visited you. He's in charge of the building. It's important that he stays informed. Have you also met the Jewish widow?" she says.

I hesitate for a moment. What does she want me to answer? "No, I haven't met her yet," I finally reply. Is she like Mr. Koch?

"There are those who say the Jews are to blame for our defeat in the Great War, that they stabbed the nation in the back. But I don't believe that," she continues speaking to me in her quiet voice. "After all, her son was killed in the war. But they say she actually opposed him enlisting and serving the Fatherland. Did you know that no Aryan woman is willing to work in her hat and glove shop? Perhaps there's truth to the rumors about the Jews," she finishes speaking and looks up the staircase toward her apartment.

"I don't know, Mrs. Vogel, I don't know her," I tell her as politely as I can, and continue up the stairs. Does she share Mr. Koch's opinion about the Jewish widow? Should we be careful about our relationship with her?

Inside the apartment, I sit with Mother in the kitchen, the brown notebook in front of us. "This is what I earned today." I pull the banknotes from my pocket and place them on the table.

Mother takes the bills and counts them slowly. "Did he give you a raise?" she asks me.

"No, why?"

"Because there's more here than last time."

I remember the money Mr. Konrad gave me for organizing the storeroom. "Yes, I received a bit more today. But I didn't get a raise. Maybe we'll get a salary increase next time."

"Why did he give you more money?" Mother asks.

"It doesn't matter," I answer. I don't want to tell her about the storeroom and the feeling of being alone with him there.

She looks at me for a moment, and says nothing. Then she lowers her gaze and records the money in the notebook, putting the bills into the small metal box. "They always think they can buy things with their money," she says, as if to herself, and we both know what she means.

"How are we doing?" I ask, changing the subject. I don't want to talk about Mr. Konrad anymore.

"If prices continue to rise, we'll be in trouble," she simply tells me, and closes the notebook. "Would you like some tea?" she asks as she stands up, moving to the kettle on the metal stove.

"Yes, please. We need to get more money," I answer. I stand up, walking into the small living room and looking around.

"Are you thinking about what we discussed back at the previous apartment?" she asks.

"Yes," I answer, "we delayed then, and in the end we didn't have enough money."

"It's not safe to bring someone into the home. There are many people you shouldn't trust."

"Do you have another choice?" I look at her. The living room is small and cramped, but we'll manage to fit a folding bed in it.

"We'll need to look for a man, their wages are always more reliable and we can charge them more," she says, lighting the fire on the stove.

"I'm not sure Mr. Koch would like a strange man living as a tenant in a house with two women," I tell her.

"Mr. Koch is not the owner of this apartment, and he doesn't yet pay our rent." She takes out two cups and places a few tea leaves in them.

"Let's finish our tea and go to the flea market, to look for a folding bed for us," I say, continuing to look around the small living room. "We'll organize the bedroom in the evening, and tomorrow I'll go to the newspaper and place an ad."

"Good morning, sir, I'd like to place an ad for a tenant," I say to the clerk the next morning at the *Berliner Volks-Zeitung* newspaper office. He sits in a small room; a wooden desk covered with black ink stains, notes and stamps stands between us. Behind the small room, the printing machines roar like a locomotive struggling to pull a freight train, and people at the side entrance shout to overcome the noise as they carry out bundles of newspapers tied with rope, loading them onto a truck.

"Only male tenants, or female tenants as well?" He raises his gaze from the wooden table and the papers spread before him, and he looks at me. His blue-gray eyes survey my lips and dress through the metal spectacles he wears. He's about fifty years old, with only sparse black hair adorning the sides of his head. Does he suspect my intentions aren't pure?

"Female tenants as well, of course," I answer with embarrassment.

"What's the wording?" He pulls out a note from one of the drawers and holds a fountain pen. His fingertips are blackened with ink stains.

"How many words do I have?"

"Fifteen," he answers indifferently.

I dictate the text of the ad to him, and he writes the words on the piece of paper. Afterward I take out the bundle of banknotes from my side bag and hand it to him, watching his ink-stained hands collect it and toss it into the wooden drawer of his desk.

"When will you publish the ad?"

"The notice will be published tomorrow, and once more next week," he answers while holding one of the stamps from the table and forcefully striking it on the note. He then places it on a pile of other notes.

"Thank you very much," I say as I leave the printing house. I need to hurry to get to work on time; perhaps I'll have no choice but to pay for a tram ticket. The main thing is that the notice will be published tomorrow, and a new tenant will come to us. We need the money. Rain begins to fall, and I quicken my pace. I'm afraid they'll throw us out onto the street again.

Chapter Four

The New Tenant

The next morning, I stop at the newspaper stand on my way to work and look for the *Berliner Volks-Zeitung*. The headline on the front page screams about a new strike by coal miners in the Ruhr region. I hold the newspaper and open it, searching for the ad I placed yesterday.

"Madam, are you buying the newspaper or not?" the vendor standing inside the kiosk asks.

"No..." I apologetically say. "I just want to see something."

"If you're not buying the paper, put it back where it belongs. Newspapers aren't free," he angrily answers.

"I'm sorry," I reply, and stuff the newspaper back among all the others competing with their black headlines about strikes and demonstrations.

At the workshop, I work at the sewing table without pause, bowing my head and concentrating on the leather straps my fingers hold. Someone will read the ad in the paper and come to see the apartment.

On my way back from work, I pass by the neighborhood bulletin boards and post notices about the available room. Some boards have large posters of cabaret performances, while others have posters from the Communist Party. But most of the Communist Party posters are hidden behind posters of the new party – the National Socialist German Workers' Party. They have a symbol of a tilted swastika. No gentleman comes to see the apartment that evening, nor the next day.

A week later, on my way back from work, I stop near the newspaper stand and look at my newspaper again. I know my ad is inside, I know someone will read it and come to us, I know the strikes will end and the economic situation will improve, it must improve.

I meet Mrs. Vogel in the stairwell. She stands in the hallway, holding a broom, wearing a brown dress that hangs loosely on her thin body. She's blocking the stairway, leaving me no choice but to pass by her.

"Good afternoon, Clara, is everything alright with you and your mother?" she stops me and speaks quietly, almost whispering.

"Everything's perfectly fine with us," I answer without thinking, though her question surprises me. Has something happened while I was at work?

"Do you have enough money?" she asks while looking side to side, as if examining the stairwell to see whether anyone else is listening to us.

"Why do you ask?"

"Are you short on money? No one has money," she quickly says, continuing to look around. "Only Mrs. Schneider has money, from her glove and hat shop. The Jews always have money, you should know, they always know how to manage. And Mr. Koch as well, because he works for the municipality, he's a respectable man," she says without pause.

"We're not short on money," I answer politely. Why is she asking this question? What does she know?

"Then who is that young girl who came to you a few minutes ago?" she asks.

"What do you mean?"

"Are you renting out a room?" Mrs. Vogel answers, but doesn't wait for my response. "I saw a note about renting a room on the bulletin board. Did you post it? Does the girl who came seem suitable to you? She looked like an irresponsible young girl to me. Young women wandering alone in the city, looking for apartments to live in. I wouldn't trust such a woman and bring her into my apartment. Does Mr. Koch know you're taking in a sub-tenant?" she speaks without stopping, and looks upward to the stairs leading to our floor.

"I need to hurry, have a nice day," I tell her, and I climb the stairs. What young girl is she talking about? Did someone come to see the apartment?

I pass by Mrs. Schneider's closed door, enter our home, and close the door behind me.

"Clara, meet Miss Krause, she's just leaving. Miss Krause, meet my daughter Clara," Mother says as I enter the kitchen. Mother stands there facing a young woman about my age, perhaps a year or two younger.

"Pleased to meet you," the young woman turns to me and politely says. "Have a nice day, Mrs. Hoffmann, thank you very much." She turns to Mother and shakes her hand. Then she bends down, picks up her simple cardboard suitcase, rises and heads toward the door. Her light hair tends toward a brown shade, gathered in a low, fashionable ponytail, and her green-brown eyes examine me for just a second as she moves towards the front door. Her skin is fair, and she wears a modern but simple dress. "Good day," she replies with either politeness or embarrassment as she passes by me.

"Good day," I mumble, and open the front door for her. What's happening here? Why is she leaving?

The door closes behind her, and for another moment I hear her footsteps on the wooden stairs. Why didn't Mother accept her? I turn and look at the kitchen entrance, where she remains standing.

"She works at a nightclub, one of the cabarets, she's a waitress or hostess or something like that," Mother tells me when she notices my look. "We don't need such women living here with us," she adds, "we need a respectable gentleman with a steady salary. I thanked her and told her that the room is unfortunately no longer available."

"But no one has come, for a week no one has come," I approach her.

"Don't worry, we'll manage. They haven't come yet, but they will," she tells me and turns her back. "Gentlemen are rare, but they too need to find rooms to live in. We'll manage in the meantime."

I breathe for a moment. I must do something, we need the money. "Mother, how will we live without money? What if they throw me out of the workshop like they did one of the other workers?" I add as I take out the salary I received today and place the bundle of bills on the table.

"Why would they fire you? You're a good worker."

"Yes, I'm a good worker," I answer, looking at the money lying on the table, "but sometimes it's not enough to be a good worker. The streets are full of women looking for work who thought they were good workers."

"We'll manage, Clara, we always manage," Mother lowers her gaze to the pile of bills thrown on the table.

"We need someone to live here, Mother, we need her to live here. We have no other choice. She's a young girl looking for a home, she's just like me."

"She's not like you, you have a home. The fact that she has nowhere to live is her problem. She's not suitable," Mother angrily answers and sits on the wooden chair.

"She needs a home too, Mother, and we need money."

"You're too good, Clara, you've always been too good to others," Mother tells me as she sighs.

"Please, Mother, at least until we find another gentleman." I lean closer to her, placing my hands on the old table. I'm so afraid they'll throw us out of this apartment. I fear the looks of passersby on the street more than whatever Mr. Koch will have to say.

For a moment I expect Mother to say something, perhaps to try to convince me that I'm wrong and she's right, but she remains silent. I turn and open the door, and start running down the stairs. "Miss Krause!" I call after her as I run, passing Mrs. Vogel who is still standing in the hallway, examining me with her gaze. "Miss Krause!"

At the bottom of the stairs I catch up with her and stand in front of her, breathing heavily. "Miss Krause, please wait," I say.

She stops and examines me with her green-brown eyes. She has a beautiful, soft face, and pink lips coated with a bit of pink lipstick. I'm not as pretty as she is; my hair is darker and my chest is too large. I also don't usually coat my lips with lipstick.

"Yes?" she asks after a moment.

"My mother was mistaken, Miss Krause, the room in our apartment is still available for rent," I tell her as I try to regulate my breathing.

"If it's still available, I'd be happy to take it. You surely know how hard it is for a young woman to survive alone in Berlin." She smiles at me with relief. "So many people don't want to rent a room to a young woman on her own."

From above I hear Mrs. Vogel's footsteps; she's probably trying to listen to our conversation, but I don't care. We need a tenant for our room. "Mother told me you work at a cabaret club," I say, and lower my gaze to her hands holding her cardboard suitcase. My gaze surveys her as I look for suspicious signs. Her delicate fingers are well-groomed and her nails are painted with light pink, shiny nail polish, in a modern style. I've always been too embarrassed to apply nail polish.

"I don't work at a cabaret," she smiles at me. "I work at the Wintergarten Club at the Central Hotel on Potsdamer Straße

5. I work there as a waitress and hostess. I had to find work, I had no choice," she adds in a quiet voice.

"I understand," I answer. From above I hear Mrs. Vogel's footsteps in the stairwell again. I need to decide. I take a deep breath.

"The rent is paid a week in advance, and it's forbidden to make noise or entertain men in the room," I tell her.

"I have money." She takes a bundle of bills out of her small side bag and shows it to me.

"Come with me," I smile at her. Maybe her money will be enough to get Mother's silver cutlery back.

On the way up we pass Mrs. Vogel, who continues to sweep the hallway and examines us with curiosity. Inside, Mother smiles at her but stays in the kitchen while I show her the room.

"You can call me Clara," I tell her as she puts her suitcase on the bed that was Mother's and mine.

"Please, call me Anna," she smiles at me. "You won't regret this. I'll be a quiet tenant." She places her side bag on the dresser and turns her back to me. She approaches the wooden closet in the corner of the room, opens her cardboard suitcase, and begins arranging her clothes in the closet.

Later, after the sun has set and we've played cards, Mother and I move aside the coffee table in the living room and open the folding bed. Then I take out the curtain from the wooden closet that will give us privacy. I carefully spread it to hide our bed from the entrance hallway; Anna is now in what used to be our bedroom.

"Did you know Mrs. Fischer's daughter from our previous building is going to marry a young man she met? They say she's pregnant. I wonder where she met him," Mother says while taking off her dress, remaining only in her camisole. She spreads the dress over the back of the chair next to the folding bed; then she sits on the bed, removes her hairpins, places them on the wooden chair as well, lies down and covers herself with the blanket.

"Did you hear there were demonstrations in the city center again today? They say the police beat the protesters." I turn my back to her and take off my dress. I don't want to talk about men and children and marriages. I also don't want to talk about Mrs. Fischer's daughter who managed to find herself a husband. The thought sits bitterly in my throat as I fold my own dress.

"Yes, I heard, the Communists were demonstrating, and opposite them the new party, the National Socialists. Come, get into bed, you'll catch cold," she tells me, and I get into bed with her. A faint smell of cigarette smoke seeps through the small crack beneath the door to Anna's room.

"I hope we won't regret taking her in," Mother says.

"It's nicer to sleep here than on the street," I answer.

"We always managed to get by, even when you were a little girl," she tells me, and I feel ashamed of what I've said. She's been raising me since Father left.

"I'm sorry," I tell her after a while.

"It's alright. It's not easy to raise a child without a father. It's also not easy to grow up without a father. Good night," she answers.

"Good night, Mother," I say, and turn off the light. I hear her calm breathing in the darkness, but I can't fall asleep. Mother's quiet breathing causes me unease instead of calming me. I'm always embarrassed to ask the question that troubles me: why did Father leave us? And what will become of me? Why don't I have a husband and children? And if I find a husband, will he leave me?

Anna's door opens for a moment, and she comes out with quiet steps, passing by us on her way to the hall. In the faint light coming through the window, I can see that she's wearing a coat. Is she going out to work now?

The soft noise of the front door closing doesn't wake Mother, nor does the soft ticking of the silver alarm clock resting on the wooden dresser in the corner of the living room. She continues to sleep peacefully.

Finally, I get out of bed and stand in front of the window, opening it and looking at the faint street lights. From afar comes the muffled noise of a demonstration and police whistles, but I ignore them and look upward. *I will succeed in finding myself a husband*, I promise myself as I look at the black sky. But no matter how much I search among the clouds, the city lights are too strong, and I can't see so much as a single star.

Down in the street, I see Anna walking toward the avenue.

A few days later, I enter the building on my way back from work. The wooden stairs creak beneath my shoes as I climb them. I try to ascend quietly so Mrs. Vogel won't come out and start talking to me, but when I reach the second floor the door suddenly opens and Mr. Koch emerges. He's dressed in a pressed dark gray suit and is wearing a tie.

"Good evening, Mr. Koch," I greet him.

"Good evening, Clara," he greets me back, his hand making a gentle motion toward his hat.

He begins to descend the stairs as I continue climbing to our floor.

"Fräulein Clara," he suddenly calls to me, and I stop. What does he want from me?

"Yes, sir?" I turn to him.

"I heard you have a new subtenant in your apartment," he says.

"Yes, sir..." I answer, searching for something more to explain, but I can't find anything else to say. He makes me nervous.

"And I understand she isn't a relative." His gray eyes look directly into mine.

"No, sir..."

"And do you know where she comes from?"

"My mother, Mrs. Hoffmann, spoke with her. She probably knows, sir," I answer, feeling tension throughout my body.

"Yes..." he speaks slowly, as if pondering the answers I'm giving him, examining each word so he can record them in that imaginary notebook he keeps in his jacket pocket. "I'm sure you wouldn't let just anyone into your home. I'm sure Mrs. Hoffmann checked her background," he adds, studying me with his eyes as if looking for a sign that I'm telling the truth.

"Yes, sir, she inquired about her," I agree. My hand tightly grips the wooden banister.

"You know, Clara, we're like family here in this building. In the end, we need to know everything about each other," he continues in the same slow speech, and gives me a small smile that only makes me more anxious.

"Yes, sir," I answer.

"Well... have a nice day. Give my regards to Mrs. Hoffmann." He again touches his hat with his fingers as a greeting, turns his back to me, and begins descending the stairs.

"Yes, sir. Good day, sir," I quietly say, continuing to hold the wooden banister. I only resume climbing the stairs when he leaves the building and I no longer hear his footsteps. Who told him about her? Mrs. Vogel? Or perhaps he'd already met her? I enter our home and close the door behind me. We're allowed to have a subtenant in our apartment. But I don't tell Mother about the conversation. I don't want to worry her. She has enough concerns as it is.

At night, after Mother falls asleep, I get out of bed and go to the kitchen, careful not to wake her. I quietly light a candle and place a kettle on the metal stove in the corner of the kitchen. When the water boils, I prepare myself a tea infusion from dried apple peels and a bit of mint.

I take Mother's brown cardboard notebook out of the wooden drawer and open it. By candlelight I examine the neat figures Mother habitually records—wages, food expenses, rent, the bold line for the new apartment, and the money we receive from our tenant Anna. Mother would be angry if she knew I was looking at her accounting notebook while she slept, but I must know our situation. I study the numbers. We have no choice, we need Anna to continue living with us. We need her money.

The sound of a key in the door makes me quickly close the notebook and slide it back into the drawer. The door opens, and in the yellow light from the stairwell lamp I see Anna's silhouette. After a moment, she closes the door. In the weak candlelight I notice her bend down, remove her shoes, and walk down the entrance hallway toward her room.

"Good night," I whisper to her.

"Good night," she whispers back.

"Would you like a cup of tea, perhaps?" I ask. We've barely spoken since she arrived.

"I'd love some," she tells me, and enters the kitchen. By candlelight I notice that a fashionable, glossy mustard-colored dress is peeking out from beneath her plain gray coat. She holds silver Mary Jane shoes in one hand, and a purple velvet clutch bag in the other.

"Come, sit," I whisper, and rise to prepare her tea. I take the metal box where we keep our tea out of the drawer and place some in the strainer. I don't want her to think we have no money. Then I pour the hot water and serve her the warm cup of tea.

"Thank you." She holds the cup with both hands and smiles at me. "It's always nice to drink tea at the end of a workday."

"Have you been working there long?" I ask as I sip my tea. The pink nail polish on her fingernails gleams in the candle-light.

"A few months," she whispers. She smells of cigarettes.

"And is it difficult work?"

"It takes getting used to," she tells me after a moment. "But I love the lights, the music and the dancing," she continues while holding the teacup with both hands and blowing on it. "There are handsome men there who invite me for drinks and want to dance with me," she quietly says, almost in a whisper, and she takes a sip from her teacup.

"Men invite you to dance with them?" I ask, trying to whis-per with indifference so she doesn't think I'm jealous. I've never been to such a club. I don't even have a suitable dress to wear. We're all women at the workshop, except for Mr. Konrad and the manager, and there are hardly any eligible men left in the city since the war and its terrible losses.

"There are nice men there, Clara. There are men who didn't return from the war on the Western Front, men with money. Men who wear suits and ties and smell of cologne, not like the simple workers at the workshops that you and I know. There are men who love to dance, men who aren't troubled by rising prices. To them, banknotes are just meaningless paper, they have plenty of them."

"It must be nice to dance with such men."

"Every woman dreams of such a man proposing to her. And until I meet the right man, it pays for my room in your apartment. It's much better than what I had before I came here," she answers quietly.

I want to ask her where she came from, where she worked before and whether she was born in Berlin, but I don't have enough courage, even though I should do it. We continue to drink in silence, her tea and my apple peel infusion.

"Good night, thank you for the tea," she finally says, and rises from her seat.

"Good night," I answer.

"You should come with me sometime, Clara, you'll love the music and the lights, maybe you'll even meet a nice man."

"Thank you," I reply, still holding my empty cup. She enters her room, and I hear her door closing behind her with a soft click. The strip of light beneath the crack of her door glows on the wooden floor for a few more minutes before it too disappears. But I remain sitting at the dining table, holding my empty teacup in my hands.

Despite seeing the men and women who drive through the streets in new cars, dressed in suits and fashionable dresses, I can't imagine a world where there's enough money. Finally I extinguish the candle and return to bed. Perhaps I'll dream of having a beautiful dress like Anna's before I wake up tomorrow to work at the workshop.

"Break time," Mr. Konrad announces a few days later, precisely at noon, and we all rise from our sewing tables and head out to the courtyard. Pleasant sunshine warms the inner courtyard, and I savor the warm rays as I eat an apple, the sweet juice running down my fingers.

"So how was it yesterday with the new guy?" Gerda asks the new worker who replaced Hildegard. Mr. Konrad brought her in the day after Hildegard shouted in the workshop and he fired her. Since then, the new worker has been sitting at her table, her fingers nimble with the needle, faster than the rest of us.

"He took me to a Fritz Lang film, and afterward we walked along Unter den Linden holding hands," the new worker excitedly recounts, her eyes bright with the memory.

"And at the movie? Didn't you do anything besides hold hands?" someone else asks her, and they all laugh, their voices echoing against the brick walls.

"He was a real gentleman," the new worker says, blushing, her cheeks turning the color of ripe cherries. "Almost a gentleman," she adds with a smile. A few more workers join the conversation, speaking quietly while giggling. I've been trying to look for Hildegard at every demonstration I see in the city since Mr. Konrad fired her. I watch from a distance, trying to identify her among the protesters raising signs, their voices raised in anger against the system.

"Will you meet with your almost-gentleman again?" Gerda asks, leaning forward with conspiratorial interest.

"He said he wants to take me to a café today," the new worker answers with a smile. She looks so young to me. Twenty or twenty-one years old. The rest of the workshop workers are younger than me too. Hildegard was my age. What will become of me? Will I always live with Mother?

"Come on, let's go in, our break is over," one of the workers says, and we all hurry back to sit at our sewing tables, the machines humming to life once more.

On my way home, I pass by the garden that surrounds the neighborhood water tower. Several women sit on wooden benches in the garden. Two of them have baby carriages in front of them, rocking them back and forth in a slow, hypnotic motion. Next to them sit two other women holding toddlers dressed in simple wool clothes. One of the women examines me as I pass, her eyes following me, but I ignore her and smile at a skinny street cat that follows me for several steps, up to the gray entrance of the building.

"Come," I whisper to it, extending my hand, but it flees from me into the bushes. I turn and enter the stairwell, climbing to the third floor apartment I share with Mother.

In the nights that follow, I lie awake in bed while Mother sleeps, staring at the ceiling's water stains. Even when I hear Anna quietly entering the apartment, I don't get up. She passes through the living room with quiet steps. Her short silver dress sparkles in the dim light like fairy wings fluttering rapidly and rustling softly. Even her dancing shoes, which she holds in her hand, sparkle like stars in the darkness, catching what little moonlight filters through our thin curtains.

After she closes her door, I turn in bed and look at the strip of light beneath her door. What is her job like? What is it like to meet men? I want to talk to her about it, but I know Mother would object. Is this my fate? To remain without a husband, together with Mother? After a few more minutes the light in her room goes out, and I close my eyes and fall asleep, dreams of a different life taking shape.

Every night I stay awake in bed, waiting to hear her come in, but one night I wait until she quietly enters and closes her bedroom door. I can smell a faint scent of cigarettes coming from her room, finding its way to the living room through the crack under the door, tantalizing and forbidden. I get out of bed and approach her bedroom door, gently knocking. I need to do this.

"Come in," I hear her from the other side of the door.

"Good evening," I hesitantly say after opening the door and entering her room. "Did you really mean it? Your offer for me to come with you to the club?"

Chapter Five

The Club

The next evening, I'm standing in the small apartment's bathroom, buttoning my coat to the very top and bending down to ensure the dress isn't peeking out from beneath the coat's hem. I'm tense.

I raise my gaze to the mirror again and run my hand over my hair, making sure not a single strand has escaped the pins holding it in place. I'm wearing no makeup. I take a deep breath and step out of the bathroom.

"Good night, Mother, I'll be back late," I tell her, trying to maintain a calm tone. She sits at the kitchen table mending holes in stockings, her fingers delicately holding the needle.

"Where are you going?" She looks up and studies me with a questioning gaze.

"I'm going out with someone, don't wait up for me," I say, forcing a smile. I don't want her to see how nervous I am.

"Who are you going out with?"

"Someone I met. You don't know him. He's taking me to a café," I tell her.

"Are you going out with Anna?"

"No, I'm not going out with Anna. I told you, I'm going out with someone."

"I saw Anna leave for her club a few minutes ago," she answers, continuing to examine me. "Why are you wearing a coat? It's not cold outside."

"Goodbye, Mother. I'll be home later," I say, hurrying out before she can ask more questions. I'm grown now, and can go to a café with a man without my mother interrogating me about my whereabouts.

I quietly descend the stairs so Mrs. Vogel won't peek at me through her peephole in search of new gossip. The rustling of the fabric beneath my concealing coat creates a sense of discomfort. Even the music emanating from the Koch family's apartment makes me anxious. It's as if everyone here always knows things about others, as if nothing in this building can be hidden from anyone.

Only when I step onto the street do I feel more liberated.

"Clara," Anna whispers to me from the alleyway, "I'm here."

"Let's go," I say to her, opening my coat slightly.

"How's the dress? Does it fit you? I thought you'd changed your mind," she says to me.

"I didn't change my mind. Mother delayed me," I lie. I had spent long minutes in front of the bathroom mirror, awkwardly examining myself. The shiny blue dress she gave me clings too tightly to my body. I'm not as thin as she is, and my breasts are larger than hers.

"I brought these for you. You can't go to the club like that."
She takes out a pair of glossy black Mary Jane shoes from her
bag. "Try them on," she adds.

I remove my plain brown leather shoes, momentarily placing my bare feet on the sidewalk, feeling the coolness of the
stones. Then I take the shoes she offers me. My fingers grip the
shoe firmly as I push my foot into it. It's too small and tight,
but I put the other one on as well and stand up.

"How are they?" she asks me.

"Comfortable," I answer, and take a few steps. I'm not used
to heels, and the shoes pinch. I feel clumsy and unstable, but
I smile at her. "Let's go," I say, and begin to walk slowly down
the sidewalk, holding my old shoes in my hand.

"What about your shoes?" she asks me.

"Just a moment," I tell her, and when we reach the garden
near the neighborhood water tower, I hide them among the
bushes.

"We need to hurry, we're late," she says, and we both walk
to the main street to catch the tram. The tram ticket is too
expensive for me, but I have no choice; we can't walk all the
way to the Wintergarten, the club is too far. I knew that when
I asked her to take me there, to see the world where men have
money and spend it on entertainment.

Inside the tram, I grip the cold nickel pole as the car trembles along the tracks. The yellowish light from the street lamps illuminates the road with a weak yellow beam. Occasionally a man in a suit riding a bicycle crosses it, probably returning home from work.

"Clara, watch out!" Anna whispers as a drunk man stumbles toward us inside the car. Her sparkling sequined dress flashes beneath her black coat as she moves toward the back of the car.

The tram is packed with people: an elderly couple whispering to each other, tired workers in dirty work clothes, men in dark coats and fedoras, and that drunk. I notice a group of young men in fashionable suits casting interested glances our way, and lower my eyes in embarrassment. Can they see my shiny dress beneath my coat? The tight fabric firmly wrapped around me makes me feel exposed under their gaze.

"Do you think they're also going to the club?" Anna whispers with a smile, shifting her leg slightly to reveal her silver dress. I grow uncomfortable and look out the window.

Even at this hour, people are still standing in lines outside the bakeries, holding baskets full of banknotes. Yesterday, when I was at the bakery, the price had doubled, and again I'd bought only half a loaf of bread. When would all this end?

"We get off at the next stop," Anna says, fixing her hair while smiling at the young men again. Her short blonde hair is so fashionable. One of the men whispers something to his friends that I can't hear. How I wish I could be as beautiful as she is.

The tram stops with a screech, and a group of workers in work clothes come aboard. They talk loudly about politics, the crisis, the Communists, and how change is needed to return to the values of the past. Some of them smoke cigarettes, and the cheap tobacco smell suffocates me. One of the men examines us with an angry look, and I want to step back, but Anna pulls my hand.

"Come, this is our stop."

We step down onto the sidewalk, and I breathe in the cool air with relief. Anna opens her coat for a moment, shakes out her sequined dress, and I do the same. The club is just a few streets away. The city is different here—there are many new cars on the street, and the men wear suits. From a distance I can already hear music—modern American jazz. I'd only heard it for the first time after the war.

"Are you ready?" Anna asks as she stops in front of the entrance and takes a silver tube out of her clutch bag. She gently pushes her finger into one end of the tube until a bright red lipstick emerges from the other end. In the light outside the club, she holds a mirror and fixes the lipstick on her lips. I've never seen such a modern lipstick tube before.

"I'm ready," I answer, feeling excitement throughout my body.

"Just a moment, don't move," she smiles and turns to me, her fingers holding the rouge. "All the men will look at you," she says quietly as she applies lipstick to my lips as well. I try not to move, to get used to the strange taste of the paste. "Now we're ready," she laughs and takes my arm, and we walk together toward the lights and sounds of the club's front door, into the Berlin night that's just beginning. I'm tense.

After we cross the front door to the club, a dark corridor leads us inside. We walk through it as if floating, flying like butterflies drawn to the lights and sounds emanating from its far end, inviting us toward them. Anna's silver dress flashes in the blinking lights, and when I lower my gaze I see my blue dress sparkling too. I feel so exposed without my coat. We'd checked our coats at the entrance with a boy wearing a round black hat standing behind a counter in a small room. Around us the men and women appear like silhouettes, some passing by smelling of perfumes and cigarette smoke, others standing embraced and leaning against the dark walls, caressing each other and kissing. But I don't stare at them, I just walk forward toward the moving lights, the loud music, and the enormous hall that appears before my eyes like a world of enchantment.

"Let's dance," I think I hear Anna shouting to me as she pulls my hand, and I follow her through all the people dancing to the loud music. They look to me like a kaleidoscope of glowing colors, sparkling without pause. Men in white shirts and black ties move to the rhythm of the music, holding women in their arms who wear short, gleaming dresses and dance without stopping, swaying their hips. Everyone gazes at the stage, where a dark-skinned man is singing, several light-skinned women dancing bare-chested behind him. I stand and watch them, amazed.

"Clara," Anna stands beside me again, holding a lit cigarette in one hand and a drink in the other. "Meet Hans." She introduces me to a young man about my age.

"Pleased to meet you, Clara." He extends his hand to me and leans closer to overcome the noisy music.

"Pleased to meet you, Hans." I smile at him excitedly. He's a bit taller than me, his brown hair carefully styled and oiled, and he's wearing a white button-up shirt.

"Dance with me," he says decisively while taking my hand and pulling me closer to the stage.

We begin dancing to the rhythm of the music; I let him lead. Occasionally he places his hand on my arm amid all the music around us, and I allow it. This is his world, he knows how to guide me.

We dance without stopping, but suddenly he disappears among the dancers. I look around, searching for him. Did I do something wrong? The women and men around me continue dancing, eyes riveted to the dark-skinned man on stage and the bare-chested women dancing behind him.

"Cheers," I hear someone close to me, and turn to see Hans standing beside me, offering a drink. He holds a second glass in his other hand.

"Cheers," I shout back to overcome the noise and drink the beverage in one gulp, ignoring its sharp taste in my throat as I continue dancing. The dark-skinned singer leaves the stage to applause from the crowd, and a tall, fair-haired female singer wearing a shiny black dress takes his place and begins to sing. I'm mesmerized by her painted red lips. Behind her the bare-chested dancers lift the hems of their short skirts, revealing legs wrapped in black stockings and held by garters. Every so often Hans pulls me closer and closer to him, bringing me more drinks which I gulp down while smiling at him. I'm completely sweaty and my head is spinning, but I don't care; I don't even mind the smell surrounding me, of cigarettes and sweat mixed with sweet perfume. I have no idea where Anna has disappeared to; when I occasionally look around trying to find her, I can't spot her in the dancing crowd. For a moment I think I glimpse her talking to one of the waiters in the corner of the club, near one of the side doors, but some dancers block my view again. When I try to search for her, she's gone. Hans disappears too, and returns after a few minutes holding two more drinks, which I consume in one gulp. The lights above me sparkle like balls of stars. His hand constantly holds my waist, and he caresses my bare back.

"Another drink?" Hans brings his lips to my ear and shouts, his hand on my waist pressing me against him.

"No..." I tell him. I'm starting to feel dizzy, perhaps from the music and noise.

"Come to the side," he shouts, and pulls me after him. I grip his arm tightly as we pass through the crowd. The noise suddenly feels too loud, and all the lights hurt my eyes. "Come here," he tells me, taking me to the dark front corridor of the club. In the darkness, I lean against the wall and breathe slowly. The silhouettes of men and women around me seem distant and remote. Only the lights of cigarettes twinkle in the darkness like fireflies. The music is fainter here. I try to steady my breathing. Only now do I feel my tight shoes.

Suddenly I feel his lips pressed against mine as he tries to forcefully kiss me, and his hands try to touch me.

"No, stop... quit it..." I tell him, and try to free myself from his kiss.

"I have to, you're so beautiful." He presses against me and tries again.

"No, stop..." I tell him again and move my lips away from his tongue, which tries to penetrate my mouth.

"This is what all of you want, free dancing and drinks and men," he whispers as he continues to caress me. His hands grip firmly my waist.

"No... stop... I'm not like that... not the first time..." I tell him, and manage to push him off me. I feel dizzy, and my head hurts.

"I shouldn't have listened to Anna. I did you a favor. I don't need you..." I think he tells me before disappearing into the darkness, but not before squeezing my breasts.

I try to push him away again, but my hands meet empty air, and I remain leaning against the wall, breathing slowly. I'm not that kind of girl.

The men and women around me continue embracing and kissing, and I lower my gaze in embarrassment, though in the darkness I can't make out who they are. Two tears roll down my cheeks. I shouldn't have come here.

I want to go looking for Anna, but I can't bring myself to return to the lights and music, which now seem frightening to me. They appear like the gaping mouth of a monster threatening to swallow me, and I remain standing in the dark corridor. Finally I walk in the opposite direction, toward the exit, occasionally leaning against the wall to support myself.

At the entrance to the small coat check room, I stop and hold onto the doorframe, entering with slow steps. The soles of my feet ache so much in the small shoes.

"Here's your coat," the boy in charge of the coats hands me mine, and I wrap myself in it.

"May I wait here for my friend?" I ask, and he nods silently. He has a small birthmark on his right cheek.

I stand in the corner of the small room, watching people checking and retrieving their coats. I'm tired and find it difficult to stand.

"Here you go, ma'am," the boy says after a while, bringing out a wooden chair from behind the counter and placing it in the corner of the room.

"Thank you," I smile at him wearily and sit in the chair. I just want to go home now. The people who come to collect their coats look at me, but say nothing.

"Enjoying the club? Is it fun to dance like that?" the boy asks me after some time.

"Yes, it's fun," I answer, even though I hadn't enjoyed it. "Do you have a girlfriend?" I ask him after a moment.

"No, not yet," he smiles awkwardly and blushes.

"When you do, take her dancing, but treat her nicely," I tell him.

"There you are, you disappeared on me," I hear Anna as she enters the room, and I turn toward her. "Shall we go home?" she asks, handing her cardboard ticket to the boy. "Let's go." She takes her coat from him and heads for the exit.

"Good night, thanks for the chair," I bid farewell to the boy, and hope he'll remember what I told him about taking a girl out and inviting her to dance.

The journey back on the tram passes in silence, the night air of the city cool and slightly damp. I shiver for a moment as I board, hugging myself.

The tram is almost empty, with only a few passengers seated. There's an old man with a wide-brimmed hat smoking a pipe, two drowsy workers at the far end of the car, and one woman clutching a small bag to her chest, her eyes darting from side to side, perhaps fearing pickpockets. I sit in one of the vacant seats by the window, lean back, and release a quiet sigh as Anna sits beside me.

Street lights pass by, creating soft reflections on the glass. Couples can still be seen shuffling down the sidewalks, along with a few cars on the dark street, but there are no longer any cyclists riding.

I touch my hair, still damp with sweat, and feel the loose hairpin. With each jolt of the tram, my eyelids close a little more. I tightly hold the small bag on my lap, and hear the wheels creaking on the tracks. Anna is also silent, lost in thought as she smokes a cigarette, ignoring the old man's critical gaze. My head aches, and I feel nauseated by the tram's rocking.

"We're here," Anna finally tells me, and we both get off and start walking home. The street is empty and quiet save for the sound of our footsteps on the stone sidewalk and the rustling of our dresses, once again covered by coats.

In the garden near the water tower, I bend down and fumble in the darkness among the bushes for my old shoes, which I'd hidden earlier. With a sigh of relief, my fingers touch those old shoes, and I sit on one of the benches. I remove the beautiful shoes Anna gave me, trying to put on my own, but my feet hurt and eventually I give up, taking both pairs in my hands and walking barefoot. The cool sidewalk feels pleasant against my wounded feet, though I feel like Cinderella turning back into a servant after attending the ball. The street is dark, with only one weak street lamp lighting its end, not like at the club. This is my place; this is where I belong. The thought of Hans with his combed hair trying to touch me stirs a wave of nausea in me.

"Are you all right?" Anna asks, and places her hand on my shoulder.

"Yes, I'm fine." I rise and take a deep breath of the cool air. "Let's go inside."

The stairwell is quiet. Mrs. Vogel is probably already asleep, and no music comes from the Koch family's apartment. I appreciate this silence, when no one checks what others are doing or tries to pry.

"Good night, thank you for taking me with you," I whisper to Anna as we enter the apartment, and I close the door behind us.

"Good night. You can come with me again if you want," she whispers back as she bends down and removes her shoes. We both walk barefoot down the hallway. I just want to get into bed and sleep, but then I see my mother sitting at the small wooden table in the kitchen. Cards are spread out in front of her in a game of Patience.

"Good night, Mrs. Hoffmann," Anna says to her. "Good night, Clara," she turns to me.

"Good night," my mother formally answers.

"Good night," I say to her as she enters her room and closes the door behind her.

"It's late," Mother says, placing a card on the table.

"Why did you wait for me? I told you I'd be back late." I sit next to her in another chair at the kitchen table.

"Because I'm your mother," she answers, and draws a new card from the deck.

"I'm an adult," I tell her. She didn't need to wait for me.

"Yes, and you also went out with a young man and happened to meet Anna in the stairwell," she answers, drawing another card.

"I didn't go to the club with Anna," I tell her as I stand up. She doesn't need to worry about me so much.

"You smell of cigarettes," she says, and gathers all the cards from the table. "Let's go to sleep. I've had bad cards today anyway."

"Mother," I whisper to her later as we're lying on the fold-out bed in the living room, "do you think it's wrong that Anna goes to those clubs?" The strip of light is still glowing beneath her bedroom door, and I can detect the faint scent of cigarette smoke lingering in the air. My fingers idly twist a loose thread in the blanket as thoughts tumble through my mind. Perhaps I should go with Anna to the club again. Perhaps I shouldn't resist so much when a man tries to kiss me after buying me a drink.

"I don't think Anna is a bad woman," she tells me, her voice soft but clear in the darkness. "I just think she has layers you haven't discovered yet. I'm not sure you'd like what you'd encounter. You're too good a woman. Even as a child, you wanted to adopt all the dirty stray kittens in the neighborhood. You have a good heart, but in our world a good heart is sometimes a disadvantage."

I try to process what she's saying, but my head throbs and exhaustion weighs on me like a heavy coat. The springs of the fold-out bed creak as I shift my position. "What do you mean?" I ask in the darkness after a while. But she doesn't answer. Perhaps she's already fallen asleep. I turn over and gaze at the thin line of light beneath her door. I think Mother is wrong about Anna.

The ticking of the silver clock irritates me, each sound like a tiny hammer against my temples. I must fall asleep; I need to get up for work soon.

Chapter Six

Collision

"Your name is Fräulein Hoffmann, isn't it?" the new worker at the workshop asks me a few days later.

"You can call me Clara," I reply, my fingers continuing their practiced dance across the leather.

"Clara," she says with obvious discomfort, shifting her weight from one foot to the other. "I've run out of thread and I can't find Herr Konrad anywhere."

I glance around the workshop, scanning the hunched figures bent over their workstations. No sign of him. Perhaps he's in the manager's office.

"Wouldn't you rather wait for him?" I continue searching for him.

"I'm afraid he'll be angry with me," she confesses.

I stop my stitching and rise from my seat, the wooden chair scraping against the floor. "I'll get you some from the storeroom. Wait here," I tell her. It will only take a moment.

"Thank you. I need black thread—I'm sewing women's shoes today," she says with a grateful smile, remaining beside my sewing table.

I make my way to the back of the workshop, my footsteps echoing on the wooden floor. The storeroom door creaks as I open it and flick the light on. The bare bulb casts harsh shadows across the cramped space. Leather hides, nails, spools of thread and cans of glue are stored on one side, while finished shoes ready for shipping line the other.

I've only been in here once before, when Herr Konrad called me to organize the shoe boxes. He's in charge of the storeroom, and is the only one who regularly enters and exits.

I approach the thread shelves, but find no black thread among the neatly-arranged spools. I bend down and begin searching the lower shelves, and suddenly I notice a large cardboard box placed at the bottom, flush against the wall. What is it doing here? Could it contain black thread, though that wouldn't make any sense?

A voice inside me whispers that something isn't right, that I shouldn't be here, but I just want to find the black thread and return to my station before Herr Konrad becomes angry with me too. I pull the heavy box from the bottom shelf, lift the lid and stop breathing.

The entire box is filled with dollar bills and French francs. The greenish-gray American notes and purple French bills are bundled together, bound with thick rubber bands. I've never seen so much non-German currency before. I've never seen so much money of any kind.

I bend down and lift a few bundles of bills to see if they're covering something else, but underneath there are only more bundles of money. The entire box is filled with American and French currency. What's happening here?

"What are you doing?" I hear Herr Konrad's voice and freeze in place, his words falling like ice down my spine.

I try to rise and turn around, but his hand seizes my gathered hair with brutal force, yanking me to my feet. I choke back a scream as pain pierces my scalp and tears spring to my eyes.

He forcefully spins me toward him, his grip on my hair unyielding. He stands so close that I can feel the heat radiating from his body, his face mere inches from mine. "What do you think you're doing?" he asks again in a whisper, his breath reeking of cigarettes.

"I'm... sorry," I manage to say, my voice trembling. "I was just looking for black thread." My head throbs from his vicious grip.

"You tried to take something that doesn't belong to you," he continues speaking quietly, his voice like the hiss of a venomous snake.

"I saw it by accident, I didn't mean to," I whimper.

"You weren't supposed to see this." He moves his face even closer to mine. I can smell the shoe glue on his fingers, acrid and chemical.

"I apologize, it was a mistake." I whisper, desperately trying to think of what to say next. What have I done? What will happen to me now? I just want to return to my sewing station, to the safety of routine.

"Apologies won't help here." He releases his grip on my hair and forcefully takes the bundles of money I'm still clutching in my hands.

"I promise, I won't tell anyone," I manage to say, my scalp still burning from his touch.

"You'll tell. Sooner or later, you'll tell. Everyone tells in the end, and I can't allow that to happen," he slowly says.

"I'm sorry," I whisper again. I just want him to release me. I'll return to my workbench and forget everything I've seen.

"You have two options," he says with a malevolent smile that transforms his face into something inhuman. "I can call the police and accuse you of black market trading and possession of francs and dollars," he continues, momentarily releasing me only to pull several bills out of the bundle and stuff them into my dress pocket. His fingers linger on my waist, and nausea rises in my throat.

"I know policemen," he continues speaking slowly, savoring each word. "They'll believe me, and you have illegal money in your pocket. You'll sit in prison, with prostitutes and criminals like yourself." His fingers stroke my waist again, and I want to scream but remain paralyzed. "Or you can leave here, shouting Communist slogans like your friend I threw out not long ago. That way I can fire you. What do you choose?" He finishes speaking and brings his lips so close to mine they almost touch. I can't move. I'm frozen with fear.

"Uhhh..." I manage to utter, trying desperately to think. I need a moment to collect my thoughts. Everything's spinning around me. Why is this happening to me?

"You need to decide, what do you choose?" he asks again, and I feel his hand stuffing more bills into my dress pocket and caressing me again, this time more crudely.

"Down with the Republic, bread and work, long live the Communists!" I manage to shout in a strangled voice, feeling his hand violently grabbing my hair as he pushes me out of the storeroom.

I had to decide.

"Shout louder, they can't hear you. I want even the manager to hear you from his office," Herr Konrad whispers as he shoves me through the hall and down the narrow passage between the workstations.

"Overthrow the government! Power to the people!" I scream with all my might, feeling like a wounded animal as his hand grips my arm with bruising force. My eyes brim with tears that threaten to spill down my cheeks.

The women in the production hall stop their work and stare at me in astonishment. I try to slow my pace, to stop for just a moment, to explain to them what happened. I desperately want someone—anyone—to come to my aid. But Herr Konrad forcefully pushes me toward the exit, his fingers digging deeper into my flesh with each step.

"Everyone continue working. I'm warning you all," he shouts at them, and every pair of eyes turns toward him. The workshop falls silent except for the sound of my ragged breathing and his heavy footsteps on the wooden floor. "Go on, get back to work, now," he barks again, and they all lower their gazes and return to their sewing, shoulders hunched, heads bowed. Only the new worker remains standing by my empty workstation, watching us both with eyes wide with fear.

"Jobs for everyone!" I shout one last time as we reach the metal door of the workshop, my voice cracking with desperation.

"Shut up, damned Communist," he hisses into my ear. "And don't you dare come back here. I have friends in the police who will take care of you." He yanks open the heavy metal door and throws me onto the street. The cold air hits me like a slap, and I stumble on the uneven cobblestones. Behind me, the door slams shut with a metallic clang.

For a moment I stand outside the workshop, disheveled and shaking, my hair coming loose from its pins as I stare at the heavy closed metal door. It was a mistake. A bad dream. It never happened at all. In a moment I'll enter the workshop and sit at my table, and start working like any other day.

But then I slide my hand into my dress pocket and feel the foreign banknotes. It wasn't a dream. He threw me out of my workplace. My cheeks are wet with tears, and I struggle to breathe. I turn and begin quickly walking down the street. I need to go, to do something, to get away from everything that just happened. The noise of the trams, car engines and horse hooves on the street around me seem disconnected from my reality. How will I find work now? Why did I open that cardboard box? Why did I think there would be thread inside?

I continue walking rapidly. The men striding down the street in their suits appear to me as dark, faceless, anonymous masses passing by. Why didn't I tell the new worker I couldn't help her and that she should wait for Herr Konrad? I shouldn't have entered his storeroom like that, trying to help her. Why didn't I look for the black thread on another shelf? What am I going to do now?

I slide my hand back into my dress pocket and feel the foreign banknotes he shoved inside. I can't use them. It's illegal to possess foreign currency. They could arrest me for that, and accuse me of black market trading. What will I do if he sends the police to arrest me? I continue walking as fast as I can, breathless, my hand clutching tightly at the bills hidden in my dress pocket, but then I remember the touch of his fingers on my waist and feel nauseated. His fingers also touched these bills I'm holding in my pocket with all my might, as if trying to cling to them. I want to vomit. I need to stop for a moment, but I can't bring myself to halt and stand still. I must keep walking, to get away from the workshop and the smell of Herr Konrad's fingers clinging to my neck and hair. A car driver honks at me angrily, and I look up in shock to realize I'm standing in the middle of the avenue. I stare at him in a panic and run to the other side. Only there do I stop, leaning against the wall with my hands and starting to cry. What will I do? I always try to be so responsible. How did this happen to me? How will I find work?

Two elderly women in black dresses pass by and look at me. For a moment they slow down, as if debating whether to stop and ask if everything is all right; but after a second they continue on their way, and only one of them gives me a sad smile. I need to keep moving, but I can't.

A newspaper boy runs toward me, shouting something while waving the paper above his head, but it seems to me like he's yelling without sound, and the printed letters in the newspaper headlines are like stains made by black birds flying in all directions, his raised hands flapping their wings as he runs down the street. From afar I think I hear the sounds of protesters and police whistles. I need to get home. I need to sit down and calm myself.

At the small park by the water tower, I pass women with baby carriages sitting on the bench. They must be watching me, examining me with their gaze. I know they're studying me. They surely know I no longer have work, and have no idea how I'll bring money home, or what will happen tomorrow, or in a week.

Only in the stairwell of the building do I feel relief, the cool air and dimness enveloping me as I slowly climb the wooden stairs, occasionally wiping away my tears. But suddenly I see Frau Schneider, the Jewish widow, in front of me. She's coming down the stairs toward me, and I grip the wooden banister and straighten myself as much as possible. She mustn't notice that something is wrong.

"Good afternoon, Frau Schneider," I greet her, trying to speak clearly.

"Good afternoon, Fräulein Hoffmann," she replies, examining me. Can she tell I've been fired? For a moment she stops, as if wanting to ask me something or tell me something, but after a moment she simply continues on her way down the stairs. I continue climbing while holding the railing. I just want to reach our apartment, close the door behind me and sit in the kitchen chair. I need to let the world around me calm down, just a little.

I quietly open the apartment door and close it behind me. Everything is silent around me, and I breathe deeply. But suddenly I hear noises from Anna's room, creaking and groaning. Her door is open.

"Anna?" I ask aloud as I stand at the end of the hallway. What's happening in her room?

The noise stops for a moment, and to my surprise I hear a man speaking. I don't understand what he's saying, but he sounds angry to me. Immediately afterward, Anna answers him. What's going on in her room?

"Anna?" I ask again. I'm afraid to move forward. I'm afraid of what I'll see.

"Clara," Anna comes out of her room. Her face is flushed, and her hair disheveled. She's wrapped in a short pink silk robe adorned with flowers. "It's not what you think," she tells me as her hands, which are holding the robe closed, try to tie it shut with a pink silk belt.

"Who is that man?" I begin walking toward her room. "Are you entertaining a man here?" I ask, though the question is stupid and I know the answer. My voice trembles. She suddenly appears blurry to me. This whole day seems blurry.

"Clara, please," she stands in front of me and stops me with her palm, "please don't tell Frau Hoffmann."

"What are you doing with him here? You know you're not allowed to do such things here," I respond. I think I'm speaking to her in anger, but I'm more surprised than anything. She promised; she took me with her to the club. Everything is collapsing around me.

"Please forgive me," she begs, her eyes expressing fear. "I have to, I have no choice. Please, go away for an hour and then come back. I promise he won't be here when you return. Please don't tell Frau Hoffmann, I need this room, I can't let her throw me out. Please go and come back in a little while, I'm begging you," she tells me quickly, as if pouring a rainstorm of words upon me while I stand and look at her, trying to understand what I should do.

"Are you coming? I'm waiting. I didn't give you money for nothing," I hear the male voice from her room say angrily.

"I'm coming," she turns her head and says to the male voice. Then she turns to me again and whispers "Please..." while continuing to block my way, her eyes pleading. "I need you to help me. One hour, I promise, even less."

I lower my gaze to the silk robe she's wearing. It's slightly open, and her breasts are almost exposed. I raise my gaze to her eyes and lips again; they tremble slightly as if she's about to cry. There are traces of lipstick too. What should I do with her? What should I do with myself?

Without saying a word, I step back toward the door. I can't think about what's happening here at home, not now.

"Thank you, Clara," she whispers to me and turns around, hurrying back to her room. The silk robe she wears flutters at her sides as if she were a flowery butterfly. I'll walk down the street, I'll stroll, I'll keep walking.

I go down and leave the building, and start walking again. But when I reach the small park by the water tower and the women sitting on the bench with their baby carriages, I can no longer continue. I sit on one of the benches in the corner of the park, at a safe distance from them. I can no longer walk without purpose; I can no longer contain everything that's happening today.

I try as much as I can to sit upright on the bench. I must remain stable, but the ground seems to shake around me and won't stop moving. Why did this happen to me? What did I do wrong? Why did I trust the new worker who asked me for thread? Why did I trust Anna, who convinced me to give her a place to stay?

One of the toddlers in the park slowly walks toward me, swaying with each step and extending his hand to me while holding a small branch. But his mother calls him, and he turns and goes back to her, stumbling to the ground and getting up again to continue walking. When will I have children? I lower my gaze to the packed brown earth. I've never done it with a man. Not even once. I haven't gone out with men in all the years since the war. There were no men left to go out with; the war had taken almost all of them. I was always busy at the workshop, making sure we had enough money and wouldn't be evicted.

I again slip my hand into my dress pocket, feeling the foreign bills Herr Konrad pushed into it, and I breathe deeply. Despite the nausea, they give me a little security. They're worth a lot of money on the black market, I don't even know how much.

I continue to breathe deeply, occasionally looking at the mothers sitting on the bench on the other side of the park. Finally, after they get up and leave with their children, I also get up and walk home. More than half an hour has passed.

To my relief the stairwell is quiet, and Frau Vogel isn't standing there watching me. Nor are Frau Schneider or Herr Koch. I hesitate at our apartment door: what if the man is still there? I breathe deeply, open the door and enter, slamming it loudly. I hope Anna made sure he's no longer here.

"Anna?" I call again, waiting in the hallway.

"Thank you, Clara," Anna emerges from her room and approaches me. This time she's dressed in a simple light blue summer house dress, and her hair is combed and gathered in a ponytail.

"Why did you entertain a man here? You're not allowed to do that," I tell her, trying to sound angry rather than sad. She promised me she wouldn't host men here.

"Because I have no choice," she tells me quietly, lowering her eyes.

"You have a job at the club, that's what you told my mother and me when you came here. Did you lie to us?"

"No, I didn't lie."

"So what about this man?"

"I work at the club, but the club is a world of men. I can get champagne and gifts there, but there's also a price I have to pay," she says quietly.

"What do you mean?" I ask, though in the pit of my stomach I feel that I know what price she's talking about. The girls at work would joke about it occasionally, saying with a smile that we're women and that we have no choice.

"I need to survive, I need money from them. What I get at the club isn't enough," she continues to speak to me quietly, and raises her gaze to me. "And if that's the price I have to pay, then I pay it. I'm willing to pay it," she says, and continues to look at me. What would she say if she knew I'd been fired?

"You can't do this. You promised you wouldn't entertain men here when I asked you downstairs, at the entrance to the building," I tell her, but the words sound hollow to me.

"Please, Clara, don't tell Frau Hoffmann. You're young like me, you have a home to live in and a mother who protects you. I don't have that."

"Where's your mother? Where's your father?"

"It doesn't matter. They're gone, it doesn't matter why," she says quietly.

"You lied to us," I answer, trying to sound angry, although I pity her and myself and everything happening around us.

"Please don't tell." She puts her hand in her dress pocket and takes out several bills, takes my palm, and places the bills in it. "I know you gave me my room because you don't have enough money. Please, take it, a little more money to help you, just don't tell Frau Hoffmann."

I lower my gaze to the money. We need this money now that I don't have a job.

"Please don't tell Frau Hoffmann," she repeats, "nobody will know I gave you this money. And if you want, you can come with me to the club again tonight. I can help you. Please take the money from me. I can get you more."

I don't say anything to her, but my fingers close around the money, feeling it burn in my palm. I need to decide what to do.

⁓⁕⁓

"Clara, why are you sitting in the dark?" Mother asks me later when she comes home. Since that conversation with Anna earlier, I've been sitting in the wooden chair in the kitchen while Anna remains in her room with the door closed. "And what's all this money on the table?" she adds when she notices the bills scattered across the wooden surface.

"I was fired," I quietly tell her, my voice hardly rising above the ticking of the clock on the wall. "They fired many girls at work today. There's no more work," I add. I'd been rehearsing what to tell her about my job since the afternoon, wondering where I might find new employment. I can't bring myself to tell her why I was really fired. I'm the one who's always dependable.

Mother says nothing. She just releases a small sigh that seems to carry the weight of a thousand worries, and she switches on the yellow kitchen lamp. The sudden light makes me squint, casting harsh shadows across the worn table and illuminating the scattered bills. She walks to the wooden drawer and takes out the cardboard notebook. Sitting down across from me, she opens it. Her reddened fingers draw a thick pencil line across the width of the page, and above it, she adds the words *Clara's dismissal* and the date.

When she finishes, she lifts her eyes from the notebook and studies me. "What is this money? How did it get here?"

"It's our money," I answer, looking at Herr Konrad's foreign bills and those Anna gave me, all scattered in disarray on the kitchen table.

"There are foreign bills here too. That's illegal," she says while examining me, her eyes sharp beneath her graying hair.

"I know. Add it to the lists in your notebook," I reply. I will never tell her about Herr Konrad, not now, not ever.

"Did you steal this?" she asks, her voice dropping to a whisper as if the walls might hear.

"You know me. I'm not a thief," I answer, folding my arms across my chest.

"I know you're not a thief. So where did this come from?"

"It doesn't matter. We need this money." The words come out harsher than I intended, but I can't retreat now.

"You're also my daughter. You don't usually hide things from me." She continues to look at me, her eyes searching mine for the truth I'm withholding.

"Please, Mother, just take it. I'm grown now. You can trust me," I say quietly, unable to meet her gaze.

"Is this connected to the girl who lives with us?" she asks without calling Anna by name.

"No, it has nothing to do with her. The important thing is that we have this money. It'll be enough for a few days." My fingers trace nervous patterns on the table's edge.

Mother continues to look at me as if debating what to say, but finally she reaches out and takes the bills. Her fingers collect them slowly, one by one, arranging them into a neat stack. Then she counts them, her lips quietly murmuring the amount. Only then does she open the notebook on the table and record the sum.

Anna's door opens, and she emerges wearing a thin summer coat. Beneath the hem of the coat I can see that same shimmering blue dress—the one she lent me when she took me to the club. "Good evening, Frau Hoffmann," she says politely, and flashes me a secret-keeping smile.

"Good evening, Anna. Are you going to work?" Mother asks while giving me a scrutinizing look.

"Yes, Frau Hoffmann." Anna stands tall.

"Have a pleasant work evening," Mother replies, her closed palm covering the money on the table.

"Thank you very much, Frau Hoffmann, and thank you for letting me live in your apartment," Anna responds as she leaves the apartment, gently closing the door behind her.

"This money will last us for a few days, Mother," I tell her, trying to sound optimistic despite the hollowness in my chest.

"Yes, we'll manage. We have no other choice." She sighs, her shoulders sagging slightly. "After all, we don't have another room we can rent out."

"We'll manage," I say, looking at her wrinkled fingers resting on the table. I'll find work. I must find work. The alternative is unthinkable in these hungry times.

"Sorry, we don't need workers. Try again in a few months," the owner of a horse saddle workshop tells me a few days later, barely looking up from the leather he's cutting.

"Sorry, we have no need for workers," the owner of a dress-making shop informs me, his eyes already moving past me to the next person in line.

"Sorry... try again in a few months," all the workshops and stores I approach tell me, the words beginning to blur together in a chorus of rejection.

Day after day I continue to wander the streets and inquire with business owners, but I feel trapped in a snare that's slowly tightening around me, leading me in only one direction—a path I fear with every fiber of my being.

At night I can't fall asleep. When Anna returns at a late hour, her quiet footsteps and the rustle of her shimmering dress remind me of a snake's whisper. Even Mother's brown notebook frightens me now; the orderly round numbers in her circular handwriting grow smaller each day. Soon we'll run out of money.

"Coal miners' strike in the Ruhr region continues due to the occupation by French military forces! Worker layoffs across the country!" a newspaper boy shouts as he races down the street, waving the paper above his head. What will I do?

At the end of the day, I turn and head home. Sweat clings to my skin from the hours spent walking through the city under the summer sun. From a distance, from the direction of the city center, the sounds of demonstrations and police whistles rise again. I slowly walk toward our building, knowing I'll have no choice but to ask Anna if she can help me.

The stairwell is cool and quiet as I climb to our apartment, but when I reach the second floor, the door to the Koch family's apartment opens and two young men emerge. I immediately recognize the taller one: Walter. He visited our apartment with Herr Koch right after we moved in. He'd stood silently then, surveying me as if trying to assess my value. As before, he's wearing a white shirt and brown tie, his short light hair meticulously combed. The moment he notices me, his gray eyes seem to pierce through me, examining me once more. The man beside him is younger. It takes me a moment to remember that this is Bruno, the younger brother. He helped Mother and I the day we carried the bed up the stairs.

"Good afternoon, Fräulein Hoffmann," Walter greets me with a small smile that seems threatening as he stands above me on the staircase, blocking my path. "Have you already met my younger brother Bruno?" he continues speaking to me while turning to his brother. "Fräulein Hoffmann lives on the floor above us. She and her mother moved in recently. They live in the apartment that became vacant, across from the Jewish widow Father and I were talking about last night," he explains to his brother.

His speech is slow, almost indifferent, but he pronounces the word 'Jewish' more forcefully, breaking it into syllables like a curse.

The younger brother extends his hand toward me. "Pleased to meet you. I'm Bruno. I don't believe we've met before," he says with a smile. He has a mischievous look, as if enjoying concealing our previous encounter in the stairwell when he helped me carry the heavy bed.

"Pleased to meet you. I'm Clara," I shake his hand and smile at him, but Walter's scrutinizing eyes make me nervous. I feel my pulse quicken under his gaze.

"Have a nice day, Clara," Bruno bids me farewell, and they both continue on their way, but not before Walter nods slightly to me and moves aside a bit to let me pass.

I climb a few more steps, but after a moment I turn and look at them. When we arrived, Frau Vogel had mentioned that no one wanted to work for the Jewish woman. Could she be in need of a saleswoman? Could she offer me employment?

I remain standing there, looking down at the empty stairwell long after the sound of their footsteps dissolves into the street noise outside. Would it be acceptable if I asked her whether she had work to offer me? What would Herr Koch think of Mother and me?

Step by step I climb the stairs, and when I reach our floor I approach Frau Schneider's door and gently knock on it. My knuckles barely make a sound against the wood. I'm afraid I'm making a wrong choice, but I desperately need work.

Chapter Seven

The Neighbor Across the Hall

Standing in front of Mrs. Schneider's wooden door, I try to steady my breathing. I can still change my mind—when she opens the door, I can say something meaningless and walk away.

I hear footsteps from the other side, and the door opens just a crack. Mrs. Schneider studies me, her eyes scanning me with apprehension.

"Good evening, Clara," she finally says, still holding the door nearly closed, her knuckles white against the dark wood.

"Good evening, Mrs. Schneider..." I reply, drawing another deep breath that fills my lungs with the cold hallway air. "I hope I'm not disturbing you. I need help finding work—things are difficult. Mrs. Vogel mentioned you're having trouble finding workers," I add quickly before I lose my nerve.

"Mrs. Vogel likes to talk," she says quietly through the door's narrow gap.

"If by chance you're looking for help, I'd be happy to work for you," I tell her, though it's impolite to speak this way without being invited inside. What will I do if she refuses me?

Mrs. Schneider observes me, then glances behind my shoulder as if expecting to find someone hiding there, preparing to rush in. "Come in," she finally says, opening the door, and I follow her into her apartment.

At the entrance to the living room, I pause for a moment and look around. The interior of her apartment is simple, but more elegant than ours. The furniture is made of heavy wood, old-fashioned but well-maintained. In the corner stands a small wooden table covered by a tablecloth that was once white, but has now taken on a slight yellowish tint. Beside it sits one chair with a faded cushion, and another chair that looks as though no one has sat in it for a long time.

"Please, sit down," Mrs. Schneider tells me, pointing to one of the heavy brown chairs. I smile at her gratefully and take a seat, the wood creaking softly beneath me.

"Would you like something to drink? Coffee? Tea?" she asks. She's wearing a simple black dress, and her gray hair is meticulously pulled back.

"Yes, please. Tea," I tell her, and she turns toward the kitchen, leaving me alone in the living room. I continue looking around: the walls are bare, and only a few books stand on the bookshelf above the dresser, some in German and others in foreign letters I can't read. A silver menorah sits on the dresser, with two photographs beside it. The first shows a man in a suit seated in a chair, next to a young woman in a floral dress. It's Mrs. Schneider when she was younger.

I shift my gaze to the second photograph. It's a picture of a young man in a soldier's uniform. He stands proud in his uniform, holding his weapon and looking at the camera with a serious expression. I turn my attention from the photographs to the heavy curtains covering the windows. New black leather gloves lie on one of the wooden armchairs, but apart from them time seems to have stood still. The room smells of old fabrics and dust, as if people haven't lived in this house for a long time.

"Here's your tea," Mrs. Schneider enters from the kitchen carrying a teapot and two cups, and pours for both of us. Then she sits in the chair across from me, her posture rigid, and watches me.

"Thank you," I say to her, taking the teacup and carefully blowing on it. The warmth of the cup seeps into my cold fingers.

"I'm listening," she quietly says.

"There's no work, Mrs. Schneider, and I'm looking for a job. I'm a hard worker, reliable with money matters, and I always arrive at work on time," I tell her while holding my teacup, the steam rising between us like a veil.

Mrs. Schneider remains silent and examines my fingers. "You know I'm Jewish, right?" she finally asks me.

"Yes, I know," I nod.

"And you know my glove and hat shop is in an area where there are many Jewish stores?"

"Yes..." I nod, though I don't know exactly where her shop is. I only know it's somewhere downtown.

"And I assume you know there are those who don't like us. You're not young anymore, and certainly not naïve," she adds. "There are those who blame us for losing the Great War," she quietly says while looking at me.

I glance momentarily at the photograph of the soldier standing tall and proud on the dresser. "Mrs. Schneider, I need work," I answer her. I'm not afraid of Jews, and I don't hate them. I don't want to hate anyone. I just want a job.

"I don't have much to pay you with. People spend all their money on food. And when people are hungry, they don't buy hats or gloves." Her voice carries the weight of these difficult times.

"Please, Mrs. Schneider, whatever you pay me will be fine."

Mrs. Schneider remains silent and holds her teacup, sipping from it slowly. What will I do if she refuses me? For a moment I think about Hans' lips trying to kiss me at the club, and Mr. Konard's fingers stuffing money into my dress pocket, touching me in the process.

"Well," she finally says, "I agree."

"Thank you very much, Mrs. Schneider." I breathe a sigh of relief. I'll have work. We'll have enough money.

"Come to the shop tomorrow at eight in the morning, at Rosenthaler Straße 39." She tells me the address and places her teacup on the table, and I do the same.

"Thank you very much, Mrs. Schneider," I say to her at the door a minute later, "I promise you won't regret it."

She just gives me a small smile, and I walk the short distance from her apartment to ours. From the floor below I can hear Wagner's music emanating from the Koch family's apartment.

"I've found work," I announce to Mother as I enter our apartment. She's sitting in the kitchen, peeling potatoes, her weathered hands moving methodically.

"Where?" she asks, smiling for the first time in a long while. The lines around her eyes soften momentarily.

"With the neighbor across the hall, Mrs. Schneider," I answer, watching her face carefully for any reaction.

"And she'll give you work?"

"Yes," I nod.

"People won't like a Christian woman working in a Jewish woman's shop." She continues peeling the potatoes, her knife never pausing. "They'll talk behind your back."

"And you?" I ask, watching her fingers holding the sharp knife. She peels the potato skins so delicately that the peelings seem thin as paper, curling in long spirals onto the table.

"I think the world is divided into good people and bad people, and it doesn't matter if they're Christians or Jews. I don't know Mrs. Schneider, but I have a feeling she's on the side of the good," she says, setting down the peeling knife. It makes a soft clinking sound against the worn wooden table. "I also think you should take some money and buy us sausage and some schnapps. We're allowed to celebrate a little today," she gives me a small smile.

At night, when Anna returns late, the rustling of her dress no longer frightens me. But after she closes her bedroom door and the house grows quiet, I think I can still hear Wagner's music from the floor below us. Perhaps I'm mistaken and simply tired, or perhaps I've had too much to drink.

Chapter Eight

The Shop at 39 Rosenthaler Straße

The door bell chimes delicately as I enter the shop the following day and close the door behind me. "Good morning," I greet Mrs. Schneider, my voice steadier than I feel. I'm ready to begin working.

A long wooden counter stands in the center of the small shop, and behind it shelves reach all the way to the ceiling, surrounding me with cardboard boxes and the scent of aged leather mingled with essence of lavender soap. I look around at the wooden drawers and shelves. At the far end of the shop, narrow wooden stairs lead up to what might be a small room on the second floor. A few simple lamps hanging from the ceiling illuminate the intimate space with a warm yellow glow that softens the edges of everything it touches.

"Good morning," Mrs. Schneider greets me and starts to explain, "these are the hat shelves, here are the scarves, and these are the gloves." She shows me the drawers one by one, explaining the different types with practiced patience. She holds men's and women's hats with gentle movements, and lets me feel the fabric between my fingertips. Afterwards she opens the glove drawers and spreads them across the counter. Women's gloves made of wool, velvet, lace and leather, and men's gloves of leather and wool, each pair waiting silently for the right hands.

Throughout the day, she patiently explains everything to me and serves the few customers who enter the shop. Finally, toward the end of the day, when the door bell rings its gentle chime and an elderly silver-haired lady enters the shop, she whispers to me: "Now it's your turn." I approach the woman, addressing her politely under Mrs. Schneider's watchful eye.

During the next few days, I nervously glance up each morning when I enter the shop at the name *Schneider* written in black letters on the tin sign above the display window. But as the days pass, I grow calmer. The important thing is that I have work.

"Good morning," a man greets us as he enters the shop two weeks after I've started working. A cool early autumn breeze rushes in with him, and he quickly closes the door behind him.

He's roughly my age, taller than me, with broad shoulders and a slightly tanned face adorned with two-day stubble and the redness of morning cold that makes his cheeks look almost boyish despite his size.

"Good morning," I answer, and he smiles at me and removes the wool cap he's wearing. Underneath it are slightly disheveled ends of light, yellowish-brown hair. He's wearing an old open wool coat, perhaps military, which reveals a simple blue work shirt permeated with the scent of diesel. Few men enter the shop, and they usually wear suits and are interested in purchasing a fedora or a gift for women.

"How may I help you?" I ask him while Mrs. Schneider goes back to organizing the glove drawers behind the counter.

"Well..." he speaks and looks around, examining the shelves as if wondering whether he's arrived at the right place, "I'm looking for leather gloves... for driving," he points to a green truck parked outside the shop, "in the morning hours, when it's already cold," he smiles at me. He has greenish-brown eyes and lowers his gaze while I observe him.

"Yes, winter is approaching," I reply. Despite his large build, I have a feeling there's something vulnerable about him.

"That's right, winter is approaching, and I needed gloves even then..." he answers, and stops mid-sentence. "Forgive me, I didn't mean to," he smiles at me awkwardly, "it's always good to have gloves in winter," he finishes speaking and places his large hands on the counter. His big hands are red, surely from the cold.

"Offer him gloves with lining, Clara, they're in the right drawer," Mrs. Schneider tells me, and I take out several pairs of gloves and spread them on the counter. I want to ask him which winter he's referring to, but I'm afraid of embarrassing him. He seems like a special man to me. Perhaps it's the fact that he didn't try to look me over as if I were merchandise for sale, but rather lowered his gaze when I spoke to him.

He tries on one of the gloves and smiles as he struggles to fit his large hand into a leather glove too small for him.

"I'll look for a larger size for you, sir." I take the gloves from him and touch his cold fingers for a split-second. The gloves will warm them.

113

Finally I manage to find the right-sized gloves for him, and he goes to Mrs. Schneider and pays her. I want to talk to him a little more, but I don't know what to say.

"Thank you very much," he thanks Mrs. Schneider, "thank you very much..." he pauses and looks at me.

"Fräulein Hoffmann. Thank you very much," I smile at him. It's the first time in such a long time that I don't hate the word 'Fräulein'.

"Have a nice day, Fräulein Hoffmann," he returns a shy smile and walks out the door. I wish he would stay, but I know that can't happen.

I watch him through the display window as he gets into the truck and starts it up a moment later, a black cloud of smoke escaping from the exhaust. I must go back to concentrating on my work.

I bend down to return the gloves on the counter to the drawer, and when I raise my head the truck has already disappeared.

"Clara, please arrange these hats on the top shelf," Mrs. Schneider points to the cardboard boxes placed behind the shop entrance door.

"Yes, Mrs. Schneider," I answer as I approach the cardboard boxes. I need to forget about him. He's just another man who happened to come here to buy gloves, and he left.

But a week later, in the morning hours, I lift my eyes to the street and see a green truck arriving and parking outside the shop.

I glance at the truck through the display window and lower my gaze, my hands smoothing down my dress. Is it the same truck driver from last week? Despite how illogical it seems, I feel a small wave of excitement washing over me.

Several pairs of women's silk gloves lie on the counter as I attach price tags to them. I hurry to put them into the cardboard box and once again run my hands over my dress, straightening invisible wrinkles.

The truck door opens, and the man from last week climbs down. He blows on his hands and rubs them together before approaching the shop door and opening it.

"Good morning, sir," Mrs. Schneider greets him, "I see you've returned to us."

"Good morning," I greet him as well, secretly wishing Mrs. Schneider would go up to the small room on the second floor where we store merchandise, and where she does the bookkeeping.

"Good morning, ma'am," he addresses Mrs. Schneider. "Good morning, Fräulein Hoffmann," he turns to me and smiles, but immediately lowers his eyes in embarrassment. He remembered my name.

"Is something wrong with the gloves you purchased from us last week?" Mrs. Schneider asks him.

"No," he answers, continuing looking in my direction. "They were excellent, but unfortunately I forgot them on a wooden crate in the cargo hold when I was transporting goods from Düsseldorf. I'd be happy to purchase a new pair," he turns to me.

"You must have been cold without the gloves," I say.

"It wasn't so bad, I've been colder," he replies.

"Have you been driving a truck long?" I ask while bending behind the counter to retrieve the box of men's gloves. I already know his size.

"I started driving trucks during the war... I was just a boy then. At first they recruited me as a horse cart driver, but after the attack on Verdun they were short of people... you understand..." He speaks hesitantly, slowly, carefully choosing his words and speaking them quietly. "Never mind, I don't want to upset you. I was a boy and they let me drive a truck. I was so proud," he smiles at me, "I've been driving trucks ever since."

I want to ask him about the war, but then I remember that Mrs. Schneider's son was in that war and I silently take the gloves out of the cardboard box. "Here's a new pair just like the ones you purchased last week, sir," I hand him a new pair of leather gloves with warm lining.

"Thank you," he says as he holds them in his hands, but he hesitates and doesn't rush to approach Mrs. Schneider to pay. "Do you perhaps have the same gloves in brown?"

"I'll check," I answer, and bend over behind the counter. Why didn't I wear my other dress today? It's prettier.

"Here you are," I place a pair of brown gloves on the counter as well.

He looks at them, tries them on, and places them back on the counter. "What do you think? Which color do you prefer?" he asks after a moment.

"They're yours, sir, you should decide," I feel myself blushing slightly.

"Mr. Berger," he smiles at me.

"Mr. Berger," I say slowly, rolling the name on my tongue.

"And what do you think?" he asks me, glancing briefly at Mrs. Schneider as if waiting for her approval to continue being in the shop, despite not fitting in with his simple clothes and the diesel scent emanating from his shirt.

"I like the brown color, I'm less fond of black," I answer him.

"Then I'll choose the brown gloves." He holds them and approaches Mrs. Schneider to pay.

I try to think of something else to say, but I have nothing and feel so awkward and boring. What did the women at the workshop talk about with men they found attractive? I lower my eyes to the black gloves that remain on the counter, and hold them in my hand.

"Thank you very much, ma'am," I hear him say, "Thank you very much, Fräulein Hoffmann." He bids me farewell and leaves the shop, heading back toward his truck.

"My son would have been like him now," Mrs. Schneider quietly says as we both watch him open the vehicle door and climb into the driver seat, and I feel a wave of sadness. I shouldn't have talked to him about the war. I look at her and try to think of what to say. Her fingers are gripping a glove box so tightly that they're white, and it seems that if she were to release the box, she would crumble into pieces of sorrow.

"I'm sorry, Mrs. Schneider, I shouldn't have spoken with him."

"You couldn't have known, you just asked him a question." She smiles sadly at me and pulls a handkerchief out of her dress pocket, using it to wipe away a tear. "He seems like a good man to me. My child was a good boy too," she sighs and bends down, placing the cardboard box inside the drawer.

"I'm sure he was a wonderful boy," I search for the right words to say, despite not having known him.

"At least you sold him another pair of gloves before winter arrives," she says as she tries to smile. "I think he likes you. I have a feeling he'll lose those too in the coming days, and return."

I smile embarrassedly, knowing it won't happen, but in the days that follow I wear my prettier dress, and on my way to the shop in the morning, as I walk down the avenue, I pause for a moment in front of the pharmacy window and look at the display of women's lipsticks. Perhaps someday I'll have money to buy myself lipstick. Inside the shop, I occasionally look out at the street while working, searching for a green truck. But no green truck stops. Mrs. Schneider was wrong; he didn't like me.

"I'm going out on errands, Clara, I'll be back shortly," Mrs. Schneider tells me at noon a few days later, and she leaves the shop.

"Yes, ma'am," I answer, turning to the shelves behind me and arranging a new shipment of men's hats.

The door bell chimes gently, and I turn to see Mr. Berger standing before me with his shy smile. He came back.

"Good afternoon," I politely say to him, but inside I feel excitement.

"Good afternoon," he hesitantly says to me.

"Is everything alright with the gloves? Can I help you with something else?" I try to think of a topic to talk to him about.

"If something isn't right, would you like to wait for Mrs. Schneider, the shop owner? She'll be back shortly," I talk without pause.

"No... no... everything's fine, the gloves are wonderful, they warm me every morning," he says, and takes another step into the shop toward the counter that separates us. "I wanted, if it's alright... and if you're available and interested, I would be happy to ask you out."

Chapter Nine

The Man with the Gloves

Two days later, as evening approaches, I rise from the chair in the corner of the kitchen and walk to the door, turning around and coming back. He should be arriving shortly.

"You can sit down, Clara, there's still time," Mother says. She's sitting in the kitchen grating cabbage, her hands moving in steady, practiced motions.

"I know there's still time," I answer, but remain standing. I can't sit. It's been so long since I went out with a man. I lower my gaze to my hands and examine my fingers. I don't like them. They're rough from all the years of working with hard leather in the shoe workshop.

"Where's he taking you?" Mother asks.

"I don't know. He suggested a café."

"Does he live in Berlin?"

"I don't know."

"How old is he?"

"About my age, I don't know."

"Invite him in," Mother says, and continues grating the cabbage with the grater, her hands moving the cabbage in strong upward and downward motions. I don't answer. I'm embarrassed to invite him into the apartment. I'm embarrassed for him to see where I live. I go to examine myself in the small mirror on the washing corner wall. Am I pretty enough? Will he like me?

A woman in a simple dress with a serious expression stares back at me from the mirror spotted with mottled, peeling patches. Maybe I should ask Anna to lend me a modern dress like the one she gave me when we went to the club? Maybe I should ask her for lipstick? I touch my lips with my fingertips. I don't want to leave the washing corner to face Mother's comments and questions, so I stay standing and looking at myself in the mirror. I'm not beautiful. I'll never be beautiful. Why would he want me?

A knock on the door prompts me to quickly leave the washing corner and go to open it.

"Good evening," Mr. Berger greets me. He stands at the door, dressed in a clean button-up shirt and an old but clean jacket. There's no smell of diesel on him.

"Good evening, Mr. Berger," I greet him in return and shake his hand.

"Please call me Hermann," he tells me shyly. He holds a small package wrapped in brown paper.

"Please call me Clara."

"Clara is a beautiful name. When I heard the shop owner call you that, I thought it was beautiful." He smiles at me. "I took the liberty of bringing you a small gift, some chocolate." He hands me the package wrapped in brown paper.

"Thank you very much." I take the package from his hands, and touch his fingers for a moment while doing so. No man has ever brought me a gift before. "I'll just get my coat and we'll go," I tell him, leaving the door almost closed. I hurry to the kitchen and place the chocolate on the table.

"Why didn't you invite him in?" Mother whispers.

"Another time," I whisper back, and hurry to take my coat from the hook. I don't want him to see the folding bed in the corner of the living room, the same bed we unfold every night and sleep on. What would he think of me if he knew I sleep in the same bed with my mother because we don't have enough money? "Goodbye, Mother," I say to her, closing the door behind me. "Let's go," I tell him, and we both descend the stairs.

On the street, Hermann opens the door of his green truck for me, extends his hand and helps me into the cabin. I've never ridden in a truck before. He climbs in after me into the driver's compartment, presses the ignition switch, moves the gear stick, and the truck comes to life like a large brown bear, growling and slowly moving across the cobblestones. Thankfully, he doesn't ask me why I didn't invite him into the apartment. Perhaps he thinks I live alone.

"Is it alright if we get coffee at the city center?" he asks me, diverting his gaze from the avenue in my direction for a moment, and I nod.

His large hands hold the truck's steering wheel as he gently moves it right and left, navigating between the horses walking slowly and pulling wagons, the bicycle riders, and the black cars moving around him. From the high truck, they look to me like nimble beetles moving in all directions. Does he notice that I'm secretly watching him like this? The smell of diesel in the truck doesn't bother me.

At the city center, he parks the truck on Unter den Linden Avenue and hurries to exit the driver's compartment, extending his hand to me. "Place your foot here," he explains how to descend from the driver's compartment to the sidewalk, his hand firmly holding mine while ensuring I don't stumble.

"Thank you," I smile at him, and we both begin to walk down the avenue. But the further we progress and I see the elegant cafés, the more I feel out of place. Everything here is so luxurious. The men on the street wear suits, and the women are in beautiful dresses, not like mine. I don't belong here. Is he trying to impress me?

"Shall we get some coffee?" he suggests, and we enter one of the cafés. I have a feeling the other people are watching us as we walk to the table, but Hermann doesn't seem bothered. He moves the chair for me as I sit, and then sits across from me.

As we wait for the coffee, he barely speaks, and neither do I. I examine his large hands resting on the small table while I smooth my fingers over the wood, searching for cracks. Why is he barely talking to me? He just looks at me and offers a small smile, and I return his gaze and smile, arranging strands of hair behind my ears with my fingers. I must say something to break the silence between us. All the people around us in the café seem so happy, while we sit in silence opposite each other.

"Did you drive a truck during the war?" I ask him, trying to start a conversation just so we don't continue with this silence.

"Yes, they were looking for volunteers, and my friend and I volunteered," he smiles at me, his large hands caressing the wooden table.

"Tell me about him, about your friend," I say. I want him to talk, I want to listen to him rather than linger in a cloud of tense silence while we look at each other and search for something to say.

"About Karl?" he asks.

"Yes. Is that your friend's name?"

"He'd been with me since we enlisted," Hermann speaks slowly, his voice warm and pleasant. "We were together in basic training. We were both the same age. He was from a small village near Stuttgart," he continues to speak and gives me a small smile. "I have no idea how he ended up in our unit, most of us were from the Berlin area. One morning, he accidentally wore his shirt inside out, we were all so tired. You know how it is in the army. And that's how he went with us to roll call, with his shirt inside out," he continues to talk to me, and smiles. "The commander conducted the roll call and didn't notice, but when he did, at the end, he yelled at us so loudly that he turned red with anger and almost choked," he continues to speak and smiles to himself, as if imagining what happened then.

"And what did you do?" I ask with a smile.

"We all laughed so much. Afterward, the commander made us run for hours in the rain, we got soaked like street cats, but we didn't mind. From then on we called our commander 'the Sausage' behind his back."

"And what happened to him in the war? To Karl?" I ask. even though perhaps I shouldn't.

"He survived. like me." He looks at me and offers a small smile, I can't tell whether it's sad or not. "He returned to his village, near Stuttgart. I heard he got married after the war, and has a little girl."

"Here you go, your coffee, and also a cookie," the waiter places two cups of coffee before us. It's been so long since I've had coffee.

Hermann thanks the waiter, looks at me and smiles. "I ordered one cookie for both of us."

"Then we'll have to share it," I answer, and hold the glass cup with both hands. I've missed the smell of coffee.

"Will you split it for us?" he asks.

I set the coffee cup down and take the cookie, ceremoniously dividing it in two and handing him the larger piece.

"The larger piece is for you." He places it in my palm and takes the smaller piece. The warmth of his fingers feels pleasant for a moment. I bring the cookie to my lips and taste it with small bites, enjoying its sweetness. I no longer care about the glances from people at the tables around us.

Later, we continue walking down the Avenue, almost to the Brandenburg Gate. Hermann tells me amusing stories from his army days and his journeys as a truck driver, and I listen to him. But there are protesters and policemen near the gate, so we turn back. I feel protected as I walk beside him.

We make the journey back home in silence, but it's a pleasant silence. By the entrance to the building, he says he'd be happy to meet me again, but he doesn't try to kiss me.

"I'd also be happy to see you again," I answer as I turn my back to him, hurrying up the stairs. I hope Mrs. Vogel isn't standing in the stairwell, waiting to ask me questions.

At night, after I tell Mother about him, I lie awake in bed, looking at the dark ceiling and smiling. I don't even mind that Anna is prettier than me, and has shiny dresses and men who court her at the club.

But in the days that follow, he doesn't come to the shop or the apartment to visit me, and doesn't make plans for us to meet again.

"Is everything alright?" Mother asks me when I return every evening from work, and I nod silently. Could it be that I said something wrong? Could it be that he's changed his mind?

"Clara, are you alright?" Mrs. Schneider asks me at work, and I tell her I am and try to concentrate on arranging the gloves, even though I already arranged them yesterday. He must have changed his mind, and doesn't want to see me anymore. Throughout the workday I try to listen to the noises outside the window, lifting my eyes and searching for his green truck. Day by day, until I hate myself.

"What's that noise?" Mrs. Schneider asks me a few days later, and I raise my gaze and look outside the window. But it's not Hermann's green truck; it's a muffled noise, voices mixing with dim rhythmic calls like I heard at the protest, from a distance.

From within the shop I see several people on the street stopping, and a man in a blue suit riding a bicycle suddenly halts and turns back. I tightly grip the purple silk scarf to which I've just added a price tag. Are they coming toward us? I feel tension crawling down my spine. I'm alone; Mrs. Schneider is upstairs, in the small room where we keep merchandise and she does the bookkeeping.

I move closer to the window and look outside. I can't distinguish them clearly, but even though the shop door is closed I can hear them. I hear the sound of boots stomping on the wet cobblestones like drumbeat, like those soldiers who marched in the street years ago, when I was a young girl and the great long war had begun. And then I see them in the street.

They aren't running or shouting, just marching in almost straight rows, as if trying to imitate a military parade. Their shirts are brown, the color of dry bread. Around their waists are brown leather belts, and they're wearing black leather boots that strike the cobblestones in a uniform rhythm. Their arms rise upward occasionally in a straight motion toward the sky. Step by step they advance down the street, like a train moving on its tracks, but when they reach the display window of our shop they stop and turn toward it. What are they doing?

A young man with short yellow-blond hair looks in my direction, his gaze fixed on me. Can he make me out from outside, despite my being in the dimly-lit shop? I take one step backward.

"*Juden raus*!" he shouts, and raises his arm in the air.

"*Juden raus*!" the people around him shout, all staring at me in the shop.

I freeze in place, looking at them in fear.

"*Juden raus*!" the young man shouts again, and raises his arm in the air.

I need to do something: to hide behind the counter, to disappear from here. Step by step I back up inside the small shop until I feel the wooden shelves against my back. I think I hear police whistles, but I'm not sure.

"Don't buy from Jews," the yellow-haired boy shouts, his mouth gaping at me like the jaws of a wolf. I can't take my eyes off him; only the display window glass separates us. Will they try to break in? The fear paralyzes me.

But then he turns his gaze away and continues marching down the street, and all those rows of people in brown uniforms continue marching with him. The sound of their bootsteps slowly fades down the street, and silence returns to the shop again.

"Are they gone?" I hear Mrs. Schneider from the second floor.

"Yes, they're gone," I answer, breathing slowly. Only then do I notice that I'm still tightly gripping the same purple silk scarf to which I'd added a price tag before everything started.

Mrs. Schneider slowly descends the stairs and looks around, like a small gray mouse peering fearfully from its burrow. "They won't come back," she tells me in a trembling voice.

"No, they won't. I heard police too," I answer, breathing slowly. Nothing happened, they're gone. I need to get back to work.

I take the pencil from the counter and write the scarf's price on the cardboard tag. But my fingers struggle to write the numbers, and my handwriting comes out crooked. What will we do if they come back?

The rest of the day passes in silence. I don't need to think about what happened. It happened, and it's over.

"See you tomorrow," I say to Mrs. Schneider at the end of the day as I take my coat.

"See you tomorrow. I'll just finish checking the accounts and will close up soon," she tells me, and suddenly she looks so alone to me.

"Do you want me to stay with you?"

"No, it's alright," she smiles sadly at me. "It's not about you, you don't need to be part of all this."

"Good night, Mrs. Schneider, see you tomorrow," I tell her, though perhaps I should stay with her after all, so she won't be alone.

I watch as she turns off the main light in the shop, leaving only a small light, and slowly climbs the wooden stairs. The glass door of the shop opens with a tired creak as I step onto the wet street and look around. And then I see them standing there.

Two policemen, standing with their faces to the street. One of them is tall and thin with a fine mustache, the other shorter and broad-shouldered. Thick leather belts fasten their long coats, and the golden police emblems gleam in the afternoon sunlight. Batons hang at their sides, and long-barreled rifles pointed upward are slung over their shoulders.

They look at me, and the shorter one takes out a cigarette and lights it, tossing the match onto the wet sidewalk.

"It's alright, ma'am," the tall policeman tells me. "We're here, maintaining order."

"Thank you, sir, have a good evening," I say to him and turn around with relief, beginning to walk home. At the end of the street, near a sign thrown on the sidewalk that has large black letters reading *Juden raus*, I turn and look at the quiet street.

The two policemen are still standing motionless by the shop. I turn and continue walking. I just want to get home, eat dinner, and recover from this day.

* * *

"Clara," Mrs. Vogel catches me as I climb the stairs, "I must talk to you about your tenant, Anna," she whispers to me, looking around as if wanting to make sure no one is listening to us.

"What is it, Mrs. Vogel?" I wearily ask.

"Do you know she's meeting with men?" Mrs. Vogel tells me quietly. "I've seen men going up to your apartment, more than one," she adds.

"That's terrible, I'll check with her about this," I answer. What am I going to do now that she knows? Why did I think Anna would stop, or that it wouldn't be discovered? I grip the stair railing, feeling like I need support.

"Lucky I'm here, to know and check. I think she's trying to hide it from you. You should thank me for watching over the building," Mrs. Vogel continues talking, her sharp face close to mine, her chin moving like the beak of a small bird of prey.

"Thank you, Mrs. Vogel," I manage to say, and begin walking up the stairs. I need to talk to Anna, even though I don't want to. Why did Hermann disappear like that?

"Mother, is Anna here?" I ask my mother as I enter our home.

"Yes, she's here. Why do you ask?" she asks me, raising her gaze from the knitting needles she's holding.

"I need to ask her something," I tell her as I approach Anna's closed door, knocking on it gently. What am I going to say to her?

"Come in," I hear her say.

I enter her room, close the door behind me, and look around.

The narrow iron bed that belongs to Mother and me stands in the corner of the room, with the cardboard suitcase she arrived with underneath it. The room smells of cigarettes.

A cracked mirror sits on the dresser in the corner, along with almost-finished red lipstick, a powder box, and a hairbrush. On the peeling wall next to the mirror hangs a crumpled picture taken from a magazine cover. It's a movie star, who also appears on film posters above the city center cinemas.

"Good evening, Clara," Anna smiles at me. She's sitting on her bed reading a book, with an ashtray beside her from which grayish cigarette smoke climbs in a delicate dance toward the ceiling.

"Good evening, Anna," I say, trying to think of what to say. "Is it possible Mrs. Vogel saw a man coming to visit you?"

Anna looks at me for a moment, as if thinking of how to answer; then she flips the book over and places it on the bed beside her. "And what if she did?" she asks.

"You can't do that, you know. It's dangerous, people talk."

"Yes..." she tells me as she takes the cigarette from the ashtray and inhales from it. "Mrs. Vogel loves to know what's going on."

"So stop it, please."

"I can't, you know that." She inhales from the cigarette again and places it in the ashtray. "I need the money, and you need me too. Your mother won't throw me out, and I know you won't tell your mother because you're a good woman."

"Anna, please, it's dangerous."

"It's not dangerous," she answers. "Dangerous is when you have no money to buy food, or nowhere to sleep, not when a gossipy neighbor who spends her life in the stairwell sees a man coming to visit you and also bringing you gifts." She finishes speaking and takes the overturned book from the bed, flips it back over, and continues reading.

"Please be careful, Anna."

"I promise to be careful, Clara," she raises her eyes from the book and takes the cigarette again, inhaling from it.

"Thank you," I say to her as I grasp the doorknob. What else can I say to her?

"And Clara..." she adds.

"What?" I remain standing by the door.

"If you need help, I'll help you too, because I'm also a good woman." She smiles at me and goes back to reading her book.

I hesitate, wondering whether I should say something more to her. Then I finally leave her room and close the door behind me. She's right, we need her money, and I would never betray her to Mother.

"What did you want from her?" Mother raises her eyes from her knitting and asks.

"I asked her about a dress I saw in a magazine photo at the newsstand today, on my way from work."

"Is it for him? Are you seeing him again?"

"No…" I sigh. "It doesn't matter."

But just then, there's a knock at the door.

"Aren't you going to open it?" Mother asks, and I get up from the chair to open the door. Could it be him? I walk to the door, feeling both tension and anticipation despite his disappearance. I carefully open the door and look into the hallway, but it's not him.

Mr. Koch's son Walter stands in the corridor, looking at me with his blue eyes, surveying me with indifference.

"Good evening," I hesitantly say. What does he want from us?

"Good evening, Fräulein Clara." He says the word 'Fräulein' as though it were a slur. "Mr. Koch is waiting for you downstairs, you need to pay the building committee fees. You haven't paid since you arrived here."

"Yes, sir, I'll bring it to him right away," I tell him, and close the door. We'll have less money for food again.

"Was that him?" Mother asks.

"No," I answer, and go to the silver metal box where we hide our money.

"Then who was it? Why do you need money?"

"It was Mr. Koch's son," I answer without enthusiasm.

"What did he want?"

"The building committee fees, his father is waiting for me to go down to their apartment and pay them." I take several bills out and put them in my dress pocket. I should have asked Anna for more money in exchange for my silence.

"Then let's go, I'm coming with you," Mother says as she rises from the chair. "People like them never want just money."

We descend the stairs and stand in front of a dark brown wooden door, almost black with age. *Mr. Koch – City Inspector* is written in stark black letters on a brass plaque attached to the wall beside the door. Music drifts through from the other side – a classical concert piece I can't quite identify, its melancholy notes adding to the heaviness in the air.

I take a deep breath, my fingers trembling slightly as I knock on the door. After a moment, it opens just a crack, and a woman peers at us.

"Good afternoon, Mrs. Koch. I'm Clara, and this is my mother Mrs. Hoffmann. We're your upstairs neighbors, recently moved in. We're here to see Mr. Koch," I say, trying to keep my voice steady.

She continues to examine us with suspicion. She's a small woman, roughly my mother's age, her yellowish-gray hair meticulously pulled back in a severe style. She's wearing a dark gray house dress that makes her blend into the shadows, while her hazel eyes survey us with quick, darting movements. Since moving here, I've barely seen her in the stairwell, as though she prefers to remain hidden from view.

"Good afternoon, Mrs. Koch. Is Mr. Koch available?" Mother asks, standing ramrod straight before her, projecting an air of dignity despite our reduced circumstances.

"What is this regarding?" Mrs. Koch's voice is thin and cautious.

"Building association fees," Mother replies matter-of-factly.

Mrs. Koch studies us for another moment through the barely-opened crack, looking frightened somehow, her fingers white around the edge of the door. "Yes, of course, come in," she finally answers as she opens the door wider, and we follow her inside.

Their apartment is larger than ours, and decidedly more elegant. The walls are covered with green floral wallpaper, and the living room features a sitting area with heavy wooden furniture. In the corner is a piano coated in dark brown lacquer, gleaming in the afternoon light filtering in through lace curtains. Mr. Koch sits in an armchair, this time dressed only in a light blue button-up shirt and tie, while his two sons Walter and Bruno sit across from him. All three men study us with varying degrees of intensity.

"Gustav," Mrs. Koch says to him, her voice softening slightly, "Mrs. Hoffmann is here with her daughter, regarding the association matter."

Mr. Koch stands and examines us both. After another moment, he moves toward us, extending his hand without a smile, his posture rigid and formal. "Mrs. Hoffmann, Clara, I've been expecting you. Please come in." He shakes our hands with cold precision.

"Thank you very much," Mother says to him, and I echo her words as we enter the living room. A gramophone sits on a wooden cabinet in the corner, playing classical music that fills the otherwise-tense silence. A chess set rests on the hosting table in the center; they'd been in the middle of a game. We're interrupting them.

"Walter, Bruno," he says quietly, and they quickly rise to shake our hands. Walter's grip hurts me intentionally, and he smiles slightly while studying my face, searching to see if I'll betray any sign of pain. But I make sure to smile politely back at him, refusing to give him the satisfaction. Only Bruno's smile feels genuine and warm as he shakes my hand, his eyes meeting mine with kindness.

"Here you go, Mr. Koch." I withdraw the money from my dress pocket and hand it to him, my hand trembling slightly. I want him to know we have enough money. Mother stands beside me, motionless, and I sense that she's protecting me, her presence a shield against scrutiny.

Mr. Koch looks at my outstretched hand with the bills, takes them and counts them slowly, deliberately, his fingers lingering over each note. "Well, as you surely know, being responsible for the association involves more than just money. Please sit down," he says while tucking the money into his trouser pocket and inviting us toward the sofas with a gesture. "Please," he repeats, and signals to his sons. Bruno, the younger one, quickly collects the chess pieces from the table and takes them to the mahogany cabinet on the far side of the room, where a porcelain figurine of a man playing a violin keeps silent watch.

"Is there some problem in the building you wish to discuss with us?" Mother asks him while still standing, projecting strength through her upright posture.

"We are neighbors, we must always look after one another. Allow me to invite you to sit," he repeats. Mother approaches and sits on the sofa, and I sit beside her, both of us straight-backed and tense against the embroidered upholstery.

Mr. Koch looks at Mother and then examines me, thinking for a moment. I turn my attention to the walls of the room, examining the paintings and the floral wallpaper. On the wall above the gramophone hangs a portrait of a serious-looking man with a small mustache.

"Please, help yourselves to some cookies," Mrs. Koch enters the room and places a bowl of butter cookies in the center of the room, then vanishes as if she'd never been there before we can thank her. Neither of us touch the cookies arranged in a perfect circle on the porcelain plate.

"We're listening, Mr. Koch," Mother begins, the table with the plate of cookies forming a barrier between us.

"I understand you're hosting a subletting tenant in your apartment," he starts, his tone deceptively casual.

"Yes, it's permitted by law," Mother answers, her jaw firmly set.

"And I understand you were fired and were looking for work, but that you found employment." He ignores Mother's answer and looks at me. Walter is looking at me too. I feel like they're investigators waiting for me to speak so they can record what I say in their hidden notebooks.

"Yes, sir, I succeeded in finding work," I answer, sitting sit up even straighter, my spine pressing against the back of the sofa.

"Yes…" he says in a contemplative voice, as if thinking of how to continue interrogating me. "And I understand that you chose to work for a Jewish woman," he continues, the word 'Jewish' hanging heavy in the air.

"For Mrs. Schneider, the neighbor across the hall," Mother says to him, her palms flat against her thighs as if she's ready for battle, each word measured and deliberate.

"And it didn't bother you that they're responsible for our failure in the last war?" He's speaking to Mother but looking at me, his eyes boring into mine. "Please take a cookie. My wife makes wonderful cookies." He extends the plate to me.

"Thank you," I say, taking a cookie and giving it a small bite. Its taste is delicate and sweet, but it somehow feels bitter in my mouth.

"Mr. Koch," Mother answers him politely, "Mrs. Schneider's son was also killed in that terrible war."

"That's what they say, the Jews, that they're part of us, that they fought with us," he answers, and takes a butter cookie himself, biting into it. "But you know," he leans slightly toward her and places his hand on his knee, "they say the Jews didn't really fight in that war. They say they fled the battlefield when bravery was required. Do you think traitors really fight? Or do they betray from within, waiting to stick a knife in our back? Look at what's happened since we lost the war. All of Berlin is full of men's clubs where you and I don't want to know what goes on, Communist cafés. Women without morals who run away from home to work in cabarets that mock tradition. Jewish businesses flourish, while your daughter is fired and works for a Jew. The Jews look after themselves, I promise you. Look at Mrs. Schneider, I'm sure she isn't suffering the crisis with her hat and glove shop." He talks without pause, his voice filling the room like it's joining the classical music played from the gramophone in the background. A few crumbs from the butter cookie he ate moments ago are still stuck to his thin lips.

"And now to you, Clara," Mr. Koch turns to me and slowly examines me.

"Yes, sir," I sit up even straighter, trying to be as upright as Mother. My fingers grip the half-eaten butter cookie that I have yet to finish.

"Are you sure you're happy at your new workplace?"

"Yes, sir," I answer, although I know he expects to hear a different answer.

"Well... Mrs. Hoffmann, it is indeed permitted by law," he looks at Mother and says with a contemplative expression, "to bring young girls as subletters into the apartment, to not insist on the purity of our people. Everything is legal..." he continues talking and stands up, signaling that the conversation has reached its end. We stand as well, facing him. "You know, Mrs. Hoffmann, many things are permitted by law, but it won't be that way in the future. The German people have no choice; we'll need to change the law. The police won't always protect those who don't deserve protection. Have a pleasant evening, Mrs. Hoffmann, Clara." He extends his hand.

"Thank you for your time, Mr. Koch. Come, Clara," Mother extends her hand to him with a confident gesture.

"Bruno," Mr. Koch signals to his son, and he accompanies us to the door.

"Mrs. Hoffmann, Fräulein Hoffmann," he says as we stand by the door, his voice softer than his father's or brother's, "don't worry about Mr. Koch. He has good intentions. In his way, he wants us all to be well here."

"Thank you, young man, have a pleasant evening," Mother says to him, and I look at him and wonder if he would still think that way if he were inside a Jewish shop during a demonstration.

"Do you think Mr. Koch is right?" I ask Mother later as we're both sitting and playing cards. The afternoon sunshine enters through the windows and colors the ugly walls with a pleasant yellow hue, warm and gentle.

"About what?" Mother asks as she puts a card down on the table.

"About how he treats Mrs. Schneider, about the Jews not fighting in the Great War, that they stabbed the nation in the back."

"I think Mrs. Schneider's son died in the Great War while Mr. Koch arranged for his son to be a clerk at Headquarters here in Berlin, with uniforms ironed like his father's shirt. The only injury his son might have suffered is some papers falling on his foot," she tells me in a quiet voice. "The only noise his son heard was the piano in hotel lobbies. The only sweat his son felt was when he danced with women in clubs here in Berlin, boasting in his clean uniform. That's what I think," she says, and places another card on the table.

"They don't like us." I put down a card on the table too.

"They don't like weak people. They're afraid it's contagious, like tuberculosis." She puts down a card on the table.

"I still think his son is kindhearted," I smile at her.

"You think everyone is kind-hearted," Mother sighs. "That doesn't make them so, it just makes you so. You also think our tenant is kindhearted, and I'm far less certain about that," Mother says, examining me. Does she know about Anna?

"She's the only tenant we could find," I answer, not telling her about what she does in the mornings when Mother is at work, although I should. Suddenly there's another knock at the door, and I raise my gaze to it. Is it him?

"Will you go open it?" Mother looks at me.

"Yes," I answer and get up. But if it's Hermann, I don't want to see him.

"Good evening, Clara," he says to me, offering an embarrassed smile, his hand fidgeting with his cap. "I apologize for not being here these past few days. I was on a work trip to Hamburg. I forgot to tell you, and I didn't know if I could write you a letter. I should've told you beforehand. I'm sorry; if you'll agree, I'd be happy to take you to a café again."

"I'm not a one-time or one-date woman. I'm not a woman that men can disappear on," I say to him while standing in the doorway, angry despite his apology. All my thoughts and fears from the past days burst out like a broken dam, flooding over the careful control I've tried to maintain.

"I know, I'm sorry," he says while holding his cap in his hand, twisting it nervously. Once again he's wearing an old but clean coat, with a simple button-up shirt beneath it. In his other hand he holds something wrapped in brown paper. Why is he coming now? I don't want to see him.

"I'm not suitable for you. I'm sorry, I'm not who you think I am. Have a pleasant evening," I say to him without thinking, my voice shaking. I can't bear him leaving me like that, and then returning only to leave again.

Hermann says nothing, just looks at me with a sad expression, and I close the door slowly, fighting back tears that threaten to spill out.

"Who was it this time?" Mother asks.

"Him," I answer as I sit back down, gathering the cards from the table with trembling hands.

"And why didn't you invite him in?"

"Because he disappeared on me, like all men, like Father." I place the package on the table and begin to deal the cards, my movements sharp and mechanical.

"He's a truck driver, Clara. That's what you told me. He doesn't disappear. He travels, but he comes back."

"How can I trust him, Mother?"

"Did he treat you with respect when you met?"

"Yes."

"Did he bring something with him? A small gift?"

"Yes, I think so. He was holding a package."

"We're in difficult times, Clara, and he cares about you. There aren't many men who would do that and respect you too," she says, and I remember that man who tried to kiss me at the club that evening, whose name I've already forgotten.

"I'll be right back, Mother. I'm going to get him," I say before rushing out the door, running down the stairs after him, taking them two at a time.

I find him by his truck, my breath coming in gasps, and I apologize and ask him to come up. At home I leave him with Mother while I get myself ready and enter Anna's room, asking her to lend me a nice dress and even applying lipstick. I want to be as beautiful as I can be.

"See how we can help each other?" she says as she helps me apply the lipstick, and I look at myself in the small mirror. The modern dress she gave me is so shiny and striking, the fabric clinging to my body, but I don't care.

"Let's go out," I say to him when I leave Anna's room, and Mother looks at me and nods her head in approval. The opened package he brought is lying on the table—a large chunk of preserved meat, more than we've had in weeks.

"Thank you, Mrs. Hoffmann," Hermann says goodbye to Mother, and by the door he holds my coat for me as I put it on, his hands gentle and careful, avoiding any improper touch. The whole day blurs together for me in a whirl of unclear emotions.

"Would you like to go dancing?" Hermann asks as we sit in the truck. The coat I'm wearing shifts slightly, revealing my shimmering dress underneath.

"No, please take me to the park, to Tiergarten. I want to walk there," I tell him, my fingers nervously playing with the hem of my coat.

In the park we walk silently side by side between the trees and stone statues. The setting sun paints the treetops in shades of gold and orange, turning the autumn leaves into molten copper. A couple holding hands passes in front of us, their silhouettes casting long shadows, yet Hermann doesn't try to take my hand.

I feel the cool breeze between the garden trees as we approach the small lake at the center of the park, and I look at the white rowboats tied to the dock, bobbing gently on the darkening water. Why did I wear this flashy dress? I'll never be that kind of woman. Will he want to keep seeing me after he discovers who I really am?

"Why do you want to go out with me?" I ask, taking a step back, creating distance between us.

"I don't understand," he quietly says, his brow furrowing in confusion.

"Why do you want to go out with me?" I repeat the question, my voice rising with each word. "You saw what kind of apartment I live in with my mother. We have no money, we're always in debt. Ever since I was a child, landlords have evicted us because we can't pay them." I continue talking, unable to stop, like a river of anger rushing out of me, crashing against rocks and stones in its path. I'm angry at him, for coming and then disappearing without my knowledge, at the demonstrators who frighten me so much, at the feeling of failure that's followed me since childhood. "Why do you want to go out with me?" I ask again, my voice trembling. "The glove shop where I work, where you came in and met me, it's owned by a Jewish woman. No one else wants to work for her, but I work there because we need money. And it's not enough for us. I sleep with my mother in the living room on a folding bed we open every night. Because we don't have enough money, we rent out the bedroom to a young woman. Her name's Anna. She goes to clubs, she's much prettier than me. Men always want to go out with her. She wears lipstick and has beautiful dresses. Even this dress is hers," I lift my coat slightly to show him the glittering dress, shining in the fading light. "Everyone only wants to go out with her," I finish in a weak voice, breathing slowly, my chest heaving.

Hermann says nothing; he just stands there watching me, his hands hanging at his sides as if waiting for me to continue attacking him. But I fall silent, and so does he. "You should take me home," I finally say. I don't want his pity.

"You know," he says to me, "three years ago I was on a work trip near Stuttgart, close to the village where Karl grew up. I remembered the name of the village, but I couldn't bring myself to enter. I found a side road and bypassed it, driving as fast as I could."

"Why?" I ask, searching for the connection to what I just told him. Why is he telling me about his friend from the army now?

"I simply couldn't enter that village, couldn't think about possibly meeting his mother," he tells me in a quiet voice that barely carries over the evening breeze.

"I don't understand..." I say, trying to look into his eyes, which seem darker now in the growing twilight. What is he trying to tell me?

"You see, after the war ended and I survived, I started imagining that Karl had returned to his village and found a nice woman, that they'd gotten married and he had a little girl he'd

145

take with him to milk the cows. He always talked about how much he loved the morning quiet during milking time. I even gave his daughter a name in my imagination." He smiles at me sadly, and I notice tears on his cheeks, glistening in the last rays of sunlight.

"Why?" I whisper, afraid of what he's going to tell me. Suddenly his shoulders seem lower to me, so much so that I could envelope them with my arms.

"It was during one of the attacks against the French, the Battle of Verdun in 1916. The first attack, or the second, the fifteenth, I don't remember anymore. They needed us to charge, to overcome the French. So we went out to attack again and again..." He speaks slowly, as if considering each word carefully, wiping his tear-stained cheeks. "We were together from the day we enlisted, and suddenly he was lying in the mud whispering that he was cold..." Hermann continues speaking, but stops from time to time and breathes slowly. "And I had nothing to give him, nothing at all, so I took out the only thing I had in my pocket, a pair of gloves, and tried to put them on him, but it didn't change anything anymore." He stops talking and wipes his cheeks again.

"I'm so sorry," I whisper and move toward him, wanting to comfort him somehow.

"I'm sorry, Clara. I've saddened you so much. I shouldn't have told you this." He tries to smile at me, though his eyes remain haunted. "The story about him finding a wife and having a daughter in a small village near Stuttgart is much nicer. But you know, Clara," he continues speaking, "I came back alive from the war. I'm a simple man. I'm a working man. I'm a man of quiet, long drives on the roads. I'm not a man of clubs and glittering dresses or expensive cafés. I'm a simple man, and I enjoy your company." He takes another step toward me and holds my hand. I feel his warm hands, calloused from work but gentle.

"What are you trying to tell me?" I raise my gaze to him with emotion, my heart pounding against my borrowed dress. I want him to embrace me.

"You're a woman who works hard, Clara, and it doesn't matter for whom. Just like I work hard. And I enjoy your company, and that's enough for me." He smiles at me, his eyes softening in the gathering darkness. "And I'd be happy if you'd agree to continue going out with me. I promise I have honorable intentions. Maybe someday, after we've dated for a while and you get to know me, you might also agree to consider marrying me."

"Please take me rowing," I whisper, and hug him with all my strength, feeling his arms wrap around me protectively.

Hermann approaches the man who rents boats at the lake and pays him, then holds my hand and helps me into the boat, steadying it as I find my balance.

In the middle of the small lake I lean back, resting against Hermann and closing my eyes, feeling the gentle rocking of the boat and the cool evening air on my face. Then I sit up and kiss his lips. He makes me feel protected, cherished. I know that in time, as we continue to see each other, I'll marry him if he just asks me, despite my fear that he'll one day discover I'm not good enough and leave me, like Father left.

ALEX AMIT

The Second Life

By the end of 1923, the German economy had managed to re-cover and Berlin was experiencing economic and cultural pros-perity. However, six years later, on October 24 1929, a day that would be known in history as 'Black Thursday,' the United States stock market crashed. This collapse led to the Great De-pression in the U.S. and triggered a chain reaction through-out the world. The German economy, which was dependent on American loans, collapsed in its wake. Within half a year, there were millions of unemployed people in Germany. Poverty and hunger prevailed everywhere, and the streets once again erupted with demonstrations and clashes between the Communists and the Nazi Party, which was growing stronger. The Nazi Party blamed the government, merchants, and the Jews for the situa-tion.

Chapter Ten

Berlin 1932, the Brownshirts in the Streets

I hold the yellowed piece of paper in my hands, unfolding it once more and reading the words Herman wrote to me two weeks ago. *My dear Clara,* he'd scrawled in his heavy, slightly crooked handwriting. I love the simplicity of his words and letters, written with a thick pencil on the yellow paper, as if they were spring butterflies fluttering toward me. My fingers trace the indentations his pencil left behind as I read the words again, despite having read them yesterday and every day since the letter arrived.

I hope this letter finds you healthy, and that you have enough food. Here in Hamburg, food is difficult to obtain, but it is less dire than in Berlin, at least according to the stories told by drivers arriving here from Berlin. I sleep in an old warehouse with several other men, trying to find work at the harbor. Sometimes they look for laborers to load ships with wooden crates or barrels, and sometimes they need help transporting goods to the port.

Every time I see a large ship leaving the harbor on a slow voyage, or watch the fishing boats rocking on the waves, I think of you.

A gust of cold air seeps through the thin window frame of our apartment. I pull my worn cardigan tighter around my shoulders before continuing.

I won't be able to send you money this month, but I hope the situation improves and I'll manage to send you something for your thirty-sixth birthday. Hamburg is cold, and it has snowed several times already, but I'm managing with the gloves you gave me and my old coat. I hope to come soon, even if only for a few days, and then we'll try again...

I stop reading and caress my belly. Sometimes it feels so empty that I want to scream.

I know the end of the letter by heart, but I still read his parting words: *missing you. Yours, Hermann.*

I gently fold the letter and place it back in the envelope bearing the Hamburg postmark. I slide it into the wooden drawer in the kitchen corner, and look around at the small apartment he and I rented together. He's been away for months searching for work outside Berlin; the walls seem grayer without him here, the ceiling lower.

I walk to the silver-framed photograph of us on the wooden stool in the bedroom, next to our bed. The mattress sags on one side—his absence hasn't changed my habit of sleeping on the right. I carefully lift the frame and kiss the image. I kiss it every time I leave the house and he's not here. I was so excited that day, when I wore the white dress. I know Hermann was excited too. His eyes shine in the photograph with hope we both still clung to then.

Afterwards I put on my coat, the blue one with the frayed cuffs I've mended three times now. I descend the creaking stairs and go out into the street. It's almost eight o'clock, and Mrs. Schneider is surely already at the shop.

There are demonstrations in the street again, and the noise of the National Socialists, but I'm used to it now.

On the corner of the street, a few steps from the shop, I stop and observe them. There are five of them, young men, all wearing the uniforms of the 'Brownshirts,' with red armbands bearing a white circle and swastika, and black boots that gleam even in the dull morning light. One holds a paint can in one hand and a brush in the other as he crouches, writing something in white paint on the sidewalk in front of the shop. Another youth watches him while the rest form a perimeter. They stand with their backs to him, in a rigid posture, arms folded across their chests, faces toward the street. What should I do? Continue forward?

I look around, but there isn't a single policeman in sight. People hurrying to work quickly cross to the other side of the sidewalk and continue onward, neither turning their gaze toward the young men nor attempting to stop what they're doing. The shop door is closed. Has Mrs. Schneider arrived yet? Is she inside?

I know I should turn around and walk away, let them finish writing on the sidewalk and leave. A few months ago they were already writing slogans against Jews on the shop wall. But what about Mrs. Schneider? What if she's already arrived and is alone in the shop? I scan the street again, imagining Hermann's green truck arriving, him driving them away, but I know that won't happen. My wedding ring feels heavy on my finger as I slowly begin walking toward the young men blocking the entrance to the shop. I'm worried about Mrs. Schneider.

When they notice me, one of the youths stands in my path. His light brown hair is combed back and slicked with oil that catches the morning light. "Where do you think you're going?" he asks, practically spitting the words at me. His eyes are filled with hatred and contempt, the blue in them as cold as winter ice.

"Let me pass," I say, trying to move past him towards the door. I'm older than he is, even though he towers over me, his shoulders broad beneath his brown uniform.

"Jews are poison. You shouldn't buy from them," he says, and for a moment he seems to lose his confidence. But two of his friends standing guard join him, and when he notices their presence, he tries to block my way again. "Anyone who buys from Jews is a traitor," he brings his face close to mine and shouts, his voice sharp and hoarse like the ear-piercing whistle of a locomotive. My entire body tenses, but I lower my head slightly and continue walking, passing them by as if I'm pushing away their shouts with my slightly-hunched shoulders, as if I'm walking through a hailstorm. I need to reach the shop door and open it. I'll be protected inside the shop from their wild screams and the spit flying from their mouths.

A split-second before I touch the door, a frightening thought crosses my mind: what will I do if Mrs. Schneider hasn't arrived yet and the shop is closed, or if she's locked the door? But I can no longer retreat. I reach for the handle and breathe a sigh of relief when it opens. While I open the door, one of the boys strikes me in the back, and I think another spits on me, the wet warmth seeping through my coat. I open the door just enough, slip inside, close it behind me, and lock the bolt. Only then do I allow myself to breathe again. Their loud shouts still echo in my ears.

"Mrs. Schneider," I call out while still holding the door handle with all my strength, despite having locked the bolt. I look back into the dimly-lit shop, but the sound of heavy knocking on the glass causes me to turn my gaze back.

"Jews out!" The boys pound forcefully on the window and shout while pressing their faces against the glass, their faces seemingly wrapped in the frightening masks of monsters carved from forest wood, distorted by hatred.

"Mrs. Schneider," I call again, trying to overcome the noise of their blows on the glass. The boy who was painting on the sidewalk is now drawing a large Star of David on the display window with the brush in his hand, while his friends continue to pound on the glass.

"Clara, come here," I hear Mrs. Schneider from the room upstairs, and I hurry up. I'm afraid, my heart hammering against my ribs.

"Are you all right?" I ask when I see her. She's standing behind the wooden desk in the corner of the small room on the second floor that serves as storage space. In the weak lamplight, she seems to be trembling. The pounding from below doesn't stop, and suddenly I hear the sound of shattering glass, and my entire body tenses.

Mrs. Schneider doesn't answer, she just continues to stand there, one hand gripping the wooden desk and the other holding a silver letter opener. What will we do if they come upstairs looking for us?

"General liquidation of Jewish shops," I hear shouts from below and the sound of footsteps on glass. "We'll help them emigrate from our nation," someone seems to reply with a shout mixed with laughter, drawers opening and wood breaking. I look around the small room, searching for a stick or rod or something else that will protect me if they try to come up, but I find nothing.

"I'll go down and talk to them. I'm like them, I'm not Jewish," I tell Mrs. Schneider, even though I know I shouldn't do that.

"No, don't go." She hurries toward me and places her hand on my shoulder. "Stay here with me. They'll leave soon, they always leave eventually," she whispers to me in a trembling voice, her fingers still clutching the silver letter opener.

"Look what I found, Jews don't lack for anything," one of them seems to say, and a moment later there are more sounds of breaking glass and strong kicks, with the sound of breaking wood following.

I'm trembling. What are they doing down there? What are they destroying? More and more blows and kicks are heard below, until finally the sound of shoes on glass stops, and suddenly all is quiet. I can hear my breathing, and Mrs. Schneider's. Are they gone?

I approach the edge of the stairs and look down toward the shop. I can see crushed and torn men's hats on the wooden floor, scattered among shards of glass.

"I'm going down," I say to Mrs. Schneider.

"Please, Clara, don't go downstairs," she tells me, but I descend the wooden stairs step by step into the shop, and when I reach the bottom, I look around. They've gone. The shop is empty.

A cold wind slips in through the broken window, and I can hear the hooves of a horse walking on the cobblestones outside. I lower my gaze to the floor, and to the shelves and drawers that were Mrs. Schneider's pride.

They've destroyed everything. Among the broken glass lie crushed hats, torn gloves and scarves. The cash register has been broken into and looted, and on the counter that had been neatly arranged with gloves, a white Star of David has been painted in ugly brush strokes.

I turn my gaze to Mrs. Schneider, who is slowly coming down the stairs. Why did they do this to her?

She gently steps on the floor, trying to walk between the ruined hats and torn scarves, but the sound of glass breaking beneath her brown shoes sounds like the screeching wail of an animal crying in agony.

I approach the broken display window and anxiously look outside into the street. Will they return?

A gray truck crosses the street and disappears, and two women pass by the broken display window. For a moment they look at me, and I try to understand what they're thinking, but after a split-second they avert their gaze and continue walking as if they haven't noticed the destruction at all. Along the way, they step past the inscription written on the cobblestones: *Jewish Shop*.

"I'll call the police. I'll find someone to help us," I say to Mrs. Schneider as I walk toward the shop door. Its glass is broken too.

"No..." she says quietly, and I turn to her.

"Shouldn't I go?" I ask her.

"Do you think it'll help? Do you think the police will help?"

"They must help. They always help."

"Not anymore," she says quietly, "they haven't helped for a long time. Many of the policemen have already joined them, frightening me more than making me feel safe."

"So what do you want to do?" I bend down, pick up a crushed fedora from the floor, and try to straighten it. "Do you want me to start cleaning up while you find a glazier?" I ask. I must help her.

"No..." she whispers, and looks at me with a long gaze.

"I don't understand," I say in confusion as I look at her. She's still holding the silver letter opener in her hand, but it hangs limply now, as if it might fall from her hand at any moment.

"No... I don't want you to clean up the shop," she slowly says, and lowers her gaze.

"Then what do you want me to do?" I place the ruined hat on the broken counter.

"Clara," she says to me as she raises her gaze and looks at me, "you're fired."

"I don't understand. Is it something I did?"

"You heard me. You're fired. I'm dismissing you. You don't work here anymore."

"But I've worked with you for years."

"You're fired. I don't have the means to pay you anymore." She indicates the destroyed shop with her eyes, and the empty cash drawer lying on the floor.

"I'll work for free now. You can pay me when you have money," I tell her, picking up a torn scarf from the floor.

"No, you're fired. Please leave my shop."

"I don't understand. Is it something I did?" I repeat the question and feel the lump in my throat growing.

"No," she sighs, "it's not something you did."

"Then what?"

"You're not Jewish. You don't need to be here. This isn't your fate."

"What?"

"You may not understand now, but someday you will. Go. I don't want to see you here in the shop anymore. Please go. Thank you for wanting to stay, but please go now," she tells me while leaning on the broken counter, and I fear that at any moment she might collapse to the floor. "Go now. I'll manage. Please," she tells me again.

I look at her for one more moment, fighting the urge to go to her and hold her so she won't fall. She looks so fragile in the ruined shop, her shoulders bent under an invisible weight. But after a moment, I turn and leave the shop. The sound of my shoes on broken glass seems to me like the wailing of an injured animal fleeing to its den to lick its wounds. But I don't turn back. I don't even search for Herman's green truck to come help us.

At home, I sit in the wooden chair by the wooden table in the kitchen corner. I take out the cardboard notebook from the drawer where I record expenses and income, and write *Dismissed from Mrs. Schneider's shop.* My fingers, gripping the pencil tightly, add a thick black line under the words I've written.

Then I open the letter Hermann sent me, and read it again.

"*My dear Clara,*" I murmur the words he wrote and begin to cry.

When will he finally come to embrace me?

The next morning, I take out the metal box that rests in the kitchen's wooden drawer, remove the remaining banknotes, take a few of them and return the rest. I'll manage, I'm already accustomed to this feeling of having no money. It always accompanies me, breathing down my neck without pause, like the whisper of a hot iron filled with glowing coals.

After kissing the photograph of us both and gently placing it back on the stool beside the bed, I leave the apartment and step into the street.

I purchase a little food at the cheapest stalls in the market and place it in a paper bag. Although I don't need to go to work, I quickly walk down the street, I'm used to it now.

Near the water tower, I pass by the garden beneath it. I don't want to look at the women who habitually sit there with their children. I don't want to feel their gazes piercing my back as I pass by. I don't want to imagine them gossiping about me.

After the garden, I walk down a side street to the old building where I lived before moving in with Hermann.

It's been eight years since I've lived there, and so little has changed since then, just tiny alterations that hardly seem noticeable at all. More of the stairwell plaster has peeled away, and there are a few new scratches in the wooden stairs.

Before climbing up, I step into the inner courtyard for a moment to see if there's enough coal to last until the end of winter; though if it's lacking, I won't have money to buy more unless I find work soon. I look around. Nothing has changed there either: the same smell of damp mildew and coal, and a few wooden crates stacked near the black coal pile. Above, on the second floor window belonging to the Koch family, dark blue uniforms hang on the clothesline. Mother told me three years ago that he'd joined them, but I hadn't seen him in the stairwell since, and I hadn't asked her about it again.

The wooden stairs creak with that familiar, pleasant sound as I climb them. Fortunately, Mrs. Vogel isn't in the stairwell to start talking to me. I pass by the Koch family's door and look at the dark brown wood. A small Nazi Party flag is now attached next to the brass plaque with Mr. Koch's name. A wave of discomfort washes over me as I remember the armbands of those young men from yesterday and their frightening faces staring at me through the display window, moments before I fled to the second floor and they shattered the glass. I take a deep breath and hurry up the stairs. Mrs. Schneider's door is also closed. It's always closed. How is she? I hesitate for a moment, but give up and walk toward Mother's apartment, knocking on the door. I didn't sleep all night after what happened yesterday. I don't know whether or not to tell her what happened.

"Good morning. Why so early? Don't you have work at the shop?" she asks as I walk into the house. I don't answer, just close the door behind me and follow her into the kitchen, setting down the paper bag and taking out the groceries.

"I don't need so much food," she tells me as I arrange the bread, butter and vegetables I managed to buy today on the old wooden table.

"I bought them while I still could. You know what the situation is in the streets," I answer, taking out most of the money I've brought with me and placing it in her round money box. "I also brought you rent for next month," I add.

"You didn't have to," she says as she sits down at the table, taking a potato and beginning to peel it.

I don't respond, I just take a knife from the wooden drawer, sit beside her, and start helping. Since I got married and left home, I've been helping her with the rent. Anna left years ago. With my help, Mother can finally sleep in her own bed, in her own bedroom.

"What about a letter? Did you get another letter from Hermann?" she asks after a while.

"No," I answer, picking up a new potato and beginning to peel it. "But he'll probably send more money soon. He's working there all the time."

"He's a good man. I know you miss him." She stops peeling and places her fingers on my hand.

"Thank you," I say, and place the fingers of my other hand on hers. I only sometimes notice that she's aging: her hair has become whiter, and she's a little less energetic. She's also barely worked since the economic crisis broke out and the layoffs began. Young girls looking for work took her position, and when someone is willing to employ her at all, they pay her less. Wealthy women prefer young women to do their laundry. What will happen to us now that I've lost my job too? I lower my gaze to her wrinkled fingers gently holding mine. How will I tell her about what happened yesterday at the shop?

"Have you spoken with Mrs. Schneider?" I ask.

"No, why? I don't see her much. Is everything all right?"

"Yes," I tell her. "There were some Brown Shirt boys outside the shop yesterday. Shall we play cards after we finish with the potatoes?" I'll tell her what happened in a few days.

"What did they do?" She releases my hand and goes back to peeling the potatoes.

"You know the Brownshirts."

"Yes, I know them," she sighs. "What did they do?"

"It doesn't matter." I don't want to tell her. I don't want to remember it.

"I'm your mother, Clara. What happened?" She stops peeling the potato and looks at me through her glasses. She's needed those in recent years.

"They destroyed the shop," I quietly say while tightly gripping the knife. "They broke the windows, broke in and destroyed the merchandise."

"They?"

"Yes, they. They were boys, but they wore their uniforms, with the symbol on their arm." I think about the things they yelled at me when I approached them before entering the shop. What would have happened if I'd turned around and left? Would they have finished writing on the sidewalk and gone away without breaking in? Could it be that I caused all of it?

"And how is Mrs. Schneider?" Mother asks.

"I think she's all right," I take a deep breath. "But she won't be able to employ me anymore. I'll start looking for work today."

Mother doesn't say anything, she just sits there and places her hand on mine again. Her warm fingers feel pleasant to me. "At least you have a husband who brings home money," she says with a sigh, getting up and filling a pot with water, which she places on the iron stove. I don't tell her what Hermann wrote to me in his letter. She wouldn't let me help her if she knew our situation.

After we play cards, I say goodbye and leave the apartment. I stop by Mrs. Schneider's closed door and look at it. Despite working for her for so long, we were never friends, and I don't know if I should ask how she is after what happened yesterday. I stand in front of her door and finally raise my hand, knocking hesitantly on the door, hoping she's not there.

From inside I hear footsteps, and the door opens a crack, but when she sees it's me, she opens it wide. She's wearing a simple black house dress, and her gray hair is loosely gathered.

"Mrs. Schneider, I just wanted to make sure you're all right," I say. She looks so lonely as she stands there in the doorway.

"Come in," she says dryly, without smiling, and I follow her into the living room. "Please sit," she gestures to one of the old leather armchairs. The photographs of her dead son and husband on the cabinet make me uncomfortable.

"Mrs. Schneider, are you all right after what happened yesterday at the shop?" I ask, unable to take my eyes off their pictures staring back at me. Did she also wish they would come to her aid yesterday?

"You know, Clara," she sits in the armchair across from me and begins to speak slowly, "I was ten years old when they came the first time," she says, without explaining who she's talking about. But I don't stop her, and she continues in her slow speech. "We were living in Kiev then, in an apartment above my uncle's bakery. I remember that beforehand, Father had said they'd murdered the Tsar and were blaming the Jews. I didn't know who the Tsar is. They came at night." She stops speaking and lowers her gaze to her palms. She has delicate hands and beautiful fingers that the years haven't marked. "I mainly remember the shouting outside, and the burning smell, and the pounding on the front door." She pauses for a moment, then continues again. "The pounding on the door, I remember that's what I feared most. My mother embraced me, but I was so afraid." She stops speaking again. "The next day we fled on a horse-drawn wagon, here to Berlin. Father said we had to escape." She sighs.

"I'm sorry," I tell her, searching for something to say that would comfort her, but I can't find the words.

"You know, Clara," she continues speaking, "the whole way here, my father said it was our fate, the fate of Jews, to wander, to move from place to place when things went bad. But I didn't want to wander. I wanted a home. I wanted to belong. And I came to Berlin as a child, I learned German, I became German. I married a young German man here in Berlin, and we bought this apartment where you and I are sitting now and talking.

And when I had a child, that child was German. And when he went to war, it was a German soldier I sent to war, and now he's buried in a German military cemetery on French soil, and my husband died of grief and is buried here in Berlin, in the Jewish cemetery. And yesterday they called me a traitor," she tells me in a trembling voice while trying to sit upright.

"You are German, you belong with us, you live here," I answer with the first thing I can think of, though I'm not sure she's listening to me.

"Do you think I should run away, like we ran when I was a child? Do you think I should escape this country?"

"I don't know. I've never left Berlin, it's the only place I know," I tell her, and think of my husband looking for work in Hamburg.

"I'm sixty-two. At my age, one doesn't wander anymore," she tells me, and I think I notice tears in the corners of her eyes. "At my age, one doesn't leave the grave plot waiting for them beside their husband. At my age, one lowers their head and hopes the storm will pass. I'm sure the Nazis will disappear soon and sanity will return, just like those rioters in Kiev disappeared. I'm just sorry you had to experience it too," she smiles bitterly at me.

"I'm sure they'll disappear soon," I say. I so desperately want to believe that.

"Thank you," she says as she rises, as if to signal that the visit is over and she's sorry I saw her in a moment of weakness.

"Thank you for giving me work when I needed it." I stand as well, and want to embrace her.

"Wait a moment," she tells me, and disappears down the hallway, returning a moment later and placing a pair of pearl earrings in my hand. "Take these. They're for you, instead of the salary I owe you that I can't pay right now."

"I can't take these, it's too much," I gasp with excitement. I've never held such expensive pieces of jewelry.

"Thank you, Clara." She ignores what I'm saying and escorts me to the door. "Thank you for being there with me when they came. Thank you for coming to visit me today," she adds, and closes the door as if wanting to escape from me back into her lonely apartment. I descend the stairs, clutching the earrings tightly in my palm. I'll save them for an emergency. But then I see Mrs. Vogel standing in the hallway, smiling at me.

"Clara, I haven't seen you in ages," she says. "I don't see your mother much either. Is everything all right?" She draws closer and asks the question quietly, so I must stop and speak with her.

"Yes, Mrs. Vogel, everything is fine," I politely smile at her while feeling a wave of discomfort. Pinned to the lapel of her dress is a small Nazi Party badge.

"I've joined them," she points proudly at the shiny party pin gleaming in the gray light of the stairwell, her thin face animated with an enthusiasm I've never seen in her before. "They say we must vote for Hitler. One can't buy anything anymore, even the prices on the black market are impossible.

They say only he will restore order. That's what Mr. Koch always says. Do you remember his children? They've really advanced. They'll bring order here. Let me tell you, Clara, we should all join them," she says in a quiet, proud voice without waiting for me to respond, her hands fluttering like anxious birds as she speaks. "Wait here, I have something for you," she adds, entering her apartment and emerging a moment later. "Here, take it, so you'll have one too. You need to join us." She places a shiny swastika pin in my palm. "You need to wear it too. Hitler will bring the change we've all been waiting for."

I close my fingers around the pin, feeling the metal dig painfully into my palm, and I raise my gaze to the wooden stairs leading up to the third floor and Mrs. Schneider's apartment. What will happen to her? What will happen if they continue to 'restore order' as Mrs. Vogel so desperately wants?

On my way home, I grip the pearl earrings tightly inside my purse along with the Nazi Party pin, the two objects feeling impossibly heavy against each other. At home, I hide them in the money box. I'll manage without them.

But in the days that follow, as I search for work, everyone refuses me just as they did eight years ago. No one's looking for workers, and I'm older now. Every morning I take a little money out of the metal container where I keep the rolled paper notes, and buy a little food for Mother and me.

Two weeks later, when the money runs out, I take some of the silverware Mother gave me for my wedding and put it in my purse. The silver spoons that once seemed like such a treasure now feel cold and unfamiliar in my hands. I'll try to sell them on the black market. I have no other choice. I'll never tell Mother where the money came from.

The cold wind slaps my face as I walk to the Anhalter Bahnhof train station, south of the city center. It's a large and crowded station; I'll try to blend in among the thousands of passengers so I can sell my silverware to one of the people disembarking from the trains. My hand grips my shoulder purse tightly. I must succeed at selling them or exchanging them for food. I haven't eaten since yesterday.

A tram crosses the large square outside the grand station, causing the cobblestones to tremble slightly beneath my worn boots. By the entrance, which consists of three stone arches, several taxis stand in a row alongside a horse-drawn carriage. The taxi drivers examine me curiously, but when they see I'm not approaching them, they return to talking among themselves and smoking, rubbing their hands together to stay warm while waiting for passengers. Is Hermann rubbing his hands like that in cold Hamburg while waiting for work? A gust of cold wind penetrates my woolen coat, making me shiver, and I quicken my steps under the stone arches and enter the large station building.

Several black trains stand at the platforms. Only one locomotive is emitting smoke, creating a whitish cloud in the vast space that slowly climbs upward until it dissipates into the metal structure supporting the high ceiling. The distant people walking across the platforms appear like ants in the gray light, hurrying about their business, their hands tucked into their coat pockets and their eyes fixed on the concrete platforms.

I stand in the corner of the station, leaning against a cold metal column and looking around, searching for someone I can approach, one hand guarding my purse to prevent pickpockets. Despite the cold, I feel my body warming from the tension, beads of sweat forming at my temples.

A soldier in a greenish-gray uniform approaches me, almost pressing against me. "Do you have cigarettes?" he asks quietly.

"I have something better than cigarettes. I'm selling pure silver at a good price," I answer, taking a silver spoon out of my purse and holding it tightly, the metal cold against my fingers.

"What would I do with that?" he scoffs and moves away from me, muttering a curse. I go back to leaning against the cold metal column and looking around hopefully. Other people will come, I know.

A woman younger than me approaches. "What are you looking for?" she asks while examining my clothes and the purse I'm holding. She wears a simple blue worker's woolen dress, wrapped in a thin coat. She too holds a purse, her hand resting on it protectively.

"I have this quality silver, a complete set of cutlery at a good price," I tell her.

"Three forks for a pair of shoes, new quality women's shoes." She takes women's shoes made of brown leather out of her purse, and mentions the name of the workshop where I once worked.

"Thank you, but no. I'm only exchanging for food or money." I look at the new leather shoe. How did she get those?

"Go away, this is my area," she suddenly speaks angrily while putting the shoes back in her purse. "You can't sell your stolen goods here," she tells me threateningly, and I feel a wave of fear washing over me. What should I do? I can't give up. I need money.

"This isn't stolen merchandise, it's mine, and I'm allowed to be here," I tell her, although she frightens me, her sharp eyes narrowing as she studies my face.

"Leave now, or I'll make sure someone else deals with you. There are plenty of police officers here that I know." She presses against me and forcefully pushes me with her free hand. Her breath smells of cigarettes.

My back hits the cold metal column. From the other side of the station, I see a police officer standing and watching us.

"Please," I whisper to her, "I need money for food."

"Go over to the end of the platform there, far away, where the trains leave. I don't care if you stand there. If you come near my area again, I'll make sure they take care of you. Go on, go," she tells me, and pushes me again.

I slowly walk backwards, moving away from her. Only at a safe distance do I turn my back to her and walk along one of the long platforms to its end, to the large opening through which the trains leave the station.

The wind is colder here, and almost no passengers come by, but I have no other choice. I'm more afraid of that woman and the police officers patrolling the station than I am of the cold wind cutting through my coat like tiny knives.

In the evening, I arrive at home and take out half a loaf of bread, soap, and two packs of cigarettes that I received in exchange for two silver spoons. Tomorrow I'll exchange the cigarettes for food. I light the metal stove in the kitchen and heat water, standing next to it and trying to warm my hands, my fingers red and stiff from hours spent in the cold.

Over the next few days, I stand at the edge of the station, the cold wind from the opening relentlessly striking my face. There are times when I walk along the platform toward the interior of the station, but when I notice that woman or one of her friends, I retreat back to my spot, a shadow among shadows.

A train arriving from Vienna enters the station and stops by the platform, and I watch people in suits and heavy woolen coats disembarking and passing by me. My hand clutches the pearl earrings inside my purse. For three days now I've been trying to exchange them. I haven't been able to sell the remaining silverware recently, and I have no other choice. These precious pearls are my final lifeline.

"Fräulein Clara," I hear a male voice and turn around in surprise. He stands before me, examining me, his gray eyes surveying me with indifference.

❦

He hasn't changed much since I last saw him years ago. His wheat-colored hair is still short, and he doesn't smile at me. He merely examines me as if I'm merchandise for sale and he's trying to assess my value, exactly as he looked at me all those times I saw him standing behind his father.

"It's been a long time since I've seen you, Fräulein Clara," he says. He wears a thick dark blue wool police coat that protects him from the cold wind at the edge of the platform. I raise my eyes to him and try to stand straight, despite his gaze making me anxious and my spine stiffening under his scrutiny.

"Herr Walter," I reply, while hesitating over which honorific to give him, "I am now Frau Berger." The golden buttons of his coat gleam in the gray light of the station. Mother told me his father helped him join the police force's Morality Division.

"Yes, I heard you got married." He speaks to me in a quiet, polite manner, but his eyes seem to be searching for cracks in me that he can bite into with his teeth. "The gossip Frau Vogel told everyone, including me. But I don't see Herr Berger here to protect you, as a man should care for his wife."

"Herr Berger is currently traveling," I answer and take a step backward, feeling the cold metal railing press against my back.

"And you?"

"I'm waiting for an acquaintance who should be arriving by train," I give him the first answer I can think of, my fingers nervously clutching the purse strap.

"The passengers have already finished disembarking. I don't think your acquaintance arrived on this train. I noticed you've been waiting on the platform since morning," he says and smiles wickedly, his thin lips barely concealing his teeth.

"I'm allowed to stand here. People are allowed to stand in a train station. I'm not doing anything illegal," I answer, feeling the cold wind striking my back, cutting through my coat.

"Not yet," he says, adjusting the leather glove on his hand, "but we record everything, in case we need to know more in the future. We always need to deal with things." He speaks, as if to himself: "What do you have in your purse?" He points to my purse.

"Nothing," I answer, "women's items."

Walter looks at me and says nothing, just signals with his hand, and I open the purse wide and hand it to him, standing before him in silence, my heart hammering against my ribs.

He takes one step closer to me, inserts his hand and inspects the contents. After a moment he takes out two silver knives, the cutlery my mother gave me. "What's this?" he asks.

"Two knives. I took them with me," I answer slowly, breathing heavily. Will he arrest me for black market trading? How much does he hate me?

Walter doesn't say a word, just releases them, and they fall onto the platform with a clatter, making a sharp metallic ring. Then he inserts his hand and continues to search, and suddenly smiles slightly. "What are these?" he asks, taking the two pearl earrings out of the purse.

"I was given them, Walter. They're mine, they're not stolen," I quickly say, panic rising in my throat.

"I'll take them. I'll treat them as property that needs to be returned to its owner," he tells me maliciously as his black leather glove closes over them. "And by the way, Clara, address me as 'sir.'" He looks at me with a cold gaze.

"Yes, sir," I answer while holding the open purse, which suddenly seems to me like the mouth of a dead fish. What will I do? I've lost the earrings, Mrs. Schneider's precious gift, my last hope.

"Now turn around and go back to the platform to wait until evening for your acquaintance," he says, tucking the earrings into his coat pocket. I must say something to him, I need those earrings.

"Yes, sir," I say in a trembling voice, bending down to collect the two knives thrown onto the platform. His black boots, polished to a high shine, are so close to my face that I can smell the wax. Then I rise and turn, starting to walk along the platform with my back to him, trying to hold back my tears. Why is this happening to me? Why couldn't I fight for my pearl earrings?

"And Clara..." I hear him calling me.

"Yes, sir," I turn to him. He remains standing upright, looking at me without moving, his tall figure silhouetted against the gray station light.

"Come here," he motions to me again with his leather-gloved hand.

I slowly walk toward him, standing before him with my eyes downcast.

"Don't say I'm not a generous man." He takes a banknote out of his wallet, approaches me and stuffs it into my coat pocket. For a moment I feel his fingers through the coat fabric and freeze in place, my breath catching.

"Aren't you going to thank me?" he asks.

"Thank you, sir," I mumble, the words sticking in my throat.

"Goodbye, Frau Clara. I have a feeling we'll meet again." He gives me another look and begins to walk away down the platform.

I remain standing there, watching his figure growing smaller among the people continuing to quickly walk through the station. Only when he disappears from my sight do I allow myself to move from my spot, my legs trembling beneath me.

"The Nazi Party under Hitler has won the majority of seats in Parliament," a newspaper boy announces as he runs, waving a newspaper above his head. "Read now in the evening edition."

I watch a man in a suit stop the boy and buy a newspaper. When will all this end? When will I not have to worry so much?

Chapter Eleven

The Winter of 1932

My dear Clara, I excitedly open the letter that arrived this morning and begin to read his words. A cold wind from early December penetrates the broken window in the stairwell, but I can't wait and lean against the peeling wall to continue reading.

It's nighttime now, and only one oil lamp burns beside me in the warehouse I share with all the other men. My Clara, in my letters I tell you about life here, about working on the ships at the harbor, but I haven't told you the whole truth. There's something else, something I've needed to tell you for some time but have been ashamed to write, ashamed that I've been hiding it from you... I lean against the peeling wall, afraid to continue reading. *But I must tell you...* I look at his words and struggle to breathe.

My dear Clara, I had no choice but to sell the truck. It had an engine problem and I didn't have the money to fix it. Without a truck, it's harder for me now to find work, but I'm working very hard so that I can buy it back. Unfortunately I won't be able to come home for Christmas to be with you, but I think of you every day... he continues to tell me in letters written in pencil on the yellowish paper, and I start breathing again. The main thing is that he's still with me, the main thing is that he hasn't left me, like Father left.

When I finish reading, I hold the paper and envelope in my hand and go up to the apartment. I arrange the few remaining pieces of silverware on the table, along with some banknotes and the Nazi pin Mrs. Vogel gave me. I look at them; I'll sell everything possible, I'll help him buy back the truck and return to me.

A few days later, I'm moving away from the sausage stand at the Anhalter Bahnhof station, heading toward the exit. The vendor promised me yesterday that he would get me sausages and meat at a special price in exchange for the last two silver spoons I had left, but he didn't keep his promise.

Three musicians stand near the station entrance, playing holiday songs on violins, with green fir branches tied to the red brick wall above them. I tighten my coat and continue walking through the cold station toward the exit.

A woman about my age wrapped in a dark blue wool coat walks in front of me, and suddenly a man in a black coat approaches her and holds her tightly, enveloping her in his arms. I shift my gaze away from them and pass by. My husband will return and embrace me like that too. I know he'll come back.

The station lights flicker for a moment, a yellow glow on the glass entrance doors as I push them and step out. The soft snow is falling on the stairs leading up to the station and the large square. The sun has long since set, the early winter darkness swallowing the city.

"Merry Christmas," one of the taxi drivers ironically calls out to his colleagues waiting outside the station. He then gets into the taxi, slamming the door shut behind him.

I cross the square, my old shoes leaving marks in the soft snow. Despite my feet aching after standing for so long on the platform, and from the cold, I continue to walk on foot. I have no money to take the tram.

On the boulevard, the slowly-falling snow looks like tiny stars in the light of the street lamps, before it reaches the ground and turns muddy gray. I lower my gaze to the snow to avoid slipping as I walk quickly. On the street, near a confectionery, a girl presses her nose against the glass, ignoring the cold and eagerly gazing at the star-shaped cookies displayed in the shop window. I smile to myself and tighten the scarf around my neck. I was once a child like her too. Soon I'll be home and will make myself a cup of hot tea.

I continue walking, turning from the boulevard into one of the dimly-lit alleys. Only the creaking of my shoes in the soft snow can be heard, but suddenly I hear thuds and voices ahead, and I stop.

"What's wrong, pervert, this isn't your club?" I hear someone laugh, followed by the sounds of blows and a groan of pain. I take a few steps closer, even though I should turn around and take another street. This street is barely lit.

"We'll cleanse the city of types like you," someone else says, and again there's a thud and someone moans in pain. In the dim light of the street lamps I can make out three silhouettes, and probably someone lying on the sidewalk being kicked.

"Police, come, they're here!" I take a few steps back and shout with all my might, even though the street is empty and there are no police officers around. My voice comes out sharp and screeching, like the unclear chirp of a wounded bird.

"Let's go," I think I hear one of the figures say.

"Filthy little fairy," I manage to hear someone curse before the silhouettes start running, moving away from me down the street into a dark area until they disappear. What have they done here? I take a few more steps back. I'm afraid to approach.

"Come, here!" I shout again with all my strength to the imaginary police officers, and remain standing while catching my breath. In the dim light I see someone lying on the sidewalk. I need to go help him, but I'm afraid.

I look around, searching for other people to come help him, but the narrow street is empty. Only I and the man lying on the snow are here.

"Are you all right?" I call to him from a distance. But he doesn't answer me.

Step by step I slowly approach him, my gaze directed toward the rest of the dark street. What will I do if they return? I'm scared and cold, my hands trembling inside my worn gloves.

"Are you all right?" I ask again when I'm close to him, but he only moans in pain. "Can I help you?" I bend down, take off my glove and extend my hand toward him. I accidentally touch his face and feel the wetness of warm liquid on his face, and he groans again.

"I'm sorry," I whisper, "come, I'll help you get up," I say as I lean over him, trying to hold him even though he's much bigger than me.

We both breathe heavily together as I help him rise, and he moans in pain. "Everything's all right, thank you, I'm fine. You weren't supposed to see this," he says when he finally stands on his own two feet and leans against the wall.

"Come with me, my apartment is close. I'll help you wash your face, you're bleeding." I raise my eyes to him, and I think I recognize him. He was younger when I last saw him, almost a boy, but it's him, Mr. Koch's younger son Bruno. Blood flows from his nose and one of his eyebrows, and his fair hair looks almost black in the light of the distant street lamp, which scatters a bit of orange light among the snowflakes. But it's him, and by his frightened expression, he recognizes me too.

"You won't tell, will you?" he asks as he wipes his mouth, turns his back to me and starts to walk with a limp, leaving the alley and moving away from me.

"I won't tell," I say to him, "but you can't walk like this. You're hurt. My apartment isn't far. I'll help you clean up."

He stops, turns around and accompanies me, and we walk in silence to the building where I live. I search for something to say to him, but can't find anything. Did they do this to him because of that word they shouted at him as they were kicking him?

At the apartment, I sit him down on a chair in the kitchen corner and help him take off his bloodstained coat.

"Come, take off your shirt. It's dirty. I'll clean it for you," I say, and he slowly unbuttons the shirt he's wearing. It also has bloodstains on it.

"Thank you for helping me. Please don't tell anyone about what happened," he quietly says, looking at the floor. He has grown up too, but something gentle remains in him from the boy I knew years ago.

I light the metal stove, fill an enamel pot with water, and place it on the stove. When the water's warm, I place the pot on the kitchen table and begin to clean his bloodied hair and face with a damp piece of cloth. "Does this happen often?" I ask, just to say something, and after a moment I regret asking.

"It didn't used to," he quietly tells me, still looking at the floor. "It's not that I could be free like other people like me; you know my father and brother, after all." He raises his gaze to me for the first time since we entered the small apartment, and smiles bitterly.

"Don't move, this will burn a little," I tell him as I go to the drawer to take out a bottle of iodine. I gently apply iodine to his injured eyebrow, and he doesn't move, just breathes a little heavily.

"Do you have somewhere to go back to? Do you still live with them?" I ask.

"I've always been afraid to go to our clubs, always learned to look over my shoulder," he tells me. "Sometimes I think I was born with a terrible disease, and that people should stay away from me. I'd love to be like them, like Father and Mother and Walter. I'd love to rejoice that Hitler and the Nazis control Parliament, that they're going to defeat the Communists, but I'm so afraid," he tells me, and I search for something to say that would encourage him. I'm afraid of them too, especially after what happened at Mrs. Schneider's shop.

"I'm sure tat if your father trusts them, you can too," I tell him, although I'm not confident in my answer. "Wait here, I'll clean your shirt." I take his bloodstained shirt to the washroom.

I open the tap and let the cold water rinse my hands, which are also stained with blood. What will happen if the Nazis take over Parliament? Will their demonstrations and those of the Communists finally stop? I gently wash the shirt and think about Hildegard, who tried to create change years ago when I worked at the shoe workshop. What became of her? Did she remain a Communist? What will happen to her now that the Nazis are winning? I continue to gently rub the fabric. I don't want to win. I just want to have a quiet job, and for my husband to come home every evening so we can have dinner. Sometimes I still dream of children, although the doctor says there's probably no chance of that anymore. He can't explain what's wrong.

I spread the shirt out and leave the washroom. "I'm finished. Now we'll just let it dry a bit near the stove," I say to Bruno, but he's not there.

The chair in the kitchen is empty, and I notice that the front door is slightly open. Cold wind slips in from the stairwell. Why did he run away?

I approach the front door and look outside, but the stairwell is quiet and dark. I hurry inside and check my bag and the metal box in its hiding place. But he didn't take what little money is hidden there. He simply ran away and disappeared, and I'm left sitting in the quiet kitchen with his wet shirt in my hands.

Later, after I eat some leftover food from yesterday, I open the brown notebook and check how long the money for food for Mother and I will last. I have no choice, I must go to him and ask for help. I've been thinking about it for several days, and can't fall asleep at night. I'm afraid of him. But he's the only one who can help me.

Toward the end of the workday, I wait for him at the corner of the street, the same street I once knew so well. Despite the early hour, it's already dark outside, and I distance myself from the streetlight's glow, moving into the shadows. The scarf around my neck protects me from the cold air, and I shift from side to side to keep warm. The cold of the sidewalk penetrates my shoes, even though I've wrapped my stockings with old newspapers.

There's still light in the high windows of the workshop. From the outside they look to me like a monster's large eyes scanning the street.

The workshop's metal door opens with a creak, and two women exit. I take a step back into the darkness, though I have nothing to fear from them. Another woman comes out, followed by two more. I try to identify them, but can't. Too many years have passed.

Finally the lights in the workshop windows go out, and after a minute the metal door opens and a man exits, locking it behind him. For a moment I fear it's not him, but when he begins to move in my direction, dressed in his black coat and wearing a fedora, I breathe a sigh of relief. He's hardly changed. My feet ache from the cold.

"Good evening, Mr. Konrad," I say to him as he passes by me, and he stops and looks at me, his hands tucked inside his coat.

He says nothing, just looks at me as if trying to remember where he knows me from. "I remember you," he finally says. "You worked here with that Communist woman who caused trouble until I fired her. You've gotten older. Though I no longer remember your name."

"My name is Clara," I answer, moving a little from side to side. "I need work, Mr. Konrad," I tell him directly. I'm embarrassed to be standing like this on the street, in front of him.

"Aren't you the one who entered the back storeroom without permission? And I caught you?"

"Yes, sir, that's me."

"I won't employ you. You're not someone who can be trusted."

"It was a mistake, Mr. Konrad. I am a woman who can be trusted," I answer. The cold hurts my cheeks and throat.

"I don't need workers, Clara. Women come to me every day looking for work. Have a nice evening." He nods to me and begins to move away.

"I apologize for what happened then, Mr. Konrad. I apologized then too. I need money. I know you sell on the black market," I quickly say to him before he can move away. He's the only one who can employ me. I have no other options.

Mr. Konrad stops and turns to me, approaching until his face is almost touching mine. "You don't know anything," he angrily tells me. "If I remember correctly, I threatened to call the police on you then. I can do that now too. I know enough police officers."

"I know you won't take me to work in the workshop. I want to sell for you." I raise my eyes to him and quietly answer with what little courage I have left.

"I don't need saleswomen. I have enough," he tells me, but at least he isn't turning to leave.

"I'll do anything, whatever is needed. I know how to sell."

"Go away, you're too old."

"Please, Mr. Konrad, I need money," I quietly tell him. I'm cold.

"I have work for you, but you're not suitable for it."

"Please, Mr. Konrad, I'll do anything. I desperately need work. I'll carry coal sacks, do laundry, whatever is needed."

"There's no work carrying sacks or doing laundry," he answers, and in the darkness I see him smiling slightly, like a wolf in the forest baring its teeth.

"Then what kind, sir?" I ask, but I feel a sense of discomfort enveloping my body.

He continues to look at me, and suddenly he brings his face close to mine until he's almost touching my neck. Then he whispers to me: "I can give you money, and you might tell everyone and yourself that you're selling shoes for me, but the merchandise will be something else."

"I don't understand," I answer without stepping back, though I'm afraid I know exactly what he's talking about.

"You're a woman. You'll get money for that. For being a woman. There are always men willing to pay. And I know such men," he whispers in my ear and places his hand on my waist, and I freeze.

"I need money, but I'm a decent woman," I tell him again, feeling as if I'm repeating myself over and over, like a cuckoo bursting from a wooden clock once an hour and making the same announcement. I feel nauseated.

"Decent women don't wait for me in the dark on a street corner begging for work," he continues to whisper to me, not moving his fingers that are touching my body. His mouth smells of unpleasant cigarettes, and I struggle with nausea.

"Please, sir," I whisper back, feeling tears threatening to burst from my eyes.

"This is the only job offer you'll get from me. I don't know if you'll be suitable, but I'm willing to try you out," he says, beginning to caress me through my coat. "This is the payment you'll need to give if you want to work for me. I have enough shoe saleswomen. If you agree, I'll also let you sell shoes, so you can tell that to everyone and your conscience." He continues to caress my waist with slow movements that make me feel as if someone is burning my skin with hot coals. "This is what people will pay you for," he says, and finally moves away from me a little. He releases the hand that was caressing me, and raises it toward me. In the dim light I see it's full of banknotes.

I need to tell him that I agree. I desperately need this money. But I can't. "No..." I finally manage to whisper, feeling the cold air wounding my throat. I'm a married woman.

"Have a good evening, Clara," he tells me indifferently. "If you change your mind and look for work, you know where to find me." He puts his hands in his coat pocket, turns around and walks away down the street, disappearing after a moment.

I feel sick, and place my hand on the wall, bending over and breathing deeply. I can't do this. I'm so ashamed of myself. But then I notice three banknotes lying on the floor at my feet. I kneel down and collect them from the wet sidewalk with trembling hands, hating myself for doing it. But I need the money.

"Stille nacht, heilige nacht..." Mother and I quietly sing on Christmas Eve, at her apartment. A single lamp spreads a pleasant yellowish light in the kitchen corner. A plate of boiled potatoes, cooked cabbage and a bit of sausage I purchased is sitting on the table. I've also decorated the table with a few small fir branches in a cup, surrounded by paper flowers I've cut out.

"Thank you for the soap you bought me," Mother smiles and places her hand over mine. I smile back at her.

"Shall we eat?" I hold the bowl of potatoes and divide the food between us.

"My wish for you is that Hermann will sit here with us too next year, that this difficult time will end and he'll earn a lot of money with his truck," she says with a smile. The stove in the kitchen warms us both. At least we're warm and comfortable.

"I'm sure he'll be with us next year," I tell her, offering her some of the sausage. I haven't told her that he sold the truck.

"You have a good husband, Clara," she says as we eat, and I think about what I'm going to do, feeling the sensation of nausea in the pit of my stomach.

"Mother," I ask after a while, "do you remember Anna the tenant? The one who lived here when I met Hermann?"

"Of course I remember her. Have you seen her? I haven't seen or heard from her since she left."

"No, I haven't seen her," I tell her, tasting a bit of sausage.

"She was a young woman. She used to entertain men here when we weren't home," she says, and continues eating.

"Is that what she did?" I try to appear surprised.

"Yes. I knew about it, and you did too," she continues to eat calmly and looks at me.

"So why didn't you say anything to me?"

"What was there to say? You were afraid we wouldn't have money, and would be thrown out into the street again. And I was afraid of that too. I didn't like her, but she paid on time." She stops eating and looks at me.

"And it didn't bother you, what she did?" I ask, lowering my eyes to the potatoes on my plate. Am I capable of doing what Anna did?

"She was a survivor, Clara. She needed to survive," Mother says quietly. "We all sometimes have difficult periods when we need to do things they've told us only inferior women do. Sometimes we find ourselves in a situation where we have no choice, and we're ashamed to look in the mirror. But we do all sorts of things."

I don't answer, and continue to eat in silence. For a moment, I want to ask her how hard it was to raise me alone, and whether she also had to do things she was ashamed of. "Thank you, Mother," I finally tell her.

"For what?"

"For this meal," I answer. I can't tell her what I'm going to do.

"You brought the groceries, I just cooked," she smiles, and I smile back at her.

After we finish eating and play cards, I say goodbye and put on my coat, leaving the apartment.

I pause for a moment across from Mrs. Schneider's closed wooden door, and consider whether to knock and wish her happy holidays. But in the end, I decide against it. She's Jewish, and doesn't celebrate Christmas.

Mrs. Vogel's and the Koch family's doors are decorated with fir branches and small Nazi Party flags. I hurry down the stairs and out of the building. How would they react if they knew about Bruno? I walk down the cold street to my dark apartment and try to warm myself with quick steps. It's hard for me to think about what I'm going to do.

A few days after the beginning of the new year, I wait for him toward the end of the workday, just as I waited for him then. I'll be able to do this. I'm already grown. I'm not a girl like I once was, so afraid of everything. I'll only do it a few times. I'll manage to get money, and my Hermann will be able to buy his truck back.

Chapter Twelve

The Bed in the Bedroom

A few days later, I pace restlessly around the small apartment. Everything is ready; I'm ready. I enter the bedroom and look around. Despite it being midday, only a little gray light enters through the window facing the inner courtyard, penetrating the flowery curtain but leaving the room in semi-darkness. Our iron bed stands in the corner, pressed against the wall and covered with a gray sheet. Above it lies a thick, coarse wool blanket; it scratches me when I sleep, but keeps me warm on cold nights. Next to the bed is a wooden stool, and on the other side of the room is an old wooden wardrobe with my sewing box on top, where I keep the letters he sends me.

When will the man Mr. Konrad sent arrive?

I sit on the bed and look at the peeling walls. I know that a picture of us with our daughter, or son, will hang there one day, even though the doctor said the chances are small. He also said it's not yet too late.

A knock at the door causes me to rise from the bed and walk there, to open it.

"Mr. Konrad sent me" is all the stranger says as he removes his hat and coat, handing them to me. I hang them on the coat rack by the door.

I don't remember what he looks like, the color of his hair or eyes, his height, or what he's wearing. Someone who isn't me takes the money from him and walks from the hallway to the bedroom, and this man follows her, and there she stares at the ceiling and imagines she's floating in a great sea full of white-colored boats, swaying on the waves and smiling.

Afterwards he leaves, and she enters the washroom, turns on the water tap and begins to clean herself.

I scrub myself vigorously, running the coarse soap over my entire body. The cold water makes me shiver, but I don't care. I don't dare look at myself in the mirror either. The main thing is that I managed to do it.

After I dress again, I take the money he gave me out of my dress pocket, slowly counting the bills one by one, and I put them in the small tin box in the kitchen. Another man will come tomorrow. I'll save enough money, and Hermann will buy his truck back, and I'll have money to buy food for Mother, and things will be good for us.

Two days later, in the evening hours, I stand at the street corner outside the workshop. The snow that fell yesterday has already turned into a gray muddy slush. One by one, the female workers exit through the main door and disappear into the darkness. Finally I see the light go out in the upper windows, and after a few minutes he emerges from the door, holding something in his hand.

This time he walks straight toward me, the cigarette in his mouth glimmering in the darkness as he stands before me. His silhouette cuts a sharp figure against the dim glow of the streetlamp behind him. "You owe me something," he says, his voice low and matter-of-fact.

"Take it, it's yours." I place the notes due to him in his outstretched palm and feel nauseated. It's money I paid for with my body. The cold air around us seems to grow heavier.

Mr. Konrad puts the money in his coat pocket without counting it. His weathered hands move with practiced efficiency.

"Aren't you going to count the money?"

"No one cheats me, I think you know that by now," he tells me, and inhales from the cigarette between his fingers. The ember brightens momentarily, illuminating the hard lines of his face.

I turn and begin to walk away, my legs cold from standing for so long on the frozen paving stones. My breath forms small clouds in the night air.

"Clara," he calls to me, and I stop and turn back to him. "Take this, it's for you, from me. New shoes. Choose one pair for yourself, and sell the rest." He moves toward me and hands me the cloth bag. It feels heavy in my hands.

"Thank you, Mr. Konrad," I say before turning around. This bag feels to me like it contains a monster that will soon emerge and swallow me whole. I just want to get to the apartment, light the iron stove in the kitchen and warm myself. My fingers are already turning numb around the bag's rough handles.

"And Clara..." he calls to me again, and I stop and turn to him.

"What is it, Mr. Konrad?"

"Always remember, people don't change," he says as he approaches me, placing his hand on my waist. I try not to recoil from his touch. The scent of tobacco and wool surrounds him.

"What do you mean?" I ask, fighting the urge to step back.

"You know, Clara," he quietly tells me, his mouth smelling of cigarettes, "since you came here some time ago and begged me to give you work, I've been trying to remember you, how you were when you worked for me at the workshop. It took time, but I remembered." He smiles at me in the darkness, and doesn't move his hand from my waist. "Even then, when I fired the Communist woman and you said nothing, I knew that one day you'd return and beg. Women like you always come back begging," he finishes and inhales from his cigarette again before throwing it onto the sidewalk, turning and walking away. His footsteps echo against the buildings, fading into the night.

I lower my gaze to the extinguished cigarette butt on the street stones. When he disappears around the corner, I return to the apartment. I should have fought then, when he fired Hildegard. I should have fought so many times, if only I'd had the courage. If only I'd known how.

In the days that follow, I continue to open the door to men I don't know. At other hours I also go to the train station and stand at the end of the platform, selling his shoes. I always keep my distance from the other women who trade in his shoes, and from the policemen. Both groups frighten me. Once I think I spot Walter standing near the entrance to the station, dressed in police uniform and questioning a woman in a dark green scarf and brown wool coat, but the rest of the time I feel safe at the edge of the platform. Few people come near the large opening, through which cold wind penetrates. For hours I let the wind burn my face; I deserve it for what I do in my bedroom.

Every evening, I count the accumulating money in the tin box and record it in my brown notebook. The small box's contents glint in the dim lamplight, coins and notes neatly stacked. The box is already almost full.

My dear Hermann, I sit and write to him a month later, my fingers clutching the pencil tightly. What should I write to make him believe me?

In recent months, I've been working at an additional job. Every day, after I finish at the shop with Mrs. Schneider, I continue working in the market until nightfall. I help carry crates and have managed to save a large sum of money... I write these words and pause, lifting the pencil from the paper and reading what I've written. How can I tell him that I miss him so much, but fear the day he might discover what I've done?

I'm enclosing the money for you, so that you can purchase the truck and continue working at the job you love so much, and so you can return to me quickly. Missing you, Your Clara.

I sign my name to the letter and feel my fingers trembling. What will he do if he discovers what I've done? Will he still believe that I belong to him and love him? How could I possibly explain?

For a moment I hesitate, considering whether to tear up the paper and throw it into the iron stove in the kitchen. Instead, I take a deep breath and carefully fold the paper, inserting it into the envelope. The paper crinkles softly between my fingers. I won't be able to write him a better letter, and he must never discover what I've done.

Afterwards, I take all the money from the small metal box and go to the post office.

The glass door of the post office creaks when I enter and close it behind me. The small hall smells of paper and dust, but at least it's pleasantly warm. Three people stand in line ahead of me: an old man leaning on a cane, struggling to take an envelope out of his coat pocket; a younger woman, around twenty, holding a package wrapped in brown paper and tied with string, perhaps clothes; and a woman about my mother's age who occasionally takes a mirror out of her side purse, looking at herself and arranging her silver hair. Her fingers move with practiced precision, tucking each strand exactly into place.

While waiting, I look back toward the street. Rays of sunlight paint it a pleasant yellow color that also enters the building. Soon winter will end, and spring will begin. The light casts long shadows across the floor tiles, a promise of warmer days.

"Madam," I hear the clerk and turn around, walking towards the counter. It's my turn.

"Good morning," I say, "I'd like to send a letter and transfer a sum of money to my husband in Hamburg."

"What's the amount?" the clerk asks while taking a form from one of the wooden compartments beside him and beginning to fill it out. His pen methodically scratches against the paper.

"Three hundred and fifty marks," I say.

"Three hundred and fifty? That's a very large sum, madam," the clerk raises his head from the form and says to me, examining me. His eyes narrow slightly behind wire-rimmed spectacles.

"Yes, sir... he needs this money..." I answer, holding my purse tightly.

"And what exactly does he need the money for?"

"He needs to buy a truck... you understand... he's a driver. It'll help him with the purchase."

"And if I may ask, madam, where did you get the money?" He continues to observe me, and I feel an unpleasant sensation ripple through my stomach.

"I've been saving... for months... I work for a Jewish woman who pays well," I answer with the only response I can think of. My throat tightens as I speak.

The clerk moves his head slightly in an almost-imperceptible motion when I say the word 'Jewish,' but he takes out another form immediately afterward and writes something on it. I try to see what he's writing, but can't manage it. Could I have made a mistake trying to send him so much money all at once? I can't back out now without arousing suspicion. The clerk's fingers move deliberately across the page, his wedding ring catching the light.

"You know that with such amounts, sometimes they check... we're required to report," he says in a quiet voice while looking at the form he's filling out.

"I have nothing to hide," I tell him in a trembling voice.

"I didn't say you did, I just said it needs to be recorded. Women shouldn't be walking around with such large sums of money," he tells me in a condescending tone.

"He's my husband," I manage to answer. There are already two men waiting in line behind me, maintaining a polite distance. I can feel their eyes on my back, curious and judgmental.

"The money, please," he extends his hand to me, and I place all the money in his palm. What if something happens to it?

The clerk quickly counts the banknotes and puts them in a wooden drawer that he locks with a key. "Sign here," he hands me the first form he filled out, but doesn't give me the second one to sign.

I sign with shaking hands, and also give him the letter. The pen feels slippery between my fingers.

"The transfer will go out tomorrow, if there are no delays," he says as he stamps the forms and puts them in another drawer. "Have a nice day, madam."

"Thank you, sir," I say before exiting to the street, raising my gaze to the sunbeams. It's a sign, spring is approaching. The warmth on my face feels like the first genuine comfort I've had in months.

"Read it now in the newspaper..." a newspaper boy shouts as he runs down the street, waving the newspaper above his head. "President Paul Hindenburg has appointed Hitler as Chancellor, read it now in the newspaper."

I ignore him and walk to the apartment. I have work to do. I need to get organized, someone will be arriving soon. The newspaper boy's words fade behind me, just another distant noise in Berlin's changing streets.

The next few days pass quietly, and I wait for a reply from Hermann. But a few days later, when I'm in the apartment and open the door expecting the man who's supposed to arrive, I see a man in a blue uniform, looking at me with gray eyes. His presence fills the doorway, casting a long shadow into my apartment.

Chapter Thirteen

The Man at the Door

"Hello, Fräulein Hoffman," he says while standing at the door. The police uniform he wears is pressed and clean, its buttons gleaming in the yellow lamplight from the corridor.

"Frau Berger," I correct him, trying to regulate my breathing. He knows I'm a married woman, so why has he come here? Is he the man who's supposed to come to me now?

"Frau Berger," Walter smiles wickedly, "I know, that's what you told me the last time we met: a married woman whose husband is away on a business trip. I haven't seen you on the platform for several days, and I was starting to wonder where you'd disappeared to. Won't you invite me in?" he says as he enters the apartment. I move aside, letting him in. I can't stop him. His cologne, sharp and official, fills the small entryway.

"Mr. Koch, Walter, you need to leave," I say while trying to organize my thoughts. What if the gentleman arrives and sees him?

"I think I'm actually supposed to arrive, and you're supposed to be waiting for me." He stops and turns to me, examining me with his gray eyes and surveying my lips. "Are you waiting for me?"

I try to think of what to answer. I mustn't ask him if he's the one who's supposed to come to me now. My heart is pounding so loudly I fear he can hear it.

"I assume you're waiting for me," he answers the question himself and turns around, entering the apartment. "I had a feeling you wouldn't be satisfied with just selling silver spoons to old ladies on the black market," he speaks, as if to himself, while standing in the small living room and looking around. "So I asked around. That's my job with the police: to inquire, to know, to receive reports." His fingers trace the edge of the small table.

"Who reported me?"

"I'm a policeman. I'm not Mrs. Vogel, who tells everyone what she knows, and I'm not a newspaper boy running down the street shouting headlines," he casually answers while approaching the kitchen corner and examining it, opening the wooden drawers, checking their contents and closing them. What does he know about me? The methodical way he's searching makes my stomach tighten.

"Was it Mr. Konrad? The girls at the train station? The clerk at the post office?" I ask, trying to organize my thoughts.

Walter ignores my question and takes out my brown accounting notebook, opening it and looking at the numbers. Then he returns it to the drawer. "It's my job, Mrs. Berger." He pronounces the name with contempt as he approaches me. "I need to know what's happening, to record, report and check."

He extends his hand and touches me, and I move backward. His touch is cold and deliberate.

"Please leave, regardless of why you came," I whisper, fighting back tears that threaten to break through.

"Since you arrived at our building years ago, you've aroused my curiosity," he tells me as he holds his tie, beginning to loosen it. "That very day you arrived, you made noise in the stairwell with your bed. There's always someone who talks about the source of the noise, whether it's Mrs. Vogel who desperately wants to be loved and is willing to trade information for it, or my naïve younger brother who thinks it's important to be good to people, and therefore helped you. That very day I came to visit with my father at your apartment, I knew the day would come when we met under different circumstances." He continues to speak indifferently as he removes his tie. "And now that day has arrived," he adds while passing by me and entering my bedroom without being invited. The floorboards creak under his heavy steps.

I walk into the bedroom after him, searching for something to say. What should I do? "You don't really want me. Aren't you married?"

"You know," he continues, ignoring my words and continuing to speak while removing his blue police shirt, undoing the buttons one by one, "I always get what I want, even if it's someone who disgraces our race and works for an old Jewish woman."

"I'm a married woman," I manage to tell him. My voice sounds distant, as if it belongs to someone else.

"Even if it's a married woman who hosts men in her home for money, I don't care. I told you my job is to investigate and to know." He places his shirt on the small stool beside the bed and continues to undress. "But perhaps it's better that others don't know. After all, you have neighbors, you have a mother, you have a husband," he says, picking up my wedding picture from the stool and looking at it. Whenever a man comes here, I turn it over so I won't be more ashamed of myself than I already am. And now he's looking at it, and I want to scream in pain and snatch the picture out of his hand. "He actually looks like a nice man," he says, placing it upright on the stool. Hermann's face stares at me from the picture with an accusing look, and there's a voice inside me that wants to fall to the floor and wail in pain. I must disconnect from myself, I must get away from here. The sunlight catches the glass of the frame through the thin curtains, making Hermann's face seem to shimmer with disappointment.

"Fifteen marks," I say. I can't say anything else to him.

"That's an expensive price," he responds indifferently and removes his shoes.

"Fifteen marks," I blurt the words out again, even though I should be silent.

"I can get someone like you for free too. There are dozens more like you in the alleys downtown, and they take five marks there," he tells me as he arranges his shoes side by side at the foot of the bed. His movements are meticulous, practiced.

"Fifteen marks." That's all I can say to him, over and over, like a cuckoo clock. I can't tell him anything else, I can't think.

He thinks for a moment, and then takes the bills out of his wallet and places them on the picture of me and my husband, who doesn't know how terrible I am and what I'm doing. The money covers Hermann's face, and for that small mercy I feel a moment of relief.

And the woman who isn't me undresses and gets into bed with him, and lets him take what he came for in order to achieve what he wanted. Sometimes she looks at the ceiling, sometimes she looks at the dirty floral curtain, sometimes she thinks she had no other choice and couldn't refuse him.

Afterward, that woman leaves the bed and walks to the kitchenette to drink a glass of water, while the man sits on her bed and puts on his police uniform.

"We'll meet again. I told you I like to win very much," that woman hears him say before he leaves and slams the door. The sound echoes through the small apartment, leaving a ringing silence in its wake.

And that woman continues to drink the glass of water she holds, convincing herself that none of this happened and that he won't return.

My dear Clara. A few days later, I'm holding the simple piece of paper and reading the words Hermann has written me. I couldn't contain myself and opened the letter while still in the stairwell, eagerly reading his words.

I have no way to describe the excitement and pride that seized me when the postal clerk transferred the money from you. You've always been a worthy wife to me, and I thank God for making me forget my gloves during that business trip years ago. I also thank Him for bringing us together in that small glove shop a few days later. With the sum of money you've sent me, I'll begin looking for a truck; not a new one, of course, but I'm sure I'll be able to find a good used one here and go back to driving and working, and also returning to you. Always yours, Hermann.

I remain leaning against the wall, wiping my tears. What would he do if he discovered where the money had come from? Would he still think I'm a worthy wife? The letter trembles in my hands, its edges worn from my tight grip. The stairwell smells of dust and, faintly, cabbage being cooked in someone else's apartment.

I continue climbing the wooden stairs, and only the sound of my shoes can be heard in the quiet stairwell. But when I reach my floor and raise my eyes, I see to my horror two policemen standing by the front door of my apartment, and I stop. Their uniforms are dark against the pale wall, their posture rigid and waiting.

"Do you live here? We've been looking for you," the taller policeman tells me, without addressing me with a polite word of 'good morning' or 'madam'. I turn around and begin running down the stairs. This is the moment I've feared. Hermann's letter crumples in my fist with each step, the sound echoing through the building like the pounding of my heart.

ALEX AMIT

Chapter Fourteen

The Holding Cell

One of the policemen catches up to me near the stairs descending from the first floor to the street, and he shoves me against the peeling wall. I crash into it and cry out in pain.

"No one runs from us," he angrily says to me as he grabs my arm, bending it behind my back. I wail, feeling blood flowing from my nose. The rough plaster scrapes against my cheek.

"We received reports about you," he whispers to me while pressing me against the wall, pressing himself against me from behind. "What's your name?"

"Frau Clara Berger," I tell him in a trembling voice.

"Show me your documents."

"I didn't do anything," I tell him through moans of pain, my whole body panting from running down the stairs. The metallic taste of blood fills my mouth.

"Is this her?" I hear the second policeman ask as he grabs my other arm. He's breathing heavily, like me.

"In the bag," I say, struggling to breathe. I feel everything around me collapsing, that I'm drowning and must breathe. The walls of the stairwell seem to close in around me.

"Take it out carefully, and don't try to run again," one of them tells me, releasing my arm while the other continues to hold me.

I take my identification papers out of my bag and he moves away from me for a moment. But I can't see what he's doing, because the second policeman forcefully presses me against the wall. His uniform buttons dig into my back through the fabric of my dress.

"Excellent, that's her," he says to his colleague.

"I didn't do anything," I tell him again, feeling tears streaming down my face.

"You'll tell that at the police station," he tells me, "and now you'll come with us. It won't hurt if you come quietly and don't try to resist."

"I'm bleeding," I whisper to him as they pull me away from the wall. I feel the metallic taste in my mouth. My hair has scattered, and I think my dress is also slightly torn where he reached out to grab me. What will become of me now? I try to regulate my breathing, and can't manage it. This isn't happening to me. This is happening to another woman.

"You shouldn't have tried to run," the larger policeman tells me. He has a black mustache and smells of sweat and pipe tobacco.

"Please, I have a husband, I have a home, please…" I tell him, but he pulls me from the wall and they both grab me forcefully, and begin descending with me down the stairwell and into the street. My legs feel weak beneath me, barely able to support my weight. Why is this happening to me?

As we walk down the street, a woman in a purple dress whom I don't know looks at me with anger and disgust, and when we pass by her she spits on me and says in a voice full of hatred: "It's about time, we don't need immoral women like you here." But all I can think about is the pain in my arms as they forcefully hold me, and force me to walk between them in the street. Everything is blurred around me: the cars, the people riding bicycles and staring at me, the tram that passes across the tracks with a metallic noise, the taste of metal in my mouth. Behind me I hear the laughter of children as they chase after us.

"Get away from here," one of the policemen turns and threatens them with his upraised hand. I turn for a moment and see three children, about six or seven years old, running after us and laughing. One of them holds a wooden stick and waves it above his head, but the policeman's shout makes them keep a safe distance from us.

"Come on, move," the second policeman pushes me forward toward a small dark blue, almost black truck parked on the side of the street. Beside it stands another policeman who opens its doors, and I feel them dragging me into the mouth of the monster threatening to swallow me. The vehicle looms before me like a predator, its metal surface gleaming dully in the afternoon light.

"Please," I whimper to the policeman with the mustache, "let me go, I promise I haven't done anything." I stand fearfully in front of the truck's door. Its interior is painted in peeling dark gray, with wooden benches attached to the walls. They want to put me inside. What will become of me?

"Come on, inside," he tells me, "you did things you're not allowed to do."

"It's a mistake," I try to tell him.

"You want to be forced in?" He pushes me forward, and I crash against the truck's floor as I'm shoved inside. The wooden planks are rough and splintered beneath my hands.

"Please don't lock me in here," I hurry to turn to them, my knees aching from the blow.

"You should have treated him with more respect," he tells me maliciously. The wooden door closes in front of me, leaving me locked inside the dark compartment.

"Please," I scream, hitting the wooden door with all my strength. From outside I hear the metallic sound of a bolt being closed. Inside, I'm surrounded by suffocating air, with the smell of wet wood and rust. The darkness presses against my eyes, and I can barely make out the outline of the benches.

"Let's go," someone says from outside and hits the wooden wall, and the truck starts and begins to move. I almost fall, and hurry to sit on the hard wooden bench. My fingers hurt from hitting the wooden door. The truck bounces over the cobblestones, each jolt sending pain through my bruised body. Where are they taking me?

A wave of cold air hits my face as the door opens. Where am I?

"Come on, get down," says another policeman I haven't seen before.

He extends his hand to me and helps me down from the truck, escorting me through a long corridor, but he doesn't grab me forcefully or hurt me. His grip is firm but not painful, almost gentle compared to what I've experienced.

He stops near one of the doors. Where am I?

"They'll ask you questions here. Answer politely, they want to find out who you are," he tells me quietly. He has a small birthmark on his right cheek. "Do you understand me?" he asks, and I nod my head. Is he on my side, or against me? His brown eyes seem kind, but I can't be sure of anything anymore.

The policeman opens the door, and we both enter a small room lit by white fluorescent light. There's a large wooden desk in the center of the room, with a policeman sitting behind it, looking at me. The light is harsh and unforgiving, casting sharp shadows across his face.

"Sit," he signals me towards the chair on the other side of the desk.

"Your name?" he asks, and begins filling out the forms laid out before him on the table. His pen methodically scratches across the paper.

"Frau Clara Berger," I answer.

"Are you married?" He lifts the fountain pen he's holding and looks at me, then shifts his gaze to the same policeman who remains standing at the entrance to the room.

"Yes, I am married," I answer, my fingers tightly gripping the purse on my lap. The leather feels slippery in my sweaty palms.

"Do you have documents to confirm this?" He returns his gaze to me, his brown-green eyes surveying me. His skin is pale, and he wears round gold-colored glasses that catch the fluorescent light.

"Here you are," I take the folded yellowish page from the municipal registration office out of my purse. My name, address and marital status, everything is written on that same purple-stamped page. It feels fragile between my trembling fingers.

"I see that you're thirty-five years old," he speaks to me while continuing to write on the form laid out before him.

"Yes, sir."

"And without children," he continues speaking casually while writing. The words hit me like a physical blow.

"Yes, sir," I answer, feeling a lump of pain in my throat.

"Occupation?"

I remain silent. What can I answer?

"Occupation?" he asks again, and raises his gaze from the form.

"I'm a merchant in a glove and hat shop," I answer, turning my gaze to the policeman with the birthmark for a moment. He looks at me, but I can't see any expression on his face.

"Address of the business?" the investigating policeman asks, and I give him the address of Mrs. Schneider's shop. If they check with her, will she confirm my words? My heart pounds as I wonder what she might say.

"And what were you doing on the street if you work in a shop?" He puts the pen down and looks at me, folding his hands.

"I wasn't on the street, they arrested me at the entrance to my apartment," I answer quickly. "I don't know why," I add. The words tumble out faster than I can control them.

"Is that correct?" The investigating policeman lowers his glasses for a moment and looks at the policeman with the birthmark who stands near the door. I also turn my gaze to him. What will he say against me?

"Yes, sir," he says, looking at me.

"So why did they arrest her?"

"We received inside information," the policeman answers. The words hang in the air like a death sentence.

The investigating policeman thinks for a moment, then takes a light blue handkerchief out of his shirt pocket, wipes his glasses, holds the fountain pen again and continues writing. The scratching sound fills the silence, each stroke sealing my fate.

When he finishes, he takes a stamp out of the drawer in the desk, hits it on the form he's filled with black lines of ink that look to me like ants that will soon attack me, and he raises his eyes. "I'm finished. You can take her," he tells the policeman by the door.

"What will they do with me, sir?" I ask, feeling my entire body be paralyzed with fear.

"The judge will decide that, not me," he tells me, enclosing the paper in a cardboard folder. His tone is matter-of-fact, as if discussing the weather rather than my life.

"Let's go," the second policeman tells me as he takes my arm, and we both exit the interrogation room. I'm so frightened that it's hard for me to walk. My legs feel like they might give out beneath me.

He takes me down the corridors of the police station, occasionally turning right and left as we walk past closed doors and concrete walls. I have no idea where I am, everything looks so similar, as if we're walking in circles. I remember how, when I was a child, Father took me to the big amusement park, and I entered the hall of mirrors and couldn't get out, bursting into tears. With each step, it's hard for me to breathe. The fluorescent lights above flicker occasionally, casting dancing shadows on the walls.

"Go in here," he finally tells me, putting me in a small room with peeling concrete walls and a wooden cot attached to the wall. I look around and hear the iron door slam shut behind me, and the sound of the bolt closing echoes in the small space, final and terrifying.

I kneel, my forehead touching the cold concrete floor, and I begin to cry, unable to stop, my whole body shaking. What have I done? How did I ruin everything I had? I only wanted to do good and preserve our family, and I destroyed everything. The moment Hermann hears what I've done, he'll leave me. I continue lying on the floor and crying, hugging myself, closing my eyes, unable to stop. The concrete is rough against my skin, but the physical discomfort is nothing compared to the anguish in my heart.

"Madam, I've brought you a wool blanket so you won't be cold, and some food." I feel someone touching my shoulder, and open my eyes. It's that same policeman who's escorted me since I arrived at the station. "You need to get up and cover yourself, so you don't get cold." He smiles at me. "Come, get up, don't worry, no one will hurt you," he tells me, and I look at the birthmark on his cheek and suddenly it seems to me that I've met him before, but I can't remember where. His face seems kind in the dim cell light, almost familiar.

"Thank you," I tell him, wiping my eyes and raising myself to sit on the wooden cot. The blanket feels rough, but warm against my skin.

"You'll have your trial soon, the judge will have mercy on you," he tells me, and I want to hold onto his words so much, even though I don't know whether I can. I look at him again. He's several years younger than me. There's something about his gentle manner that reminds me of something.

"Thank you, sir," I tell him, wiping my eyes.

"I'll bring you more food later, madam. Is there someone who cares about you? Would you like me to notify someone?" he asks.

"Yes, please," I answer, even though the last thing I want is for someone to know I'm here.

Two days later, the detention cell door opens with a grating metallic screech as I'm sitting on the bench. I raise my gaze to the gray metal door and see a policeman I don't know. "Someone's come to visit you," he tells me as he moves aside, and I straighten up as much as I can and run my fingers through my hair, trying to arrange it as best I can. My hands shake as I attempt to make myself presentable.

Mother enters the small room and stands in the center, looking around and then at me. She's wearing that same simple dress she always goes out in, and there's a small cloth bag in her hands. I examine her, thinking of something to say, but I'm unable to come up with anything. What does she think of me? Her face is composed, unreadable, but I can see the weariness in her eyes.

She also doesn't say anything, she just approaches and sits beside me on the wooden bench. It creaks under our combined weight, a sound that echoes in the small space.

Then she places her hand on my knee, still not saying anything. Her touch is warm and familiar, a comfort I hadn't realized I desperately needed.

I feel the warmth of her palms through the fabric of my dress, and again feel the tears beginning to flow from my eyes. The concrete walls seem to close in around us, but her presence makes the space feel less suffocating.

"Did they tell you why I'm here?" I finally ask.

"Yes, they told me," she answers, her hand still resting on my knee. "Is it true?"

"Yes..." I nod, and we both return to silence. The weight of that single word hangs between us like a physical presence.

"Have you heard from him?" she asks after a few minutes.

"He wrote me a letter before I came here," I whisper to her. "I haven't heard from him since."

"Does he know?"

"No. He'd leave me if he knew." I want her to hug me, but she was never the type of mother to give hugs.

"You're a good woman. I know you, I'm your mother. You didn't do this for no reason," she quietly answers.

"He mustn't know," I say, lowering my gaze to her cracked fingers holding my hand. The years of hard work have left their mark on her hands, but they're still gentle.

"He's your husband, he'll know in the end. It's not something you can hide, someone always talks in the end, a neighbor, someone. Someone always talks."

"Yes, someone talked," I bitterly say, thinking of Mr. Koch's son. Was he the one who sent the police to take revenge on me? The thought makes my stomach clench with fresh anger and fear.

"He needs to know," she sighs.

"He won't forgive me," I answer, looking at the closed iron door and wiping my eyes.

"You should have told me you needed money," she says, sighing.

"You know we need money, Mother. We always need money. We've needed money since I was a child."

"And what about the silverware I gave you for your wedding? What I received as inheritance? You could have tried to sell them."

"I did sell them," I tell her quietly, continuing to hold her hand. The admission feels like another small defeat, another piece of my dignity stripped away.

Both of us sit in silence. She'll have to leave me alone again in a few minutes. "He'll leave me, like Father left," I finally say.

"I'll be alone, like you." Two tears slide down my cheeks, wetting them, but I don't wipe them away. I don't care anymore. What does it matter?

I hear footsteps from outside the cell, but after a moment they fade and disappear.

"You were a little girl. Only eight years old, not even nine," she finally says. "He went to Frankfurt on business matters, or so he told me, and that was it, he simply disappeared. We lacked money even when he was there, he loved to drink," she continues speaking slowly. "It's hard to be married to someone who loves to drink, someone who comes home drunk in the middle of the night." Her voice carries no bitterness, only the flat resignation of someone who has made peace with old pain.

"I didn't know," I quietly tell her, remembering the nights I would hear noises from the other room and Mother would tell me those were wolves scratching at the wall, but that I shouldn't worry and that she would protect me, that they wouldn't come.

"In the end, I didn't care when he left," she sighs. "It was better for me that way, better than sitting awake every night and worrying whether he'd take all the money I'd saved in the tin box and spend it on beer or schnapps or brandy, or on other women. Even if we never had money, I preferred that it just be the two of us," she continues speaking, and I release my hand from under her fingers, holding them between my palms. "Your father didn't leave because of you, Clara. Your father only cared about his alcohol. He left because of me, because I wanted him to work and be responsible, to be a parent to a family."

"I didn't know, you never told me," I tell her, caressing her fingers.

"Mothers shouldn't tell their daughters such things."

"And now I'll be like you," I sigh, continuing to caress her palm.

"No, Clara, you won't be like me. Hermann is a good man, a man who works, and he'll forgive you."

"Mother, who would want to be with a woman who was with other men for money?" The question tears free from my throat, raw and painful.

The iron door opens with a screech, and I raise my gaze. "The visit is over," the policeman announces.

"Take this, it's for you. I've brought you clothes to change into." She stands and gives me the bag she's holding. "I'll come visit you again in a few days," she says.

"You need to leave, madam," the policeman tells her.

"Goodbye, Clara. I'll come again," she says, exiting through the door. I watch the metal door close, hear the sound of the bolt from outside, but I smile for the first time in so many days.

A few days later, the bolt opens again and the policeman announces that I have a visitor. I stand and arrange my dress a little, waiting to see Mother, but instead he enters the small detention cell, stops and looks at me. He's wearing that same old military-style coat I know so well, and a work shirt smelling of diesel. My heart stops, and for a moment I can't breathe.

"You came back," I tell him as I stand to face him. I can't manage to find any other words to say. I'm so ashamed that he's seeing me like this, standing before him in prison. But I've also missed him so much. I want to approach him, to take those two steps that separate us and hug him, but I'm afraid of his reaction. I'm afraid he'll push me away. I'm afraid he'll never want to touch me again for the rest of his life.

"Yes, I came back," he says, removing his wool hat and holding it tightly in both hands. I need a hug so badly right now. His familiar presence fills the small cell, but it feels distant, unreachable.

"You've lost weight," I tell him, restraining myself from reaching out and touching his shoulder, wrapped in the rough fabric of his coat.

"You too," he says as he continues examining me, his eyes surveying my simple dress.

"I'm fine, they give me enough to eat here," I answer, smoothing my hand over the dress Mother brought me. Why is he examining me so much? When will he tell me he's leaving me? The silence stretches between us like a chasm. "Shall we sit?" I finally ask, pointing to the wooden cot attached to the wall. He nods, and we both sit on it at a distance from each other.

"Did Mother tell you?" I ask.

"Yes, she wrote to me. She told me that I'm your husband, and that I need to know." His voice is flat, controlled, giving nothing away.

"And do you know?"

Hermann holds the wool hat in his hands and nods, his fingers crushing it forcefully. Why doesn't he say anything? I don't care what, as long as he says something. Let him be angry at me, let him yell at me, let him hit me, I don't care, so long as he's not silent like this. I feel my entire body freeze with tension.

"Did you buy a truck?" I finally ask. I can no longer bear the silence.

"Yes," he answers, looking at the floor.

"What color?"

"Dark green, similar to the truck we had." His answers are clipped, mechanical, as if each word takes effort.

"The same model?" I ask, even though I have no idea what truck we had before.

"No, a different model," he tells me, explaining something to me about engines and wheels that I don't understand. But afterwards, he returns to his silence. The technical details wash over me meaninglessly; all I want is for him to keep talking, to fill this terrible quiet.

"Please say something," I finally tell him. I can't bear this silence.

"I have nothing to say," he answers, continuing to knead the wool hat he's holding. "You know I'm not a man of words."

"Still, say something," I whisper.

"You should've told me."

"It's not something you say. You needed a truck, we needed money, for me it was enough to do everything I could," I quietly say, lowering my gaze to the concrete floor. He still hasn't touched me since entering the small cell. The distance between us on the narrow cot feels like an ocean.

"I'm sorry, I need to go," he says and gets up, knocking on the metal door. "Guard," he calls through the small barred window. I remain sitting, and struggle not to burst into tears. The sound of his voice calling for the guard feels like a knife in my chest.

"Will you wait for me until I get out of here?" I raise my gaze to him, but he doesn't answer and exits through the open door. Again it slams shut with a grating metal screech. How will I continue from here?

A few days later, the cell door opens and the policeman with the birthmark on his cheek stands in the doorway. "Madam, you need to come with me now, your trial is about to begin."

I rise in panic, straightening my dress and walking after him. What will they do to me? My legs feel unsteady beneath me, and my heart pounds so loudly I'm sure he can hear it.

I follow him and do what he tells me to, shaking hands with a man in a three-piece suit who introduces himself as my lawyer, though I don't remember his name. He has black, shiny, greasy hair that he arranges with a comb he takes out of his suit pocket. His smile is practiced, professional, but there's no warmth in his eyes. Then I sit on a wooden bench in the empty hall and look around, but neither Mother nor my husband are there, only myself, the lawyer with the shiny hair, the police representative and the judge who asks both him and I questions. I give the answers my lawyer told me to say. I feel so alone on the wooden bench, while everyone stares at me as the lawyer with the shiny hair extends his hand and points at me. Everything seems like a carousel filled with lights and colors and blurred figures around me that aren't connected to me, appearing for a split-second with noise and melody and then disappearing again.

Finally the judge strikes his gavel, and again the lawyer shakes my hand and promises me that my situation is excellent because they have no evidence. A second later, he shakes hands with the police representative, and they both disappear through one of the wooden doors on the side of the hall.

"Come, madam, we're finished," the policeman with the birthmark tells me, escorting me through those same long corridors that never end. I feel so lonely. And then suddenly I remember where I know him from.

"Excuse me, sir," I stop and tell him, "I think I know why you're familiar to me."

He stops and examines me. "I'm sorry, madam, I haven't met you before."

"Did you ever work at a nightclub?"

He stops, surprised by my question. "Years ago, when I was a boy, I worked in a cloakroom for a short period before I enlisted in the police," he tells me.

"You gave me your chair to sit in one night."

He looks at me again, as if trying to remember. "Sorry, madam," he finally says, "but I can't remember you. There were so many people there every evening." His voice carries a note of genuine regret.

"It doesn't matter, thank you for how well you treat me here."

"You seem to me like a good woman, madam. When all this is over, go learn a profession, be a typist, a secretary or a telephone operator, professions that will always need working women, so you won't have to do what you did," he tells me as he puts me back in my cell and closes the door behind me.

I sit on the wooden bench again, waiting for the sentence.

"Frau Berger," a policeman opens my cell door two weeks later, "please come with me." I hurry to gather my few belongings and follow him through the mazelike corridors. Where are they taking me? My heart pounds with uncertainty.

"Go in here," he tells me, and follows me into a room that looks like the interrogation room I sat in the day they brought me here. What will they do with me? Will they transfer me to prison? The familiar wooden desk and harsh fluorescent lighting make my stomach clench with dread.

"Sit," the policeman tells me, pointing to the empty chair facing the desk. Then he begins filling out a form without talking to me, signing and stamping it with several stamps. The sound of each stamp feels like a nail being driven into my coffin. "Take her," he says to the policeman standing by the door.

"Sir, what's happening to me?" I tell him, gripping the chair tightly. Where are they taking me?

"You're being released, madam. They hired a new lawyer for you, and he convinced the judge that there's no reason to keep you in detention any longer. Have a nice day, madam," he says, closing the cardboard file and putting it in the desk drawer.

"Come with me, please," the policeman tells me, and he escorts me out through the corridors. I search for that same policeman with the birthmark in order to thank him, but I can't manage to find him.

"Have a nice day, madam," the policeman tells me as he opens a final door, and I exit into the street and stand there for a moment, blinded by the winter sun. The light feels almost violent after so many days in artificial illumination, and I blink rapidly, trying to adjust.

It takes me a moment to get used to the street noise and the people around me. I breathe in the cold air and look around, and I notice him.

He approaches me slowly, facing me and remains silent. His familiar presence feels both comforting and terrifying. I still don't know what he's thinking, what he's decided about us.

"Thank you for coming to get me." I hold his hand, even though I want to hug him. His hand is warm and calloused, exactly as I remembered during the long nights in my cell.

"Let's go home," he tells me and takes my hand, begins to walk with me toward the subway station.

"Aren't we going in your truck?" I ask.

"I sold it, we needed the money. It was much more important than the truck. I'll find work as a truck driver, you'll see, it'll be fine," he tells me, continuing to hold my hand as we walk toward the underground train station. I don't say anything to him, but I hold his warm palm so tightly that I feel I'm managing to convey to him how much I missed him.

"Large fire in the Reichstag, the Communists are guilty, the President has signed an emergency decree for the benefit of the Führer," a newspaper boy shouts as he crosses us at a run. His words drift past me like smoke.

"Come, let's get on," he tells me when the train arrives, and throughout the entire journey he continues holding my hand. I feeling the warmth of his palm, which calms me and makes me feel safe. I lean my head on his shoulder and let my tears flow down my cheeks. I don't care about what the newspaper boy shouted, I don't care about all the swastika flags hanging in the underground train stations either. He stayed with me, he didn't leave me, despite what I did.

The Third Life

After the Nazis rose to power in 1933, Germany became a dictatorship based on terror, propaganda and racism.

The Nazi regime worked to reduce unemployment through large government projects and accelerated armament while violating the Versailles agreements, which led to an impressive but artificial recovery. In 1938, Germany annexed Austria and Czechoslovakia.

During those years, racism toward Jews intensified through racial laws and nationalization of property. It reached its horrific climax on Kristallnacht, when hundreds of synagogues were burned and Jewish shops were destroyed throughout Germany. The German Army invaded Poland in September 1939, and World War II broke out. In May 1940, the Germans surprised the West and conquered Holland, Belgium and France. The feeling was that Germany was unstoppable, and Britain would be next.

ALEX AMIT

Chapter Fifteen

Berlin 1940, A Brilliant Victory

"The Führer in Paris! The Führer in Paris!" a young boy shouts as he runs along the train station platform, waving the newspaper above his head with youthful enthusiasm. "Read now: France belongs to us! Hitler visited the Louvre and gazed upon the Eiffel Tower!" he continues shouting, stopping in front of a man about my age, a bit over forty, who extends a coin and takes a copy of the newspaper from him.

"The Führer in Paris, the Führer in Paris..." the boy waves the newspaper above his head again and continues running along the platform. His cap is secured to his belt with a thin leather strap so it won't fall from his head as he runs.

I look up at the row of large Nazi flags hanging from the station's roof, red fabric banners with white circles at their centers containing black swastikas. The flags seem to me like rows of large eyes watching from above, surveying me and all the people around me.

The warm summer afternoon sunlight penetrates the glass panels of the station roof, painting the platforms a light gray. I quicken my pace toward the station exit, passing a group of soldiers in gray-green uniforms and politely smiling at them. The soldiers on the platform stand out in their gray-green uniforms, filling the station with green dots of nature against all the concrete platforms, conspicuous among the men in suits and women in summer dresses. The soldiers have been filling the train station platforms throughout the recent months, since the invasion of Poland and the start of the war; they carry large knapsacks on their backs and gather in groups. That same newspaper boy is now running along the platform, shouting with pride, telling of their victories.

I exit the station onto the street and cross towards the shops on the other side, walking quickly between the cyclists. Only one private car crosses my path; fuel rationing was introduced . when the war began last winter, and private vehicles have almost disappeared from the streets.

Today, on Victory Day, there is meat is written in chalk on the wooden board standing outside the butcher shop, and I take my place at the end of the line of women waiting patiently outside the door.

"We finally beat them," a woman in a light green dress says with satisfaction as she stands in line in front of me.

"The Führer promised he would lead us to victory, and he delivered," a tall, thin woman my age adds. She's wearing a small blue hat, her voice filled with conviction.

"It's about time we took what's rightfully ours, it's time they paid for what they did to us in the last war," another woman adds, joining the conversation, her tone bitter with old resentments. "It's time the Parisians stood in line to buy meat with ration coupons, not we here in Berlin," she adds, and they all nod in agreement.

"Now it's the English's turn," says the woman in the light green dress who started the conversation, leaning forward conspiratorially. "I heard we've already started attacking London."

"They'll surrender, you'll see they'll surrender soon," another woman replies confidently. "No country will dare fight us after the Führer's brilliant victory," she adds as we all slowly move forward in the line outside the butcher shop. Soon it will be my turn.

One woman takes her ration booklet out of her purse and counts the small pages, biting her lip as her fingers flip through them. "I have extra coupons for oil and sugar, would you like to trade them for meat coupons?" she whispers to me.

"No, I'm sorry, I need my meat coupons," I answer, gripping my cardboard booklet tightly.

A young soldier in uniform walks down the street with his girlfriend, passing us on their way to the train station. He's dressed in a clean gray-green uniform with a large square canvas bag over his shoulder, a rolled-up wool blanket tied to its top. I watch the young woman's hand gripping his, as if trying to tie her fingers to his in a knot so tight that no one will be able to untie it. They're both so young. When they part at the train station in a moment, he'll travel to the front; will she wait for him here, in the streets filled with victory flags and long food lines? I mustn't think about Hermann, but I can't help myself as I continue watching the soldier and the woman beside him, until they disappear into the train station that seems to swallow them whole.

"Your turn, madam," the woman behind me in line says, and I enter the butcher shop.

The butcher shop is narrow and deep, with a floor of worn gray-white tiles. An old ceiling fan lazily rotates, dispersing a bit of air through the space. The saleswoman stands behind the counter with an indifferent expression, extending her hand to me.

"I have two coupons." I give her my food coupons, placing them on the counter.

"Two families?" she looks at me suspiciously while examining them.

"Yes," I answer.

She looks at me again, then cuts them with a sharp motion, turning to the refrigerator behind her and pulling out a small piece of meat wrapped in yellowish wax paper. A metal sign hangs above her head on the wall: *Attention: Supply is limited, no complaints are to be made to the workers.*

"This is the double portion," she says, placing the chunk on the white scale. I watch the black needle barely move. "This is what there is this week," she tells me, noticing my gaze and pointing to the sign above her that calls to avoid complaints. "Maybe they'll bring us meat from France now, as well as champagne and good cheeses," she adds, and I can't tell if she's saying this ironically about the food rationing or joyfully about the conquest.

"Thank you very much," I tell her, and take the small amount of meat.

"Cook it with onions and potatoes, you'll have a tasty stew," she tells me. Then she turns to serve the next customer who enters the butcher shop, extending her hand to take the meat coupon from her.

I exit the shop onto the street, passing the line of women waiting in front of the door, hoping there will be enough meat for everyone.

"This is a brilliant victory by the Führer," I hear a man in a suit walking ahead of me explain to the woman beside him, his voice full of confidence. "You'll see, soon the British will raise their hands in surrender to us, we'll bomb London until they give up," he adds. I walk behind them for a few more steps and stop at the end of the line of women waiting outside the bakery.

"How are you?" I ask Mother as I enter her apartment, placing the groceries in the kitchen.

"Could be worse. As long as I wake up in my own bed and not in a plot of earth, everything's fine," she says while helping me unpack the groceries. Her hair has turned completely white in recent years, and she's more hunched over than before. She no longer works, but years of hauling loads of wet laundry have left their mark on her bent back and weathered fingers.

"At least you have your own bed," I tell her with a smile.

"My bed suits me perfectly, I don't need another. Is this all the meat you got? Did you use my ration booklet too?"

"This is what they distributed today," I answer. "At least there wasn't a long line at the bakery. Did you hear the news?" I take out a knife and begin cutting the small chunk of meat into cubes.

"I heard today's news, and I heard yesterday's news, and I'm sure I'll hear tomorrow's news too," she grumbles, settling into her chair with a weary sigh. "Frau Vogel makes sure to report to me every day on what's happening, and how proud she is of the brilliant victory the Führer has brought with him, first over Poland and now over France."

"And what do you think of it?"

"About Frau Vogel?" she responds while sitting down and beginning to peel potatoes, her practiced hands moving with automatic precision. "Frau Vogel won't change. At our age, people don't change."

"No, about the conquest of France. They're praising Hitler in the street for his strategic vision."

"We're women, Clara, we're not supposed to understand strategic vision; that's how the men explain it to us, at least. We're supposed to produce children for the good of the nation, and send them to war for the sake of victory. That's what his Minister of Propaganda explains to us all the time, and that's also what Frau Vogel explains to me." She sighs heavily, her voice carrying the weight of experience. "They promised us great victories in the last war too, and look how that ended."

"Yes, Frau Vogel doesn't have children or a husband to send to war," I respond, remembering the young woman today who walked hand in hand with the soldier.

"Frau Vogel has a new armband she loves to wave around and annoy all the neighbors with. *Luftschutzwart*, air raid warden," Mother pronounces the title mockingly. "People like to feel important in this war."

"How is she?" I ask Mother, nodding towards the door.

"Frau Schneider? She's aging, like all of us," Mother tells me, looking at me through her glasses with tired eyes. "Mr. Koch's eldest son wants her apartment, but she refuses to give it up. She's stubborn, I'm not sure how wise that is on her part."

"Mr. Koch's eldest son wants many things," I tell her, putting the meat, onions and potatoes into the pot. Even though several years have passed, I haven't told anyone that he also visited me in those days, not even Mother.

"Koch's son learned how to be dangerous from his father. It's not wise to refuse him, especially now that he's in the Gestapo."

"It's never wise to refuse people like him," I respond while rising from my seat and beginning to wash the dishes. I'll never tell her that it was he who informed on me.

"Leave the dishes," Mother says to me. "I'll wash them in a moment. Sit, rest. Have you seen his younger son lately? His father arranged a job for him at City Hall."

"No, I haven't run into him," I answer, remembering that night when they beat him in the alley. I haven't seen him since then.

"That whole family loves flags and symbols and honor far too much," she says.

"Too bad they're your neighbors," I tell her while I keep washing the dishes. She's washed too many dishes in her life.

"I'm used to them by now. I'm not afraid of Mr. Koch. He's aged just like me. Nothing stops old age, not even being an enthusiastic Nazi. Besides, it seems to me that such neighbors exist in every building in Berlin nowadays. At least I know these ones and know who to watch out for," she says as I dry my hands with a towel and take the deck of cards out of the wooden drawer in the kitchen.

Later, after we finish eating and playing cards, I put part of the stew into an enamel pot that I brought with me.

"Take more, I don't need so much," Mother tells me, but I don't listen to her and divide the stew precisely: half for me and half for her.

Afterward I look in her pantry, making sure she's not missing anything, and I say goodbye to her. "Goodbye, Mother. I'll come visit again in a few days," I tell her, stepping out into the dark stairwell. We're not allowed to turn on the light. We're at war.

I walk carefully through the darkness in the stairwell, holding the pot in my hands. I brush my arm against the peeling wall to maintain my balance, but before I begin to descend the stairs, I stop in front of Frau Schneider's door and knock gently, the sound barely audible in the silent building.

She opens the door just a crack, and examines me. Weak yellow light glows behind her, from within the apartment.

"Good evening, Frau Schneider," I quietly say to her.

She looks at me for another moment, as if trying to ascertain that it's really me standing before her in the darkness. "Come, come in," she whispers, hurrying to close the door behind me.

"I've brought you some food," I tell her as we stand in her living room. I speak quietly, even though we're inside her home and I don't need to whisper.

"You didn't have to," she responds, but takes the pot from me with trembling fingers.

"I have enough food, I don't need so much now that I'm alone, and I know you don't receive rations like we do," I answer. She's still standing before me with that same upright posture she's always maintained, dressed in the same black dress she always insisted on wearing. Her white hair is still neatly arranged, but her eyes have grown dim in recent years. Since the war broke out and rationing was introduced, Jews have been forbidden to purchase meat and chocolate, and a whole list of other products. Every few weeks the Nazis add more products to the list.

She smiles at me sadly, her fingers tightly gripping the enamel pot. "Please, at least let me give you the rations I've received in return, a small payment from an old Jewish woman," she says, disappearing into the kitchen while holding the pot. After a moment she returns with her ration booklet, which has the letter 'J' stamped on it in red, and places it in my hands.

"I don't need it, I don't eat much, I have enough food from my own rations," I lie to her. I know I'd be ashamed to take this booklet out at the bakery or grocery store. I'd be ashamed of the red letter stamped on it.

"You need it, we all need it, if not now then for the future. Please take them."

"Alright," I finally relent and put them in my purse, even though I know I won't use them.

"Thank you, Clara," she says, taking my hand, and I notice a spark of emotion in her eyes. But suddenly there's a knock at the door, and we both look at each other with alarm.

Without saying a word, she releases my hand and approaches the door. I remain alone in the living room, looking at the photographs of her husband and son that gaze back at me. After a moment, I walk to the corner of the living room; I don't want whoever's at the door to see me from the hallway, even though I have no reason to hide. I'm not doing anything illegal. It's permitted to meet and speak with Jews.

I hear quiet talking from the direction of the door, and after a few moments it closes. Frau Schneider returns to the living room, approaches the window facing the inner courtyard, and runs her hand over the black opaque fabric covering it, making sure it's tightly pressed against the wall.

"Who was it?" I ask.

"Frau Vogel," she answers with a weary sigh, moving to the second window. "She said she did an inspection from outside, and saw a sliver of light escaping from the window. She warned me. She's now volunteering for civil defense, didn't your mother tell you about that?"

"Yes, she told me," I say as I approach the window, running my hand over it. The fabric is firmly adhered to the wall. "I don't think light could escape from your windows," I tell her.

"I'm Jewish, Clara," she quietly says, her voice barely audible. "Do you think I can afford to violate their air raid regulations?"

"I understand that Mr. Koch's son was here to see you," I tell her. She looks so small and alone as she stands by the window, running her hand over the black fabric again and again.

"He wants me to leave. Your mother also thinks I should give up and go. But where would I go?" she says while continuing to run her hand over the fabric pressed against the wall. "I have nowhere left to go. The only place remaining for me is beside them." She looks at the two photographs on the sideboard, her eyes lingering on the familiar faces.

"You'll be fine, you don't need to be afraid of him," I tell her, even though I too am frightened when I think of him.

"It no longer matters whether I'm afraid of him or not," she sighs as she accompanies me to the door, her footsteps slow and deliberate. "I simply have nowhere else to go. I need to be like the cypress that bends before the strong wind, waiting for it to pass. Thank you, Clara, for the food you brought me. You should go now. It's late. Be careful in the dark on your way home." She says goodbye to me, and I descend through the darkness down the creaking wooden stairs, exiting onto the street.

The dark street surrounds me like a heavy cloak. In the distance I hear the rumble of a truck, but aside from that everything is quiet, the street empty. The people who were moving about in the morning have disappeared into their homes, and the street lamps that once burned brightly are now extinguished.

Only the sound of my footsteps echoes on the cobblestones. At the end of the street, I place my hand against the wall of the shadowy building and peer down the dark avenue. For a moment it seems I've gotten confused in the streets, and I cross the road, only relaxing when I nearly bump into the metal door of the small cobbler's shop. I raise my eyes and can barely make out the black iron shoe mounted above the shop; I'm on the right street.

The buildings around me are black, like dark masses encircling me in the gloom. The sound of a streetcar on the tracks running down the center of the street causes me to stop and look back. It moves with slow, deliberate motion, only two small slits of light protruding from its headlamps as it approaches me, passing by with a gentle clatter. In the weak light from the streetcar's lamps I can see wooden crates arranged outside one of the shops, waiting for morning, and a wooden cart standing at the side of the street like a sleeping animal. Three more streets and I need to turn onto mine. I continue walking along the avenue, occasionally touching the walls of the buildings to feel secure in the darkness. From the other side of the street I hear footsteps, but I can't identify who's walking there, so I stand still, waiting quietly until they disappear into the night. I've almost arrived.

At the building's entrance, I again feel my way toward the stairwell, placing my hand on the mailboxes and counting them with my fingertips. The fifth box is mine. I open the metal latch and push my fingers inside; there's a letter.

I excitedly grasp the wooden banister and climb through the darkness to my apartment. I can only turn on the light inside my home, to read what he's written me. This must be a letter from him.

Inside the apartment, I light a candle and walk through the house, moving from window to window, checking that the black fabric sheets are properly closed. Only when I've finished do I turn on the light and blow out the candle. All this time I'm holding the letter tightly between my fingers.

I recognize his handwriting on the simple yellow military envelope. I love reading my name written in his hand. Above it, the ugly red seal of an eagle clutching a swastika has been stamped, and adhesive paper is crudely stuck to the envelope: the work of the censor who read the personal words he wrote me before I did. But I don't care, the important thing is that I've received a letter from him.

I carefully open the envelope, take out the simple paper, and begin to read.

My dear Clara,

Who would've believed that I would ever reach Paris with my unit? I'm the oldest member of my transport unit, and the young soldiers like to jokingly call me "Papa," but I don't mind.

The city of Paris is so beautiful, like in the postcards we once saw in the bookshop as we were walking together. I even got to see the Eiffel Tower.

The commander told us that after our victory, we'll probably get leave. He thinks the war will end soon. The other soldiers like to photograph themselves in every square and also sit in cafés, singing and celebrating our victory. But I don't join them. I remember the last war and how it began, how happy and proud I was when I went to the front then. I also remember how it ended.

I miss you so much, my dear Clara, and I truly hope the British will surrender now so we can get leave and I can return home, perhaps forever.

You didn't tell me about work in the letter you sent me. Have you managed to find new work yet?

Missing you, Hermann.

I fold the letter carefully and hold it against my chest, feeling the weight of his words and the distance between us.

Chapter Sixteen

The Broom Workshop

The newspaper advertisement in my hands reads *Wanted: Experienced secretary for workshop*. I raise my eyes to the white sign hanging above the iron door, and to the black letters written on it: *Weidner – Workshop for Brooms and Brushes*. This is the address. I fold the newspaper, put it in my purse, take a deep breath and enter.

The workshop resembles the shoe workshop where I worked years ago. The same space lit by yellow lamps, the same workers bent over metal machines, the same incessant noise, the same smell of glue and wood, the same tall windows divided into squares within iron frames, and the black curtains that were added to the windows since the war began.

The work supervisor notices me and approaches. I show her the newspaper advertisement and she politely smiles at me, pointing me towards the corridor at the back of the workshop. I thank her and approach the door, beside which the words

Mr. O. Weidner – Manager are engraved on a brass plate. Again I take a deep breath, straighten up, gently knock on the door and wait.

"Yes, come in," I hear from inside, and enter the room.

There's a smell of ink and mildew in the small room. Mr. Weidner sits behind a brown wooden desk, upon which piles of papers and documents sit. Behind him are filing cabinets with drawers. He's about my mother's age, around sixty, perhaps a bit younger. His thin gray hair is combed back and oiled, and he wears a simple brown suit with a bright yellow handkerchief protruding from the front pocket. When he notices me, he stands and looks at me through his thick black-framed glasses.

"Hello, good morning. My name is Frau Clara Berger. I came regarding the advertisement you published in the newspaper," I tell him while standing upright before him.

"Yes, welcome, Frau Berger. Please, sit." He shakes my hand and gestures for me to sit in the chair facing him. He seems like a good man to me, like a kind grandfather from the children's stories I believed when I was a little girl. "Please tell me about yourself," he says to me, settling down as well while looking at me through his thick glasses.

"I'm forty-three years old. I learned touch typing at night school, and I have experience," I tell him while taking documents out of my purse and handing them to him.

Mr. Weidner holds the documents, brings them close to his eyes, reads them slowly and finally places them on the desk among all the other documents and papers. "It says you've already worked as a secretary," he tells me.

"Yes, sir, for the last three years. At the Berliner Feinweberei Müller & Sohn textile factory," I answer, feeling the pressure from the questions that will come momentarily. My fingers tightly grip the handles of my purse resting on my lap. I've been looking for work for several months now. There are people who find it harder to get jobs in recent years.

"And why, if I may ask, did you stop working there?"

"The accounting manager wanted all employees to be politically reliable," I answer, knowing the interview will end soon.

"And you're not politically reliable?"

"I'm a loyal German," I answer, trying to sit upright in the chair facing him.

"Then what do you mean by politically reliable?" he asks.

I hesitate for a moment, and finally answer: "I don't have a Party membership card, sir."

"Why not?" he asks, going back to examining the documents, bringing them close to his eyes again.

"I didn't join the Party," I quietly answer. The air in the room around me is compressed. They wouldn't have accepted me if I'd tried to join after what I did then, years ago. In recent months, all other workplaces have rejected me for the same reason. He wouldn't accept me either if he knew what I did then.

"We're a small workshop, but we supply our products to the Wehrmacht. We're also among those contributing to the war effort. We're considered an essential factory," he tells me.

"I'm a loyal German. My husband serves in the army, he's conscripted now," I answer, fearing he won't be satisfied with this answer.

"There are those for whom that isn't enough. They want to see certificates. Things are simpler when you have certificates," he says while continuing to examine me through his thick glasses. "What's your opinion on German workers who aren't pure Aryans?" he asks, and I lower my gaze to my fingers as they tightly grip my purse resting on my lap. Why is he asking me that question? Is he testing my loyalty?

"I have no answer, Mr. Weidner. I don't know. I'm a loyal German who loves my country. I don't hate anyone," I try to give him an evasive answer while thinking of Frau Schneider. In a moment he'll ask me to leave.

"Yes, I don't hate anyone either," he says in his slow speech. "Not everyone wants to work here, Frau Berger, despite the fact that we serve the German nation and the Wehrmacht, and despite the fact that we pass all their inspections and audits." He speaks slowly, as if searching for the right words.

"I would be happy to work here, sir. I need work. I'll be a good employee," I answer. I must have this job.

"This workshop, which I founded, also employs blind people and those with visual impairments. If you noticed, my eyesight isn't good either." He smiles warmly at me for the first time while raising his hand and touching his thick-lensed glasses. "If you work for me as a secretary, you'll need to be my eyes, read documents to me, go in my place to all the places that require permits and forms, and read me the newspaper every morning."

"I'll do it. I can do it," I quickly answer.

"And one more thing," he adds while momentarily removing his glasses, rubbing his eyes and putting them back on. "Everything is of course under permits and supervision, but the workshop employs women who aren't pure Aryans, those whose identity cards register them as Jews. The police and Gestapo tend to check on us again and again. They check licenses, authorizations, work permits. You need to know this too if you work for me. Know that they might check you too someday," he quietly says while momentarily removing his glasses and cleaning them with the handkerchief from his jacket pocket.

I look at the pile of papers on his desk, and at his fingers holding the cloth. I need to give up this job. I was with Frau Schneider when they entered her shop. I met Mr. Koch's son, I was arrested. I know what they're capable of. I know they'll come check on me. But what other choice do I have? I'm already among those women who have a black mark.

"I'd be happy to work for you at this workshop, sir," I tell him. I need this job. I just want to work and earn money, and no other workplace will accept me.

"If so, it seems you can start tomorrow," he tells me, standing and shaking my hand. "Shall I show you the workshop and the workers?"

Later that night, in my apartment, I read my husband's latest letter. Then I turn off all the lights in the house and approach the window, removing the black fabric and gazing out at the dark city. I very much want to believe that the war will end soon.

The first thunder comes late at night, two months after I've started working for Mr. Weidner. After that I hear another thunderclap, closer, and then another. Autumn is approaching; surely rain will begin soon. A few more rumblings are heard.

I've covered myself with a blanket and turned off the light when I suddenly hear the wail of a siren, screaming in the street outside like a wounded animal. What's happened?

I stand in the dark room, confused, wondering what to do. The siren isn't stopping, rising and falling again and again. Is someone attacking us? Civil defense instructions say to go down to the shelter in case of a siren, but this can't be, Berlin is safe. The newspapers I read to Mr. Weidner every day say that London is being bombed and that the British are on their way to surrender. I stand motionless in the dark room. From the stairwell I hear footsteps and shouts, while outside the distant thunder grows stronger, and suddenly it's joined by cannon fire. A cold wave passes through my body. I must get out of here. I don't want to die.

I grope my way through the darkness to the front door, take my coat off the hook and put it on over my nightgown. My trembling hands struggle to open the latch, but I finally succeed, opening the door and stepping out into the dark corridor. The pressure makes it hard for me to breathe. Are the English attacking us? How is someone attacking us?

Someone shouts from below: "Everyone to the shelter, now!" I grope my way through the darkness, stumbling, getting up, gripping the banister and beginning to descend. I must hurry. How did their bombers manage to reach us? More doors open in the building, and there's the sound of people's footsteps on the stairs. People are talking, someone is shouting loudly and one young girl is crying, looking for her doll in the darkness. A woman scolds her, but the girl doesn't stop crying. I want to cry too, but I can't. Another explosion sounds, this time stronger. Even the glass panes in the stairwell window are shaking. I must go down faster, I'm so afraid.

"Come on, here, hurry!" I hear a call, and see the glimmer of a flashlight illuminating the stairs to the basement. I run toward the point of light, followed by that woman holding the girl's hand.

Only when I'm standing in the center of the basement, looking around at the people sitting on old chairs, do I think of Mother. What about her? Is she okay?

"Sit, madam," a man about my age says as he gets up from his chair and offers it to me. I thank him and sit down. What about Mother? Everything around me suddenly seems blurred: the people holding candles in the small basement, the man illuminating the room with his flashlight, the muffled thunder in the streets, and the girl sitting in her mother's lap, wiping her nose, the tears on her cheeks glistening in the candlelight. What's happened to us?

"This is a mistake," a young woman beside me whispers, her voice barely audible. "He promised they would never attack us."

"This isn't a mistake," an elderly man with white hair answers while holding an unlit pipe in his mouth, his voice grave. "They've reached Berlin."

"What will happen now? They promised us we won. Isn't it enough that there's no food in the stores?" the woman asks the basement space, not directing her words at anyone in particular.

"Don't speak against the Führer," a woman answers as she chain-smokes cigarettes, her voice sharp with warning. "Those are words of treason."

The woman doesn't answer her and we all fall silent, watching the smoke rising from the cigarette held by the woman who believes in victory and Hitler.

Time passes slowly. I watch the yellow candle flame illuminate the faces of the people sitting in silence, pressed against the walls on wooden benches and chairs. Even the little girl has stopped wiping her nose and fallen asleep in her mother's lap, her head resting on her mother's shoulder. The thunder of the bombs has also stopped.

"You can go out," the man holding the flashlight finally says when another siren sounds, this time not rising and falling. Everyone slowly gets up and exits the basement, beginning to climb the stairs, but I leave the building and begin quickly walking down the street. I must know what's happened with Mother.

In the darkness, the quiet street seems even more threatening to me. In the distance, above the dark buildings, I see searchlights wandering across the sky like a giant directing enormous flashlights toward the clouds, playing and moving them in all directions.

No one is in the street; the sound of my footsteps echoes off the empty façades.

"Stop," I hear a voice and halt in alarm, blinded by a flashlight shining into my eyes. "What are you doing in the street at such an hour?" a man's voice asks. I can't see who's speaking to me.

"I'm on my way to check on my mother, after the bombing," I answer, shielding my eyes from the flashlight's glare.

"Papers," the voice tells me.

"I have them," I answer, "in my purse."

The man in front of me lowers his flashlight and illuminates my purse. After several seconds, when I've adjusted to the darkness again, I can see a man and a woman standing before me. He's in a short black leather coat, she's in a dark dress. Both have dark armbands on their arms with the word *Luftschutzwart* embroidered in white letters, and the woman is holding a large leather notebook.

"Here you go." I take my papers out of my purse and give them to them. The man illuminates them with his flashlight and carefully examines them.

"We need to check," he tells me while still holding my papers, "we make sure there are no traitors revealing secrets to the enemy. Spreading fear also strengthens our enemy. It's preferable that you not wander around like this at night. The enemy seeks to find the cowards among us who fear victory."

"Yes, sir," I agree.

"Good night, Frau Berger. Don't do this again," he tells me, while the woman writes something in her leather notebook. What is she writing?

I take my papers from his hand and move away from them. This time I walk more quietly, trying to listen and make sure I don't encounter more civil defense volunteers.

"Mother, are you okay?" I ask her the moment I enter her apartment.

"I'm fine," she answers, walking to the kitchen with her characteristic steady gait. "A few British bombs won't frighten me. And it's not the end of the world if I sleep a little less."

"What about everyone in the building, is everyone okay?"

"There are always those who are fine and those who are less so. Would you like tea?" she asks while placing a kettle on the stove and lighting the flame by the light of a candle.

"What do you mean?" I ask, settling into the kitchen chair.

"They didn't let her into the basement. Mr. Koch forbade her from entering the basement. He told her it wasn't meant for Jews."

"Do you think it was intentional? What Mr. Koch did to her?" I ask Mother as we drink tea in the kitchen, lit by candlelight.

"Despite being retired, Mr. Koch wears his suit and tie every day, with his white button-down shirt. He doesn't do anything that isn't planned in advance," she answers while sipping her tea with deliberate slowness.

"I feel like they're a pack of wolves, slowly closing in on the Jews until they devour them," I answer quietly and sip my tea, the warm liquid doing little to ease the chill in my chest. "Once I didn't believe there could be so much evil. Now I don't know anymore. I think she needs help."

"Yes, she needs help, even though she's too proud to ask for it. The Nazis and Gestapo have made them into targets, and when we're at war everything is permitted, which is why they love the war," Mother answers.

I continue drinking my tea in silence. What would I have done if I'd been there in that basement tonight? Would I have tried to help her, arguing with Mr. Koch, or would I have stayed silent and let him drive her away?

"It's already late, you need to return to your apartment," she tells me after a while.

"Yes, I need to go back," I answer, remembering the civil defense volunteers who shone their flashlight on me just minutes ago. "Can I stay over with you tonight?" I ask. I don't want to return in the darkness and encounter them again.

Mother says nothing, she just gets up from the kitchen chair and goes to the washing corner. Afterwards I follow her and prepare for the night. It's been so long since I've slept with someone else that I'm not used to it. She makes room for me in her bed, and I take off my dress and join her. The warmth of her body and her familiar scent remind me of all those years when I was younger.

"Do you remember when we used to sleep like this?" I whisper to her in the darkness.

"We slept like this for too many years," she answers, her voice soft in the quiet night.

"It was nice," I answer. When I was a child, I always loved sleeping in her bed; it was a substitute for all those hugs she never gave me.

"We shouldn't sleep like this," she answers from within the darkness, her voice carrying a note of practical resignation. "You have your husband, even though he's in the army now, and I have my old age and my habits."

"Good night, Mother," I smile at her, even though she can't see.

The city is quiet again. But I can't fall asleep. I can't stop thinking about Frau Schneider, who tried to go down to the basement and was driven away. How would I feel if they drove me away?

The next morning, on my way home, I knock on her apartment door, but she doesn't answer. Maybe she went out early, though she hardly leaves her home anymore.

"Frau Schneider," I whisper to the closed door, "it's me, Clara."

But she doesn't answer, and I finally give up and go down the stairs, hurrying to work.

The street is wet from the rain that fell at dawn. I quickly walk to work, looking around. In the daylight I search for signs of the bombing that occurred last night, but it seems nothing has changed. The same women are hurrying with shopping baskets, the same men in suits are riding bicycles, the same children are walking to school and carrying brown leather schoolbags on their backs. It's as if nothing happened at all last night.

I approach the newspaper stand and look at the hanging papers. The headlines scream words of rage and revenge: *The Führer will respond with force! The Luftwaffe will take revenge on London!* Black words printed on white newspaper.

"Give me the Berliner Morgenpost, please," I tell the seller in the short leather coat with a cigarette stuck in his mouth, placing a coin in his hands. He pulls out the newspaper and I place it under my arm, continuing to walk to the workshop.

"*Goebbels promises revenge on London*," I read the newspaper headlines to Mr. Weidner later. "It says the bombings caused no damage at all, but that the Luftwaffe will turn London into ruins," I continue reading him the article.

Mr. Weidner sits quietly behind his desk and listens to me. He leans back in his leather chair, his fingers interlaced. "Thank you, Frau Berger," he tells me when I finish. "Did all the women come to work today? We have a shipment of brushes that needs to go out to the German Army tomorrow."

"I'll check, Mr. Weidner, and I'll handle the shipment," I answer, folding up the newspaper.

"Thank you, Frau Berger. We need to continue being efficient, so they don't think the bombings are affecting us."

"Yes, sir," I answer, turning to my tasks. The Jewish women are quieter in the workshop. They work in silence at their tables and machines, as if trying to ensure that no one from the police or Gestapo will come and blame them for what happened last night.

More air raid sirens sound in the city at night during the coming weeks, shattering the silence with wailing screams.

I sit among neighbors in the basement, trying to calm myself and not look up at the basement ceiling. Will it protect us in the event of a direct hit? It seems to me the neighbors always say the same words and voice the same opinions about the war and the British, sitting on wooden benches and chairs in the same fixed places under the command of the shelter warden illuminating us with his flashlight. How is Mother managing? I no longer go out to see how she's doing after the bombings. I don't want the civil defense people to catch me again. And what about Frau Schneider? How does she feel in her apartment, alone, when the anti-aircraft guns fire non-stop and she's not protected at all?

"The main thing is that London is burning," says the neighbor who usually smokes, and the man who usually sits beside me agrees with her, nodding his head with grim satisfaction.

"You can go out," the shelter warden finally says, and we climb to our homes, until next time.

In the streets, winter has already arrived, and with it the cold and snow that covers the city in a white blanket. Every day I walk to work, passing the gray buildings decorated with enormous red flags adorned with swastikas.

Christmas will come again soon, but there's rationing of butter and meat, and I'm already slowly hoarding, so there will be enough left for the holiday meal.

I stop by the newspaper stand as I do every day. "Give me the Berliner Morgenpost, please," I tell the seller in the short leather coat, placing a coin in his hands.

A column of young soldiers passes down the street in front of me. Their uniforms are new, and their polished black shoes strike the cold pavement with rhythmic precision. People stand on the sides of the street and watch them. An elderly man in a brown wool coat salutes them, and several women wave in greeting. I also watch them as they pass me by, their gazes fixed forward on the back of the soldier ahead of them in the column. They seem so young to me, like children. I remember what Hermann told me about joining the army in the last war, how young and proud he'd been to enlist. But he was never willing to talk about the war itself. When I'd ask, he'd say I wouldn't be able to understand. Another moment passes, the soldiers disappear and I continue on my way. Several women are talking at a café, and in an alley near the workshop some children are playing with a rag ball, running and kicking it with sounds of laughter, ignoring the cold air.

"Good morning," I greet the workers and enter Mr. Weidner's office in the back.

After I read him the morning newspaper, I fill out forms for City Hall, print letters and receipts, and examine the inventory. Towards noon, I approach the work hall to speak with the supervisor about shipments that need to go out later in the week, and merchandise that needs to arrive.

"Frau Berger," Sarah, one of the workers, approaches me as I wash my hands in the tin sink in the back part of the hall. "Could you... perhaps help us with a small matter?" She speaks quietly, lowering her eyes with nervous hesitation. Behind her stand two other workers, Miriam and Esther.

I look at them. They seem to be examining me, waiting and tense for a sign of refusal. "What is it?" I ask her.

Sarah takes a carefully-wrapped blue cloth handkerchief out of her dress pocket. She slowly opens it, and removes a golden pocket watch with a delicate gold chain. "This belonged to my husband," she says, her voice barely above a whisper. "He's... no longer with us. And I have no use for it. We've received an order to pay a tax... and we have no other way."

"I don't understand," I tell her, looking at the watch she holds in her delicate hands.

"We've received a demand from the authorities, from the Nazis," Miriam whispers to me, taking another step closer. "We, all Jews, must pay them sums of money they've determined for each of us. We're trying to sell goods to pay the tax," she says, looking back fearfully. "We thought maybe you'd want to purchase it, the watch."

"I'm sorry, I have no need for a watch," I tell them.

"I need money. I'll sell it at a good price, only eighty Reichsmarks," Sarah tells me. There's a look of pleading desperation in her eyes.

"I'm sorry," I tell them. "I don't have that amount of money."

"I can lower the price. I can also sell it for thirty," she tells me, her lips trembling with barely-contained emotion.

"Sarah," I tell her, and all three look at me with hopeful eyes. "You know there are places where you can sell such things. You can go there and try."

"We know about those places, Frau Berger," Miriam answers, her voice heavy with resignation. "But if the police or Gestapo catch us there and see that we're..." She doesn't finish the sentence.

"It's too dangerous for us. Some tried, and were caught; they look for Jews like us there," Esther adds, protectively wrapping her arms around herself.

I look at the three of them. What would I feel if I were in their place?

"I'm sorry, I can't help you," I answer after a moment. I mustn't do this. It's dangerous for me too. I was arrested once before, even if it was years ago. I know what the Gestapo and police are capable of.

"Thank you for listening to us," Sarah says sadly, wrapping the watch in the blue handkerchief again and putting it back in her dress pocket.

I return to the office and continue typing orders and documents, but I can't stop thinking about them and the gold watch. What would I do in their place? Would I take the risk or would I give up? My fingers continue typing mechanically.

"I'll be right back, Mr. Weidner," I finally tell him, and approach the hall again. Sarah is sitting at the third table on the right side, and I approach her and whisper: "If you want, you can give me the watch, and I'll try to sell it and bring you what I can get for it."

I know I shouldn't do this and that I'm taking a risk, but if I were in their place, I would want to not feel so alone when facing the people in black leather coats. I'll manage to get by without getting caught.

At the end of the workday I board the tram, and get off at a side station near the old market of Wilmersdorf. I'm afraid to enter the train station with the watch, it seems too dangerous to me. Before I begin wandering around the market, I stand and observe. A man wearing a fedora sits on the bench outside the market, reading a newspaper with studied casualness. A woman in a brown dress and apron stands with a baby carriage by a cauliflower stand, and doesn't move. Another man stands by one of the trees, with several sacks lying on the ground beside him. Which of them are traders? Is there someone among them who's an informant for the Gestapo?

I begin moving slowly, looking around. As I pass the woman with the baby carriage, she whispers to me: "Butter? Eggs?"

"I'm selling jewelry, interested?" I whisper back to her, but she shakes her head and I continue walking among the market stalls.

I stop by the seller at a used clothing stand. She's a bit older than me and is wearing a simple worker's dress, her hands stained and weathered.

"Are you buying or just looking?" she asks me with hostility, her eyes sharp and assessing.

"Do you also purchase things, or do you only sell?" I ask in a whisper.

"I'm a trader, I don't say no to good merchandise," she tells me, glancing to the sides with practiced wariness.

"I have a watch, gold," I whisper to her.

"I'm a market trader, lady, I don't run a watch shop," she tells me and laughs, her yellow teeth prominent as she opens her mouth.

"I'd prefer to sell it here," I tell her, taking the blue handkerchief out of my purse and showing her the watch for a moment before returning it.

"Are you Jewish? Getting rid of property?"

"I'm not Jewish. Are you taking it or not?"

"They need money, the Gestapo takes all their property," she says, and laughs with cruel satisfaction. "If they don't pay, kaput." She makes a cutting motion across her throat with her finger.

"Are you taking the watch or not?"

"I'm willing to take it, but this is what I have, you won't get even one mark more for it." She takes several crumpled bills out of her purse and shows them to me. "I can also add some sausage, Jews dream of sausage." She bends down and pulls a crumpled newspaper out from under the stand, spreading it and showing me a chunk of reddish sausage. Her hand grips the package tightly, so that I won't try to snatch it from her.

"Give it here." I hand her the watch and take the money and sausage, hurrying to stuff them into my purse.

"If you have more things, I'll be here tomorrow too. Jews won't have property much longer," she tells me, laughing as she hides the blue handkerchief with the watch under the clothing stand.

I say nothing to her, and hurry to distance myself from her and the market stalls. My hand tightly grips the money bills and the chunk of sausage wrapped in newspaper. Tomorrow I'll bring them to Sarah.

On the way to my apartment, I occasionally stop and look back, making sure no one is following me. And the next morning I approach her table, lean close to her and give her the money and the sausage.

"Thank you," she whispers to me emotionally, her eyes glistening with grateful tears.

During the lunch break they approach me again, asking if I can sell more things for them.

I look at them for a moment, remembering the throat-cutting gesture of the seller at the market, and then I agree.

In the following days, I board the tram at the end of each work day and travel to the market, but every few days I change which market I visit. I look around all the time, searching for people in long leather coats, wondering which of the people in the market are their informants. I know it's only a matter of time until he comes to me again.

The pine forests of Poland, June 1941,
My dear Clara,
For one moment we passed through Berlin, on our way from the streets of Paris to the pine forests of Poland. I wanted so much to stop, just for a moment, to see you, but I couldn't. We had to continue on the road to the place where I am now, hiding among the trees and waiting.

In the evening I look up at the treetops and remember that time we walked together in the Tiergarten, when we had just met and I told you I would be happy if you one day considered becoming my wife. I'm so glad you agreed.

I've been riding the same truck since everything began. Sometimes I feel its bolts are getting tired along with me. I'm learning to recognize vibrations according to the type of road. A good road feels like your hand holding mine when we sit together to eat dinner at our kitchen table; a bad road, like those difficult days of the last war.

I won't tell you much about what they say will happen soon. Perhaps that's for the best. It seems to me that in this place it's not proper to say aloud what's in my heart, but I suppose you will understand between the lines, as always.

I'm forty-four years old, Clara. Four times eleven. That's too whole a number for adventures. My heart wants only peace, to see winter descend again on our street, to smell your soup from the hallway when I return from a day's work.

I hope you are well. Don't worry about me too much. I know how to take care of myself. When I was young, back in the Great War, I learned what happens when you believe too much in others' slogans. I know that you also know how to choose between good and slogans of power.

Forever yours,
Hermann.

I look at the words written on that simple paper again, and wipe the tear in the corner of my eye. I'm already used to my husband's absence and to loneliness. Afterwards I look at our wedding photograph, that same photograph beside our bed. I think our marriage has been spent more apart than together. Perhaps this is what I'm already used to, living alone, without children and with a husband who loves me from afar. *A husband of letters*, I privately refer to him. But every time I receive a letter from him in a yellow envelope with the military censor's swastika stamp, I read his words and am moved anew.

His slightly crooked handwriting on the paper I'm holding now makes everything around me seem a bit simpler: the endless food lines, the food coupons that keep shrinking, the nighttime air raids, sitting in the basement in fear. Sometimes I think his letters are what give me the courage to do what I do for the Jewish women at the workshop.

I carefully fold the sheet of paper and put it in the crumpled envelope. I gently smooth my fingers over the eagle stamp clutching a swastika in its talons, partially covering my husband's name. Who knows how many days it spent on the road, how many hands it passed through until it reached my fingers? Then I carefully place it in my purse and exit the building onto the street on my way to work. I need to hurry, I delayed too long reading the letter. But when I approach the newspaper stand to purchase the daily newspaper for Mr. Weidner, I see several men and women by the stand. I move a few more steps closer and see the headlines of all the newspapers hanging outside on clothespins: *The Führer addresses the German people*

– Germany responds to the Bolshevik threat. The Wehrmacht storms Russia.

Chapter Seventeen

The Yellow Badge

"*Bolshevism crumbles under the might of the Wehrmacht, brilliant victories in Minsk*," I read the newspaper aloud to Mr. Weidner as we both sit in his office, several weeks after the offensive began. What about my husband? Where is he now? Is he fighting alongside all of them?

"What do you think, Clara?" Mr. Weidner asks, his weathered fingers drumming lightly on the desk.

"About what?" I reply, startled by the question.

"About the war, about the Wehrmacht's advance."

"I don't think anyone can stop him. I believe Hitler is going to conquer Russia as well." The words feel heavy in my mouth, like stones I'm forced to swallow.

"Yes..." he sighs deeply, removing his thick spectacles and rubbing the bridge of his nose. "I also think no one will succeed in stopping him. Could you continue reading the newspaper to me?"

"Yes, sir," I tell him, lowering my eyes once again to the newspaper I'm holding. Until today, Mr. Weidner had never expressed his opinion of Hitler. "*In a blitzkrieg attack, Wehrmacht armored forces have encircled hundreds of thousands of Bolshevik soldiers...*" I continue reading.

Suddenly there's a knock at the office door. I stop reading and go to open it. To my surprise, Miriam stands before me, visibly agitated. Beside her stands a man in a dark brown suit, a white shirt with a black tie, and a fedora. "Frau Berger, Mr. Drexler has come to meet with Mr. Weidner," she quietly says, as if struggling to get the words out of her mouth. Her hands tremble slightly as she speaks.

"It's alright, thank you," I tell her, studying the man before me. He's younger than I am, around thirty. He removes his hat and holds it in his hand, which is covered by a black leather glove. "Please, come in," I say to him. Something about his confidence frightens me. Is he one of those people Mr. Weidner warned me would come?

"Thank you very much," he says, entering the office as if he owns it. Inside, he stands before Mr. Weidner and pulls a notebook out of his jacket pocket, opening and examining it. "Mr. Weidner," he reads from the notebook, then closes it with a sharp snap, "according to the records of the Third Reich's Security Department, you employ women in your workshop who are not Aryan, women who are not racially pure, and full Jewish women, enemies of the Reich."

"Mr. Drexler," Mr. Weidner responds slowly while remaining seated in his chair, his knuckles white as he grips the armrests. "Our factory produces brushes of excellent quality for the Wehrmacht. Shoe brushes, horse-grooming brushes, brooms. I'm sure this is also recorded in your Security Department files. Clara, could you please show him the documents that prove we are an essential factory?"

"Yes, sir," I answer, and hurry to the filing cabinets. I retrieve the appropriate folder, pull out the document and hand it to Mr. Drexler. My hands shake slightly as I pass it to him.

He takes the document I offer him and reads it carefully, then he briefly pulls out his notebook, writes something down and returns the document to me. "Well then," he says to Mr. Weidner, "starting September 19th, new regulations will take effect regarding all the workers I mentioned earlier." As he speaks, he pulls a brown envelope from his jacket's inner pocket and places it on the desk without removing his gloves.

"Guidelines regarding what?" Mr. Weidner asks him, his voice barely concealing his apprehension.

"Guidelines for marking," he coldly answers. "Have a pleasant day." He puts on his hat and exits the office, his footsteps echoing with authority.

I walk behind him, escorting him to the door. As we walk through the production hall, he stops and observes the workers who sit with their backs to us, facing the tables and machines, working with quick, practiced movements. None of them turn to look at us. The sound of machines creates a steady rhythm that suddenly feels ominous. After a few moments, he again writes something in his notebook and heads toward the exit.

"Good day, Mr. Drexler," I bid him farewell at the workshop entrance, forcing politeness into my voice.

"And you, madam?" he asks, his light brown eyes surveying me with cold calculation.

"What do you mean, sir?"

"What is your racial group?"

"I am a pure Aryan, sir," I answer. The words that come out of my mouth sound broken between my teeth, like glass shards cutting my tongue.

"Excellent. I'm sure you'll know how to convey the message appropriately. This is a mandatory regulation starting September 19th. It is in the interest of every loyal citizen to take care of the matter." He smiles at me coldly and removes the leather glove for the first time, extending his hand to shake mine.

"Yes, sir," I answer, shaking his outstretched hand. His grip is deliberately and painfully firm.

"Have a pleasant day, madam," he touches his hat in farewell and walks to the black car waiting for him beside the workshop, his silhouette dark against the grey sky.

I hurry back to the office, open the brown envelope and pull out the printed paper. The eagle clutching the swastika is embossed at the top of the page, and below it are several stamps and signatures.

I read the decree aloud to Mr. Weidner, line by line, going over the words as he remains silent, leaning back in his chair, holding his thick glasses in his hand. "Clara," he sighs when I finish reading, his voice heavy, "please gather everyone and read the decree to them."

"Yes, sir," I tell him as I rise from my seat, walking toward the production hall. I feel as if the eagle printed on the paper is gripping me in its talons, wounding my fingers holding the printed decree. The weight of what I must do settles on my shoulders like a shroud.

"Police Decree for Reich Security, Berlin, September 5th, 1941." I stand in the workshop, reading the decree aloud, my hands trembling like autumn leaves in the wind.

"Marking obligation for Jews within the German Reich's territory: in accordance with the Führer's directives and the decree of September 1st 1941, every person defined as Jewish according to the Nuremberg Laws is obligated to wear the Jewish symbol on their outer garment – a yellow Star of David, measuring at least 10 centimeters across, with the word 'Jude' written in clear black letters..." I read the paper, my voice becoming smaller with each word. All the women stand before me, watching me in a silence that feels heavier than stone.

"The symbol shall be worn on the left side of the chest, at heart level, whenever the person is outside their residence. It is absolutely forbidden to remove or conceal the symbol. Violation of this section will be considered an act of subversion against Reich security and will result in severe sanctions..." I continue reading, the words sticking in my throat like thorns. The workshop is silent, the machines still, the women saying nothing. Sarah, Miriam and Esther stand in the front row, headscarves covering their hair, staring at me with eyes that seem to bore into my lips as they speak words that wound them like bullets.

"Jewish children aged six and above are also obligated to wear the symbol in accordance with these instructions. Jews working for public institutions or German businesses must wear the symbol at their workplace as well, without exception..." I want to take a breath and stop reading, but I can't. I can't lift my gaze

to look at the women standing before me in their devastating silence. The yellow lights above cast harsh shadows across their faces, making their expressions appear as though they're carved from marble.

"The symbols will be provided by the Jewish communities, and the responsibility for obtaining and using them rests with each Jew individually. This decree will take effect starting September 19th, 1941. In the name of the Police Command for Reich Security, Berlin."

I finish reading and lower my gaze to the floor, unable to meet their eyes. The paper crumples slightly in my sweating palms.

The women say nothing. They ask no questions and voice no protest. One by one they turn and walk to their work tables with measured steps. They start their machines, and the noise gradually returns to the hall. The familiar scent of glue spreads through the air again, but now it smells different, bitter, tainted with something I can't name.

"I apologize," I quietly say before folding the terrible paper I'm holding, but I don't think anyone hears me. My words are swallowed by the mechanical hum of the machines, and the weight of what has just been spoken.

I need to go to Frau Schneider, to tell her about the decree. No one else will do it.

A few days later, I'm walking down the avenue at the end of the workday, clutching a slip of paper with the address Sarah had written for me. Occasionally I stop and look at the house numbers, checking my location. I'm getting close now.

The avenue is nearly deserted save for a military truck slowly passing by, overtaking a horse pulling a wooden cargo cart behind it. The clip-clop of hooves echoes against the empty buildings.

I see it further down the street, a large building with two towers and a great dome built into its upper section. I lower my gaze to the note I'm holding. This is the address. I take a few more steps closer and observe the building. It looks abandoned; part of its façade bears scorch marks from fire, and the glass of the large windows facing the street is shattered, reflecting the gray afternoon light in jagged fragments.

I continue advancing toward the building, but then I notice the black car parked on the other side of the street, and the man in the black leather coat and cap standing beside it. His posture is too alert, too watchful. I stop in my tracks, my heart hammering against my ribs. Is it safe for me to continue walking? What will I tell him if he stops me and starts asking questions?

The cold wind strikes my face and penetrates my wool coat, chilling me to the bone. If I continue standing like this, I might arouse his suspicion. Three men in coats pass by me, walking down the street with purpose, and I walk behind them as if I intend to continue down the avenue. Only at the last moment do I turn and approach the side door to the right of the large, abandoned building. *Berlin Jewish Community*

Office is written beside the door on a small metal plaque, the letters worn and faded.

I place my hand on the handle and open the door, entering quickly and hurrying to disappear from the street and the scrutinizing eyes of the man standing beside the black car. My breath comes in short puffs in the cold air.

The door creaks as I close it behind me and look around. There are several wooden tables in the small hall, behind which sit men and women hunched over papers and forms. One woman on the other side of the room is using a typewriter, the rhythmic clacking of keys the only sound breaking the oppressive silence. A woman about my age, wearing a simple dress and a scarf over her head, raises her gaze to me. Her eyes look tired. "Yes?" she asks in a quiet voice that barely carries across the room.

"I came... on behalf of my acquaintance, Frau Rachel Schneider. She's an elderly woman, she rarely leaves the house. I need a yellow badge for her," I say, placing the note with the address on the table as if it's authorization I need to provide.

"I need an address and date of birth," she tells me, her pen poised over a form.

"I don't have the birth date, only the address," I tell her, then quickly add: "But she's a widow. I know her son was killed in the Great War in 1916, at the Battle of Verdun." I tell her everything I know about Frau Schneider, hoping it will be enough.

"Wait a moment," the woman says as she approaches one of the other tables, speaking with an elderly man sitting at one of the desks. He has a gray beard, and wears a black suit that has seen better days. I can't hear what they're saying, but they glance at me several times. The typewriter continues its mechanical clacking, and people speak in whispers as if afraid to wake a monster that might burst in at any moment. Finally the woman goes to a back room, and returns after a few moments holding a form.

"Frau Rachel Schneider, born in Kiev on October 5th, 1869," she sits down and reads the form to me. "Ten pfennig per symbol," she says, opening a wooden drawer in the table and taking out a cardboard box containing yellow fabric Stars of David. In the center of each symbol, the word *Jude* is embroidered in black letters so bold, so prominent, they seem to shout their purpose.

"Give me six, please. It's just for her, I don't need any, I'm not..." I say, extending the money to her. But when she hands me the yellow badges, I'm afraid to touch them, as if they might transform me into one of them. I put my hand in my purse, pretending to search for something. My fingers won't obey me; I'm afraid to take them from her.

"You also need to confirm that this is the address where she lives," the woman tells me, placing the yellow badges on the table like dangerous objects. "I need to fill out this form as well," she adds, raising her gaze to me with an apologetic look. "They want to know everything."

"That's her address. I confirm that's her address, and that she lives alone. She's a widow."

"And what's your name?" she asks while filling out the form, her handwriting careful and precise.

"Clara Berger," I tell her apprehensively, then catch myself. "Sorry, I made a mistake, Clara Hoffman," I give her my maiden name and sign the form she hands me. The pen feels heavy in my trembling fingers. Then I take the yellow fabric stars lying on the table, push them deep into my purse, and hurry to leave the building, my heart racing.

Outside the building, I turn back and walk as fast as I can, making sure not to look behind me even though I fear the people in the black car might follow me. The weight of what I carry feels heavier than it should. I haven't broken any law, have I?

"Frau Schneider," I knock on her apartment door later that evening, my knuckles barely making a sound against the worn wood.

"Good evening, Clara," she opens the door for me. Each time I come to visit her, she seems a little smaller to me, as if she might disappear at any moment. The hallway light casts long shadows that make her appear even more fragile. I close the door behind me and follow her to the living room, my footsteps echoing in the quiet space. How do I tell her about the yellow patch?

"Frau Schneider, I've brought you some food I managed to purchase, some sausage." I take a chunk of sausage wrapped in newspaper out of my purse, the ink smudging slightly on my fingers. "And also some chocolate." I retrieve a small package wrapped in brown paper with the Wehrmacht symbol, cut it in half. I managed to purchase the half-package at the market in exchange for two oil ration coupons, a small victory in these impossible times.

"Thank you, Clara. You're a good woman, but you don't need to bring me food. I manage fine. At my age, I'm like the birds, I make do with crumbs," she says, but despite her words she takes the sausage and chocolate from my outstretched hands with grateful fingers. "Would you like tea?"

"Yes, please," I tell her as she walks to the kitchen, her slippers shuffling against the floor. "And Frau Schneider... there's something else..." I say in a hesitant voice, the words catching in my throat. "There are new orders, regulations, for all Jews."

Frau Schneider doesn't answer, and I wait quietly in the living room, looking around at the furniture and the photographs of her husband and son. Their faces seem to watch me in silent accusation, and I feel ashamed before them, lowering my eyes to study the worn carpet beneath my feet.

"Thank you," I say when she hands me the tea, the cup warm against my cold palms. "Frau Schneider, there's a new regulation from the authorities. You must wear a yellow badge." I place the teacup on the table and take the yellow badges out of my purse, gently laying them on the table like fragile, dangerous things. They frighten me with their stark symbolism.

"I heard about it," she sighs, her voice carrying the weight of years. "Rumors travel fast among us Jews, through the neighbors, through the walls, through the wind. They reach us whether we want them to or not."

"You must sew them onto your clothes, Frau Schneider. You can't go out into the street without a yellow patch. It's dangerous, I saw the decree myself."

"Clara," she answers sadly, settling deeper into her worn armchair, "maybe I should simply stop going out into the street. Maybe I should stop eating altogether. In any case, you can't purchase anything with the rations they distribute to us Jews. Maybe I should just give up and sell the apartment to Mr. Koch's son, even though he's offering me an amount that would last me a month of living." She speaks slowly while sipping her tea with deliberate care. "Maybe I should just give up."

I watch her and search for something to say, something that might encourage her. The silence stretches between us like a chasm. "Don't give up," I finally tell her, leaning forward in my chair. "You'll see, they're just making threats. The yellow patch, the registration of all Jews, Mr. Koch's son, they're just threats. You once told me that Jews always had to bow their heads and let the storm pass. You just need to bend. You'll see that things will be good here again."

Frau Schneider looks at me and smiles sadly, her eyes reflecting decades of survival. "Thank you so much, Clara, for trying to encourage me. But I have a feeling they mean business this time."

"Then at least let me help you sew the yellow patches onto your clothes."

"Thank you, Clara, but it's not necessary. I'll ask your mother to help me tomorrow. You have enough work, and you help me plenty already," she says as she stands up, as if wanting to signal that the conversation has ended. Her movement is deliberate, final.

I bid her farewell, and all the way home I think about the fabric Stars of David that remained lying on the table in her living room. How would I feel if I had to wear such a mark? The thought follows me through the empty streets like a shadow.

At night, I turn off the light in the bedroom, and when the room is dark I push aside the black curtain and open the window. The city outside is dark, without a single spark of light. The blackout regulations are enforced with German precision. I lean on the windowsill and let the cold wind strike my face, breathing in the night air that tastes of smoke and uncertainty. Will the wind really pass? And what's happening in the east, in Russia? The newspapers constantly promise victories, but I have a feeling the storm is only getting stronger, gathering force for something terrible yet to come.

A few weeks later, I'm riding the tram, my hands gripping the metal rail as the car sways along the tracks. I need to renew work permits for Jews at that building, the one everyone fears. Gray clouds of early winter cover the sky like a shroud, casting everything in somber tones.

On the street near that building, I lower my gaze to my feet lest they think I'm looking in its direction. It seems to me that other people are doing the same, and no one dares to look directly at it out of sheer terror. Even when the tram stops beside it and two men in dark brown suits board, I continue to keep my eyes down, staring at their polished black shoes as they stand beside me in silence. Their presence fills the car with an oppressive weight.

At the next stop, I get off the tram and begin walking back on foot. I have no choice, I must enter.

From a distance it looks similar to the other buildings at the city center. The lower floor of the large structure is covered with bricks and small windows, and three taller floors rise above it, with large windows embedded in the facade facing the street like malevolent eyes watching me.

To my surprise, there are no police or guards outside the building, only one black car parked by the steps leading to the entrance. Two people in long coats stand by the car, smoking. Perhaps guards aren't necessary in a place like this; fear itself serves as the sentinel.

I pass by the two men who survey me with their gazes, lowering my eyes to the sidewalk, tightening the hem of my coat and climbing the steps. I pass beneath the enormous Nazi flag dangling above the entrance like a banner of doom and enter through the open door, which seems to be waiting to swallow me whole.

"Yes, please?" the clerk at the entrance asks me. He's dressed in civilian clothes, but his haircut is military style: short, precise, authoritative.

"I need to get to the Department of Jewish Affairs," I answer, trying to stand upright despite the tremor in my voice.

He looks at me, surveying me with his eyes, his gaze lingering for a moment on the left side of my coat lapel where the yellow Jewish patch is sewn. "Identity card," he says after a moment, his tone flat and bureaucratic.

I hand him my cardboard document, watching his fingers open it, his gaze comparing me to the photograph. Then his hand grips a pen and writes my name in the large entrance log before him. Each stroke of the pen feels like a nail being driven into a coffin.

"Department IV B4, second floor, left side," he tells me, and returns my identity card with mechanical efficiency.

I climb the wide stairs to the second floor and walk down the corridor. The walls are white, devoid of pictures, and gray light enters from the windows facing the street, painting everything in pale gray like a hospital. Nazi flags hang between the windows, and beneath them stand tall wooden cabinets topped with bronze busts of the Führer. Several dark wooden benches are pressed against the white walls, and three men in suits stand near one of the closed doors, speaking quietly while smoking. Everything here is so quiet; only the sound of my footsteps echoes in the corridor, each step announcing my presence.

IV B4 Department of Jewish Affairs is written on a small brass plaque, and I enter the room, feeling tension throughout my entire body like electricity crackling under my skin.

"How can I help you?" the secretary asks me, not looking up from her typewriter.

"Good morning," I tell her, forcing politeness into my voice. "I need an extension of work authorization permits for Jews at an essential factory." This room is also white and lacking any pictures except for the Führer's portrait hanging on the wall, watching me with painted eyes that seem to follow my every movement.

"Documents, please," she says with indifference.

"Here," I take the workshop certificate and all the workers' cards out of my purse and hand it to her. This is the first time I've done this, the first time I've been in this building, and every fiber of my being wants to flee.

"Wait outside, they'll call you," she tells me as she takes the documents and enters one of the inner offices, her heels clicking on the polished floor.

I go outside and sit on the bench, tightly gripping the purse on my lap. Everything's fine, this is a routine bureaucratic procedure. At least that's what I tell myself, though my racing heart suggests otherwise.

I don't know how long I sit like that, but finally the clerk comes out and calls me, and I enter behind her. "Room three," she tells me, and I enter the room and sit across from an official in a suit.

He's about my age, wearing a dark gray suit, balding, and he removes his glasses from his nose and wipes them with a bright yellow handkerchief he holds between his thick fingers. His movements are deliberate, calculated.

"You're requesting work permits for twenty-seven women," he says, putting his glasses back on and fixing me with a stare that makes me feel like an insect under examination.

"Yes, sir. These are essential workers for the workshop. We also manufacture for the Wehrmacht, we have permits, they're attached," I quickly say, the words tumbling out in my nervousness.

"Yes, I saw," he says with indifference. "Well then..." He begins reading the names aloud. "Bella Levinson, approved," he places her card on the right side. "Greta Mandel, approved," he places her card on the right side as well. "Ruth Neumann..." He goes through name after name with mechanical precision. "Esther Spiegel, not approved," he places her card on the left side, and I want to stop and ask him why, but he continues reading the list and I don't dare interrupt him. "That's it," he says, placing the last card down and beginning to stamp them with red stamps. "Twenty approved for continued work, seven not," he casually tells me, his hand holding the stamp as it moves from card to card, striking each one with force.

"Excuse me, sir, why didn't you approve those seven women?" I ask despite his frightening indifference. "We need them for work, they're diligent workers." I search for something to say to him. Sarah, Miriam and Esther didn't receive work permits. What will they do without them? "They contribute to the Wehrmacht," I desperately add.

"Not anymore. They have a date." He stops stamping the papers and looks at me with eyes devoid of humanity.

"What do you mean?"

"Within four days they need to report to the Jewish community offices."

"For what?" I ask, though part of me already knows I don't want to hear the answer.

"That's no longer up to me. I'm only responsible for the lists," he tells me and again grips the stamp, dismissing my question with bureaucratic finality.

I stare at the pile of forms. I could ask him to switch the names and keep Sarah, Miriam and Esther – the ones I know best – instead of others. Sometimes we stand and talk together during lunch breaks. What difference does it make if he keeps them and sends others? I tightly grip the handles of my purse on my lap and breathe deeply, but I'm unable to ask. I'm too afraid. The cowardice burns in my throat like acid.

Name after name, he stamps every last remaining card.

"Here you go," he hands them to me.

I take them in silence and leave the building. I should have asked him to keep them, and replace them with others.

"I'm sorry," I tell Mr. Weidner as I enter his office and place the list of workers on his desk. "Of all the workers, they didn't approve seven," I add, sitting in my chair, the weight of failure pressing down on my shoulders. I want to burst into tears right there, but I force myself to maintain composure.

Mr. Weidner takes the list and brings it close to his eyes, examining it slowly. His well-groomed fingers hold the paper gently as it almost touches his nose, then he places it on the desk with a heavy sigh.

"You did what you could, Clara. They don't want the Jews, Hitler has been saying it for years."

"So what can we do?" I ask, staring at the list, my heart breaking as I think of Sarah, Miriam and Esther. What will become of them?

"You know, Clara," he quietly says, leaning back in his worn leather chair, "six months ago, when you came to me looking for work, I hesitated about whether to accept you. But I know I wasn't wrong. I know you're a good woman." He smiles at me with tired eyes.

"But I feel like it's only getting harder," I tell him, the words catching in my throat. I feel so terrible about all those whose work permits were canceled, as if I've personally condemned them.

"Yes, that's true. It's going to get harder. We'll need to do everything we can, even if it's not much." He smiles at me sadly, his weathered hands folded on the desk like a prayer.

"Thank you, sir," I say, looking at the list lying on the table like a death sentence. How do we tell the women?

"Do you want me to tell them about the permits?" he asks, his voice gentle with understanding.

"No, sir," I tell him. It's my job, my burden to bear.

I take the list and go out to the production hall.

In the workshop hall, I stand for a moment and observe the women working. They work with their backs to me, some unaware of what I'm about to tell them. Only the supervisor notices me and approaches, her face creased with worry. She knows I was at Gestapo Headquarters today.

"Are there permits?" she asks with an anxious look.

"Not for everyone," I tell her, feeling the lump in my throat threatening to choke me. "Could you gather them?"

One by one they stop working and turn off their machines, rising from their work stations and standing before me. They say nothing, but they all stare at the work permit forms I'm holding in my hands. The yellow patches on their dresses stand out so prominently, like accusations directed at me. In the quiet workspace, I feel like the Angel of Death bearing terrible news. I need to tell them I'm sorry, but I'm unable to say anything.

In silence, I approach the women one by one and give them their work permits. Each woman who receives the paper that will allow her to get food rations and continue working here takes it quietly, with an embarrassed smile, and returns to her work station. Finally, seven women remain before me and my hands are empty. "I'm sorry," I whisper, lowering my eyes to my fingers, unable to look into their eyes.

They stand there for a moment, as if trying to digest the news, then they approach the workshop exit, take their coats hanging by the door, and disappear into the cold street. Their footsteps echo in the sudden silence like a funeral march. One of them – I think it's Esther but I'm so sad I'm no longer sure – approaches me and says: "It's alright. You did everything you could." Her voice carries no bitterness, only acceptance that breaks my heart even more. Then she turns toward the exit door as well, takes her coat, and disappears into the gray afternoon.

I watch the remaining women who continue working in silence, their movements mechanical, haunted. I escape to the inner office. I have reports to print, papers to file, anything to keep my hands and mind busy.

At the end of the workday, I walk through the cold city, feeling the mass of tears in my throat threatening to burst. I so desperately want someone to embrace me.

Russia, November 1941
My dear Clara,
So much time has passed since I wrote you last, but I think about you every moment. You're the only thing that warms my heart in the frozen wastelands surrounding us. Everything here is cold and frozen: the ground, the food, the metal sides of the truck, and the things we do here. I write to you while my hands tremble from cold, and I know I can never tell what my eyes have seen... I examine the continuation of the following lines. Two of them have been blacked out with ink by the censor who read these words before me, and decided what I'm forbidden to know. The dark strokes cut across the page like scars, hiding secrets I'm not meant to bear. *...even if I'll never believe we did it,* he finishes telling me about things I'll never know.

My Clara, I converse with you in my imagination while driving for long hours on frozen dirt roads. The conversations with you, knowing there's one woman in the world whose goodness of heart shines all the way to me, to Russia, give me hope even when the sun disappears and is replaced by darkness. Already waiting to return home and embrace you.
Yours,

Hermann.

I carefully fold the paper like I'm handling something precious and fragile, return it to the envelope and kiss it, even though the black stamp of the swastika and censorship is imprinted on it. The official mark feels cold against my lips, but I don't care. What matters is that he's alive; what matters is that I warm his heart across all those frozen miles.

I tightly close my coat, wrap my neck in the wool scarf, and hurry to the office through the cold streets. The morning air bites at my cheeks, turning them red, but Hermann's words echo in my mind like a prayer. If he can cope with that black winter in Russia, facing whatever horrors the censored lines conceal, then I too can endure.

A few days later, as I'm printing a production report for the Wehrmacht, the door opens and I raise my eyes. Before me stand two young women, both around twenty, maybe a bit younger. "Excuse me, are you Frau Berger?" the one on the right asks me. They resemble each other closely; probably sisters, maybe twins. Both have dark brown hair and fair skin. The one on the left wears thick glasses similar to Mr. Weidner's.

"Yes, I'm Frau Berger," I answer, studying their faces with curiosity and concern.

"I'm Marlene Ehrenstein, and this is my twin sister An-nemarie," she tells me while standing upright before me, her posture defiant despite her circumstances. "They told us you might be looking for workers, so we came to check if you could give us work." Both wear yellow badges sewn onto their coats.

"How old are you?" I ask. They look so young.

"We're nineteen, ma'am. We're already adults," she answers as if she's prepared the response in advance, her chin lifted with forced confidence.

"And who sent you?"

"From the Jewish community. They said you employ people like us, and also sometimes accept people like my sister." She momentarily moves her hand and touches Annemarie's, who stands beside her and remains silent the entire time. There's something protective in her gesture, an older sister's instinct, even though they're twins.

"What about your parents? Don't you have parents?"

"We have a mother," she answers, and it seems she struggles to articulate the words, her voice catching slightly. "But a few days ago they took her. She was supposed to arrive at the Jewish community offices. They took her from there, to a train heading east," she quietly speaks.

"And what about your father?"

"He left," Annemarie opens her mouth and speaks for the first time, and for a moment I think about myself. What would I have done if I'd been left alone at their age?

"And where do you live?"

They're silent for a moment, then Annemarie answers: "We manage, ma'am. We know how to get by."

"And do you have documents? Work permits? Have you worked somewhere before?" They seem so young to be in this city without a mother, and without a place to live.

"I worked in a munitions factory," Marlene answers, "but they brought forced laborers from Poland and France, so they fired me." She places their identity cards and her old work permit on the table with careful precision. "We're both diligent workers, ma'am. We know how to work hard," she adds, while her sister nods in confirmation.

I hold their documents and examine them, though I already know what I'm going to do. The decision has already formed in my heart. "Please wait here," I tell them as I enter Mr. Weidner's office. He raises his gaze to me.

"There are two young women outside asking to work here," I tell him, placing their identity cards on the table. The letter J, stamped on the brown cardboard documents, stands out starkly.

He looks at their cards for only a moment, then raises his gaze to me. "What do you think we should do?" he asks.

"I think we should hire them, if we can get approval."

"Try to get them hired. We need workers. That's what you'll tell them. Tell them we need more workers to support the Wehrmacht's brilliant victories." His voice carries the bitter irony of a man forced to speak in the language of his oppressors.

"Thank you, sir. That's what we'll do," I tell him, taking their documents from him. "Come with me," I say to them as we go to the production hall. Inside, I speak with the supervisor, arranging their placement at the very workstations recently vacated by women who would never return.

"Thank you, ma'am. You won't regret it, we're dedicated workers," Marlene tells me, smiling sadly for the first time. I smile back at them and hurry back to the office. It's hard for me to see them sitting at the empty workstations of Sarah and Esther.

Later, I again board the tram with their identity cards in my hand, and again enter the frightening building, and again wait at the second floor of Department IV B4. This time the clerk stamps the forms without question, and I return to the workshop and give them their permits. Despite their grateful thanks, I hurry back to my office. They've replaced women who were sent east, and the weight of that exchange presses on my conscience like a stone.

On the way home, I can't stop thinking about them. If I had two daughters, would they be nineteen today? Would they look like them?

I banish those thoughts and look at the queue outside the bakery. I need to think only of the here and now, and how to continue existing in this gray city with all the queues and the cold and the food that's becoming increasingly scarce.

A few days later, I'm at home, getting ready to go to one of the subway stations and try to trade some butter I managed to obtain. Afterwards I'll continue to my mother's, and help her cook. But suddenly there's a knock at the door.

I approach the door and open it just a crack, peering into the dark stairwell.

He stands before me, studying me with those cold, calculating eyes. He stood before me like this once before in this apartment. And now he's come again. I knew he would one day, I just didn't know when.

"Won't you let me in?" he asks, but I feel my entire body frozen with fear and tension, unable to answer him.

In the weak light of the stairwell, he looks exactly as he did ten years ago, when he entered my apartment. Those same gray eyes examining me with indifference, the same pressed suit, the same fedora, and that same evil smile. Despite aging, and his once wheat-colored hair now being streaked with white, it seems to me he's remained the same person, a predator who has found his way back to old hunting grounds.

"What do you want?" I ask, finally managing to break free from my paralysis. My hand grips the door handle with all my strength, though if he tries to push me and enter, I won't be able to stop him.

"I came to visit, to see how you're doing. Won't you invite me in?" He studies me with those calculating eyes that seem to strip away all pretense.

"I don't do those things anymore," I answer. I can't think clearly from fear. Why has he come to me? The question echoes in my mind like a death knell.

"I know exactly what you do and what you don't, that's my job," he answers, with indifference that chills my blood. "You know I'm nice. If you refuse to let me in, others will come. You know they won't be as nice as me."

"Please come in," I say, managing to step back and open the door for him, my body moving against my will.

Walter enters the apartment, brushing past me. He smells of sweet aftershave, and I follow him without saying a word. He stands in the center of the small living room and looks around, exactly like last time. The familiarity of his movements makes my skin crawl. "I see not much has changed since I was here last, Clara," he says after a moment, his voice carrying the casual tone of someone inspecting property.

"My name is Frau Berger. What do you want?" I answer, trying to summon some dignity.

"I still don't see your husband here with you." He approaches the sideboard and examines the photograph of the two of us. "I see your photo together has moved from the bedroom to the living room," he says, holding it as if it were a worthless object, his fingers leaving smudges on the glass.

"My husband is in the army, fighting for the homeland, despite his age," I answer angrily. I want him to leave my house.

"Yes..." he answers thoughtfully while placing the photograph on the sideboard and approaching the black curtains that block the light from escaping the apartment. "First he was in France, now he's in Russia. He also writes you touching letters. I checked." He seems to be talking to himself as his hand touches the black fabric, violating even this small privacy.

"He's my husband," I answer, feeling nauseous at the possibility that he might have read Hermann's letters to me. The thought of his eyes on those intimate words makes me want to retch.

"Does your husband know what you used to do?" He continues touring the house, approaching the pantry and checking the empty shelves with the thoroughness of a customs inspector.

"I don't do that," I answer, watching as he examines the little sausage I'm saving for an emergency. He brings it close to his nose, smells it, and returns it to the shelf with deliberate slowness.

"Yes, they told me you don't do that anymore." He approaches the back door of the apartment, the one that leads to the service stairs behind the building, used when more respectable families lived here with servants. He places his hand on the door handle and tries to open it, but it's locked. "Do you use this to escape our visits?" he asks casually, as if inquiring about the weather.

"You know there's a door like this in every apartment in the building," I answer angrily, my voice shaking with suppressed rage.

"Yes, I know. It's our job to know. And what about your husband?" He turns to me, his gray eyes boring into mine. "Does he know you continue to love Jews? Does he know you work in a workshop that employs Jewish women?"

"It's a workshop that manufactures brushes for the Wehrmacht. We contribute to the war effort," I manage to say courageously, though my voice betrays my fear.

"Yes... for now." He brushes past me and enters the bedroom without my permission. Does he want to do it with me again? I follow him angrily, my footsteps echoing my indignation.

"Please leave this room, Mr. Koch," I tell him, remaining at the entrance to the room.

"You know, Clara," he looks at me with his cold eyes, "you always chose the wrong side. You always chose the weak. And we always know everything about you. We do our job, we know." He calmly looks at my bed, as if appraising its worth.

"I'm not doing anything illegal. They have work permits," I answer from the room's threshold, my voice growing stronger with desperate defiance.

"Yes, I know. You were also at Gestapo Headquarters twice to get permits. You're a diligent worker. But you don't really love the German nation and the Third Reich." His words are like ice water poured over my spine.

"I'm loyal to the Third Reich, just like you."

"Years ago you received a Party pin from Frau Vogel and have never worn it, not even once. I know everything about you, Clara, I'm in a position where I need to know." He walks toward me, but again brushes past me and exits my bedroom. Despite my terror, I feel the tension in my body dissipate slightly as he moves away from that intimate space. "There's always someone who comes and talks to us. Someone who's afraid, someone willing to trade what their eyes have seen." He approaches the kitchen, opens the kitchen drawers, checks their contents, and takes out a large knife. "They support us, the Third Reich." He again examines me with his cold gaze, his hand gripping the knife. What is he going to do to me? I feel a wave of cold throughout my body.

"Please leave, I'm begging you. I haven't done anything," I tell him in a trembling voice, my words barely audible.

"Of course..." He smiles at me while speaking slowly, savoring my fear. "By the way..." He takes a piece of paper out of his jacket pocket and places it on the table with theatrical precision. "This is for Frau Schneider, whom you got yellow badges for."

"What is it?" I look at the folded paper form lying on the table.

"It's a relocation letter, to the east. You'll probably be happy to give it to her personally, since you love working with Jews," he tells me maliciously, forcefully striking the form on the table with the knife, embedding it in the paper and the wooden table. The knife remains upright, quivering like a gravestone marker.

I try to stifle a scream, unable to move from sheer terror. The blade catches the dim light.

"Have a pleasant evening, Clara," he nods his head slightly and touches the tips of his fingers to his hat, turning toward the door.

I can't answer. I just remain standing in place, trying to restore my breathing.

"And Clara... one more thing," I hear him from the direction of the door. "This whole Jewish business, it's temporary. It'll end soon. In the end, you'll go back to being who you were. I told you once, people don't change. When you want to earn money like last time, you know where to turn." Then I hear the door open, and the sound of his footsteps going down the stairs.

"Do you have anything strong left to drink, Mother?" I ask as I burst into her apartment like a storm. I haven't stopped running from my apartment to her building, ignoring the sharp pain in my ribs that cuts through me with each breath.

"Is everything alright?" she asks as she approaches the kitchen, taking down a half-empty bottle of schnapps from the upper shelf and giving it to me. "Take this. I save it for bombings, so I can calm down afterwards," she tells me.

I take a glass, pour myself a generous portion, and drink it in one gulp, feeling my throat burn and my eyes fill with tears. Only then do I sit in the chair by the table, lower the glass and breathe.

"What happened, Clara? Is everything alright?"

I don't say anything to her, I just take the paper Walter Koch left on my kitchen table out of my purse and place it before her. I haven't stopped looking behind me all the way from my apartment to here, certain that he or one of his men is following me, that eyes are watching from every shadow, every doorway.

"What is this? Why is it torn?" Mother asks as she takes the paper, puts on her glasses, and begins to read it. I grip the bottle and pour myself another drink, swallowing it in one gulp, trying to wash away the taste of fear that coats my mouth like ash.

"They want to take her?" she finally asks.

"Yes," I nod.

"And you'll give it to her?" She reaches for the bottle, takes the glass I'm holding, pours herself a bit of schnapps and drinks it, sighing audibly.

"I have no choice," I answer, my voice hollow. "I have to."

"How did he get to you?"

"It doesn't matter." The memory of his presence in my home makes my skin crawl.

"Maybe you shouldn't have gotten involved," she quietly says.

"How uninvolved are we supposed to be, Mother?" I ask, wanting to drink more of the schnapps, but I already feel nauseous. I'm nauseous from the schnapps, nauseous from the black words written on this paper, nauseous from the smell of Walter Koch's sweet aftershave that seems to cling to my clothes, my hair, my very soul.

"I don't know how uninvolved we're supposed to be," she sighs.

"Neither do I," I answer.

"I sewed the yellow patches for her. I also bring her food from time to time. I know you do too," she tells me while holding the empty glass, her fingers tracing its rim absently. "Do you want me to give her the letter?"

"No, I'll do it." I take the paper and rise from my seat. I'm no longer a little girl who needs her mother to protect her.

At the door I turn around, return to the kitchen, and hug Mother for a moment. Only then do I leave an walk those few steps to Frau Schneider's apartment.

A few days later, I enter Frau Schneider's apartment. She stands upright in the center of the apartment, dressed in her simple black dress, her posture dignified despite everything that's about to unfold. Beside her stands a single suitcase, exactly as written in the instructions on the paper I gave her. By the sideboard, a man in a long brown wool coat stands with his back to me. He holds a small wooden clipboard with a form attached, moving from one piece of furniture to the next in the living room, cataloging each item with mechanical precision. I look around: everything is exactly as it was, except the two photographs that were on the sideboard have disappeared.

"Sir, what are you doing?" I ask the man, my voice sharper than I intended.

"I'm just doing my job," he answers without turning around, his tone flat and bureaucratic as if he's inventorying office supplies.

"Shall we go?" Frau Schneider says to me, her voice trembling slightly, though she fights to maintain her composure.

"Yes," I answer. I approach the waiting suitcase and bend down to grasp it, even though I want to stop this rolling train that seems unstoppable.

"These are the house keys," Frau Schneider tells the stranger as she places a bunch of keys on the sideboard.

He doesn't answer, just approaches the sideboard and takes them, slipping them into his pocket as if they were always his. Then he approaches a landscape painting hanging on the wall and begins recording its details, his pen scratching across the paper.

"Let's go, Clara. This house is no longer my home, they've taken it from me," she says in a broken voice, exiting through the door.

I stand there for another moment, watching the stranger who's taking her apartment piece by piece. I want to do something, but I know it's already too late. The machinery of dispossession has begun, and I am powerless against it. I follow Frau Schneider out of the apartment.

We walk in silence all the way to the Jewish community building near the great synagogue. She tries to walk upright, maintaining her dignity, and I walk beside her, holding the suitcase.

People on the street fix their gazes on us, moving their eyes from the yellow badge on her coat to me. Do they think I'm also a Jew trying to hide my identity? I continue walking beside her, fighting the urge to distance myself from her. From a distance, I can already see the large dome of the abandoned synagogue. Several people carrying suitcases are entering through the small door of the community building.

"Come," I tell Frau Schneider, trying to inject hope into my voice. "We're almost there."

"No," she quietly tells me as she stops, looking at me with eyes that have seen too much. "From here, I continue alone."

"I don't understand," I tell her.

"Come with me for a moment," she tells me, and walks toward a small alley that branches off from the avenue.

"You have to go, those are the orders," I tell her. "You'll return soon, you'll see. Like you told me, like the cypress tree in the wind that bends until the storm passes. You'll reach the new place and write to me, tell me how they're treating you." I continue talking, trying to fill the silence with words.

"Clara," she smiles at me, "you know I'm too old to wander. You also know I'm not coming back, we both know that."

"You're wrong. You'll see that you'll be fine in the east," I tell her, though I don't believe the words coming out of my mouth.

"Thank you, Clara. Thank you for being by my side for so many years when I was alone," she tells me in her quiet voice. "And one more thing," she adds, "I want to give you two things." From an inner pocket of her wool coat, she removes a silver menorah that gleams in the gray light of the alley. "This is a silver menorah. Sell it, it's worth a lot of money. Don't keep it, it's dangerous to keep it. Sell it." She gives it to me, the metal cold and heavy in my hands.

"And one more thing. I'm giving you my son's photograph." She takes the photograph of her young son out of the other side of her coat. He looks at me with pride, dressed in a German Army uniform, before he was killed in the Battle of Verdun in that Great War.

"I can't take this photograph," I whisper.

"My husband's photograph will go with me, Clara, but my son's photograph will go with you, so you'll always remember there was once a good Germany here, a Germany we were proud of."

I search for something to say, but I can't find the words.

"Goodbye, Clara. Don't follow me." She takes the suitcase from me and walks slowly, a thin, elderly woman holding a single suitcase.

I remain standing in the alley for a few more moments, wiping my eyes as tears I can no longer hold back fall freely.

When I emerge from the alley onto the avenue and look toward the synagogue and the community building, I no longer see her. She must have already gone inside, to the assembly point, as was written in that terrible paper.

I walk home with the menorah hidden in my coat along with her son's photograph, the son who was once proud of Germany. I wipe my eyes and wonder if I could have offered Walter something that would have changed the order to take her.

Chapter Eighteen

The Transports

Berlin-Anhalter Bahnhof
Station, February 1942

The cold penetrates the wool coat I'm wearing as I stand motionless on Platform Four. My hand tightly grips the envelope I received from him two weeks ago. He didn't write much, just a few words, but the important thing is that he's coming home for five days of leave.

Every few moments I turn my gaze to the large clock on the station wall, and then to the railway track coming from the east. I'm tense. How will our meeting go? The question gnaws at me like hunger, mixing anticipation with inexplicable dread.

A train begins slowly moving to Platform Three, filling the station hall with the screeching sounds of metal grinding against metal, and the smell of soot and steam. Other women stand on the platform, waiting for their loved ones like I am, and perhaps trying to trade on the black market with the soldiers who will soon arrive.

The announcer's metallic voice sounds over the loudspeaker: "Military train from Smolensk via Warsaw will now enter Platform Four." All the women step forward to the edge of the platform.

From a distance I see the black locomotive slowly entering the station, like a great draft horse straining to take a few more steps while dragging a heavy freight car behind it. The women on the platform walk excitedly along the length of the train, looking at the cars and searching for their loved ones. Here and there they call out with joy and wave their hands, while I stand frozen, unable to move from my spot. I miss him so much, and yet I'm so afraid of this reunion.

Another moment passes, and the train doors open. Soldiers begin descending onto the platform in their long coats, some with quick steps and others walking slowly as if carrying invisible burdens. The platform becomes a tumult of voices and a mixing of colors, gray-green with burgundy, blue, brown and black. Around us are footsteps and the conductor's whistles, and wounded soldiers descending with slow steps, trying to stabilize themselves on the concrete platform. And then I see him.

He's in a simple military coat with a leather knapsack on his back, standing and watching me as I walk toward him. I can't run, my legs feel weighted with lead and uncertainty.

"You've arrived," I whisper as I raise my hand, gently caressing his cheek and examining him. He hasn't changed at all; he's still my Hermann, whom I love so much, but his eyes are tired, and his face is weathered from summer sun and winter cold. His short hair is also filled in with more white strands, like frost that has settled permanently.

"I've arrived, for five days." He opens his arms and hugs me tightly, and I try to sink into the warmth of his body that I've missed so much. But for a moment it seems to me that he's trying to hold onto me in order to stay stable, rather than fall on the platform. There's something fragile in his embrace, as if he's the one seeking support.

"Shall we go?" I finally ask, and we walk along the platform toward the exit. His hand holds mine, but it feels to me like he's so far away, as if part of him remains somewhere in those frozen wastelands he's traveled from.

"Do you want to go straight home, or should we stop to drink and eat something at a café after the long journey?" I ask. Suddenly I'm so afraid of arriving home with him and undressing before him. What will he think about how thin I've become since he left?

Hermann doesn't say anything, just shrugs his shoulders, and we both walk to a café adjacent to the train station. From time to time I study him secretly: his eyes wander around as if still examining the snowy wastelands of Russia, as if his thoughts have remained there in that distant place.

At the café, we sit facing each other. He remains in his coat, as do I. The small space is barely heated by a single coal stove, casting dancing shadows on the walls. I place an order with the waiter, and after a few moments he brings us two cups with coffee substitute, and two slices of simple dark cake made from butter substitutes.

"I'm sorry there isn't more, everything is rationed," I tell him as I sip the bitter coffee, the taste sharp and unsatisfying.

"It's alright," he tells me, sipping his coffee. His eyes seem to look at me for the first time since his arrival, trying to understand who I am and how I belong in his life.

"The important thing is that you're here." I place my hand on his where it lies on the table, but even this simple touch feels strange, unfamiliar.

In the following days we're together all the time: in the apartment, on the gray city streets, at the cinema showing a film about the triumph of the German spirit. But in all that time, I feel I can't express what I'm feeling. I can't tell him about the Jewish women working in the workshop who barely receive food rations; I can't tell him about Frau Schneider who was apparently sent to resettlement in the east, and from whom I haven't received a letter since; the endless queues for food; the night air raid sirens that frighten me so much; the clean and quiet Gestapo building; or about Mr. Koch's son's visit. I feel that he can't tell me what's in his heart either, and the whole time he looks at me, his eyes see other sights that don't belong to me. We walk through the streets more and more, but I feel that we're both being propelled toward the last day of his leave, as if time itself is pushing us apart.

Five days later, we're standing on the platform together again. I hold Hermann's hand and look around at all the women holding their loved ones. Do they also feel as I do, that the war is taking the souls of their beloveds? That the war is taking their own souls as well?

"Military train to Smolensk via Warsaw will now enter Platform Two," the announcer announces in his metallic voice, and I feel my body tremble for a moment. The snow has returned, and small chunks of ice are dripping outside the station.

"I work with Jewish women," I whisper to him, the words bursting out like water through a broken dam. "There are only Jewish women in the workshop. They're being treated terribly," I begin telling him, unable to stop myself. "They constantly need permits, and must wear yellow badges, and they keep cutting their food rations. Some of them are simply taken, disappearing into the east. Sometimes there are air raid alerts at night, the British bomb us, I sit in the basement and I'm so afraid." I grip his hand tightly with all my strength, until I fear my fingers will break from the pain.

Hermann remains silent, his gaze again wandering over the platform. "We're doing terrible things in the east," he finally says, as if speaking to an invisible figure who isn't me. "Things that can't be told or written," he continues speaking slowly, as if to himself. "Things people should never do." He lowers his eyes and looks into mine, as if noticing me for the first time during this entire leave. "I'm constantly fighting with myself to remain the same person I was, Clara. Promise me you'll also remain the same woman you were." He places his hands on my shoulders and grips me forcefully until he's hurting me, his fingers digging into my coat with desperate intensity.

"I promise," I tell him, but the sound of my words mixes with additional announcements from the announcer, the noise of the locomotive's steam exhaust passing by us as it stops, and the doors of the cars opening with the tumult of people around us.

Hermann pulls me tightly to him and whispers something in my ear that I can't manage to hear over the chaos, and then he releases his grip on me and enters the car. By the time I manage to wipe my eyes, he has disappeared among all the soldiers walking into the car, swallowed by the machinery of war once again.

Another moment passes, and the doors close with a bang as the conductor whistles. Again the tired black horse pulls the cars out of the station, with a steam exhaust that sounds like a dying breath.

Even after the train disappears, I remain standing on the platform for long minutes. Along with the feeling of sadness and longing that's already beginning to form within me, I also feel a sense of relief, of returning to the familiar world that has enveloped me, and to which I'm accustomed. Finally I turn around, tighten my wool coat and walk along the platform, exiting the train station. I want to return to the familiar routine of the workshop and the Jewish women, despite how frightening it is. But first I want to know, I need to know what happened to Frau Schneider, and to Sarah, Miriam and Esther. I'm afraid to ask him, but perhaps his younger brother could help me. On the cold street, I tighten the scarf around my neck and walk down the gray street towards City Hall. All the way there, I try to think of what Hermann had whispered to me that I couldn't hear, but I can't remember.

The heavy wooden doors of City Hall creak slightly as I push them inward, and they close heavily behind me. The air in the lobby is somewhat compressed, saturated with the smell of paper, ink and cigarette smoke. Next to the curved staircase leading up is a large wooden bulletin board, with recruitment notices, examples of rationing orders, and a small red sign announcing the office hours of various departments pasted on it.

I stop for a moment, take a deep breath, and approach the front desk. Behind the glass sits a clerk in a suit, with a red Nazi Party armband on his sleeve.

"Good morning," I quietly address him.

"Yes...?" he asks, looking at me with cold eyes.

"I'm looking for Mr. Koch, Bruno Koch."

"Did you schedule an appointment?"

"No, sir."

"He's busy," he answers indifferently, already looking past me as if I've ceased to exist.

"He knows me. We're acquainted," I answer, trying to smile. I feel that wherever I turn for help, I'm trying to swim against a river current that's getting stronger, threatening to sweep me away entirely.

The man looks at me for a moment, then lowers his gaze to the papers lying by the counter. Finally he says: "Second floor, third door on the left. Wait in line if necessary."

"Thank you very much," I tell him as I turn toward the stairs. I just want to know where they took them, and why Frau Schneider hasn't written to me yet. Surely there's an explanation.

I wait for a long time outside his room, until the secretary instructs me to enter. I approach the door and gently knock. He'll help me, he's a good man. The memory of that night I helped him gives me courage.

"Come in," I hear, and enter, closing the door behind me with a soft click that echoes in the small space.

The room is small and cold, with a weak bulb casting light from the ceiling. In its center is a simple wooden desk, and behind it, wooden filing cabinets full of drawers. "Hello, Mr. Koch. Bruno," I say, waiting for him to invite me to sit. He's barely changed since that day I helped him in the alley. His face remains young.

He looks at me, and for a moment it seems he doesn't recognize me, or is pretending not to know me. But after a moment he recovers, rises from his seat, and points to the chair facing him. "How can I help you, Fraulein Hoffman?" He sits down and gives me a polite smile that doesn't reach his eyes.

"I've been Frau Berger for many years now," I smile hesitantly. "I'm sorry to bother you, but I'm looking for information. I thought perhaps you could help me," I add, my words careful and measured.

"Yes... certainly. What subject are we talking about?" He examines me. He's wearing a clean blue suit, and the signs of the beating from that night have disappeared without leaving scars.

"I'm trying to find out where in the east a Jewish woman was sent. Frau Schneider. You know her, she was your neighbor too. I accompanied her to the Jewish community building two months ago. They told her they were taking her for 'resettlement' in the east, but she hasn't sent me a single letter since," I tell him, trying to sit upright.

"Frau Berger, you're an intelligent woman... you know that's not a question that can be easily asked," he answers politely, interlacing his hands on the desk as though he's creating a wall between us. His fingers are pale, manicured.

"But you knew her. Your parents still live in that building, they know her too. So does your brother," I tell him, even though perhaps I should listen to him and stop asking. I can't stop myself; I'm the one who accompanied her to the transport. "There are also three other women who worked in the workshop where I work, they took them too. I just want to know where," I say before I regret it.

"Frau Berger... Clara," he tells me quietly, his voice taking on a more official tone. "I'm sorry, but I don't handle such matters. I don't deal with population registration. I'm a simple clerk who handles tax collection."

"I just want to know they're alright, Mr. Koch, please," I tell him, desperation creeping into my voice. "You were at my house then. I took care of you then, after what happened with those men," I add, playing the only card I have.

He remains silent, seeming to retreat slightly. His fingers tap gently on the desk's wooden surface, a nervous rhythm that belies his composure. "Frau Berger," he finally answers in a cold voice, "I don't know what you're talking about, I was never at your house. But because you were once my neighbor, I'll check. Please write down the dates they were sent, and their names." He hands me a sheet of paper, his movements precise and bureaucratic.

I write down the names as he requested, and he takes the paper, studying it briefly. "Please wait here," he says as he rises, exiting the room and leaving me alone in the empty space that suddenly feels like a trap.

I look around fearfully, having no idea whether I was allowed to tell him what I did. I also don't know how much time has passed. I sit motionless, feeling like someone's watching me constantly, even though the room is empty.

Finally the door opens and he returns, sitting in his chair. He holds a page in his hand, from which he reads to me: "Frau Schneider was sent to the city of Lodz, and from there to an unknown destination. You won't receive any more letters from her. The others were also sent east, you won't receive any more letters from them either. Don't look for them anymore," he answers me dryly, folding the paper he's holding. "Frau Berger," he adds in an official voice, "I expect you won't come to my workplace anymore."

"Thank you, I understand…" I tell him as I rise, though I'm not sure I understand. Did they do something to them?

"Clara…" he suddenly says in a weak voice, and I stop and look at him. "I'm sorry," he adds, his official mask slipping for just a moment. "I'm in danger too, even more than you. I'm exactly like them," he adds quietly, his voice barely above a whisper. "Do you know what they'll do to me if they find out I provided you with information? Do you know what they'll do to me if they discover who I am? They'll send me where they send them, I'll disappear exactly like they did." He looks at me with a sad gaze.

"I understand… I'm sorry…"

"The Gestapo, they send people away. These aren't rumors." He looks fearfully at the room's walls, as if he's afraid someone's listening to us. "My brother sends people away too. He's a man of power, but even he mustn't know who I am. They don't have mercy on anyone," he adds.

"Sorry... I'm sorry... thank you..." I tell him, leaving his suffocating office.

On the way to the workshop I try to cry, but the cold wind freezes my tears before they can fall. Why did I convince Frau Schneider to travel east?

I grip the cold door handle and enter the workshop. I stand in the hall, looking at the women working with their backs to me. The important thing is that there are women for whom I managed to obtain work permits. The important thing is that we're managing to save some of those women.

A few days later, I enter the workshop in the morning, holding the newspaper in my hand.

"Clara," the work supervisor approaches me with a worried expression, "two women didn't come to work today. They took them."

"Who took them?" I ask, though I know the answer.

"The Nazis. They took them. The other girls told me," she quietly says. "They didn't give them time to organize, didn't notify them in advance. They simply came to their building and took them out," she tells me, and I see the fear in her eyes. The yellow patch embroidered on her wool dress seems to glow like a target.

"But they have work permits, they're valid," I tell her.

"That didn't matter to them. One of the girls told me, she lives in a neighboring building. They simply took all the Jews in the building and escorted them outside, all of them, regardless of work permits."

"And where did they take them?"

"To the community building, the usual place. From there they take them to the train heading east."

"Does Mr. Weidner know about this?"

"Yes, he knows."

"I'll see what I can do," I answer as I enter Mr. Weidner's office. Suddenly the newspaper I'm placing on his desk seems utterly insignificant.

"Good morning, Clara," he tells me in a tired voice, "did you hear the news?"

"About our workers?" I ask, sitting in the chair facing him.

"It's getting worse," he quietly says, interlacing his fingers like a man in prayer. "They're closing in on them."

"Maybe we can try to get them back from the transport east," I tell him, though the words sound hollow even as I speak them. "Maybe it's a mistake. They have the documents. Maybe we can free them, I can go to them."

"We won't succeed," he quietly tells me. "They're too strong. Everyone in this city is afraid of them. We can only try to delay the end and act quietly, like mice. To look for places where they can hide."

"I want to try, sir. Maybe we can get them back." The words come out with more conviction than I feel.

"You're a brave woman, Clara," he smiles at me tiredly, "not like all the other people in this city."

On the tram on the way to Gestapo Headquarters, I tightly grip my purse with the work permits, trying to think of something to say to the clerk. Why did they take them despite them having work permits?

"Department IV B4, second floor, left side," the clerk at the building entrance tells me indifferently as he returns my ID card.

"Room Four, you can enter," the secretary at the Department of Jewish Affairs tells me, and I rise from the wooden bench where I've waited for the past hour. I approach the door, knocking gently.

"Yes?" asks the man behind the wooden desk.

"Sir," I tell him, introducing myself and my workplace, "we are a workplace that supports the Reich's war effort. We employ filthy Jewish workers who will help the Reich, and despite this, you ordered two of them to stop working, even though they have permits. You took them to the Jewish community building," I tell him without stopping, the words tumbling out in desperate haste. "They are essential workers, they're the only ones who know how to operate the machines they work on."

"Frau Berger, what is this department?" he smiles at me politely while lifting the pencil lying on the desk and holding it between his fingers.

"The Department of Jewish Affairs," I answer, confused by the obvious question.

"Exactly," he quietly answers, "this is the Department of Jewish Affairs for the entire Third Reich. And this is the department that will handle all Jews," he begins speaking in a louder voice, each word carefully enunciated. "I decide how many food rations they receive each month, and I decide the size of the yellow patch they wear." He raises his voice even more, his face beginning to redden with controlled fury. "And they'll wear three yellow badges rather than one if I want them to, they'll only walk on the road rather than the sidewalk if I want them to. And if I decide to send two women to the east, they'll go to the train and board it. And no one," he continues speaking angrily, his face red and his eyes fixed on me, "no one, not someone from the Wehrmacht who thinks they're essential, not a policeman, and certainly not a secretary, will come here to complain and try to change my decision!" He screams with rage and crushes the pencil he's holding between his fingers, the sharp crack echoing like a gunshot in the small room. "Do you understand, Frau Berger?"

"Yes, sir," I answer in a trembling voice.

"Have a pleasant rest of your day, Frau Berger," he returns to the calm demeanor he had when he received me, taking a pencil out of his desk drawer and continuing to fill out the form, ignoring the pencil fragments scattered on the desk.

"Thank you, sir," I manage to say as I rise, hurrying to leave the building.

Outside the building, I walk quickly; I must get away from this place. The echoes of the clerk's voice and the sound of the broken pencil still reverberate in my ears like thunder. From time to time I turn around fearfully; could he have recorded my name as being dangerous to the Third Reich? Will they follow me? I have trouble breathing, and despite the warm sun I feel sweat on my back. But the street in front of Gestapo Headquarters is empty, with only two black cars parked in front of it like sleeping predators. It's as if all the people of this city are afraid to pass in front of the swastika flags that fly over the building's façade.

On the tram, I almost press my face to the glass and look at the people walking in the streets beneath the swastika flags. The sharp black lines look to me like the claws of an ancient monster that will soon devour the people beneath it. Are they as afraid of the Nazis as I am? Do they also continue going to work day after day in silence, thinking this is just temporary and they need to wait, like Frau Schneider who disappeared and will never return?

I look at the people sitting around me on the tram. Would they be willing to do something for the Jews? What does the woman in the beige dress sitting on the other side of the aisle, who isn't smiling, think about the Jews? If I tried to help them and she discovered it, would she inform on me to the Gestapo? And what about the man in the suit sitting in front of her, reading a newspaper?

Three workers in overalls board the tram, smelling of sweat and diesel, and I look out the window again and see that I've missed my station by two stops. I get off at the next station and wait for a tram to take me back. The dress sticks to my sweating back. I'm afraid to do this.

But at the workshop, I enter Mr. Weidner's office and tell him, despite my fear: "If there are other ways to help besides going to Gestapo offices, I want to help. I want to find places to hide mice in."

The next day, I walk through the Wilmersdorf neighbor-hood in the western part of the city, searching for the ad-dress I keep repeating in my memory like a prayer. The quiet streets frighten me: everything is so peaceful, yet I feel tension throughout my entire body, as if the very air is charged with danger. When I reach the address, I climb up to the apartment on the second floor and knock on the door. I have no idea who will open it for me.

"Yes, madam?" A man of about fifty opens the door for me. He's dressed in tailored pants and a white button-down shirt.

"They told me to give you this," I hand him a sealed brown paper envelope with nothing written on it.

"Thank you, madam. Good day," he tells me as he shuts the door in my face. I turn around and return to the workshop, my footsteps echoing in the empty stairwell. I have no idea what was in the envelope or whether Mr. Weidner is testing me, but I want to help.

Three days later, I deliver another envelope with ration booklets and money to another address in the north of the city. I don't know how much I'm helping; another worker didn't come to work because they took her and her family to the hall where they gather Jews, despite her having a work permit.

A week later, I enter the workshop office while holding the morning paper. To my surprise, there's a young woman in the office, sitting in a chair facing Mr. Weidner. She's about thirty, wearing a simple green summer dress. When I open the door, she turns and looks at me, her brown hair gathered carefully. I examine her with growing curiosity. There's no yellow badge on her dress.

"Clara," Mr. Weidner tells me, "this is Frau Fischer."

"Very nice to meet you," I tell her, and she rises toward me, extends her hand and shakes mine, but doesn't say a word.

"Frau Fischer is not from Berlin, and I need your help to take her to this address," he tells me, showing me a handwritten note.

"Welcome to Berlin. Where are you from?" I ask her.

She remains silent and looks at me in confusion, but Mr. Weidner answers for her: "From southern Germany. She needs to reach her family, at the address in the note."

"Certainly," I tell him, continuing to look at the woman. Her brown shoes are simple and slightly torn, and her handbag is made of cracked and worn leather. I offered to help, and it doesn't matter who she is. "Shall we go?" I turn to her and leave the room, and she follows me in silence like a shadow.

We silently walk down the crowded street, passing through the main avenue. I walk quickly, and she adjusts her pace to match mine. Although we're no different from any woman on the street, every man who passes and examines us seems suspicious to me, as if our guilt is written across our faces.

"Come this way," I tell her, turning onto one of the side streets. It's quieter here, and only the sound of our footsteps can be heard on the sidewalk. A few shops are open between the walls of the aging buildings, but they're almost empty. We're not far now, but suddenly I notice several people standing in a small square, at a safe distance from an open military truck with a small Nazi flag flying on a small pole above the front headlight. I continue walking, we can't stop, but Frau Fischer halts in her tracks.

"Come on, it's alright," I tell her, though I'm also afraid. But she looks at me with frightened eyes that seem to see something I'm missing. "Come, you're with me," I tell her, feeling a wave of cold throughout my body. They could suspect us and ask to see our documents if we stop. What if she doesn't have documents?

She begins walking slowly beside me, trying to stay upright as we approach the people in the square and the truck. We must not arouse suspicion.

The men stand at a safe distance from the truck, but two Gestapo men in black coats stand by the building's front door, one of them holding a notebook like a ledger of the damned.

We're already close to the truck, whose rear section is open. A woman emerges from the building. She's very thin, and barely manages to carry a heavy suitcase. Behind her come two children, a girl and boy, about seven and five years old, holding hands with the desperate grip of siblings. The smaller child is clutching a rag doll in his hand. A man follows, dressed in an old brown suit and hat, with another Gestapo officer behind him.

"Rosenberg family, four souls," the Gestapo man says as if talking to himself, writing something in his list.

"Keep walking, don't look at them," I whisper to Frau Fischer.

The Gestapo man holding the notebook raises his gaze and examines us for a moment, surveying us. My entire body is tense, but I continue looking ahead with an indifferent gaze, fighting the urge to grab Frau Fischer's arm as she slowly walks beside me.

"I left a key with you, in the mailbox," the woman quietly says to one of the men standing on the sidewalk.

"Come on, up, we don't have all day," the policeman tells her, giving her a light push toward the truck. Just a few more steps, and we'll pass by the truck and this scene.

I still manage to see the man give the woman his hand and help her climb into the back of the truck. Then he grabs the child, lifts him up, and hands him to the woman. She extends her arms and hugs him tightly.

At the end of the street, I turn again onto the main avenue. It's safer here, trying to disappear among the people who continue their daily lives as if nothing extraordinary is happening just a few streets away.

In the evening, when I return to the apartment after bringing Frau Fischer to the correct address, I check the mailbox. But no letter has arrived. I climb the stairs, wish my neighbor a quiet night and enter the apartment, preparing myself an evening meal.

Before sleep, I play cards alone by the light of a candle. From time to time I look at Hermann's photograph, and beside it the photograph of Frau Schneider's dead son that I placed on the sideboard. Both look at me with serious gazes from within the black and white photographs, their eyes seeming to judge me. Would they be proud of me for what I did today, or would they tell me I'm risking too much?

"Thank you for your help, Clara. Frau Fischer reached her relatives successfully," Mr. Weidner tells me a few days later at the end of the workday.

I wonder whether to ask him who she was, whether her last name was really Fischer, but I stop myself. It's better that I not know everything. The important thing is that I'm helping.

"What about all the women here? What will happen to them?" I ask.

"They'll take them all in the end. We won't be able to stop it. Maybe we'll manage to find a corner for some to hide in, with a new identity. In the end, Clara, they'll defeat us. They're too strong." He looks at me sadly.

"What about the Russians? The Americans?" They've joined the war, after all.

"Do you think they'll succeed in defeating the Wehrmacht? Do you think they'll succeed in stopping the Nazis?" He places his hand on the newspaper, which reports that the German Army is again fighting heroically against the Russians.

I don't answer, and accompany him as he takes his brown leather briefcase and we both leave the office.

Mr. Weidner approaches the work supervisor and gives her the envelopes containing the salaries of all the workers. They rise from their places, turn off their machines, and approach the work supervisor. I watch the twins Marlene and Annemarie, the youngest of all the remaining workers. They always stand at the end of the line.

One by one the workers extend their hands, receive the money, approach the workshop door and go out into the street.

"Thank you," Marlene tells the work supervisor as she takes both their money and puts it in her purse, and both exit the workshop. Where do they sleep at night, after they took their mother away and sent her east?

I hurry to go out after them, seeing them walk close to the building wall as if trying to be absorbed and disappear, to become invisible.

"Annemarie, Marlene," I call to them as I walk toward them.

"Yes, Frau Berger?" Marlene answers as both turn around and face me.

"I wanted to ask," I stand there, facing them, "do you have somewhere to stay?"

"Thank you, Frau Berger, we manage," Marlene answers while Annemarie looks at me through her thick glasses.

"What do you mean? Do you have a home to go to?"

"No..." she answers, confused, "but we manage."

"So what do you do?"

"We walk around on the streets," she answers.

"It's nice outside now, it's summer," Annemarie adds. "It was harder in winter."

"And where do you sleep?"

"Sometimes in parks, if it doesn't rain," Marlene answers, "or in the changing rooms of clubs, those that are still open. Sometimes the owners agree in exchange for payment, even though we have..." She touches her dress where the yellow badge is. "They agree for money."

"Or public restrooms, there's no one there at night," Annemarie adds.

"We're fine, Frau Berger, we're like U-Boats," Marlene smiles at me.

"I don't understand," I tell her. They seem so young to me. How do they manage to get by alone?

"The U-Boats," she explains again, "the navy's submarines, the Kriegsmarine. We're like them: we try to disappear so they don't see us until morning, and then we return to work."

I continue to look at them, surprised that they're using a military term that doesn't suit 19-year-old young women. But maybe this whole war and the Gestapo chasing them shouldn't be happening to 19-year-old young women. "And they've never caught you?"

"Two policemen once found us sleeping at night on a garden bench," Annemarie tells me, "but we managed to convince them our house was destroyed in a bombing, and that we're essential workers."

"We had the documents you brought us," Marlene tells me with a smile.

"But don't worry, Frau Berger, we manage," Annemarie tells me, "and after that night, we make sure one of us is always awake, so we can escape if someone's coming."

I look at them for another moment, at their stance trying to project self-confidence. "See you tomorrow," I finally tell them, "take care of yourselves."

"Thank you, Frau Berger, see you tomorrow," they answer and turn around, beginning to walk, and after a moment they disappear among the people, as if they were submarines that have disappeared and will resurface tomorrow.

As evening approaches, I slowly climb the wooden stairs of my mother's building, the thin fabric purse hanging on my arm. My feet hurt after standing in line for almost two hours to receive the egg ration that didn't arrive in the end.

Frau Vogel stands on the second floor, shaking out a small rug. She raises her gaze as I approach, her sharp face looking at me. "Hard day, Frau Berger?" she quietly asks.

"Same as yesterday," I answer politely. I don't want to talk to her. Everything I tell her, she'll pass along.

"There are those who know how to manage," she whispers, looking at the Koch family's door. She smells of sour sweat and simple soap.

"We're all trying to manage," I answer.

"But they manage better. Their father arranged good positions for his sons. You surely know about the eldest son," she continues whispering, "but do you know that he also arranged for his younger son to work at City Hall?"

"Yes, I know. Mother told me years ago."

"And what about you? What about your work? Are you still working in the city at the workshop? Sometimes I ask your mother, but she doesn't tell me much," she continues asking, while looking at me with big owlish eyes.

"Everything's the same with me," I answer, and suddenly I hate her so much. For her treatment of Frau Schneider, for all the things she heard and passed on to Walter. For all the pieces of gossip she collects like a squirrel gathering nuts for winter, waiting to trade them for something better.

"And do you have enough money? Don't you need to trade on the black market?"

"Trading on the black market is illegal, you know that. We all need to support the Reich," I answer loudly, as if expecting that if someone's listening to us from behind the Koch family's door, he'll hear my words.

"You know..." she whispers, "at first I supported them, I even wore a pin with the Party symbol, but now they say the army is going to lose in Russia, and that the Führer will bring disaster upon us. All we'll have left in the end is lines for bread and butter, and British bombs. Did you hear that the Americans are also starting to bomb us?"

"Those are just rumors, Frau Vogel. We mustn't believe them. We must continue believing in the Führer. Good day," I answer, trying to control my hatred, continuing to climb the stairs to the third floor.

Frau Schneider's apartment door looks at me accusingly, and I turn my back to it and hurry to enter my mother's apartment, closing the door behind me and leaning on it for a moment as if I've reached safe shores.

Then I approach her in the kitchen, unload the groceries on the table, sit quietly and begin cutting potatoes.

"You're not talking much," Mother tells me after a while.

"There's not much to talk about. Every day is the same," I answer.

"Have you heard from him?"

"No," I reply, no longer sure who she means. Is she asking about my husband, Hermann? Or perhaps she's referring to Frau Schneider? Or maybe she means the war itself – the endless radio broadcasts reporting victories no one believes anymore.

"New neighbors have arrived," she says after a while.

"In her apartment?"

"Yes," she nods, "the widow of a military man from Düsseldorf. Her house was destroyed in a bombing, so they housed her here," she says.

"Alone?"

"No, she has two children, a son and daughter."

"I thought Mr. Koch's son wanted the apartment for himself," I quietly say, feeling nauseous that we're talking so indifferently about Frau Schneider's apartment.

"Her husband was apparently an officer of high rank, higher than Walter's influence. But Walter made sure to take all the valuable paintings out of there. Those expensive paintings now decorate the walls of his apartment. Believe me, he didn't care about the apartment, he wanted the paintings, they were worth a lot of money."

"How do you know all this? Did Frau Vogel tell you?"

"I live here, Clara. I don't need Frau Vogel to know what's happening with my neighbors."

"I'm sorry," I place my fingers on her old hand.

"Did you hear anything from her?"

"No," I tell her. I can't tell her about the visit to Bruno Koch at City Hall.

"She was a good woman," she sighs. "She's probably well in the east."

"Yes," I answer, though neither of us believe it.

"Walter surely knows where they sent her."

"Yes, he surely knows," I answer. He's one of them. I could turn to him for more information, but I'm afraid of him and the price he'd want in exchange. I also know she won't return, and that I accompanied her to the transport.

Two months later, they arrive in their long leather coats, the black ravens who bring the transports. They enter the office and stand at the door. "Mr. Weidner," the shorter one says, holding a notebook, "your workers' permits are canceled."

"Sir," Mr. Weidner tells them while rising from his chair, "we're an essential factory. The Wehrmacht needs our production. Our workers are professional and essential."

"Your workers are moving east. From now on, if you want to employ workers, you can employ racially pure Aryan workers. We can also provide you with a cheap labor force of forced Polish workers. You're welcome to contact the appropriate department at Gestapo Headquarters tomorrow," he answers indifferently, closing the notebook as they both leave the office.

Mr. Weidner and I hurry to leave the office after them. All the women in the workshop stand facing them in a straight line, the yellow patches on their dresses prominent in their bright color.

"The work permits," the taller of the two says to the supervisor, and she hurries among the women, taking the permits that grant them the right to food rations and protection from deportation.

"Here," she hands them to him.

"Yours too," he tells her, his leather-gloved hand holding the signed papers.

She hurries to take out her work permit and place it among the others he's holding, careful not to touch his black-gloved hand.

"Tomorrow morning, at 8 o'clock, you must all be at the collection point at the Jewish community offices. One suitcase per person," he says, and both leave the workshop, slamming the iron door behind them.

Mr. Weidner moves among the workers, pays them their salaries, and whispers a few words to each one. One by one they quietly approach the entrance, take their coats and disappear through the workshop door.

I watch the twins, who remain last as usual.

"Thank you, Frau Berger," they tell me as they approach the door, take their coats, and exit. I look at the closed door. What will their fate be?

"Marlene, Annemarie," I shout as I hurry to leave the workshop, searching for them before they can disappear among the passersby on the street, submerging and vanishing forever.

Chapter Nineteen

The Twins

"Come with me," I tell them.

"Where to, Frau Berger?" Marlene asks, standing close to her sister as if trying to protect her.

"Just come," I tell them, and begin walking home. I don't know what I'm planning to do, but they no longer have work permits. I can't leave them on the street.

I walk quickly, and they walk with me, making sure to stay slightly behind me. Two strange women in blue dresses approach us and look me over. Do they suspect that I'm with Jews and want to hide them? It seems to me that my thoughts are laid bare before every man and woman who pass us by.

I look around, searching for more people on the street with yellow patches, but I can't find any. There were always a few, walking with lowered gazes close to building walls, but now I can't even see one. Have they already taken them all?

A wave of fear washes over me, an unclear fear, and I turn from the main street into one of the alleys, even though this lengthens the route. If we meet policemen or the men in black coats here, we'll stand out more. Still, I feel safer in the quiet alleys, as if the building walls are protecting us.

"Follow me," I tell them when we reach the building, leading them into the inner courtyard. "Wait for me here," I add.

Both nod their heads and press against the inner wall.

I climb the stairs, see that there are no neighbors in the stairwell, and come down to them. "Come," I quietly tell them, "if we see anyone, you're my mother's relatives from Munich."

They nod their heads again, and the three of us climb the stairs.

Only when I bring them into the apartment and close the door behind me, locking it and closing the bolt, do I understand what I've done.

They look at me in confusion, expecting me to tell them what to do, even though I have no idea what I need to do now.

"Are you planning to go to the pickup point tomorrow?" I ask while the three of us stand close to each other in the apartment's front hallway. I can still send them outside, or host them for just one night.

Both shake their heads.

"No one writes back from the east," Annemarie answers, looking at me through her glasses. "From the east, only terrible rumors come."

"And what will you do?"

"We'll manage, Frau Berger. We have no other choice," Marlene tells me.

"You have yellow badges. They'll catch you."

"Do you know what the punishment is for a Jew they catch without a yellow badge?" one of them answers. I look at the yellow badges embroidered on their coats, and at the old torn leather shoes they wear. I'm afraid of what I'm about to do.

"Give me your coats," I tell them, extending my hand.

They take off their coats and give them to me, but instead of hanging them on the coat rack at the entrance, I take them with me to the kitchen and place them on the wooden table. To my surprise, they're still standing by the front door.

"Come," I call to them, and they enter with hesitant steps, looking around.

"Sit," I tell them as I go to the bedroom, taking the sewing box down from the closet where I keep my Hermann's letters. I take out a seam ripper and return to the small kitchen. "Should I remove them?" I ask while holding the seam ripper before them.

They look at each other, then return my gaze and nod.

I gently begin ripping out the yellow badges, slowly freeing them from the coats. I'm very tense; I have a feeling there will be a knock at the door any moment, and police or Gestapo will arrest all of us.

After a few minutes, the yellow badges lie between us on the wooden table.

"And now the dresses," I tell them.

They rise quietly and undress, remaining standing only in old, slightly torn white cotton undershirts and simple underwear. Their delicate fingers place the dresses on the wooden table before me. Then they cover themselves with their hands while watching me rip the yellow badges out of the dresses, until they too lie between us on the table.

"It's done." I hand them back the dresses, and they put them on again. Suddenly they look like regular young women on the street, without the very identifiable yellow stain on their clothes. "What about your documents?"

Both take out their cardboard identity cards, with the letter 'J' stamped on them in prominent red.

"What will you do with all this?" Marlene asks.

"I think we have to burn it," I quietly tell them.

"Mother embroidered the yellow badge for me," Annemarie whispers, and I see a tear rolling down her cheek.

"Burn it," Marlene tells me, placing her hand on her sister's.

"Alright..." I quietly say I rise from my place, take a candle out of the wooden drawer in the kitchen, place it on a ceramic plate in the center of the table, and light it with a match. I burn the yellow badges, one after another, followed by the documents. The three of us silently watch as the flames consume them. There's no way back now.

"Stay here for now," I tell them. "Did you eat anything today?"

"No," they shake their heads.

"Are you hungry?"

"Yes," they nod.

"Wait for me here. I'll return later. Don't open the door for anyone," I tell them as I rise from the table, go to the bedroom closet and remove the silver menorah Frau Schneider gave me. Their fate will not be like hers.

I walk down the street, gripping my purse tightly, placing my hand over it to protect it. From time to time I look around; the sun will set soon, and the sky is already gray. There are fewer people in the street, as if preparing for the darkness and shadows that will come at any moment. I turn and descend the stone steps in the narrow side alley near the train station, beneath the bridge where the railway tracks pass. It's too dangerous to try exchanging goods at the train station, especially the goods I want to exchange.

The stone steps descending to the abandoned space are full of moss, and wet from the rain that fell earlier. Above us, low iron arches stretch out, supporting the railway tracks like the ribs of an ancient giant beast. Several lightbulbs hang around on exposed iron wires, illuminating the shadows of people on the walls like black dancing figures. Here, in the world beneath the city, you can get everything that can't be obtained in the long lines at the empty-shelved shops on the streets.

People stand close to the basement walls, enveloped in the sharp smell of cheap tobacco, vinegar, sweat and moldy sausage. At their feet lies merchandise wrapped in blankets or packed in canvas bags.

I slowly walk among the people, gripping my purse tightly.

"Real cigarettes, quality tobacco," a boy whispers to me. He's about nine or ten, wearing short pants and a jacket that's too big for him.

An old man sits by the wall, and on the basement stones in front of him lie several fountain pens on cardboard, arranged in a row. Two elderly women stand beside him, holding sausage wrapped in newspaper. I continue walking until I stop in front of a large man behind a small wooden table with two candlesticks placed on it.

"Are you buying or are you getting out of here?" he asks me angrily. He has a broken tooth.

I reach in and take out the menorah wrapped in a scarf, slowly removing the covering. It sparkles in the dim yellow light like a lighthouse shining in the darkness. "Will you buy this?" I ask.

"Beautiful," the large man tells me, his eyes gleaming. "This is Judenstück, eh?"

I stand before him silently.

"What do you want for it?" He reaches out and feels it, but I continue holding it tightly.

"Four hundred Reichsmarks."

He laughs. "You'll only get four hundred for it if you bring two pigs with it. One hundred. I won't pay more."

I stand before him, quiet. I need more than that, I have nothing else to trade except the menorah.

He leans closer to me. "Listen... there won't be any of them left at all soon. Hitler is cleaning out the country once and for all. And all their gold, silver, houses... everything will return to us. But if you know how to get their property, you'll probably know how to get more."

I don't answer. I think of Frau Schneider, who would light candles in this menorah, and feel nauseous, but I remain silent.

"One hundred thirty Reichsmarks, and that's only out of pity, yes?"

"Two hundred Reichsmarks," I answer.

"One hundred fifty, you won't get more."

"One hundred fifty, and I need something else."

"What?" He looks at me, his broken tooth like a hole decorating his mouth.

"I need forged identity cards," I whisper.

He laughs mockingly. "A poor-quality document costs two thousand Reichsmarks. If you want one that will pass Gestapo inspection, you'll need to bring me five thousand, not a menorah you stole. One hundred fifty, and go bring a lot more money."

"Give me the money," I tell him, extending my hand.

He takes the bills from his pants pocket and places them in my hand, and I hand him the menorah.

"Beautiful," he says to himself while holding it. He spits on it, and rubs the saliva with a piece of cloth he took from his pants pocket. I turn around and move away from him, fighting the tears in my eyes. At least this menorah will serve a good purpose. I continue moving among the sellers, and buy food for the twins. I buy the cheapest things, so the money will last a long time.

Up on the street, the sun has almost set. I turn into an alley outside the train station, and then I see her.

She's standing under an unlit streetlamp, leaning against it. Her hair is braided carelessly, her coat too short. She holds a cigarette between her fingers. So many years have passed since I last saw her, when she lived with Mother, when we went to the club together, but I'm almost certain it's her.

"Anna?" I call to her.

She turns around and examines me. Her eyes widen, as if she recognizes me, but after a moment she turns and disappears into one of the dark openings, as if she never existed.

I remain standing there for another moment, but then I continue on my way to the apartment. The twins are waiting for me alone there.

Before I enter the apartment, I stand in the hallway and press my ear to the door, waiting to hear voices. It's possible that someone from the police followed me and is waiting for me inside. I remain standing in the dark hallway, listening. After several minutes of quiet, I open the door with the key and enter.

They sit in the darkness on chairs in the kitchen, in the same place where I left them a few hours ago. I light a candle and walk through the house, making sure the black curtains cover the windows well. Then I turn on the weak lamp in the kitchen. The whole time, they follow me with their gazes.

"I brought you food." I take the bread, potatoes and butter out of my purse, and the three of us prepare the food together. They follow me with their eyes and do what I ask of them. It feels strange to eat with them like this; I'm used to living only with Mother or with Hermann, and suddenly it's as if I have two more young women who could have been my daughters.

Later they wash up in the tin bathtub in the washing corner, while I spread a blanket for them on the bedroom floor. Their quiet movements remind me how young they are, how careful they've learned to be.

"Good night, Frau Berger," they tell me when they lie down to sleep and I turn off the light.

"Good night, Marlene, Annemarie," I tell them, feeling as if I'm responsible for them. I need to remind myself that I'm not their mother. They're here only for one night, and tomorrow I'll think of what to do with them.

But the next day, when I get ready for work, I tell them to stay until evening, and then we'll see.

Several German women sent by the Reich's labor office arrive at the workshop. They enter the office one by one and proudly present their identity cards, which aren't stained with the red letter J. One by one I show them the work stations, remembering the names of the women who worked there until yesterday, wondering what would become of them, and whether they were taken east on the transport that left today. Their eager faces contrast sharply with the fearful expressions I'm used to seeing.

At the end of the day, I buy food for the three of us. I'll let them stay with me for another day, and tomorrow we'll see.

Two weeks later, I again stop on the way home to buy them food. Again it seems to me that I see Anna standing in one of the alleys. Between the boy who sells cigarettes and the large man behind the wobbling wooden table, I exchange a little bread and cabbage for the last bills I have left. I'll need to divide the food I buy with rations into three portions from now on.

Every night they lie down on the blanket spread on the floor and wish me good night, and every night I wish them good night and decide that tomorrow I'll watch over them too. Every night I feel more like their mother. And every night I decide that the photograph of my husband and Frau Schneider's dead son looking at me from the sideboard are the ones watching over us.

The siren's scream wakes me in a panic, and I sit up in bed completely tense. They're coming again. I get out of bed and turn on the light, and I see Marlene and Annemarie looking at me, expecting me to tell them what to do. I look around, searching for a solution while the sirens outside continue wailing without end. They can't come down to the basement with me, they must stay here.

"Quick, under the bed, hide, I'll be back," I whisper to them. They bend down and hurry to squeeze under my bed. I put on my shoes, rush to the door and put on my coat, turning off the light and going to the stairwell. For a moment I stand and regulate my breathing. The apartment is empty, there's no one inside, it's just me in the building.

"Come on, hurry," I hear the voice of the building's basement supervisor from below, mixed with the sounds of people going down the stairs and the crying sounds of a baby. "Come on, the planes are coming," I hear him again, hurrying down toward his flashlight, which glows like a small star in the darkness. From above I hear them, like the slow growl of a large, angry dog before it starts barking and attacking.

In the basement, filled with people, I walk by the light of the flashlight and sit on a wooden bench close to the wall, beside the neighbor from the first floor. Everyone has their permanent place by now, where they sat the first time we came here over a year ago. Like the permanent places, the smell also remains constant: dust, mold and fear. But the smell of fear has grown stronger in the past year.

The neighbor from the first floor holds his fedora in his hands, his fingers crushing it so hard that it almost loses its shape. The woman sitting across from me tries to calm her baby by singing a quiet lullaby, but he refuses to stop crying. Another woman sits across from me wrapped in a blanket, eyes closed, whispering something to herself that I can't understand. And above everything, the growl of the angry engines in the sky grows stronger, and then I begin to hear the rattle: the incessant rattle of anti-aircraft gun batteries, shooting like the clicking hooves of a herd of horses ceaselessly running on cobblestones, more and more, joined by the sound of explosions. At first it's a muffled sound, almost inaudible, but it grows stronger like drums in a military parade, slowly approaching.

"It's the Americans, you can tell by the engine noise," says a man slightly older than me wearing a light button-down shirt. He lives on the second floor.

"Shoot them down already, why don't they shoot them down?" his wife angrily says, hurling the words into the compressed basement space and lighting herself a cigarette, inhaling from it with nervous movements.

Her husband tries to explain to her, telling her something about darkness and nighttime, and how our fighter planes can't identify the enemy bombers, and searchlights, but I don't hear his voice, I only see his lips moving constantly in the weak yellow lamplight that scatters black shadows on the walls. My eyes focus on the tip of the woman's cigarette as it lights up every few seconds. I feel tension throughout my entire body. Now the sounds of explosions are like heavy hammer blows that can't be stopped. I grip the wooden bench with all my strength until my fingers hurt. The wooden beams in the basement ceiling shake, and a little dust falls on the back of my neck. *Please let them continue onward, please don't let them drop their bombs on our building.* Marlene and Annemarie are upstairs alone in the apartment. They're so alone. Outside, everything sounds like a confusing mix of sounds: the horse hooves of the cannons and the thundering drums of the bombs. The woman sitting across from me strokes her baby's head again and again, and kisses him constantly, and the man beside me says something about the Führer that I can't understand. What will happen to Marlene and Annemarie if a bomb hits the house? What about Mother? Did she go down to her building's basement? I lower my gaze and focus on the tips of my shoes, wanting to scream in fear, but I'm unable to do so. Only the wave of pain passing from my fingers as they grip the wooden bench assures me that I'm still alive. Another round of galloping horses, and another, in a rhythm that doesn't end. Finally they move away, slowly, and the drum sounds fade too. I've survived.

"The Jews finance the American bombers with their money," I think I hear the smoking woman whisper as she lights herself another cigarette. But no one answers, everyone sits quietly, and only the woman with the baby continues to gently stroke and kiss her son's head.

A long siren from outside makes my body tense again for a moment, but then it relaxes. The attack is over.

One by one, people get up and leave the basement, not even waiting for instructions from the building's defense supervisor to confirm that we can leave. I remain seated on the wooden bench, not knowing what to do, who to see first, Mother or the twins hiding in my home.

"It's over, Frau Berger," the defense supervisor tells me, shining his flashlight on me. I thank him and leave the basement, turning at the exit to the dark street and beginning to run. In the distance, between the black buildings, I see an orange glow, and hear screams and the sickening sound of burning fire. I must know that Mother is alright.

"She's alright, the fire is far away," I whisper to myself as I run breathlessly. The light from the fires is reflecting off the clouds in the sky, coloring the darkened streets a weak yellowish gray. Her house is fine, I know, these are distant fires.

I almost trip over brick fragments scattered in the street. Shouts from rescue teams come from one of the buildings, and flashlight beams flicker momentarily between broken walls. I hear glass under my feet, but I continue running, stopping only when I'm standing in front of her building. It's intact, standing in the dark, with fire and people's shouts coming from a building that was hit further down the street.

I run up to the third floor, breathing heavily as I open the door and call: "Mother."

"I'm here," I hear her, and approach the weak light in the kitchen. She sits by the table, playing cards by candlelight.

"Mother, are you alright?" I approach and hug her.

"They cut the electricity, so I had to light a candle. I think I'm fine," she answers quietly, placing another card on the table.

"There are fires outside," I tell her fearfully.

"Yes, they're getting closer," she answers while examining the cards in her hand. "What are you doing here?" She raises her gaze to me. "You don't need to worry about me so much."

"I'm your daughter." I sit beside her, even though I must return home to see the twins.

"I'm your mother. It should be the other way around, a mother should worry about her daughter."

"You always worried about me, I know."

"Do you want to play a game before you go home, fleeing the Führer's security guards as they make sure citizens don't wander around at night to see the damage he causes?" She places another card on the table, and smiles at me.

"I'll play with you tomorrow. I'll also bring more food tomorrow. Right now I'm tired." I place my hand on hers and say goodbye. I still need to evade the civilian patrol and get home.

I approach the door, but turn around and come back.

"What is it?" Mother raises her gaze from the cards and looks at me.

"I need to tell you something," I tell her, and sit in the chair facing her.

She says nothing, just continues holding the cards and looking at me, waiting for me to speak.

"For several days now, I've had two young women, nineteen years old, living in my house. They have nowhere to go," I quickly tell her before I regret it.

"Why don't they have anywhere to go?" she asks, her eyes examining me in the candlelight.

"They want to take them," I tell her quietly.

"Like Frau Schneider?"

"Yes…"

Mother is silent for a moment, places another card, and finally says: "I know you want to help the weak, Clara, but are you sure you want to do this?"

"Mother, do you remember when I was a child, and we slept in the same bed?" I ask. I must make her understand me. "I was so afraid, but I knew you were protecting me. They don't have a mother, they took her. They need someone to protect them."

"You're not their mother, Clara, you never will be," she tells me in her quiet voice. "When you were a child and slept with me in the same bed, I protected you from the monsters in fairy tales. But the monsters chasing them are real. They have black cars and black coats."

"Yes, I know. I'm not a child anymore, and they're not children either. Still, they need someone to hide them and keep them alive until the war ends."

"The war will never end. The monsters won't let it end, they love war. This isn't about protecting them for a day or two."

"I'm trying to get them forged identity cards. I'll succeed."

"You don't have enough money to get them such a thing. No one does."

"I'll manage, Mother. They're only with me for a few days."

"Do you know what they do to those they catch hiding Jews?"

"Yes, I know," I answer fearfully.

"You need to hurry and leave, so they don't catch you at night. You mustn't give them any reason to suspect you," she finally tells me.

"Thank you, Mother," I tell her, and hug her again. Even though she doesn't hug me back, it seems pleasant to her. "I promise I'll be careful," I tell her before leaving through the door.

Again I walk carefully through the streets, breathing easily when I return to the building. What would my fate have been if I'd been one of the twins, without identifying documents?

I quietly climb the stairs and open the apartment door in darkness, entering and closing it behind me. "Marlene, Annemarie," I walk through the dark apartment and whisper, "Marlene, Annemarie." The sound of glass comes from under my shoes. Is everything alright?

"We're here," I hear a whisper from the bedroom. "Don't turn on the light, the window shattered."

"Are you alright?" I ask.

"Yes, Frau Berger, we're fine. We were worried about you. Are you alright?"

"Yes, I'm fine," I answer, though I feel so exhausted. It's as if I've boarded a train traveling speedily toward a bridge that's about to collapse, and no one can stop the locomotive anymore. I also no longer have any idea who the enemy is, and who will help me. What will the Gestapo do to me? And what about the Americans who are bombing me? Maybe my neighbors, like Frau Vogel and the Koch family, are my enemies? "You can come out," I quietly say, walking into the bedroom in darkness. I can no longer get off this train, I must continue traveling to the bitter end.

They come out from under the bed, and the three of us make sure the black curtain is covering the broken window. Only then do I light a candle.

We sit around the kitchen table, even though I'm tired and I'm sure they are too. I can't sleep.

"Were you afraid when the bombs came close?" I finally ask.

"We played the game," Annemarie answers.

"What game?" I ask.

They hesitate for a moment, and Marlene finally says: "It's a game we started playing after they took Mother."

"When we slept alone outside, in a garden or public restrooms. But only when we were really afraid," Annemarie adds.

"Or when we were really hungry," Marlene says. "We would imagine what we'd eat after the war ends. How we'd go to the market and buy lots of food."

"And sausage," Annemarie adds.

"And Mother would return and make us a really big meal, like she used to for Friday evenings, before the Sabbath, when we were little."

"And that's how we'd pass the time until morning, in the game, imagining what that meal would be," Annemarie says.

I look at them and want to hug them, but I can't. They're not my daughters. They have a mother who disappeared in the east, and all three of us know what has probably happened to her, though they still believe she'll return.

Later, when we go to sleep, I lie in bed and open the letter Hermann wrote me so long ago, reading it by candlelight.

My beloved,

So much time has passed since we parted on the train station platform, and I don't know if it's been weeks, months or perhaps years. We were together during that leave, but I missed who we were so much, before everything began. Despite the distance, I never stop thinking of you on the long roads of Russia. I know life forces us to make difficult decisions, but these decisions are who we are, and they're what made me love your determination and your desire to help others without fear. I eagerly await my next leave, or for the war to end, so we can repair and return to being us.

Love, Hermann.

I go over the words by candlelight.

"Annemarie, Marlene, are you hungry?" I ask while folding the letter and carefully returning it to the envelope.

"A little, Frau Berger," Marlene answers, "but it's alright. We're used to it, it doesn't bother us."

I get out of bed, go to the pantry and take the sausage I saved for myself, dividing it in two and returning to the bedroom, and giving it to them. I never want to reach a point where I need to dream about food.

"Thank you, Frau Berger," they whisper.

"Is it alright if we smell it for now, and save it for when we're really hungry?"

"Yes, it's alright," I answer in the darkness, looking at the black ceiling. I'll go meet him tomorrow. I did it years ago, I know how to get money, I know how to do it. He was right, he knew I'd return to him for money. I'll make sure they have forged documents and food rations, and the three of us won't need to be so afraid. They won't be sent east like Frau Schneider. They won't need to save sausage and just smell it.

Chapter Twenty

U-Boats

Spring 1943

"He'll be here in a few minutes," I tell the twins a few days later. I'm tense.

"It's alright, Frau Berger, we're used to it," Marlene answers.

They're both standing by the door to the building's rear stairwell. They're dressed like other young German women in the city during wartime: simple dark dresses, old leather shoes, hair gathered with scarves on their heads, and no makeup.

"Remember to come back in about three hours. Enter the inner courtyard and look at the laundry hanging from my apartment. This is the shirt I'll hang on the line after he leaves." I show them a green shirt lying in the stainless steel bucket in the kitchen corner.

"Thank you, Frau Berger. We'll submerge for a few hours and return. Don't worry," Annemarie tells me. Marlene opens the back door and closes it behind them with a gentle thump.

I turn in a circle, making sure no sign remains of two other women living here. I hide the photograph of Frau Schneider's dead son, the one who watches over me, and place my husband's photograph on the chair beside the bed. Then I stand before the mirror and arrange my hair. If I had lipstick, I would apply it to my lips so he wouldn't notice the tension, and to create a protective layer between them and his body.

A few minutes after the time we set, there's a knock at the door. I approach and open it, looking at him. He's wearing the same suit he wore a few days ago, when I visited him at the Gestapo building and told him I'd changed my mind. He holds a bottle of schnapps in his hands, as if he comes to celebrate his victory.

I don't say a word, helping him remove his leather coat and hanging it behind the front door, letting him enter the apartment.

He doesn't speak to me, but places the bottle on the kitchen table, goes to the bedroom, sits on the bed and begins undressing.

Someone who isn't me lies on the bed and does everything she needs to do so he'll be satisfied, and will want to return to her again. Someone who isn't me doesn't feel nauseous, and doesn't hate herself for what she has to do to earn money from a man. And someone who isn't me whispers to herself that this will soon be over, that she's doing this for the children she doesn't have but so desperately wishes she had.

After everything is done, I get out of bed, go to the kitchen, bring the bottle of schnapps and pour some for him. He remains lying on the bed, his clothes placed on the chair beside it, on top of the overturned photograph of me and my husband.

"You know," he tells me, sweat still glistening on his chest, the half-full glass of schnapps in his right hand, "we've cleansed Berlin of Jews. A whole city without a single Jew. There are still a few in hiding, but we'll hunt them down. It's a real pleasure to hunt them," he says with a smile, while his eyes are closed.

I don't answer. I mustn't say anything. If I try to tell him I've become a Jew-hater, he'll suspect me.

"I have a whole network of spies searching for them," he continues speaking with a smile. "They hunt them throughout the city. I knew you'd come to me, even though you love them. People like you are weak, exactly like the Jews are weak."

"I'm not weak. I want money. Living in this city with Mother during wartime requires money, just like ten years ago during the great depression. I'm sure Frau Vogel tells you that too," I tell him.

"Yes," he says and smiles. "In the end, you always chose money. That's your weak point." He reaches for his pants, thrown on the chair beside the bed. Then he takes out his wallet, pulls several bills from it and places them on the bed. "I love identifying people's weak points. You're exactly like the Jews, you love money and are afraid of power. The last shipment was two weeks ago. A whole train, children, women, the elderly, almost no problems. They saw our black coats, entered the train cars like sheep, didn't even scream or resist. Goebbels announced to the Führer that Berlin is clean of Jews. My power definitely pays off." He sips from his glass, emptying it completely.

"I'll continue choosing the power of money," I tell him, trying to control my words.

"Maybe I'll send my friends to you too. They'd surely be happy to be in bed with the one who, despite loving Jews, now gives personal care to Gestapo men because she ran out of Jews to care for," he says and laughs. "They love to win too, exactly like me."

I fight the feeling of nausea and pour him more schnapps, forcing myself not to recoil as I run a finger over his shoulder. "And what do they do with Jews in the east?"

He thinks of his answer for a moment, then he places the schnapps glass on the floor, takes out a pack of cigarettes from his shirt pocket and lights one. "This is what we do with them," he says, blowing the cigarette smoke upward into the room.

After he leaves, I get out of bed, go to the washing corner and wash myself, scrubbing myself constantly with cold water and hard soap. Then I dress again, returning the photographs to their place, collecting the money and counting it. Every bill is a small measure of my body's revenge against him and the rest of the black-coated men he'll make sure come to me. When the money is hidden in the tin box in the kitchen, I hang the green shirt on the line, approach the back door facing the stairwell and open it. The stairwell is empty. Where are they now? Where were they hiding all this time when I was with him in the bedroom? I pour myself some of the schnapps and down it in one gulp. The burning pain in my throat mixes with the nausea from his hands and lips that touched this glass and me. I wipe the tears welling up in my eyes and place the glass in the sink. I have a goal, that's what matters. My body is just a tool to achieve that goal.

"May we enter?" Marlene whispers from the back door after a long time. I'm standing in the kitchen. By the yellowish light of the weak lamp, I slice three thin slices of bread and spread a thin, almost transparent layer of beet jam on them.

I don't answer and just nod my head, and they both slowly enter the small kitchen. The important thing is that they're alright.

"They closed the market early today," Marlene says as I place the plates on the table.

"So we went through Tiergarten and sat in the garden. It's almost empty all the time," Annemarie adds.

"So you sat there the whole time?" I ask, slowly nibbling my slice of bread.

"More or less There was a man in a blue work coverall who passed us by several times, so we got up and left."

"Then we tried to enter the cinema on Kurfürstendamm Street, just to sit in the lobby, not the hall, but the ticket seller looked at us too much, so we went outside and continued walking until it got dark," Marlene tells me, taking small bites of her bread.

"Be careful of train stations, and people who start asking you questions," I tell them, remembering Walter's words about Gestapo informants searching for fleeing Jews. I don't want to frighten them more than they already are.

"We're careful," Annemarie answers, looking at me through her thick glasses. "Marlene describes people who seem suspicious to her, and I need to remember them in case we encounter them again. I give them names so it'll be easy for me to remember." She gently touches the thin jam layer on the slice with her fingertips, and licks them.

"We make sure to be non-existent," Marlene adds.

Later that night, as I lie on the bed with them on the blanket spread on the floor, I look at the black ceiling and try to forget him. In a few days he'll come again, along with his friends.

"Tell me, Frau Berger," Annemarie asks in the darkness, "do you think the war will end one day, and we won't need to hide like this?"

"I'm sure the war will end soon. We've been at war for four years already, it must end soon," I whisper in the darkness, even though I know I'm lying to her and to myself.

In the following days, I slowly fill the tin box with money that comes from the leather wallets of strange men, and during this time Marlene and Annemarie continue to be non-existent. And after each passing day, I look at the black ceiling at night and wonder when one of us will make a mistake.

One afternoon a few weeks later, the three of us are sitting in the kitchen. I write the amounts of money in the cardboard notebook while Marlene delicately embroiders and fixes holes in stockings, and Annemarie peels potatoes. They'll need to go get ready soon. A man will arrive later. Suddenly there's a knock at the door. I close the notebook and look at them. They return looks of fear.

"Quickly," I whisper to them. There are still dirty dishes from lunch on the table. Everything must be cleaned. There's another knock at the door. Marlene quickly takes the dishes to the sink and begins washing them, and Annemarie gathers the potatoes and stockings, holding them while standing in the center of the kitchen, searching for something to do with them.

"Shhh..." I whisper to them, and they freeze in place. I approach the door and grasp the handle. No one must suspect that I don't live here alone.

"Good evening," the man at the door tells me, removing his fedora and holding it in his hand. "Have I arrived at the right place? I think I'm a bit early." He's wearing a light brown suit and black tie.

"Good evening. Could you give me two minutes to get ready? You're a bit early," I manage to tell him, my heart racing.

"I apologize," he answers as he steps back. "I'll certainly wait."

"Two minutes," I whisper to him with the most seductive smile I can manage, and close the door. What do we do now?

"Give me that, go get ready," I whisper to Annemarie, taking the bowl of potatoes and stockings from her and pushing them into an empty pot which I place on the stove. "You go too," I whisper to Marlene, who runs to the bedroom, coming out after a moment holding her shoes in her hands, followed by Annemarie. "Take care of yourselves, wait for the signal," I whisper to them as I close the back door behind them. I straighten up, arrange my hair with my fingers, and approach the front door.

"Please come in," I give him a big smile that hides my fear. "You've arrived right on time. I apologize for the delay."

After he leaves and I close the bolt, I go to the kitchen, take the potatoes and torn stockings out of the pot, and place them on the table again. Then I hang the green shirt on the line and wait for them. Soon the sun will set, and then they'll be in greater danger of being stopped by civilian defense teams who will ask to see their documents.

I try to count the money in the tin container, and can't manage it. I'm completely tense while thinking about them. Finally I get up, approach the back door and stand in the darkness, waiting until I hear them climb the stairs and enter the apartment. We've managed to get through another day.

Three months have passed since I was here last. I'd bought food in other places every other time, being careful not to return to the same place twice. I descend the stairs leading to that basement beneath the railway tracks. I'm not looking to buy food this time.

I quickly walk among the people, passing the boy trying to sell me cigarettes and reaching the man with the broken tooth who stands behind the wobbling wooden table.

"You were with me once," he tells me, looking at my hands which tightly grip my purse. "You sold me Jewish property," he adds, smiling with satisfaction.

"I need identity cards, two of them. I told you then," I quickly tell him.

"And I told you then that they're expensive and hard to obtain."

"Do you know how to get them?"

"I know how to get everything," he answers with a short laugh. "If you want a Luger pistol, a tank or a submarine, I can get you anything."

"I need good-quality identity cards for two women."

"People don't just lose identity cards. They can go to City Hall and report that their building was bombed and they've lost their documents. Why don't they do that?"

"That's not your business."

"Are they Jewish?" he leans toward me and whispers.

"That's not your business. Can you get them for me or not?"

"A good identity card costs five thousand Reichsmarks," he answers, continuing to examine me with his small eyes.

"I'll give you five thousand for both," I answer. I don't have that much money.

"Go to someone else, not to me."

"Six thousand, final price." I take some bills out of my purse and show him.

"Six thousand," he nods. "And only because you love trading in Jewish property, you probably get a commission from them," he tells me, laughing evilly.

"We're all traders, not just you," I answer, fighting the feeling of nausea.

"Go to this man, he'll photograph them, then come back to me with the photos and half the amount." He gives me an address and a person's name. "Tell him I sent you."

"What's your name?"

"Describe me to him, he'll know," he answers.

"And how do I know I can trust you?"

"You don't. If you want to trust someone, you're welcome to go to City Hall, they'll be happy to provide you with identity cards."

"I'll return in a few days," I answer, moving away from his stall and going to buy some food for the twins. I don't trust him, but I have no other choice.

After I finish, I leave the basement and begin walking home, moving away from the smells of cabbage, potatoes and moldy leather. The sun will set soon.

"I see someone's returned. She must have money to buy things here," I hear a voice from the alley and turn toward it, noticing Anna, the same Anna I'd tried to call to then. She'd run away from me.

She approaches me slowly, her worn shoes clicking on the sidewalk stones. A cigarette is stuck between her lips, smeared with dark red lipstick that looks like it was applied with an unsteady finger, rather than in front of a mirror. I try to look at her face, her hair that was once bright blonde and is now a lifeless shade of gray-yellow. She's wearing an old, tight green dress that reveals some of her thighs, with high gray wool stockings on her legs, torn in places.

"It's been a long time," I tell her.

"Yes, a long time," she smiles at me tiredly and takes the cigarette from her mouth, holding it between her fingers.

"You were working at the club then," I say, searching for something polite to say to her.

"Yes, I was young. I could work in clubs, earn well and lend dresses to friends," she says, inhaling from her cigarette. "It's harder to make a living when you get older."

"Yes..." I answer, lowering my gaze to her worn shoes with their mismatched laces.

"And what about you? What happened to you during those years? What about that man you knew then?" She inhales from the cigarette in her hands, blowing the smoke upward.

"He's my husband now," I smile awkwardly.

"One of us got a husband and the other didn't," she answers, playing with the lit cigarette between her fingers.

"He's in the army. He was drafted."

"What about your mother? Still in the same apartment?"

"Yes, like all of us, getting through the war," I answer, feeling uncomfortable with her questions.

"Yes, this war doesn't bring enough livelihood for women like me. People don't have money to spend on luxuries. What about children?"

"None," I shake my head sadly.

"Yes, I don't have any either." She throws the cigarette on the sidewalk and crushes it with her shoe. "It's better that way, fewer hungry mouths to worry about feeding."

"Have a pleasant evening. I was glad to talk," I tell her as I begin to move away.

"You know," she says, "I watch you from a distance, from my corner. A married woman like you doesn't need to come here, especially if she doesn't have a reason to exchange goods among all the rats wandering around here, selling stolen property."

"Everyone needs something. You live in Berlin just like I do," I answer carefully. What does she want from me?

"Don't look surprised," she tells me while taking out another cigarette and lighting it. "I'm not stupid, and I have eyes. Everyone who comes here has something to hide, and you surely have something to hide. People don't just approach the toothless man to talk, I saw you. On the other hand," she inhales from her cigarette, "I can always go to him and find out the reason. He's been looking at me for months, wanting me to be nice to him for a few minutes." She takes the cigarette out, holding it between her fingers.

"What do you want?" I angrily ask.

"I just want to talk," she smiles slightly, "and smoke my cigarette," she adds, her speech slow as if savoring every word, remembering those days when she was twenty and could control her life. "Or maybe I'll talk to someone who'd like to hear what I have to say. There are always those who like to listen, you know," she inhales from the cigarette again. "One of them once told me that women like me are the best communication network in Berlin, better than the telephone network." She blows out the smoke again and smiles at me.

"We've known each other for twenty years. I helped you then," I answer, thinking about Walter Koch. Does she know him?

"We knew each other twenty years ago, and I helped you in return. Maybe it's time you help me again. I'm always happy to receive five Reichsmarks without having to lift my dress," she examines me. "On the other hand, maybe it's time I get more curious about the reason you wander around here."

"I'm not doing anything illegal, certainly not like what you're doing. And all you needed was to ask, like you asked twenty years ago," I answer, taking out a five Reichsmark bill and placing it in her outstretched palm.

"So I've asked," she smiles at me and clutches the brown bill in her hand like a treasure, hiding it in the small purse hanging on her shoulder.

"Have a pleasant rest of the evening," I tell her, turning around and beginning to walk quickly.

"A pleasant rest of the evening to you; see you next time you come to visit my workplace," she tells me, but I don't turn around or answer her.

On my way to the apartment, I stop from time to time, hiding behind a parked car or freight cart on the side of the road and looking back, checking to see if she's following me. But I can't identify her, I only see men in suits and women in simple dresses hurrying home before the sun sets and we gather in that silent fear, waiting for the bombers to come.

My hand tightly grips my purse with the money in it. I was right to give her that amount. After all, we both work in the same profession, but I have a home, and I can't take risks, not now when I already have almost the entire amount I need.

"Meet me downstairs on the main street in a few minutes," I tell the twins the next day at noon as they exit through the back door. I close the door behind them, and exit through the main door, going down the stairs toward the street exit. "Good afternoon," I tell the smoking neighbor from the shelter as I exit into the main street. The sky is gray, and rain will soon fall.

The three of us walk among all the people on the main avenue, myself in front and them a few steps behind. In my mind, I repeat the name and address of the man who will photograph them for the forged documents.

I examine the people passing in front of me, the tram traveling down the center of the avenue, the military truck passing slowly with its canvas cover shut. But then I notice them.

There are four of them standing at the street corner beside a black car, talking with two people they've stopped for inspection. They wear black boots, and their peaked caps cover their eyes. I look around; two more policemen in blue uniforms stand on the other side of the street, with two more people in black coats and black boots behind them, questioning a woman. I must continue walking, I can't arouse suspicion, but I slow my steps. What's happening here? To my left, on the other side of the street, another man in a brown suit leans against a streetlamp, pretending to read a newspaper, but he's watching the people advancing toward the policemen and Gestapo at the end of the street. What can I do? I can't turn around, the man in the suit is watching and surveying me.

I look right and continue walking, slowly approaching the side of the sidewalk, but there's no alley we can turn into between the shops, only a bakery with a long line, a houseware store, and a cinema. I turn toward the cinema, pushing the glass door and entering the lobby. I hear the twins' footsteps behind me. I don't dare look back to check if any of the policemen suspect us and have entered after us.

The lobby is warm and dimly lit. There's a scent of tobacco and mold around us. A cashier about my age raises her eyes from behind the counter and surveys us with indifference.

"Three tickets, please," I tell her, taking a bill out of my purse.

The cashier points to the clock standing on the wall, covered with yellowish wallpaper. "The screening started a few minutes ago."

"It doesn't matter," I tell her. "We were delayed. We'll see the rest."

She shrugs and hands me the change and three pieces of paper that suddenly seem precious to me.

"Let's go inside," I tell the twins, and the three of us approach the elderly usher standing at the theater entrance in his dark blue uniform. We hand him the tickets and enter through the curtain into the darkness.

Inside, there's a smell of cigarette smoke and old velvet fabric. I feel like a fleeing animal with her two cubs, trying to blend in among the people sitting quietly and watching the black and white rectangle projected on the wall. We find empty seats near one of the back rows and sit, looking at the screen while the projector above us chatters with gentle, slow noise.

In the newsreel being shown, proud pilots run to their planes and take off to meet the enemy, while the announcer enthusiastically explains the victories against the Communists and the American air force. Then they show the Führer standing beside a large map, pointing at it while all the generals around him listen, standing upright without movement.

I look around at the people. Some nod in agreement with the announcer's words, and several even applaud. Only one woman on the other side of the row sits in darkness and doesn't nod in agreement. Has she lost someone in the war? Is she like me, waiting for a husband who has disappeared from her life for so long? Or maybe she's simply afraid of the endless war and the bombings that are getting closer, or of the Gestapo? The film begins, and the heroes on screen stand and talk to each other, they argue and reconcile and are happy, but to me they appear blurred and unclear like an approaching waterfall preparing to drown me, and I can't do anything to stop it. Every move I make only slightly delays the end, and I just want to rest a little.

"Frau Berger," I hear a whisper and raise my eyes, looking around. The lights in the theater have come on, and the people around me are getting up and leaving. "Frau Berger," Marlene quietly tells me, "the film is over."

We exit the hall, blending in with the audience and turning into the street. The people in black boots and black coats have disappeared. The man who was reading the newspaper is also gone. Only a woman in a short coat, her lips painted red, stands at the darkening street corner, talking with a man in a dark blue suit who stands with his back to us. The important thing is that they'll have forged documents in a few more days.

The knock at the door two days later surprises all three of us.

The twins look at me for only a split-second before they rise, quickly gather their belongings, and disappear through the back door as if they never existed. I stand for another moment, looking around, making sure no sign remains, rubbing my hands on my dress to dry the sweat. Then I take a deep breath and approach the door, opening it a crack and looking through it.

I open the door. She's standing before me in her thin coat and a dark blue headscarf. "I was starting to think you weren't home, I was getting ready to leave," Mother tells me while standing in the doorway. She's holding a small fabric basket. "I was at the grocery store, used my rations, and wanted to see how you were," she adds as she enters the apartment.

"You didn't need to come," I tell her, bringing her into the apartment. "There could be a bombing when you're outside, they're bombing during the day as well. You're not young anymore."

"No, I'm not young anymore. You're not young anymore either. None of us are young anymore with this war." She places her shopping basket on the kitchen table. "I brought salted fish and sugar, they received a shipment today and I assumed you were short. I even managed to buy two apples." She takes them out and places them on the table, looking around.

"Thank you, you really didn't need to. You need this food for yourself."

"Are they here?" she asks, continuing to look around, surveying the apartment with sharp eyes.

"Are you sure you want to know? Maybe it's better that you don't know."

"I already know. It's too late to hide it from me," she tells me as she enters my bedroom, examining it.

"When someone knocks on the door, they escape through the back entrance," I quietly tell her.

"And do they need to escape often?" she asks, bending down and looking at the blanket hidden under my bed.

"They need to escape. Does it matter how often they need to escape?"

"I'll wait," she answers. She leaves the bedroom again, goes to the kitchen and sits in the wooden chair.

I debate whether to try and convince her to give up. She's sitting upright in the chair, her chin raised while the groceries she brought lie on the table. It's better that she not be involved; if they catch us, it's better if she has no connection to this. But after a moment I give up and approach the back door, opening it slowly and whispering to them: "Come."

They enter, but when they see Mother they freeze in place, panicking as they stand at the entrance to the kitchen. Mother turns her gaze to them and slowly surveys them. "Sit," she finally tells them, and they approach and sit facing her.

"What are your names?" she asks them.

"Annemarie."

"Marlene."

"Where are you from?"

"From Berlin," Marlene answers.

"But we were born in the east, in Königsberg," Annemarie adds.

"And your father? Do you have one?"

"No father," they shake their heads.

"And your mother?"

"No," they again shake their heads, and I see hints of tears in their eyes.

"And where were you before you came here?"

They don't answer, just shrug their shoulders.

"Take these, they're for you," she hands them the two apples.

"Thank you, ma'am," they answer simultaneously as they hold the apples, gently caressing them as if they were precious jewelry.

"Eat, don't be embarrassed. You must be hungry," she tells them, and they gently bite the apples they hold as if trying to get used to their sweet-sour taste.

"Should I make myself tea? Do you want some?" She rises from the chair and approaches the stove, taking the kettle sitting there.

Later, after we've had tea and she's continued asking questions and they've answered her, she rises from the chair and approaches the door, and I accompany her.

She slowly puts on her coat and headscarf, her hands moving slowly, as if tired of the continuing war and of life.

"I won't ask you how long they need to hide, and what you do when they hide," she tells me.

"Please don't ask."

"They're good girls, Clara, but you're risking your life. I assume you know that."

"Yes, Mother," I whisper. "I know that."

"And you're not their mother."

"They don't have a mother."

"Still, you're not their mother."

"I know that, Mother."

"Good. Put a thicker blanket on the floor for them, it must be cold for them at night."

"Yes, Mother."

"And I'll try to see if I can bring more food."

"You need that food for yourself."

"They need it too, they're too thin," she tells me as she exits through the door, heading down the stairs. I follow her until the sound of her footsteps can no longer be heard in the stairwell, and only then do I close the door, wipe the tears from my eyes, and return to the twins sitting in the kitchen corner.

They look at me silently, following me with their gaze as I sit facing them.

Finally Marlene asks: "That was your mother?"

"Yes," I nod.

"And she knows that we're...?"

"Yes," I nod again.

"Does it bother her?"

"No," I shake my head.

"She worries about you?"

"She's my mother, she always worries about me."

"She must be very proud of you."

"Yes..." I answer. I can't tell them about her concerns.

"She's similar to you."

I look at her. "What do you mean?"

"Not in appearance, but in the way she speaks. The way she acts, the way she cares."

I want to smile, but can't. I'm too worried. They'll have forged documents soon, but even then they'll need a place to live. They're only nineteen-year-old girls, after all.

"Let's go to sleep, it's late," I finally tell them as I go to the closet, taking out another blanket to put down as a mattress for them so they won't be cold.

Two nights later, we hear shouts from outside the apartment: "Police, open the door."

I jump out of bed and go to turn on the light, but at the last moment I change my mind and leave the apartment dark. "Marlene, Annemarie," I whisper. My entire body is shaking despite the warm air.

"What?" I hear one of them, their voice drowsy.

"Quick, get up, they're here." I bend down to the floor and shake them. I hear more pounding from the direction of the hallway, but not on our apartment door, and someone calls again: "Open up, police."

"Come on, flee," I whisper to them, grasping one of their hands and lifting her up. One of them grabs me forcefully, as if trying to cling to me. "To the back door, quietly, don't turn on the light," I whisper. Only the pattering sound of their bare feet is heard as they exit the bedroom toward the back of the house. Who informed on me? I bend down and push their blankets under the bed, there's no time to hide them better. In the distance I hear the sound of a door being broken down, and the apartment's back door closing with a slam.

I feel my way to the front hall and peek through the peep-hole, but I can't see anyone in the weak light of the hallway. They're not on my floor, they'll come up here soon.

I press my ear to the door, hearing sounds of banging and a door breaking. "They're on the floor below," I whisper to myself. A rustling behind me makes me turn around in fear. Have they entered here too? My body freezes and I can't move.

"There's someone on the back stairs on the floor below, Frau Berger, there's a man there in a long coat," Marlene whispers, both clinging to me in fear.

"Quick, under the bed," I whisper to them. "Did you lock the door?"

"Yes," she whispers to me, but both remain standing beside me like chicks trying to cling to their mother. I lean against the wall and try to calm myself. It's not at our place, it's at the neighbors'. But I know that in a moment they'll come and break down the door, and take us. We have no way to escape.

I manage to turn to the door and open it a crack. Behind me I hear Marlene and Annemarie's breathing, and feel the warmth of their bodies. The sounds of boots are heard in the stairwell, and something below us breaks, a vase or something else made of glass. "Two Jews, arrest them," someone says, and I hear more screams and wailing and crying. "Them too," the loud voice adds, and I hear the sound of weapons being loaded.

I want to scream, but no sound comes out, and I stuff my fist in my mouth and bite it.

"Please, no," someone begs, and someone else speaks in Polish. There are more sounds of dragging, probably furniture, and more screams, and suddenly the sound of boot steps in the stairwell again. I close the door quietly and lean against it with all my strength, waiting for the knock and the blow that will break it down. I know I won't be able to stop them, but it's already too late, there's nothing else I can do. Marlene and Annemarie cling to me, and also lean against the door with all their strength. Only the sound of our breathing is heard in the night's silence. Why aren't they coming?

But they don't come. Another minute passes, and another, and the building is quiet. I want to know what happened down there at the neighbors' apartment, who they caught there and why they didn't come to us, but I'm afraid to open the door, and we continue leaning against it in silence for a long time. I'm certain that if I just open it a crack, they'll burst from their hiding place again, strike the wooden stairs with their boots, reach us and take all three of us.

As morning approaches, we return to the bedroom, but all three of us curl up tightly on my iron bed, close to each other and unable to fall asleep. At least they didn't take us this time.

The next day, I prepare to leave the apartment. "Don't open the door for anyone," I tell them. They don't say a word, just look at me and nod, their eyes wide with understanding.

I put my old coat on, struggling with the stubborn buttons, and leave the apartment, making sure to check that the door is properly locked behind me.

As I descend the stairs, I keep glancing downward, searching for police officers and Gestapo agents, ready to flee back upstairs at the first sign of danger. But the stairwell remains quiet and empty, filled only with the musty smell of old wood and dampness.

One floor below, the Becker family's door is open. The wooden door sways slightly in the morning breeze, its hinges creaking softly. The metal lock is broken, and wood splinters are scattered across the floor near the entrance. From the hallway I can see into the living room, where a brown wooden armchair with dark green upholstery lies on its side, and white porcelain fragments are strewn across the carpet and wooden floor. I mustn't think about what happened there yesterday. I need to get to work. I barely knew them, they were a quiet family. The last time the Americans bombed at night, I sat beside him in the shelter while he gripped his fedora tightly and muttered something about the war.

"Did you see what happened there?" I hear a voice behind me and turn to see Frau Schäfer, the neighbor from the first floor. She stands by the stairs in a gray dress, holding a cigarette between her yellowed fingers.

"I heard it during the night..." I answer, my voice barely above a whisper.

"I'm the one who reported them," she says, taking a drag from her cigarette, looking at me with a satisfied smile spreading across her thin lips. "It's our civic duty to report such things."

I look at her, trying to hide the wave of fear that washes over my body, but I don't think she notices. She just continues smoking her cigarette and keeps talking: "I'd suspected them for some time now. They were bringing in too much food from the market. I saw unfamiliar people several times. Any decent citizen would have been suspicious." She exhales the cigarette smoke and moves closer to me, also peering through the open door into the apartment's interior.

"What did they do to them?"

"They took them all, the police, the Gestapo, does it matter who? The Jews they were hiding, and them too. They were hiding a man and woman."

"But the Becker family had a small child."

"Yes, but it's our duty to report such things. Even a small child is subject to the law. No one is above the law, that's what keeps us strong as a nation," she says, almost to herself, while placing her hand on the doorframe and examining the apartment with the keen eye of someone savoring their victory.

"I didn't suspect anything," I manage to say, finding it difficult to continue standing so close to her in the doorway, the smell of tobacco and stale perfume overwhelming.

"That's our job, to be suspicious. Only thus will we win." She takes another drag from the cigarette she's holding. "I saw two young women on the back stairs a few days ago. I don't know if they came to steal or to hide, but I'm watching. We won't let anyone tear us apart from within."

"I'll keep watch too. Good day," I tell her and walk away, hurrying down the stairs. My legs feel weak from fear, each step uncertain. What will happen if she sees them again? How long will it take her to report me? Only when I reach the main street do I stop for a moment and breathe, the cold morning air filling my lungs. What am I going to do?

After work I hurry to the apartment, standing by the door and examining it carefully. It's intact, no one has broken in and is waiting for me inside.

I enter and close the door behind me, sliding the bolt into place with trembling fingers. All day long I couldn't concentrate on work, my mind constantly returning to Frau Schäfer's satisfied smile and her chilling words.

Marlene and Annemarie emerge from the bedroom and walk to the kitchen corner, settling into the wooden chairs like they're waiting for me and whatever news I might bring.

"The neighbor from the first floor reported them, Frau Schäfer. They took them all," I finally say, letting out a heavy sigh, feeling the weight of the day settling on my shoulders.

They remain silent, watching me with those young, frightened eyes.

"She saw you on the back stairs. She's suspicious," I add.

"We'll leave," Marlene tells me, her voice steady despite the fear I can see flickering across her pale face.

"You can't leave, you have nowhere to go," I tell them. They're so young, barely more than girls, really.

"We'll survive, Frau Becker, just like we've survived until now," Annemarie answers, trying to sound brave.

"How will you survive?"

"Thank you for everything you've done for us," Marlene says, her hands clasped tightly in her lap. "We'll wait until nightfall and leave. Really, thank you," she says quietly, but I can see on her face that she's emotional, perhaps terrified.

"Stay here. I'll be back soon," I tell them and stand up, smoothing down my worn skirt. "Don't open the door for anyone," I add, and step through the door. There's one more place where I might be able to ask for help.

Chapter Twenty-One

Just a Little More Time

"Do you have any schnapps left, Mother?" I ask as we sit in the small kitchen of her apartment.

"No, I finished it during the heavy bombing two weeks ago. There's far too much war here. I'm not sure there's enough schnapps in the world for this war," she sighs, her weathered hands smoothing down her apron. "Would you like some tea?"

"Yes," I answer, looking around the familiar space. Why did I even come here? She won't be able to help them either. No one will be able to help them, it's far too dangerous.

"Here you are," she hands me the cup of tea and sits across from me, holding her own cup and watching me, waiting for me to tell her what's wrong. She already knows me too well.

"The Gestapo raided the building," I quietly say, wrapping my fingers around the warm ceramic. "In my neighbors' apartment, on the floor below me. They caught Jews there. One of the neighbors informed on them."

Mother doesn't say anything, just slowly sips her tea, her old hands gripping the cup tightly, knuckles white with tension.

"She suspects there are more Jews in the building," I add, my voice barely above a whisper. "She saw the twins going down the back stairs."

"Aren't they in the apartment all the time?"

"You know they're not, we've talked about this. They have to go out sometimes. I have to let them out," I tell her, taking a small sip of the tea and feeling the hot liquid burn my tongue.

Mother again says nothing, just continues to watch me with those knowing eyes that have seen too much.

"I need money," I continue speaking, setting the cup down with shaking hands. "For months now I've been feeding three women on one woman's ration cards, and even those aren't enough. I need to get them forged identity papers that cost thousands of Reichsmarks. There's only one way to do that, and I'm using it," I tell her, lowering to my hands clasped around the warm cup.

"Does Hermann know?" Mother asks. To my relief, she doesn't lecture me about morality.

"No…" I shake my head. "He doesn't know about anything, not about the women I'm hiding, not about the men, not about the money I'm trying to save to rescue them, and not about what it's like to be alone for three years during a war, without a husband, while still needing to survive and make decisions."

"Maybe it's good that he doesn't know," she says, lowering her gaze to her tea cup.

"I need to get them out of the apartment. This neighbor is too dangerous, and what I'm doing is too dangerous."

"Where will they go?" she raises her eyes and asks.

I lower my gaze and don't answer her. I'm the one who will have to make the hard decisions.

"How much more do you need for the forged papers?"

"Not much. I've managed to get most of it already, they already have photographs. In a few more weeks I'll manage to get the full amount."

"Bring them to me," she says, and I freeze.

"To you? Do you remember what you said to me when you found out about them?"

"I'm your mother. It's a mother's job to say those things to you," she answers calmly and continues sipping her tea as if we're discussing yesterday's rain.

"It's just as dangerous for you as it is for me."

"I don't have a suspicious neighbor here."

"You have Mrs. Vogel here, with her nosy eyes and big mouth, and there's the Koch family who look like Nazism was built around them," I answer.

"Clara," she looks at me, her eyes steady and determined, "I'm sixty-eight years old. I've lived for many years, and seen far too much war. I'm no longer afraid of Mrs. Vogel, the Koch family or the Nazis. I've also lived to see them take my neighbor Mrs. Schneider and make her disappear, and you and I know where they took her," she quietly says. "I won't lie and tell you I'm not a afraid, and I won't tell you it's not dangerous, but you're my daughter, and you're doing something brave. Now it's my turn to help you do something brave."

"And what will happen if they do something to you?"

"What will happen if they do something to *you*? How will I feel then?" she returns the question, her voice firm but gentle.

"You should go bring them now. Don't leave them alone for so long."

"Are you sure about this?" I study her face, searching for any sign of doubt.

"I said it once. I don't think I need to repeat myself," she answers, and continues sipping her tea with the same calm determination I remember from childhood.

"Thank you, Mother," I stand and embrace her.

"Go on, hurry. It'll be dark soon," she scolds me, but hugs me back tightly.

"One more thing," I tell her as I'm already standing by the door, my hand on the worn brass handle. "If something happens to me, try to get the twins to Mr. Weidner, the manager of the workshop where I work. He's a good man, he'll try to help."

The three of us walk through the dark streets, our footsteps echoing softly against the cobblestones.

Each time we reach a street corner, they press themselves against the building wall while I advance several steps, standing still and listening to make sure no civilian guard patrol is approaching. Only when the area is clear do I return to them and signal to continue following me. We could have left earlier, but then we would have risked them encountering Mrs. Vogel in the stairwell.

From time to time I stop and listen, waiting to hear the distant rumble of bomber engines approaching. But tonight is quiet, and only a single vehicle can be heard driving down one of the nearby streets. The city is dark and silent, as if waiting for morning.

At the entrance to the building, I signal for them to wait in the inner courtyard again. I remove my shoes and climb the stairwell to make sure no one's there. When I see it's empty, I come back down to them. They also remove their shoes, and all three of us climb barefoot to the third floor, holding our shoes in our hands.

Mother opens the door for us without a word, and all three of us enter. "Come with me," she tells them, and takes them to her bedroom. In the dim light I can see the blanket she has spread on the floor.

I place the basket with what little food I've brought on the kitchen table, and follow them into the bedroom. "This is only for a short time," I tell them, "until you have papers, and we manage to find a better arrangement."

"Thank you," they both say to me, seeming to search for something more to say, but they remain silent in embarrassment.

"You should go, I'll walk you to the door. Don't delay," Mother tells me, and we both walk down the front hall.

"Thank you," I tell her. "I'll come again in two or three days. I'll bring more food with me."

"Don't worry, Clara. I'll watch over them. I also have ration cards, and I also know how to go to the market and buy food."

"Thank you, Mother," I hug her and begin to descend the dark corridor. Behind me I hear the wooden door close with a gentle click. They're safer here. I acted correctly.

Three weeks later, I'm descending the stairs to the basement near the train station. I approach the man behind the wobbling wooden table, and stand before him.

"It's still not ready, madam. Three more days."

"You said that two days ago. I've already given you a lot of money," I tell him while gripping my purse tightly. All the remaining money is in there.

"I'm not a swindler, madam, even if I'm standing here among all these people," he looks around and answers me angrily. "We're at war, and even if I say something, it doesn't mean it will happen exactly on time. I'm not a train station conductor."

"Someone is waiting for these papers," I answer.

"Believe me, there are also those who always want to know what's happening. I promise you there are many here with big noses," he says, his eyes darting nervously around the crowded basement.

"I'll come back in a few days," I tell him and walk away, thinking about Anna. Was she the one who tried to find out from him what was happening, or was it someone else? I look around as I exit the basement and begin walking toward the apartment. But it doesn't matter. There are too many Gestapo informants in this city, it's not just her. A man in a suit riding a bicycle passes by me, and then I hear it, the wail of sirens.

The people on the street stop for a moment, frozen exactly as if a photographer in a studio were shouting at everyone not to move. But after a moment, they begin to run. A woman ahead of me drops a basket of potatoes while running, and they roll down the street. A child of about five or six stands in the street, screaming in fear while a man shouts back at him. The cyclists disappear from the street, as do the trams and the military truck that had passed just moments before. And then I hear the ominous rumble, like the dull growling of a large, angry dog.

I raise my eyes and see them, small dots in the gray sky approaching in slow motion, looking like an orderly pattern on a gray blanket of clouds, symbolizing approaching death. Then the incessant drumroll of anti-aircraft guns paints small patches of black and ugly smoke around the advancing crosses above me, coloring the sky. All around me I hear the whistles and screams. I cover my ears and begin to run.

A distant building ahead transforms into a mushroom of smoke and dust. A strong wave hits my face, knocking me to the ground. A loud noise strikes my ears, and maybe people are screaming around me, I no longer know. I just have to reach Mother's apartment, to see that everything's all right.

"To the shelter, madam!" A man in a gray dust-dirty suit lifts me up and seems to be shouting at me, but I continue walking slowly down the street. I must see that they're all right. Mother and the twins are all I have. My ears hurt, but I don't care. The main thing is that I keep walking.

Five streets of smoke and the burnt smell of rubber and wood, people walking slowly, policemen running around, an overturned cart in the middle of the street with all its contents scattered, and smoke from fires, so much smoke. A building on the street looks like it was cut in half, exposing bedrooms as if it were a giant dollhouse waiting for a child to play with it. Three policemen stand around a metal cylinder on the road, keeping everyone away and shouting that it's an unexploded bomb. Two more streets to walk. My ribs hurt from the fast walking, but I don't stop. The main thing is that the building is intact, though there's glass scattered everywhere and windows have been torn from their frames. I climb the stairs, gripping the swaying railing, ignoring Mrs. Vogel who tries to stop me. The door to the neighbors' apartment, the one that belonged to Mrs. Schneider, is broken and leaning to one side, as is Mother's apartment door.

"Mother?" I quietly say, entering through the door leaning on its side, but no one answers me. "Mother?" I repeat the question while running through the rooms. Kitchen utensils are scattered on the floor, and the windows are broken. But the apartment is empty. Mother and the twins aren't there. I go out to the hallway and lean on the rickety railing, looking at the floor and trying to overcome the feeling of fear.

"Clara," I hear Mrs. Vogel. "Clara," she calls to me.

I ignore her and begin descending the stairs. I'll search for them in the street, they must be somewhere. I have to find them. I'm sweating all over from the fast walking and fear.

"Clara," Mrs. Vogel calls to me again, grabbing my arm as I pass by her on my way down. "Clara, stop," she says, and I stop and look at her. I mustn't delay.

"Clara," she whispers to me again while looking to the sides. "Come with me," She opens her apartment door for me, continuing to hold my hand so I won't run away from her.

I follow her inside like a rag doll, and there in the corner of the small kitchen sit the twins, huddled together like small puppies, looking at me fearfully.

"Clara," she whispers to me, "your mother went out to the market earlier, and I knew they were with her," she whispers.

"I don't understand," I tell her, looking at the twins who smile at me slightly.

"That night, when you brought them, I saw you through the peephole," she says. "And today, when the bombing was so close and your mother wasn't here, I didn't want someone else to discover them," she tells me while staying close to me, her birdlike chin suspiciously moving from side to side.

"And Mother?" I ask, looking at the twins, still refusing to believe they're here.

"She should be back soon," she continues talking to me non-stop while I try to digest what she's saying. "I know you think I support them, but I don't. I haven't supported them for a long time. I didn't want them to take Mrs. Schneider," she continues talking, almost clinging to me. "I didn't want so many people to die. I didn't want this war. I just wanted us to return to what was once here. Your mother is a good woman. I just want to help her."

Only later, after Mother returns from the market, do I leave her apartment and head back home, but not before I hug her with all my strength and thank Mrs. Vogel.

Before I leave, I help Mother and the twins position the door to block the entrance, making sure they move the dresser from the guest room to block it so no one can enter.

"Go already," Mother tells me. "They're with me, I'm watching over them. You need to stop worrying so much."

"See you tomorrow. I'll bring food and try to find work tools to fix the door," I tell her, and hug her one last time before descending the stairs.

The city is quiet. A few people are hurrying to return home before sunset, and I walk slowly, trying to calm myself after this entire day.

This time, when I climb the stairs to the apartment and see them, I don't try to flee. I know there's no point.

Both of them stand by my broken apartment door in their black leather coats, waiting for me. Beside them stands Anna, dressed in her short coat and torn high wool stockings, with red lipstick on her lips.

One of them grabs my hand firmly, hurting me, and begins to descend the stairs with me. He doesn't even ask my name.

"I had to tell them something. I had to give them names," Anna shouts to me before one of them silences her and she whimpers in pain. "I only told them you were trading on the black market."

Chapter Twenty-Two

The Building on Prinz-Albrecht-Straße

The metal chair rocks slightly, though I'm not sure if it's the crooked floor or my trembling knees.

The room around me is gray, with exposed concrete walls, and there's nothing in it except for the lamp hanging from the ceiling, the table that separates us, and his eyes examining me.

He lowers his gaze to the open folder before him, silent. He looks like an ordinary man, like a bank clerk, dressed in a gray suit and a white button-down shirt.

"Your answer again, please," he says in a quiet, almost pleasant voice.

"I didn't sell anything," I tell him again. "I only bought a few items, some soap, butter, like everyone else."

He nods his head as if he understands, as if he's on my side and agrees that I've arrived here by mistake.

"In exchange for what?" he asks.

I remain silent for a moment. Was Anna the only one to betray me? Maybe it was also the man with the broken tooth and the wobbling wooden table? "I gave a silver menorah," I finally say.

"A menorah," he smiles slightly. "So you're trading in Jewish property? How interesting."

"I needed the money. I managed to obtain it," I tell him, swallowing my saliva. How much does he know about me?

He stands up and begins slowly walking around the room, pacing from side to side in slow movements. "You know, many people need money, not just you," he approaches me and places his hand on the back of my neck, grabbing my hair. I scream in pain. "You're a whore who entertains men, you don't lack money," he whispers to me quietly, like a snake's hiss.

"I spent it all," I whimper, feeling his hand gripping me forcefully.

"On what?" He releases my hair and returns to sit by the table, again becoming the same polite bank clerk he'd been just minutes before.

"On drink, on every drink I could manage to buy," I tell him, feeling my tears streaming down my cheeks.

"You know, Clara," he tells me calmly, raising his gaze again from the folder lying before him, "I'm not a violent man. I won't hurt you anymore."

"Yes, sir. Thank you, sir," I manage to tell him.

"I'll go home for dinner with my family soon, and play with my little boy, he's already six," he smiles at me. "And then

I'll listen to the radio and read about the battles we've won in today's newspaper. And the Third Reich will continue to exist, with or without you."

"Yes, sir," I answer quietly, trying to understand what he's going to do to me.

"And you have two options," he continues speaking to me quietly in his polite voice. "Tell me what you did with the money and why you traded on the black market, and whether you helped hide Jews," he smiles at me, "or join them in one of the camps in the east, where we send them."

I look at him for another moment, feeling the tear on my cheek dripping down my neck. "All the money went to drinks, sir," I quietly say. I can't endanger Mother. I can't send the twins to their deaths.

Autumn 1944, the Zillerthal-Erdmannsdorf forced labor camp, a sub-camp of the Groß-Rosen concentration camp, southwestern Poland

I walk among the women hunched over sewing tables in the workshop. Sometimes I imagine that nothing has changed, and this is the same shoe-sewing workshop where I worked when I was young, or Mr. Weidner's broom and brush workshop. But everything has changed.

An inverted green triangle badge is embroidered on my prisoner uniform. This is the sign for women like me, who were sentenced for moral crimes and black market trading. The other women in the workshop have yellow badges, just like at the workshop. From morning to night they sit in their chairs, hunched over sewing machines, sewing uniforms for the Wehrmacht, keeping alive the Nazi monster that wants to kill them. But they have no other choice, everyone here wants to live just a little longer.

The type of badge is the key between life and death, the class rank that decides the fate of every woman in this camp. The green triangle patch makes me responsible for them, and turns them into replaceable ammunition in the workshop. They must obey me, or they'll be taken from here and I'll never see them again. It grants me larger food rations and better treatment from the guards. It promises that maybe I'll stay alive, and not be sent to those death camps whose names pass in whispers like wind blowing through the leaves of trees surrounding the camp.

"Morning count," I tell them every morning when I take the Jewish women under my responsibility, from the barracks to the workshop. "Evening count," I tell them every night after I escort them to the barracks, and they stand in the endless line for the pot of thin soup and half-loaves of bread. Sometimes I give them some of mine; even though I'm hungry all the time, they're always hungrier.

"Come on, move along," the prisoner responsible for the soup pot tells them indifferently, ladling one scoop of soup for each of them. A red triangle patch is embroidered on her uniform, indicating she was suspected of Communism.

Sometimes I search among the Communist prisoners for that one who worked with me years ago, but I've forgotten her name. Hunger makes me forget many things here. In the men's camp on the other side of the dirt road are those suspected of homosexuality. Sometimes I wonder if Bruno Koch managed to hide his identity, or whether the Gestapo's cleaning machine managed to lay its hands on him too, and he's housed in that camp. Sometimes I imagine that Mother managed to get by and the twins managed to escape, but I know it's just my imagination. I didn't manage to escape from them, no one will manage to escape from them. I only hope that Hermann is okay, and that no one has told him what's happened to me.

"Lights out," I tell the Jewish prisoners at night. In the darkness I walk among them, and take the five cigarettes I received today from a Ukrainian guard out of my pocket. They lie in their bunks and remain silent before I turn off the light. Those who know me extend their hands as I place a cigarette in each. I make sure to give them to the weakest ones, so they can exchange them for extra soup or bread. Sometimes they thank me, sometimes they just look at me and their eyes thank me. Then I turn off the light, and they close their eyes and try to sleep. The barbed wire fences will stop all the dreams of those locked up in this camp.

The only thing the barbed wire fences can't stop is rumors. I have no idea how they manage to cross rivers, floating between the spruce and pine trees surrounding the camp, and slipping in between the barbed wire fences and the watchtower guards. But they arrive, in fragments. We know the Allies have landed in Normandy and liberated Paris. We also know the Red Army is advancing in the east, and is no longer far away. Sometimes we see formations of large bombers in the sky, and one quiet morning it seemed to me that I heard muffled sounds in the east. "It won't last much longer," a Croatian guard told me a week ago as he gave me two more cigarettes.

"Morning count," I say the next day as I lead them to the workshop, watching the freight cars on the railway platform unloading new prisoners.

"Evening count," I say at the end of the day when the new prisoners stand in formation, their faces bearing that same surprised look due to their shaved head and itchy prisoner uniforms.

"Lights out," I say, and begin walking among the bunks.

"Clara," a veteran prisoner with brown eyes calls out. She arrived here shortly after I did. Beside her lies a prisoner who arrived today.

"Yes," I answer.

"She wants to ask you something," she nods to the new prisoner.

"Are you from Berlin? Is your name Clara Berger?" the new prisoner quietly asks me.

"Yes," I answer as I look at her. She's not familiar to me.

"I heard about you," she says, "in Berlin."

"What did you hear?"

"I heard that you helped, I heard they're okay, that's all I heard. But I heard your name."

"Did you hear anything about my mother?" I ask, gripping the wooden beam that supports the prisoners' bunks.

"No, I'm sorry. Just someone who whispered your name to someone else, and that they're okay."

I search for a way to answer her, but I can't, so I continue walking among the bunks and finally turn off the light. A few minutes later, as I lie down to sleep, I manage to digest what she said to me and I feel a tear rolling down my cheek.

In the quiet night of the camp, I hear the ominous hoot of an owl that must be perched on the barbed wire fence. I must continue to believe that this will end soon. I must continue to believe that she's not mistaken, and that Mother is okay too. I must stay alive.

I look at the barracks ceiling and imagine the meal that Mother, the twins and I will prepare when all this is over. It'll be a meal with soup and delicious sausage, it will fill the plate with potatoes and cabbage, and for dessert a sweet cake with the scent of cinnamon, like the one at the pastry shop on the main avenue, the one destroyed in the bombings.

Chapter Twenty-Three

The Rowboat

Mittelbau-Dora forced labor camp, Germany, April 11 1945. V2 rockets were being built in this camp under terrible conditions by forced laborers, and toward the end of the war, prisoners from the east were brought there.

"Drink some water, you have to," someone tells me as they lift my head, bringing a metal cup to my lips. I have no idea how long we've been here, maybe weeks, maybe more. We haven't received food in recent weeks. Over the past few days I've been unable to stand. I'm surrounded by women with yellow stars embroidered on their prisoner uniforms. Sometimes, when I open my eyes, I think I'm surrounded by glowing stars that are keeping me alive.

"They're gone, the camp is empty," I think someone says.

"Drink, you must drink," someone else tells me, and again lifts my head and tries to moisten my lips with some water.

I close my eyes and float, hearing voices in a language I don't understand. When I open my eyes, the sun blinds me and I see two soldiers in green uniforms carrying me on a stretcher. I smile and grip the metal poles tightly, careful not to fall, imagining that I'm sailing in a boat on the blue sea, swaying between the waves like the picture in the only book of poems I had when I was a child, the one that Mother used to read to me.

The End

Chapter Twenty-Four

Epilogue

The Mittelbau-Dora camp was liberated on April 11, 1945 by soldiers of the US Army's Third Division.

The Jewish woman who arrived at the concentration camp and told Clara that she'd heard about her was not mistaken. Clara's mother Marga and the twins Marlene and Annemarie Ehrenstein managed to escape the Nazis and survived.

After the war ended, Clara returned to Berlin with ten marks in her pocket, and discovered that the building where she'd lived had been destroyed in the bombings.

In the following years, Clara tried to rebuild her life in the ruined city along with her husband and her mother. These were difficult years, and she finally died in poverty in 1977. Only after her death, in 2012, did she receive recognition for her actions in saving Jews during the Holocaust.

This book was inspired by the life of Hedwig Porschütz Völker, 1900-1977, and although it I gave myself considerable literary freedom in writing this work of fiction, the foundation of facts and events did indeed take place in Berlin between 1923 and 1945.

A year ago, while reading an article about Berlin during the war, I happened to encounter a short paragraph describing her life. At that moment I decided that I wanted to write a book about her that would tell the story of a brave woman who, despite being poor and struggling all her life to survive, risked her life to save Jewish women during the war.

There are no words I can write that would express my appreciation for her actions, and the courage with which she acted.

Alex Amit

Chapter Twenty-Five

Author's Note: Pieces of History

The end of World War I in 1918, and the Treaty of Versailles that was signed in its aftermath, were among the factors that led to the outbreak of World War II twenty-one years later. The treaty obligated Germany to pay reparations for the war, which led Germany into severe economic distress. This distress became fertile ground for the rise and establishment of the National Socialist movement.

Despite the accusations by Hitler and the Nazis that Jews had fled from the war, approximately one hundred thousand Jewish soldiers fought loyally in the German Kaiser's army, seeing themselves as patriots like any other German. Thirty thousand of them received medals, and about twelve thousand of them were killed in battle, one of them being Mrs. Schneider's son.

Despite all this, anti-Semitism toward Jews increased after the war, with the rise of the Nazi movement along with claims that they had fled from battle.

The opening point of the book is 1923. This year marked the peak of the economic crisis following World War I. During this period, the young 26-year-old Clara struggles to survive economically along with her mother, and they are evicted from their old apartment. During this time of terrible poverty, in which money has no value, Berlin was a city of contrasts. Alongside the hungry people on the streets, many cabarets and clubs operated where wealthy people continued to celebrate. Anna, who arrives as a sub-tenant, works in one of them. Alongside Communist demonstrations and numerous strikes, Hitler began establishing his position as leader of the National Socialist Party during this period, and the Party began to grow.

On November 8 1923, Hitler attempted to seize power in Bavaria and from there march to Berlin, an action that would later be called 'the Beer Hall Putsch.' Hitler was captured and sentenced to five years in prison, of which he served one year. During that year he wrote *Mein Kampf*.

In the book, Clara's first period of life ends with hope when she meets her future husband Hermann.

After 1923, the Weimar Republic managed to stabilize the state, and the economy began to recover. However, the Nazi Party grew stronger throughout those years, as did the Communist Party opposing it. The United States stock market crash in 1929 once again brought down Germany's economy.

Clashes between Nazis and Communists intensified. Stalin ruled the Soviet Union during this period, and Communism was presented as the main threat to democracy. At the same time, Nazi anti-Semitism also grew. The depiction of Mrs. Schneider's shop being destroyed by members of the Hitler Youth takes place during this period. Despite threats to freedom from both Communists and Nazis, Berlin was still a city with great openness, and many homosexual clubs operated there, although they were already under threat. Mr. Koch's son Bruno is attacked by thugs near one such place, and Clara tends to him.

During this period, Clara trades on the black market and begins engaging in prostitution to survive. In 1934, she is sent to prison for nine months on charges of extortion.

Her release and her meeting with Hermann constitute the end of her second period of life. By the time she's released, the Nazis have already taken control of the state through emergency laws, and Germany is no longer a democracy.

Clara's third period of life begins in 1940, almost a year after the outbreak of World War II. Despite his advanced age, her husband is drafted into the Wehrmacht as a truck driver and serves throughout the war, leaving Clara alone in Berlin with her mother.

In 1941, Clara begins working as a secretary in Oscar Weidner's workshop. The character of Mr. Weidner is inspired by Otto Weidt, a German businessman who operated a workshop for brooms and brushes during the war, and employed thirty Jewish women who were deaf and blind. Mr. Weidner appears in the book as a secondary character, but in history Mr. Weidt indeed obtained approval for an essential factory for the Wehrmacht, and operated a network during the war that dealt with hiding Jewish women from the Nazis. Some of them were hidden in his Berlin workshop, at 39 Rosenthaler Straße.

The treatment of Berlin Jews, and Germa [ALEX AMIT] changed gradually after the outbreak of Wor. the war, 75,000 Jews lived in Berlin. A poll tax w Jews in March 1941, which is mentioned in the st three Jewish women approach Clara and ask her ι .chase their property. The Nazis sought to take control of Jewish property through the poll tax. In October 1941, regulations were tightened and Jews were required to wear yellow badges that could be purchased at Jewish community offices. That month also began the concentration of Jews at Jewish community offices, and their dispatch to the east. Initially Jews were sent to ghettos in Poland and Czechoslovakia, and later directly to Auschwitz. The collection and dispatch of Jews is mentioned in Mrs. Schneider's story.

By April 1943, the Nazis were engaged in deporting all Berlin Jews, and on April 11 1943, Goebbels recorded in his diary that Berlin was clean of Jews.

Out of 75,000 Jews, approximately 1,500 Jews remained throughout the city, looking for places to hide. They indeed slept in public parks, clubs and bathroom stalls, as described in the girls' story. Many of them could not find a permanent apartment where they could hide, and during the war they wandered through several apartments of good people who were willing to hide them. They lived in constant fear, and the term "U-Boats", the nickname for German submarines in the war that the twins use, is a real term fleeing Jews would use to describe their situation: an attempt to submerge within the city, and an attempt to avoid capture by the Gestapo and the many informants who aided the Nazis.

During this period, Clara takes two young twin women into her home and hides them for half a year. In reality, Hedwig took in two additional women in March 1943, and hid them. She was using the apartment to entertain men at the time, and the women had to go out and wander the city during those hours.

In the summer of 1943, the situation became too dangerous due to a Gestapo raid on another apartment in the building. Two women moved to live with Hedwig's mother, and two others were sent to another apartment in Berlin. Three of the four women survived the Holocaust.

Throughout this entire time, Hedwig continued to deliver food packages and forged documents to Jews.

In September 1944, she was arrested for "food hoarding" and sentenced to a year and a half in a labor camp, on charges of black market trading and prostitution. Hedwig remained in a concentration camp until the end of the war.

Her actions were only recognized by the city of Berlin after her death, in 2010, and a memorial plaque was placed outside the apartment where she lived at the end of her life. In 2011, all charges for which she had been accused and imprisoned under the Nazi regime were dropped.

It wasn't simple for me to write the story of her life, spanning three such turbulent periods of life in Berlin. I have tried to understand what would lead an ordinary woman to risk her life so much for the sake of saving others, to imagine what she thought and felt.

I hope I've succeeded.

Thank you for reading,

Alex Amit

Printed in Dunstable, United Kingdom

72883276R00234